Drowning in Gruel

Also by George Singleton

These People Are Us

The Half-Mammals of Dixie

Why Dogs Chase Cars

Novel

Drowning in Gruel

GEORGE SINGLETON

A Harvest Original • Harcourt, Inc.

Orlando   Austin   New York   San Diego   Toronto   London

www.HarcourtBooks.com

Library of Congress Cataloging-in-Publication Data
Singleton, George, 1958–
Drowning in Gruel/George Singleton.—1st ed.
p.   cm.
"A Harvest Original."
1. South Carolina—Social life and customs—Fiction.
2. City and town life—Fiction.   I. Title.
PS3569.I5747D76   2006
813'.6—dc22   2005017974
ISBN-13: 978-0-15-603061-8   ISBN-10: 0-15-603061-6

Text set in Van Dijck MT
Designed by April Ward

Printed in the United States of America

First edition
K J I H G F E D C B A

In memory of River, Inky, and Nutmeg—at my feet during these stories—fearless warriors against land developers

.

In memory of River, Inky, and Nutmeg—at my feet during these stories—fearless warriors against land developers

Contents

Drowning in Gruel

Runt

WHEN THE STRAY, bighearted, mixed-breed female birthed twenty-four puppies all the exact size of a canned Vienna sausage, Watt Pinson made the mistake of calling up a friend of a friend who had an acquaintance at the local news station sixty miles away. At this point Watt hadn't even named the dog, hadn't let her in the house. She had been circling his property for a couple weeks, and ate what scraps he set out at dusk. Sometimes she slept next to the woodpile, other times Watt found her beneath his work van or in a tamped-down section of monkey grass edging his back deck. Watt's wife, Mattie, left the back door open one Thursday evening, the dog flashed inside, and began the long process of exuding a litter of runts between the couch and wingback chair. Watt came home, saw the mess, and remarked how lucky he was to own a carpet cleaning company.

Mattie said, "I wasn't paying attention. I left the door open while I took out the garbage. I didn't even see her around."

"Twenty-four has to be some kind of record. Even if it isn't a record, I bet if we get one of those fancy scales that drug runners use, we'd find out that all these dogs are the same. That never happens. There's always one big pup, and one really little one that usually dies off from not getting to a teat."

Mattie went and found an old comforter in the garage—something that a client gave them when even industrial steam cleaning couldn't get out the stains—and wrapped it around the bitch. Mattie said, "I'm tired of these yuppies driving all the way out here when they're bored with their dogs and throwing them out. Or when the dog eats upholstery."

The Pinsons owned another ten dogs, all ex-strays, that found their way from crossroads, around woods, through haphazard trailer parks, past a Christmas tree farm, to the Pinsons' yard in Gruel, South Carolina. They'd spent five grand to have a back acre fenced off, bought upwards of seventy pounds of dry dog food a week, and employed two different veterinarians—one for spaying and neutering, the other who made yearly shot house calls.

Watt pulled a hardback chair out of the kitchen and set it down five feet from the stray. "This dog must be Catholic or something, what with this many kids. Let's name her Sister. Like a nun, you know."

Mattie didn't say anything about how a nun wouldn't have kids. She looked at the dog and said, "Is your name Sister? Do you want to be named Sister?" in her highest voice.

The dog weighed not more than forty pounds, and looked mostly mottled hyena. Sister wagged her tail, raised her head, and nosed newborns toward her belly. "I need to call somebody up and see what the story is with hand-nursing these puppies. There ain't no way they'll survive otherwise."

Then Watt called his friend Yarbo, who called his friend Brewer, who called the man at WYFF to say that there was a human interest story going on somewhere in the middle of nowhere, between the towns of Forty-Five and Cross Blood. By the time Mattie had a saucepan of milk warmed on the stove and Watt found an eyedropper and an ear syringe beneath the bathroom sink, a news crew was on its way.

There aren't twenty-four people I know who'd take a free dog apiece, Watt thought. Mattie won't take a dog to the pound, and there's no way I can take another dog. He stuck the ear syringe down to one of the all-white puppies and said, "This might make you moo instead of bark."

Then he thought of how there was an empty burlap fertilizer sack in the garage and the Saluda River not two miles away.

Mattie scooped up two handsful of puppies and said, "Sister looks like a calico cat. I wonder why all these dogs are either all-black or all-white. I wonder who the father was."

Watt thought about taking a drywall bucket out back, filling it with water, and drowning one—maybe two—puppies at a time and nestling them back down in the ruined comforter after his wife went to bed each night. He said, "I don't understand the genetic makeup of people, much less dogs."

He knew that he couldn't harm Sister's puppies, though. He'd gone out of his way, while cleaning the carpet of a near Italian restaurant on Friday nights after they closed, of shooing cockroaches instead of sucking them up into his machine. He'd driven his van on two wheels for twenty yards once while veering from a raccoon blinded in the road. There were flying squirrels in the attic and mice living in the crawl space that he couldn't harm—vermin too smart to enter the live traps he set out. He held a one-ounce puppy and eased milk into its mouth.

"These dogs are so small I can't even tell which are male and which are female. They're like kittens," Mattie said. "It won't cost much to get them fixed, at least."

The other ten dogs—all relegated to the backyard while Sister continued her motherly functions—began barking. The cameraman and reporter pulled into the long gravel driveway, their high beams on.

"How'd y'all find out about this?" Watt asked. He didn't open the front door more than two feet.

The reporter was Celine Ruiz, and Watt recognized her. She appeared to be half Hispanic and half Asian, and much shorter than she appeared on the TV. Sometimes at night he'd watch the eleven o'clock news before going out to a carpeted Pizza Hut, Shoney's, or Kampai of Tokyo that he had on contract some fifty miles away. Watt's clients trusted him enough to give him keys, and most of the restaurant managers said he could partake of the beer coolers, the soft drink dispensers, that he could make a pot of coffee if he cared. Watt worked from midnight until six in the morning many days, came home to take a nap, then fulfilled his residential orders between noon and five. When he got enough steady clients Mattie quit her bank telling job, learned how to operate the steamer, and came along. Mostly she moved chairs and tables from one side of a dining area to the other, then back. She drank free Sprite some nights, Dr Pepper the others. Mattie liked to take a salt or pepper shaker, sugar packets, the cayenne pepper containers from the pizza joints. "I like to live dangerously," she said more than once.

"I'm Celine Ruiz," the reporter said. "We hear you have an amazing litter of runts on your hands here."

She was beautiful, with long straight dark hair and

almond-shaped eyes. Watt Pinson said, "I gave at the office," because he could think of nothing else.

"This could make you famous," the cameraman said. He had his camera running. "Man, I've seen this happen before." The cameraman appeared to be an albino black man, an ex-student who studied communications in college before a professor finally said something like, "People will fear you giving their news, even the sports. And especially the weather."

"You *are* Watt Pinson, right?" Celine said. "Are you the man who owns Pinson Carpet Cleaner? We got a call."

Watt Pinson wanted to plain call his place Pinson Cleaners, but knew that PC might turn off prospective clients. He said, "Yeah, we got a dog in here with twenty-four pups. But I don't want to talk about it. We got a bunch of dogs, and some people might think we're weirdos or something." He looked at the cameraman and said, "Please turn that off. I don't want that on TV."

The albino said, "Oh, we promise not to show this part."

Celine Ruiz slipped through the door, and held her microphone up like a torch. The albino followed. Mattie Pinson got up from the floor, an eyedropper in one hand and a black puppy in the other. She said, "Hello."

Celine nodded. She looked back at the albino and said, "Hit that light switch behind you. I'll stand right here." She turned forty-five degrees. She backed up toward Sister and almost stepped on her front paws.

The albino said, "Whenever you're ready."

Celine did a countdown and said, "We're here in the den of Watt and Mattie Pinson, and it appears that a miracle has taken place between Forty-Five and Cross Blood. Twenty-four puppies were born to a stray dog that showed up in their yard not long ago." Watt Pinson looked at his wife and shrugged his shoulders. Why did he ever call up Yarbo? he thought. Why did he give up so much information? The cameraman zoomed in on Sister nursing a dozen of the puppies. Celine turned to Watt Pinson and said, "Mr. Pinson, come on in here and tell us about how all this got started."

"I wasn't there when it got started," he said. "It's not like I'm the father." He said it in all seriousness. "This poor dog showed up at our place a couple weeks ago, but she was so skittish she wouldn't come near us. I set out food for her, you know, because that's what you do. We just named her Sister a couple hours ago. She somehow snuck in and started dropping puppies like a faulty gumball machine."

Mattie said from off camera, "All those goddamn yuppies keep throwing dogs out their car doors, especially right after Christmas," but it got dubbed out before the piece aired on Friday's *Hey, South Carolina!* morning show.

Celine said, "And what kind of dog is Sister?" Celine nodded her head up and down.

"I'd say she's part spaniel and part Lab. Or she's part shepherd and part something else. She's part, that's all I know. She seems to be a good mother."

Celine Ruiz turned her body toward the albino, held the microphone to her mouth, and said, "She's part. Just like the Carolinas are becoming more and more homogenized, so are our dogs." She turned back to Watt. "What're you going to do with all of these puppies, Mr. Pinson?"

Watt Pinson raised his eyebrows. He said, "If I find the man or woman who threw Sister out here in the country, I'm going to let them know how they don't belong in the human race. As for the puppies, I ain't going to drown them or anything."

Celine Ruiz didn't expect such an answer. She gave big eyes to the cameraman to keep his lens pointed at the litter. In the morning, she had voiced over, "So if anyone is interested in owning a miracle puppy, you might want to contact the station," even though Watt Pinson had said nothing about this option.

Afterward, Watt only thought about how he should've made a plug for his carpet cleaning business, how difficult it was making a living in an area that didn't attract new subdivisions, businesses, restaurants, and/or clumsy, wine-spilling communioners.

Between the next morning's weather report and a segment on the president declaring war on everyone who didn't agree with him, Celine Ruiz aired her segment. It wasn't 5:10 A.M. yet. Mattie said, "I only saw one camera in the house. I look forty pounds fatter." Mattie was a striking woman with eyes the color of an aloe plant. She weighed less than 140 pounds, and stood five-eight. "I'm hoping I look fat only because these puppies are so small."

The Pinsons had stayed up the entire night, watching Sister, trying to interpret squeals, grunts, and shifts of position. They watched their interview again at 6:10, and by noon the item had evidently been picked up by CNN. By the puppies' four o'clock feeding Mr. Bunky Tucker, the famed agent to many of Hollywood's leading child actors, had called the house to pitch what he could do for the Pinsons.

"I've already got you lined up to visit Humane Societies, PETA meetings, local SPCAs, and a couple of state fairs with Sister and her litter," Bunky said over the telephone. "I've done the research for you—a Saint Bernard in England gave birth to twenty-four pups, but a Saint Bernard's a purebred. And England's not America. So what we have here is a mixed-breed American dog, just like all of us are mixed-breed Americans.

Listen, I got connections that you could never have, Mr. Pinson. I can get you on the *Today Show* and the *Tonight Show*, not to mention every midday show from New Orleans to Boston, from Milwaukee to Miami."

Watt looked across the bar that divided his kitchen from his den and dining room. He said, "What? Who are you again?"

"I know your name already," Bunky said. "Listen, good state fairs pay upwards of a couple thousand dollars for a four-hour appearance for something like what you got. People are numb to fat ladies and three-legged midgets. I can get you an advance, plus a piece of the door. I'll take care of getting your plane reservations, your hotel rooms, and your meals. I mean, wherever you go, they'll take care of your transportation." Bunky Tucker listed off every child actor he'd brought into the business, then saved again after their ruinous ways. He mentioned how he represented every parent in North America who gave birth to quintuplets and beyond. "You've seen how they bring those seven kids out every year on their birthday? I can't tell you how much money they take in in donations from people who feel sorry for them. The same thing will happen to you, I promise. You'll be opening up envelopes with all kinds of dog food cash inside."

Watt didn't listen closely. "I don't think I'd be willing to check my dog and her twenty-four puppies in an airplane's belly, sir. Sorry about that."

On the other end of the line Watt heard a bell ring, similar to one that a short-order cook might ding when somebody's fried eggs and hash browns were ready for the waitress. "You're exactly right!" Bunky said. "I can see that you've thought this through better than I have. How about we get you an RV? And a driver?"

"That would be much better," Watt said.

"Who are you talking to?" Mattie mouthed from the den. "I need some help in here."

"I get fifteen percent of your gross, of course. I wish I could do all of this out of the kindness of my heart—and I do have a kind heart, Mr. Pinson—but I have bills to pay, too."

"Uh-huh. Listen, I have to get back in there and help out my wife. A couple of the runts are looking runtier and need to be hand-fed."

The bell went off again. Watt pictured this stranger slamming down his palm out in California whenever an idea hit. "This show has to begin within the week, let me tell you. And it won't be able to go on for more than a couple months. Three at the most."

Watt looked at Mattie and wondered what to do. "I'll have to talk this over with my wife. We have a business to run. We run it together."

The bell didn't ring. Bunky Tucker was silent for a five-count and then said, "Do you people make upwards of three thousand dollars a day? You do a Humane Society fund-raiser at noon in Nashville and a fair in Louisville that evening. You do a state fair in Lexington the next morning and a PETA fund-raiser in Cincinnati that night. I'm talking off the top of my head, but that's part of the tour I have set up for you so far."

Watt looked at his wife. She stroked Sister's head. He tried to figure up three grand multiplied by seven days, then by eight weeks. Minus fifteen percent. He said, "We've always wanted a lake house, or a cabin in the mountains. But I still got to talk to her. Could I give you a call back tomorrow?"

Bunky Tucker said he'd make the call, and asked Watt to go find a calculator.

"That was some kind of agent, manager, and publicist all wrapped up in one. He says you and I can make a lot of money off of Sister and her litter."

Mattie didn't make eye contact with her husband. She said, "I heard you mention lake house or mountain cabin. Why would you lay out our private daydreams to a stranger?"

Watt crouched down and stuck the ear syringe in the milk saucer. He picked up two black pups and said, "Y'all want to travel the country?" To Mattie he said, "What the hell's PETA?"

She said, "It's fancy bread."

Sister and her pups traveled in what Watt considered the largest rubber container ever invented—six feet long, by four feet wide, by three feet deep. The patented burp top had holes in it the size of fifty-cent pieces, and was donated by Tupperware. Bunky Tucker had arranged it all, thinking that Sister might distract the driver if she took to sniffing the accelerator, or got carsick, or smudged windows with her wet nose.

Mattie had agreed to run the carpet cleaning business while Watt traveled around, promised to videotape any segments that aired nationwide, and bought him a cell phone so he wouldn't have to use hotel phones or pay phones. When the Winnebago appeared in their driveway, the Pinsons were surprised to find it driven by a woman named LaDonna, a woman who worked in Bunky Tucker's agency and handled clients on the road more often than not.

"I don't like this," Mattie said. "You failed to mention how you'd be out on the road for however many months with a woman."

Watt said nothing. He stared up at the large windshield, at the beautiful woman behind the steering wheel who unwrapped her shoulder harness with one hand and waved with the other. "How're my puppies doing?" LaDonna said, jumping down. She stuck her hand out to Mattie first and introduced herself.

Mattie said, "I was thinking about meeting up with y'all at some points. You know, if the carpet cleaning business slows down. Do you think that would be okay?"

LaDonna stood straighter than anyone Watt had ever seen. She wore what Watt considered a regular one-piece bathing suit, low-slung blue jeans covering the bottom part. For Watt, she seemed the epitome of a fireball—maybe five-three, her shape like that of an *S* and its reflection. LaDonna said, "The more the merrier. I'm sure that Sister would like to see her own mother some weekends." She used a similar high-pitched voice as Mattie's.

Mattie didn't nod or blink. She didn't say how she wasn't the dog's mother. She wasn't pleased with LaDonna's response, though in later years she admitted that nothing this woman could've said might have eased Mattie's sudden jealousy. Sometimes when she was a bank teller running the drive-through window, Mattie would send a dog biscuit through the pneumatic tube to women who she knew hired her husband out. Although no Girl Scout troop ever existed in this area of South Carolina, every woman could boast a thousand badges for marking territory and catfighting.

Watt piled Sister and her pups in the comforter-lined Tupperware bin. He took his three hard, gray Samsonite suitcases and set them on a couch inside the RV, then came back for an ice chest Mattie had filled with luncheon meats, loaf bread, a jar of sliced dill pickles, and a jar of mayonnaise. LaDonna pet Sister in the back of the RV after checking the oil, radiator, and tire pressure.

Mattie pretended to check the leaves on a Japanese plum for beetle damage. She thought of every movie she'd ever seen. Should she make a big kissing spectacle with her husband before he embarked? Should she act nonchalant, maybe wave him off with the back of her hand?

When Watt came up behind her and placed his hands around her waist, she didn't move visibly. Watt said, "You have to trust me, Mattie. That's all I can say. And think about how our life together will be so much better. Two or three months apart isn't much when it comes to what will pretty much be a free lake house or mountain cabin. Or even beach house. We ain't even middle-aged yet. Think about the times ahead."

Mattie turned around. Peripherally she saw LaDonna strapping herself in the driver's seat. The RV started with a rumble not unlike Watt's steam cleaner. "If you don't call me every morning and every night I'll know why."

Watt Pinson thought about thanking his wife again for taking care of the business, but figured that she knew.

The itinerary included stops in Asheville, Knoxville, Nashville, Memphis, New Orleans, Jackson, and Oxford during the first week. Bunky Tucker arranged for a veterinarian to check out Sister there in Oxford, to make sure she withstood the pressure fine. Then they were off to Birmingham, Atlanta, north to Nashville again, Lexington, Louisville, Cincinnati, Cleveland, and Akron. There would be a two-day layover, unless Bunky could talk some Shriners in Detroit to find a way to shove Sister into their schedule.

Watt looked over the schedule from a captain's chair behind and to the right of LaDonna. There were stops in Iowa City, Madison, Milwaukee, and Minneapolis. Boston and New York City came later, toward the end, before traveling south to D.C., Charlottesville, Richmond, Raleigh, Chapel Hill, and Columbia, South Carolina.

Sister slept the hundred miles to Asheville, where they'd be shown off to a lesbian action group called Sisters in Heat, and for an extra two dollars any of the participants could leave the ChiliFest and view Sister and the runts in a back room of the Unitarian church. LaDonna said, "A lot of our male clients don't trust my driving the RV. I appreciate your not saying anything yet. I've had to drive everyone from writers to ex-politicians on the lecture tour."

Watt said, "How old are you, LaDonna?"

She looked to be about twelve to him. "I'm thirty-two. See, I studied American literature with a minor in public relations. And then for some reason I decided to get a chauffeur's license, back about my junior year in college. I made some money, let me tell you. And it's come in handy since."

Watt thought, I'm thirty-five. Mattie's thirty-four. There must be some difference in our lives and that of a woman who got brought up outside of South Carolina and garnered work in California.

He got up and walked back to his dog. "I went to college for a couple years down in Georgia and about took everything there was at least once. I never cottoned to any of it." He held Sister's muzzle.

LaDonna's voice came over an intercom. "I didn't like any of it, either. To be honest—not that I'm not looking forward to spending the next few months with you, Watt—I wish I'd've either studied archaeology to discover what ancient people made, or woodworking so I could make something that future people will discover. Does that make any sense?"

Watt leaned down and kissed Sister's snout. He said to the dog, "We'll stop off up here soon and feed your boys and girls, whether you like it or not. You have to eat, Sister. You have to eat."

Later, when he picked up one of the white male dogs, she turned and nipped his wrist, which made a mark but didn't bring blood to the surface.

All went well for the first six appearances. LaDonna stopped at nice hotels and got two rooms. Every hotel employee cooed over Sister and her pups, and Watt always had two queen-sized beds in his room in case Sister wanted to pile out of the Tupperware and take a snooze for herself. Watt would find a chocolate mint on his pillow and a rawhide chew on Sister's.

It was in a hotel stuck next to the Superdome in New Orleans that both Sister and Watt realized that they couldn't take it, though. Humane Society groupies waited for them, held signs that read WE LOVE YOU SISTER, and WE LOVE ANY MAN WHO LOVES DOGS.

Watt said to LaDonna, "What's this all about?" when they pulled the RV into the parking garage.

"You're a celebrity, Watt. Live it up. Glory in it all, as you people say down here."

"My dog underwent a strange and unusual litter. I don't see why they would love me. Hell, it ain't even my dog, officially."

LaDonna hit the brakes halfway between the second and third floor. She said, "Sister is your dog, and those puppies are your puppies." She set the brake right there on the ramp and came back to where Watt sat cross-legged beside the dog. She bent down and grabbed his neck, nestled her bosom straight into the back of it, and said, "I know how much pressure you're under. But you have to keep it up. We have a long way to go. If Sister ever has a bigger litter, I promise we won't undergo such a big tour. We'll cut it down to ten cities." She kissed Watt on the mouth, stood up, and pulled at her brassiere in the front. LaDonna walked back up to the driver's seat, released the brake, and continued driving to a spot on the roof.

Down in the hotel's Magnolia Room where the Louisiana chapter of PETA met—and normally they talked about alligators, snapping turtles, and nutria—five hundred men and women waited for the appearance of Sister and her puppies. Watt pushed the full Tupperware bin in via a dolly supplied by the hotel. When the crowd broke out in applause Sister tried to jump straight through the perforated top. No one seemed to see how she shook, how the puppies trembled between her limbs, around her muzzle, near her sagging belly.

They lined up for photographs—something Bunky Tucker thought up himself—that would cost them five dollars each, unless they chose to hold one of the puppies. Then it cost ten dollars. If Watt stood there with a big fake smile on his face it cost twenty.

I need to call Mattie, Watt thought. He thought, There's an hour time change. It's almost eleven o'clock home. "Hey, can I take a cigarette break?" he said to LaDonna, who wore a purple sequined miniskirt. SISTER spangled out across her T-shirt.

She nodded. "Go on. Of course you can." She shook her breasts unintentionally. "I'll tell anyone that you had to go out and get some vitamin tabs for Sister. They'll see you as a great, great father."

In the hotel room Watt pulled out his cell phone and called home. The answering machine picked up. He heard his wife say, "There's no one here right now, so leave a message." When he left home with Sister and LaDonna, his own voice told incoming calls to leave a message. Mattie's voice then said, "I'm off doing my husband's work right now because he's not man enough to do it himself, evidently. If I'm not doing that, I'm outside with our other ten dogs, taking care of them."

Watt tried to think of what restaurant he and Mattie normally cleaned on . . . he didn't know if it was a Monday or Tuesday. Was it the Pizza Hut? Was it the Denny's, or Shoney's, or Capri's Italian? He couldn't even remember what the number was for information.

"Honey, I'm in New Orleans with the dog. You wouldn't believe how many people are here wanting pictures of us. And they're doing this new thing where they stick Sister's paw on an ink pad so they can get her print on an eight-by-ten. It's weird. Hey, I'm sorry it's so late. I forgot about the time change. I love you, and I promise to call in the morning."

Watt hung up. He tried not to think about how, the entire time he spoke into his own answering machine to his wife, he only thought about how LaDonna could shake her breasts left and right.

Back downstairs, more women lined up. They clamored. They held photographs, and newspaper and magazine articles about Sister the Wonder Dog and Her Amazing Runts. Watt walked in to find LaDonna leaned over kissing his dog right on the nose, stroking her head, cooing into her ear.

The veterinarian in Oxford, Mississippi, said that Sister and her puppies withstood the pressure better than Faulkner on a book tour back in the old days. He said that there didn't seem to be any side effects, that Sister didn't seem to be the kind of mixed breed who needed to drown herself in bourbon and/or dog treats. Watt said to the vet, "Hey, you wouldn't have any kind of sedatives for me, by any chance, would you?"

The vet's name was Dr. Furr, of all things. Watt Pinson

trusted him only because of that—like he was born to be either a veterinarian or mink coat dealer. The vet said, "Let me call up Bunky. I can probably get you a little something if he tells me you're on the up-and-up."

LaDonna had gone up to a bar called City Grocery to talk to a bartender named Whitey who—every time she handled Bunky Tucker's other clients—poured heavy on the bourbon. "People in the South love dogs," LaDonna said after Watt got Sister and the puppies settled down at the University Inn. "This is a town where all dogs are revered. Any new dog can walk around the square and get pet on its head nonstop by complete strangers."

Watt sat up at the bar and looked at Whitey. He said, "I better just have a beer. I just took a painkiller."

Whitey nodded. "I'm giving you a light beer, then. I don't want to be known as the man who killed a celebrity." He pushed a ten-ounce glass Watt's way.

Watt held it up to LaDonna and said, "To the best and brightest and most beautiful driver in the world."

LaDonna said, "Shucks, Watt. I'm just doing my job," but giggled, and grabbed his right arm above the elbow. "Hey, I don't want to tell you how to run your homelife, but you might want to call your wife and let her know you're doing all right."

Watt looked past LaDonna. In the corner, two women stared at him, all smiles. "She doesn't like to talk to me when I'm fucked-up. It makes her worry too much."

LaDonna slugged back her bourbon and pointed for another. "You're a good man, Watt Pinson. Not too many men would consider a wife's feelings, you know."

He felt his head begin to numb. "Tell me again when I'm going to get all of this money that Bunky told me about?"

17

LaDonna went into great detail about how checks were sent to the office first, and then Bucky took anywhere from 90 to 180 days before subtracting his cut, and then the money showed up. She said, "Don't think about the money. Is there anything I could do to make you not think about the money? I should tell you that I'm a licensed massage therapist, too. I took a course my senior year in college."

Whitey said, "How'd you handle that light beer?"

Watt tried to make his speech not slur. He said, "I'll take a Southern Comfort and Coke. I promise it'll be okay." To LaDonna he said, "'*Licensed*,' huh?"

The noonday anchorpeople didn't do much homework. They brought Sister in, accompanied by Watt, and asked, "So! Where'd you come up with the name Sister?!" and such.

Watt Pinson didn't say anything about Catholicism. He always answered, "We call a bunch of people 'Sister' in the South, whether they're related to us or not."

"Can you name all of the puppies' names off in order?" they always asked. Either the man or woman anchorperson always held up one of the white dogs, and shoved it toward the camera.

A couple times Watt actually had to wear makeup. He hoped that no one back in South Carolina had a satellite dish. The makeup woman always said, "We don't want your face shining so much that people notice you more than they notice what they're supposed to be looking at."

"Say, what does a man do with twenty-four dogs and a mother?" the anchorperson would eventually say. "You have enough dogs to play a game of football, both sides. And some left over."

It wasn't until Memphis, on *Alive at Nine!*, when Watt thought to say, "I have enough to buy a case of beer and each have one."

The man, Alex, laughed. The woman, named Marybeth, said, "I'm an animal lover, and let me tell you that it's detrimental to give a dog beer. It should be against the law."

Behind the running cameras LaDonna bobbed her head up and down. Watt said, "Yes. Yes it is. I know that. It was a joke, Marybeth. I was only kidding."

Marybeth looked at the camera and said, "Okay. Well. Twenty-four puppies! Coming up next, we're going to show y'all how to bake the *perfect* peach *cobbler.*"

Watt Pinson would remember this segment as being the most effortless, the easiest, the most almost lifelike.

In the Midwest—in Iowa City, Milwaukee, Madison, and Akron—Watt Pinson encountered card-carrying PETA women who either wanted to laud his efforts or steal Sister away. There were women who thought that he only exploited the stray and her puppies, and that he had pushed pet ownership back a hundred years. And then there were women who believed that, if it weren't for Watt, Sister would've birthed her brood out in the wild, and that these dogs, more than likely, would either terrorize small children or be hit by cars on country roads.

In Madison, Wisconsin, both factions showed up in full force, and it was there at a local fair that a woman from the you're-exploiting-Sister group tried to steal the puppies. When both Watt and LaDonna grabbed the woman, one of the white puppies dropped, fell on its head, and died on impact.

Later on during the local news, another woman from that faction said, "Well, that puppy was better off dead than being paraded around the country. What kind of life is it being paraded around the country?"

"Twenty-three runts is still an American record," Bunky Tucker called to say that night. "I'm sorry for your loss, Watt, but it's still a record. And you won't believe the press you're getting. *Entertainment Weekly*'s running an article on 'Fun Things to See This Season,' and you're going to get a B plus. How about that? Hey, it's not half bad. The baby pandas down at the Atlanta zoo only got a B minus. Some kind of laser show in Michigan's Upper Peninsula got a C."

Inside the Canterbury Inn bed-and-breakfast—where they got the Miller's Room—LaDonna said, "This kind of publicity will only bring in more money, Watt. Believe me. One time I was handling a novelist who got arrested for indecent exposure. He pulled out his thing and waggled it in front of a woman who wanted him to travel for free six hundred miles to talk to her book club. Well, he got arrested. But when it made the papers and national news, his book went to something like number eight on Amazon.com."

Watt held his dead puppy in a paper bag that he got from a guy who sold vegetarian hot dogs. Sister didn't take her eyes off of the sack, as if she knew. Watt couldn't look at his own dog, for he knew that her eyes watered, that she mourned. He wanted to call Mattie, but didn't know how to tell her what occurred earlier in the day. He said, "I guess we need to drive out in the country somewhere and bury this little boy. I keep thinking it'll kick back to life. Kind of like when my carpet cleaner takes a mind of its own."

LaDonna moved from a wingback chair and rubbed Watt's shoulders. Sister sat in her Tupperware bin next to the window, which overlooked a bookstore downstairs. "We're going to tell the press that that's what we did," she said, "but right now we have to go take Sister and the other puppies down to a local TV station for the eleven o'clock news. We don't have time to drive around looking for plots, Watt."

She turned her head toward the bathroom.

Watt said, "You ain't going to flush this puppy down the toilet, I can tell you that right now."

LaDonna moved her hands farther down, to the small of Watt's back. She said, "I don't want to bring up how you signed a contract that stated how we would know what's best. That you had no say in what we thought was best." She cradled Watt's neck with her breasts, like some kind of airline's U-shaped comfort pillow.

"I need to call my wife," he said. He thought, I need to see how much money it would cost to fly home with Sister and her puppies and forget about this here arrangement. "There'll probably be something on CNN about that woman killing this puppy."

LaDonna kneaded and kneaded. She said how Bunky probably took care of anything airing on CNN that didn't need airing.

Mattie Pinson didn't forget what she said about how if Watt didn't call one night then she would know what had happened. On the evening of the first puppy's death Watt never called. Mattie drove the Pinson Carpet Cleaner van out to Wingding's Wings and Things—a place that only got its carpet cleaned once a month at most. Watt hated the joint, and made mental notes as to how teriyaki sauce sucked off a carpet much easier than honey and mustard or Fireball 666, how a special Memphis BBQ blend almost gripped itself into the nap.

Mattie opened the door at one in the morning and locked it behind her. She didn't pull in her hoses. She didn't go straight to the Sprite or Dr Pepper dispensers.

Mattie hit the liquor shelf, and took down a mini-bottle of amaretto, another of Jim Beam, and another of cheap cognac—three things she didn't make a point of drinking, ever. She turned on the television and sat at the first cushioned barstool with the channel changer.

Wingding's Wings and Things' manager Tony Rice came out of the storage room. "What're you *doing?*" He looked like an ex-fraternity boy who waited only for his next yearly homecoming. Under "Things" on the menu he offered a side order called "Tony rice."

Mattie jumped up. She said, "Oh, goddamn it, I didn't think anyone was here. I'm sorry, Tony."

He said, "You're Watt's wife, right?"

"Watt's off with our dog touring the country. I'm supposed to be running the show alone. I just needed to sit down and take a break. If I'd've known someone was here I would've yelled out something."

Tony Rice walked behind the bar and pulled another mini-bottle of Jim Beam off of the shelf. He poured it into a short glass without ice, and topped Coke into it. "I heard about that wonder dog of y'all'ses. How many puppies did she have, like eighty?"

"Twenty-four." Mattie slugged down the cognac in two gulps. "Two dozen. All of them were runts. Hell, I guess if everyone's a runt, then they could all be alpha dogs."

Tony Rice stared at Mattie. He had no idea what she meant. "I thought about pledging Kappa Alpha, but didn't."

Mattie pushed the remote past sports stations and settled on CNN. "I'll be pushing the tables aside and cleaning the carpet in a minute, I promise. And I'll pay you for this here booze." She looked up at a piece about how the president would bomb anyone who didn't agree with him, then another about how the president's economic team quit en masse.

Tony Rice brushed back his sun-bleached hair, fingered his loop earring, kept breathing through his mouth. "I'd help you, but I have to meet some people over at Ricky's Got a Hangover bar. They stay open till four, you know. You get this place all cleaned up and can meet us over there if you want. I'll put you on the guest list out front. It's a private club, but they don't care. It's open till four, you know."

Mattie twisted the top off of the amaretto. She took one swig, not knowing how sweet it would be. Mattie tried not to make a face. Tony Rice pointed at the television.

"Where's the volume on this remote?" Mattie yelled out.

There was a picture of Sister and her puppies, with Watt standing behind them, his arms spread out. It was a promo shot that Bunky Tucker sent all around. By the time Mattie got the volume turned up, she and Tony only heard from the anchorwoman, "So, sadly, there are only twenty-three left."

Then the news went on to some kind of supposed cure for Alzheimer's that involved a concoction of wormwood seeds, milk thistle, fennel, pokeroot, and high dosages of vitamins B and C. Tony Rice left through the back door. Mattie Pinson got up from the barstool, moved half of the room's chairs and tables to one side, then sat back down. She drank the bourbon. She got up and grabbed three more mini-bottles of bourbon.

They always show these news items every hour, she thought. I can wait an hour and they'll show what's going on with Sister.

She turned the TV's volume up all the way, and waited. Mattie didn't steam-clean the carpet. She lost patience, and left for the after-hours club one segment before the story of Sister's dead puppy re-aired.

Runts two through eight died natural deaths right after being handled by some of the college interns who worked for *Good Morning America*. Nine through sixteen died the next day, on a Sunday morning when Sister was supposed to show up live on CBS. LaDonna took care of the dead puppies both times, and Watt knew not to ask questions. In the RV, out of New York City, he said, "I don't know why we should go on with this."

"As long as Sister doesn't die, we have something America wants to see," LaDonna said. "She's a fucking martyr, as a matter of fact. It might be best if all of the puppies died. Then we have something for people to feel bad about. No. We have something so people can feel *better* about themselves. It's like catharsis."

Watt didn't say anything about how he needed to find a Laundromat. He got up, walked two steps to the RV's kitchen, and pulled out a bottle of bourbon, some Coke, and made a drink. He thought about how his liver probably suffered over the last couple months, that when he got back home with Mattie he would fall into her arms, and curl up, and let her heal him as she always did when he couldn't take the pressure of carpet cleaning.

LaDonna drove down I-95. Watt sat in the back with Sister and her eight puppies, all of which now weighed in at about four ounces each. Sister had gotten to the point where she couldn't even lift her head. A couple hundred miles down the road he said, "I know that word. I know the word *catharsis*. Don't think I don't know what that means." Watt kept his face close to the intercom.

"I didn't say that you didn't," LaDonna said. In her voice Watt heard a strain, a tenseness, a snap. "I'm demanding a raise," LaDonna said under her breath, while wheeling through Delaware.

All of the puppies died by Washington, D.C. Watt said he couldn't go on. LaDonna called Bunky Tucker on the hour. Tempers flared. Sister mourned.

When LaDonna pulled the RV back into Watt's driveway a day later she didn't say a word. She didn't say, "Well that was a magnificent tour and we made a bunch of money." She didn't say, "The big markets didn't do so well, but boy, we sure did do a killing with the independents," meaning the SPCAs were moneyworthy even though the state fairs weren't. She didn't say, "I hope we can do this again real soon."

LaDonna pretty much quit talking—or giving massages—when Watt Pinson said he didn't want to do a photo book of Sister, or a Sister cookbook, or a Sister twenty-four-month calendar.

LaDonna let Watt out with his sad, confused dog in his front yard. She kept the Tupperware kennel. LaDonna backed up onto the road, and drove off without honking the horn, without waving, then drove west.

This was at two o'clock in the afternoon. Watt's carpet cleaning van wasn't parked in the driveway.

Sister took off running after the RV for a good hundred yards down Old Old Greenville Road. Watt chased her, and called. The dog, though, didn't turn her head. Then she vanished into the tree farm, the place from which she entered Watt's life.

Watt took out his key to enter the side door but found it unlocked. He walked inside, put down his suitcases, and smelled the difference. There was no carpet anymore. He only smelled wood, or grainy chemical particleboard.

Watt walked in, and saw where Mattie had taken up every square foot of Berber. All of the furniture stood against the den's south wall—couch, chairs, end tables, television set, useless armoire, thin bookshelf. Watt yelled out, "Mattie! Hey, Mattie, I'm home."

He walked into the bedroom, the guest bedroom, the dining room. Watt stepped into the living room and yelled out his wife's name twice.

It wasn't until a telemarketer called at eight o'clock that night and he didn't answer the phone that Watt heard the outgoing message. Mattie's voice went, "I'm not here. Leave a message for the son of a bitch."

Later Watt told anyone who would listen at places like Roughhouse Billiards about how he got ruined by the media, that he got all caught up in the spotlight. Everyone looked at him like he made it all up, for within a year no one remembered Sister the Wonder Dog. At nearby convenience stores and flea markets and trade shows Watt Pinson found ways to tell stories of his old life. He went to state fairs in North and South Carolina, in Georgia, and in Tennessee to find people who underwent similar circumstances.

"I had this dog had twenty-four puppies, and the next thing you know I'm being seduced by a woman who drove me around the country in an RV, I lost my business, and my wife ran off and left me," he started off most conversations. Men and women alike looked at him, and nodded in the way they might nod at a person who purported to have a direct line to God. "It's true," Watt said. "It's true. It's true, it's true, it's true."

Bunky Tucker sent Watt's large share of the money six months after Sister's tour. Watt spent a portion of it on telephone calls trying to get LaDonna to move south. More often than not she said, "Hey, it's great talking to you again, Mr. Pinson, but I have to go. I'm about to embark on another tour," involving an actor or writer or ex-child actor.

Watt bought ten doghouses for his other strays, and set them out equally in the backyard. He bought and paid for a three-foot-deep swimming trough so the dogs would never want of water or exercise. At night Watt went out and called for Sister, but she never returned. He waited at home for Mattie to call, so he could explain everything, so he could apologize, but she didn't.

He kept thinking about that first dead puppy. At night he dreamed of the Madison woman yanking that dog's head and body away.

Then Watt Pinson bought two shotguns, in case one didn't work right.

Migration over Gruel

MARKHAM ZUPP WENT BY MARKHAM—not Mark, Marky, Ham, Hammy, not even Zupp—and whenever someone made the mistake of offering an endearment, like I did, something occurred from deep within Markham's malformed sense of recognizing social pleasantries. He squinted. His lip curled to one side and he pulled his head upward. Markham inflated his chest and bowed his back. He turned one foot—usually the right one—inward pigeon-toed. Then Markham, inevitably, either popped his so-called accuser in the chest a couple times with the flat of his palms or threw a roundhouse outright.

I had seen it happen on a few occasions, usually in Roughhouse Billiards, when either Larry or Barry tired of miscalculating trick shots and said something like, "Hey, Mark-o, the table's yours," or "Hey, Zuppinator, the table's yours," or "Hey, Mark-ham-on-rye-wha'Zupp? the table's yours."

Normally I pretended that I didn't know Markham about the time his first punch landed, then Barry or Larry beat the shit out of him. Oh, I might've stepped in on a couple occasions, but mostly I looked at Jeff the owner and lifted my finger for the tab.

We sat on a bench on Gruel's square, right beside the statue of Colonel Dill, Civil War hero. This was October, and we awaited the first-annual fake hawk migration. Birdwatchers from as far away as west Texas surrounded us, all holding live white mice, barely weaned bunny rabbits, the occasional brown trout all gasp and wiggle.

The hawks weren't fake, but the migration was. In an ongoing process to reinvent Gruel and bring in some kind of tourist trade, members of the volunteer Chamber of Commerce came up with the hawk migration concept, though most hawks came south for the winter following the Appalachian Trail, the Blue Ridge, fifty miles one side or the other, on their way to wherever. Paula Purgason bought ads in *Southern Living* and a couple bird-watcher trade magazines for upcoming festivals and such. She promised thousands of swirling redtails, kestrels, and Cooper's hawks performing gyres overhead during a weeklong spree.

I said to Markham, "Hey, a dyslexic might accidentally call you Zuppo Markham—almost like Zeppo Marx. I never thought about that before." We didn't buy live mice or bunnies or fish from Victor Dees, who ran a makeshift concession stand there on the square. Supposedly, according to him, the hawks would come down and take prey from one's hands. Everyone from far away wore those big leather gloves that one lacking tongs might wear when pulling a hot, hot raku bowl out of the fire.

Markham stood up and said, "Stand up." I did. Because he tilted his head upward I thought maybe some migrating hawks arrived.

He pushed me hard on the chest, right above my nipples. I fell back on the ground, of course, and my shoulders hit a khaki pants-wearing woman in the back of the knees, thus causing her to fall over. Unfortunately, she held binoculars to her eyes, and when she hit face-first immediate bruises formed in such a way that made her look like a raccoon. I thought to myself, Oh God, I hope some wayward hawk doesn't look down from the sky and attack her. To Markham I said, "Hey, man," and punched him twice in the Adam's apple, hard. To the woman I said, "Let me help you up," and did.

She said, "Ow, ow, ow!" like that, and some people turned around momentarily until they saw her stand up. Then they stared back to the northeast, waiting for birds that would never appear. Maybe they thought she said, "Owl!"

Markham said, "Goddamn you, son of a bitch," and took one of those long, long swings at me, but I ducked, then got him with an uppercut right in the solar plexus, like a champ. He sat back down on our bench.

The woman said, "I've lost a contact! I've lost one of my contact lenses! If these hawks show up and I don't see them I'm going to send you the bill for my KOA campground and rental car fee."

Man, she was gorgeous, outside of the purpled rings around her eyes. I said, "That man over there fell into me, and I fell into you. I apologize." I stuck my right thumb toward Markham Zupp. "I think he's drunk or something." I said, "Let me run over to the concession stand and see if I can get an ice bag. I'm thinking that fellow has some fish on ice to slow them down a bit."

I looked over at Markham Zupp and fake-lurched his way to let him know that I might, at any moment, decide to turn unpredictable bird-watching redneck on him. "I appreciate it," the woman said as we headed over to the concession stand.

To Victor Dees I said, "Hey, man, let me buy some ice off you."

He said, "I got Italian ice for two bucks each. You want orange, cherry, cola, pineapple, blue, or mixed?" Victor Dees wore mirrored sunglasses and a camouflaged outfit. His hat advertised 3.

I said, "I just need some ice. Shove over one of those fish and give me some ice."

"That'll cost you extra," he said.

I turned around to point at the woman, who now crawled around Gruel Square looking for her contact lens. I said, "I'll take two blue, that's it."

I gave Victor Dees a five and told him to keep the change. He whispered, "Hey, that's good, Freddie Kerns. Make people think they's birds really on their way." Dees bounced his eyebrows up and down a few times until the hat fell off the back of his head.

I didn't punch him in the nose, even though I only went by Fred, not Freddie, not Frederick, not Frederich. Not Kernels. Not Kern-dogs. I said, "Uh-huh. I don't want to tell you how to keep up your business, but when the hawks don't show up you can keep your dead fish and rodents for the first-annual fake black buzzard migration. They travel, too."

"We gone have one them coming up?" he asked.

I showed up with my two blue sno-cones to find the bruise-eyed woman seated next to Markham, though he was more heaved forward than seated. I said, "Here. I know you might think it weird, but take one of these in each hand and stick them to your eye sockets. It'll be a lot like when you had binoculars to your face."

She said, "Thanks. My name's Sharon. I'd shake your hand but I don't want to lose my ice."

She didn't need to tell me that she was from the lower part of the state. It sounded like she said, "I'd shake your hand but I don't want to lose my *ass*."

I said, "I'm Fred. Now time's a-wasting. Stick your *ass* up to your eyes," of course.

Markham Zupp, to whom I will forever be grateful, said, "Sorry about that. Good punch, Fred."

I looked upward to the bleak, blue, empty sky. "You got to get ahold of yourself, man. You might want to look over some psychology textbooks and see what makes you act thusly."

Sharon stood there with two sno-cones to her face, the paper cup tips stuck out like a porno bra. "Are you some kind of paramedic, or athletic trainer, or doctor? How'd you know to do this so fast, Fred?"

I said, "Uh-huh," even though I only used Gruel to hide out in while I waited for one of the big companies to buy out my invention. I said, "Well not really—I just know, you know."

Markham Zupp sat up straight and took two or three deep breaths. He winked at me and said, "Man, is that a sharp-shinned hawk flying in? Is that a broad-winged?"

Sharon took the ice from her face, causing the frozen balls to hit the grass. She blinked toward the sun, then stuck the empty paper cones to her eyes. I said, "Mean joke, Markham. Mean joke, Markhamisole. Markhambodia. Markhamembert cheese. Markhamomile tea. Mark-hamfiregirl."

Sharon pulled the cups from her eyes and said, "Don't start."

Markham said, "Fred's just jealous 'cause they ain't no hawks coming today to show you off to."

I bent down toward ring-eyed Sharon and said, "Please trust me on this one." I took her by the elbow and led her in the direction of off-the-square. She didn't resist. "I'm always glad when people come visit here, but in another way I'm embarrassed about it. There's really nothing to do, except find a way to make a fool out of yourself in front of strangers."

Sharon said, "I've never spent time with the voodoo people from down where I live, but I have this suspicion that we've all been duped to come visit Gruel. Should I feel this way?"

"Tell me about it," I said.

Then I walked her around the corner to the Gruel Ice House, the only thriving business in town. Their motto, nearly flaked off atop the entire cement block facade, read, THE WORLD'S HARDEST ICE.

I wanted to hear Sharon say that, I'll admit.

The Old Gruel Cemetery holds the remains of about a dozen families—mostly Cathcarts, Deeses, Purgasons, and Downers. Because I imagined how disappointed—and perhaps litigious—Sharon might become once the hawk migration ruse became obvious, I felt it necessary to divert her attention to an ancient tombstone I had discovered during my first expedition through Old Gruel. There in the back corner stood a ragged-edged piece of limestone with NOVEL AKERS—WASHED ASHORE printed on it.

Sharon retracted two plastic bags of crushed ice from her sockets and squinted at the headstone. She said, "What does this mean, 'washed ashore'? No way. What, did the guy drown somewhere else and they moved his body here?"

I said, "I have no idea. When I asked some people about it, they either said they didn't want to talk about it or that some things were better off unknown."

"I doubt the Atlantic Ocean ever came this far north. I think it stopped somewhere around Columbia. Even if it did, that would be long before the English language arrived, you know. My *ass* is melting."

The ground in front of NOVEL AKERS—WASHED ASHORE barely grew new grass. It must've been some kind of Gruel inside joke, I realized, or maybe it was a dog buried there. No other headstone advertised a member of the Akers family. I suddenly felt like an idiotic and love-ravaged schoolboy showing off a secret hiding place or buried trivial treasures to a sixth-grade girl. I said, "Well this is Gruel. There's this washed ashore thing, and then there's a couple boys at the bar who try to do trick shots all the time."

"No hawks flying overhead on cue," Sharon said. "No birds of prey whatsoever. Not even geese."

I said, "You'd have to talk to somebody else about all that. The Chamber of Commerce woman. I only moved here some few months ago."

We walked back to the square. Sharon threw her ice bags in the garbage and said, "I'm still young enough to look punk. People will think I'm only wearing a lot of mascara and eye shadow. I used to dress up like that at my last job, but I think my boss didn't like it."

"Where'd you work?" I figured she worked for a zoo or something, what with traveling all the way from the lowcountry to watch some birds fly by. I figured she ran a homeless shelter, or a clinic for people who suffered from insomnia.

"I was a teacher for four years. Then I sold cell phones. Then I went back to being a teacher for four more years. It got to the point where I couldn't keep a job where everyone watched your every move. And no, I didn't teach biology or ornithology. And I don't think my mother and father were rein-

carnated into hawks, though I can tell you that more than a few people over there"—she pointed across the street—"are hopeful to remeet their relatives in the sky."

We approached Victor Dees's concession stand. I said, "What grade did you teach?"

Sharon looked up and northeast. She pushed the middle three fingers of each hand to her cheekbones. "Second. I need a headache powder. Say, what made you move here?"

I said, "They sell Goody's powders over at Roughhouse Billiards. I need a drink anyway." Then, for no rational reason, and against my better judgment, I said, "You ever see those wooden triangles with golf tees in them, like you see on the tables at Cracker Barrel? You know, you jump tees and see how many you have left at the end? Well my father invented that thing. Ever since, my entire family's lived off the royalties. And then I became an inventor, too."

She said, "Bullshit. That was invented by someone at Junior Achievement. Along with that weird board with two metal rods trying to get the big ball bearing to travel uphill to five hundred points."

I couldn't picture the metal rod game. And deep down I kind of knew that my father didn't really invent the triangle game. Right as I opened the heavy glass door to Roughhouse Billiards I said, "My latest invention ain't really that much of an invention." We walked six steps and pulled out stools at the bar. "It's more of a concept. I want to package a DUI retardant."

Jeff the owner said, "We got a special for middle-aged men going through a midlife crisis today, Fred. Bourbon and Pepto." To Sharon he said, "Lady, I can tell you right now that I'm in no need of free-range eggplant." He pointed to the purplish rings around her eyes. Let me say right here that I was

35

kind of amazed at Jeff's acumen in regards to quick-witted observations vis-à-vis people with physical abnormalities. I knew right away that I'd try to patent his abilities.

Sharon said, "I just want a beer."

"My DUI retardant is kind of a care package, you see. It'll have a tin of those Altoid things, of course. But I also want to put in there a choke collar and leash and some dog biscuits so that when the cop pulls you over, you only have to say, 'Hello, Officer. I'm out looking for this obviously beaten and pregnant stray dog I saw yesterday, and I want to get it to my vet.' Also, in my package, there'll be a fake poster of a missing child, so if you get pulled over by a cop you can say that you were looking for some little girl you thought you saw. See, most of the time you'll get caught for weaving, and there's a reason to be weaving if you're looking for a stray dog or missing kid. On top of all this, there's two or three empty Styrofoam take-out boxes with MEALS-ON-WHEELS printed on the lids, so if a cop pulls you over, you can say you were swerving while trying to read house numbers. You see? Isn't that a great idea? Can you see it? It's like a little box—maybe one-by-one foot—and you keep it right there in the passenger seat ready to open up if you've been out boozing it up and a policeman pulls you over."

Jeff the owner handed over a bourbon to me and a bottle of Pabst to Sharon. She said to me, "Tell me the real reason you had to move here. I've known some inventors in the past, and they don't like to talk about what they're in the middle of inventing. I met an old man up in Greenville one time named Townes who won the Nobel Prize for inventing the laser. He still won't talk about it."

I looked at my glass of bourbon, but didn't grasp it. "Well it's the truth," I said.

"Tell her about that other thing you thought up," Jeff said. To Sharon he stuck out his hand and said, "I'm Jeff, the owner."

Sharon said, "Sharon." She didn't say anything about how I almost knocked her eyeballs out.

"No," I said.

"Go ahead, man. Tell her why you're here, Fred."

I drank from my bourbon. Outside the window it looked as though people searched the sky for skydivers or the Second Coming of Jesus Christ. "It's not like I'm part of the witness protection program," I said.

"Tell me," Sharon said. I wanted to run over to Gruel Drugs and see if Bobba Lollis still sold sunglasses.

I finished my drink and said, "We came over here for some Goody's powders. You still sell them back there, Jeff?"

"We can't get them no more." He poured me another and said, "When you think those hawks will ever show up? They been like clockwork, how many years now?"

Markham Zupp came into the bar and said, "There's a guy out there who doesn't look like he's part of the bird-watchers, Fred. I don't like to cast aspersions or make generalizations, but he kind of looks like one of those gun guys who's after you."

I had invented a lock for pistols and rifles that fit onto the trigger. Not only did it take a secret code and a Social Security number to open, but it also recognized fingerprints and irises. Forty-nine state legislatures wanted to enact a law that would require any gun buyer to purchase my Secur-a-Shot upon purchase of his or her gun. Unfortunately, the thing added quite a hefty sum to even a cheap, cheap pistol.

The South Carolina legislature, though, felt it an unnecessary intrusion. Thus my move to Gruel.

I got death threats from the NRA, the United States Turkey Hunters Federation, some fellow who said he ran the mob in Boston, the owner of a dozen shooting ranges in Demopolis, Alabama, and so on.

I said, "Where?" and looked out the window.

Sharon turned her bruised face and said, "What's going on?"

I told her my entire story. She said that she'd expect me later on that night, at campsite 22 in the KOA campground. "I love a man who makes decisions," she said.

I decided not to tell her that the hawk migration wouldn't take place anytime during her vigil here.

I'd never undergone sexual intercourse with a woman who looked like she held afterburners to her face. The man who Markham Zupp thought might be after me ended up only being an angry golfer lost, looking for a course somewhere over on Strom Thurmond Lake and Resort thirty miles to the west. Sharon pulled out afterward a fold-up nylon chair with drink holders in the armrests and said, "There is no migration, is there. You can tell me. I won't let on to anyone else staying over."

I said, "There *might* be. I mean, there's a possibility. Hawks migrate, and sometimes, I'm sure, they veer from the normal course. The Capistrano birds have done it before, I read somewhere."

"Actually, they haven't. But that's okay. It might be a good thing that all these birders came out and saw nothing. That'll make their next experience that much more exciting. Yin-yang."

The smell of veggie burgers and tofu dogs wafted our way. No one cooked chicken, that was for sure. I said, "Let me get this straight. You taught school for a few years, then sold cell phones, then taught again. What are you doing these days?"

"I've never taught a day in my life," Sharon said. "And I've never even used a cell phone. I kind of feel bad about lying to you, Fred. It's a defense mechanism. Most men get repelled by elementary school teachers, don't they? Don't they look into the future and only see a wife coming home with snot on her hands and a load of homework to grade? As for the cell phones, I figured some people still believe that brain tumor story—about how people develop brain tumors if they're around cell phones too much."

I reached into her old-timey metal Coke cooler and pulled out two cans of beer I'd brought over. "I'm no saint, but when I think of elementary school teachers I think of rare angels. When I think of cell phone salespeople I think of desperation, mostly." I handed Sharon a PBR. "Gruel somehow missed all of the economic recovery that went on throughout the rest of the country during the Clinton years. Hell, Gruel missed out during the Reconstruction, too. Some of the people in the community are just trying to bolster business."

Sharon drank from her beer. Her eyes had gotten worse in regards to color, but the ice seemed to halt swelling. "Maybe I'm with Mothers Against Gun Control. Maybe I'm with Women in Need of Guns."

I sat up out of instinct. "Maybe I'm a maxillofacialist, or whatever they're called, and I push women down in hopes of drumming up some cheekbone cosmetic surgery."

We both went "Ha ha ha ha ha ha ha" like that, as if we'd practiced for years.

Outside it was dark completely. The other disappointed and befuddled birders stood around their own fires, most of them still looking to the sky. I heard someone yell out, "You've heard of nighthawks, haven't you? You've heard of goddamn nighthawks?"

Sharon said, "I used to be a history professor down at the College of Charleston. That lasted only seven years. Straight out of graduate school, then I got the job, got tenure, and quit last year. I don't know if it was some kind of midlife crisis—if it *was* I should only live to be sixty-six—but something told me that talking about the past all the time wasn't all that constructive. It certainly wasn't meaningful to me."

I was just about to say something like, "Hey, back there in the tent, that was really fun, wasn't it?" but then I would have been talking about the past.

"I'm not even here to see the birds. I just happened to be passing through Gruel, saw all the people, and thought there was some kind of fair or bazaar going on. I rented those binoculars from your friend at the ice station, and joined the crowd. I was really on my way up to Asheville for the Women in Numbers festival. Bo Derek was one of the speakers."

"Because she was in the movie *10*? Is that what it means?" For some reason it didn't seem politically correct to have Bo Derek speak at a women's conference.

Sharon, for no reason that I could ascertain, took off her shirt and sat back down in the chair. "It's supposed to be a history conference. People go up on this stage and say, '1884,' and then talk about how that was the year of Eleanor Roosevelt's birth. Well, actually it would be the birth date of Anna Eleanor whatever-her-maiden-name-was. I've been going to the festival for about five or six years now. It's very empowering. Women in numbers."

I looked around to see if anyone else sat around half nude. There weren't any. I said, "Not that it's bothering me any, but there are probably laws around here against being topless, Sharon."

"There's one more day. The festival's still going on tomorrow. Why don't you and I pack up and go there? No, I tell you what—I'll leave my tent here, and pay the guy for an extra couple days. Then you and I can go up there, see how we get along, then come back." She said, "Take off your pants and underwear right now, and let's talk about the plan."

I've never been the smartest man in the world, but I foresaw what would happen. She and I would leave. I would be the only man in a group of a thousand women lined up and down McDowell Street. All of the women would notice Sharon's black eyes, and conclude that I was some kind of wife beater. I would hold up my hands and say, "Stop making snap judgments," and then go into great detail about how I invented the Secur-a-Shot, but no one would believe me, just like they didn't truly believe my story in Gruel. Before long there would be a mob scene, and no one would hear what Bo Derek had to say about, oh, Marie Magdalene Dietrich being born in 1901 and her importance to women in the film industry.

I said, "Asheville's a couple hours away. Thomas Wolfe used to live there. I think he invented some things. Well he invented the really, really long novel, for one." I got up, and pulled off my pants and boxers, then walked to the car and opened the passenger door.

On our way out of town—and this would be either a great or horrendous omen, with nothing in between—a flock of flamingos, confused and wayward, passed in front of us, their heads turned our way, those unblinking eyes red, red, the tufts of fine pink feathers as startling and defined as the woman seated next to me, her hands folded into her armpits like wings.

Christmas in Gruel

BECAUSE HE HAD SCOURED both public and private properties
over the year, Godfrey Hammett knew where to cut down
small perfect cedars, eight-foot spruce look-alikes, and Leyland
cypresses that might pass for Christmas trees once heavily
decorated. He took notes, drew out maps, kept a mental image
of where to go and what tools he needed. On Thanksgiving
Day he poached these lands alone, armed with an ax, a handsaw, and a tarp. Godfrey fell three or four trees at a time, loaded
them up, and drug them out. It took almost thirty trips, back
and forth. He placed his trees in the pickup truck he usually
used spring and summer to transport cantaloupes, tomatoes,
cucumbers, and watermelons to the Forty-Five Farmers Market a half hour away from his ten acres outside Gruel, the
pickup he used in the fall to transport pumpkins, gourds, the
occasional one- or three-gallon azalea. He worked alone. He
told himself that no one should have to spend fifty dollars on
a Christmas tree, the price he'd seen the previous year up in
Greenville when he had to visit a certified oncologist.

Seeing as there aren't but a dozen families still living in Gruel proper—people who could only visit Roughhouse Billiards, Victor Dees's Army-Navy Surplus, Gruel Drugs and its adjacent Gruel Home Medical Supply store—Godfrey plans to set his $10–$20 Christmas Trees for Sale stand out on Highway 25 near the Ware Shoals exit, on a piece of flat hard clay at the top of the ramp. From the beginning he foresaw men and women driving the back roads between Greenville and Augusta, between Atlanta and Charlotte—people scared of I-85, I-26, and I-20—stopping by to strap a nice Christmas tree atop their new SUVs, their old station wagons, on *bent backs* if mopeds were their modes of transportation.

Godfrey erects a simple sign: GODFREY'S CHRISTMAS TREES. He stands his wares upright, so that—taking hints from an article he read about how funeral directors set out display coffins from medium prices, to most expensive, to cheapest—possible buyers will wade through the twelve-fifty pines, then the fifteen-dollar cedars, then the twenty-buck near spruces before seeing the ten-dollar scrub Leylands.

On the Monday after Thanksgiving Godfrey's first customer drives up near noon, a woman in an El Camino. She says, "Man, you got some kind of nerve, boy. 'God's Christmas Trees.'" She points at his sign. "I saw that from a half mile away and had to stop."

Godfrey turns around to see how one of his trees blocks part of his sign, blocks the *frey* of his own name. To the woman he says, "God made the trees as an act of celebration. It's in the Bible. I think God made the trees on day three. Am I right or am I right? Genesis, chapter one, verse eleven. Something about the earth bringing forth grass and the fruit tree yielding fruit after its kind, and so on." He can't believe he remembers the first book of Moses. He feels glad to have been forced to undergo the strict Bible-knowing tenets of Gruel Normal back in the mid-1960s.

The woman says, "I don't know about all that." She meanders through Godfrey's maze of poached trees until she reaches one of the twenty-dollar pines. Then she backpedals to a fifteen-dollar variety, pulls it toward her, and says, "I'll take this one."

Godfrey wonders how she gets her hair to stand so high, and why she doesn't tend to her roots better. "Y'all look good standing aside one another," Godfrey says. "This'll look good in your house."

"I live in a trailer."

"This'll look good in your house trailer," Godfrey says. But he thinks, I am God. I am God Hammett. "Fifteen dollars. I forget what the tax is on fifteen dollars. Oh, heck, just give me fifteen dollars even."

He carries the tree to the woman's El Camino and sets it into the bed like an offering. The woman says, "I'll tell my friends about y'alls'es place." She winks at him, jerks her head down once. "My three boys gone like this fine."

Godfrey thinks, Did you start having children at the age of twelve? He says, "You tell your friends that God's price can't be beat."

After she drives off, Godfrey thinks, This might be too easy. He thinks, I might have some explaining to do later on in life.

Then he looks to make sure that the cedar tree still covers part of his sign. Godfrey feels his jaw, tries to spit, and remembers that he can't. He walks back to his car and gets a jug of tap water out. He wishes that his salivary glands weren't burned up from radiation.

———

There was a time when Godfrey Hammett's father stood in front of Gruel Five-and-Dime with a hanging pot, dressed as Santa Claus, in order to solicit and collect money for nearby William Byron Strom Bryan Dorn Thurmond Jennings Boys Home of the South. Godfrey's father ho-ho-hoed, and rang his bell, and looked in the kettle for silver dimes and quarters, for wheat pennies. As a child Godfrey stood beside his father and yelled things out like, "Won't you please hep boys who can't hep themselves, please? The children are our future. Won't you please hep boys who can't hep themselves, please?"

Godfrey didn't know that his father took kettle money daily to the William Byron Strom Bryan Dorn Thurmond Jennings Boys Home of the South and said, "Man, these people of Gruel ain't exactly putting out money for orphans. I'm sorry. I ring and ring and ring my bell, but they walk on by like I'm not there."

Godfrey couldn't have known back then, when he was five to twelve, that his father pretty much siphoned off more than half the money. How could he? Godfrey stuck his arms out toward townspeople, and pled in a way that could've gotten him any part in a Little Theatre production should said theater run a Charles Dickens extravaganza.

When his father died, though, the only inheritance that Godfrey attained was a backyard map of buried coins with a hopeful note that the numismatic scene would rise incredibly. It would, certainly, Godfrey thought, if he lived another couple hundred years or thereabouts.

Most of the good Mercury dimes weren't worth more than a couple dollars each, Godfrey knows. And seeing as he doesn't have health insurance, sooner or later he'll have to sell them off.

Or find another way to pay for his oncologist bills.

Godfrey perfects his odd monologue over the first ten days: "Ma'am, what you got there is a genuine southern blue-green short-needle spruce known only to a patch of ground between here and Asheville, between maybe Elberton, Georgia, and Gaffney, South Carolina. You seen that giant peach water tower over in Gaffney on I-85? The last of these blue-green short-needle spruces stops about right there. Let me tell you—this tree won't shed like some them other ones you see being sold. I got bass fishermen coming by to buy these things—not for Christmas trees, but to sink down in their favorite fishing holes."

"Well that's something to think about."

She's driving a new dark blue VW Beetle, and already Godfrey can't figure out how to tie it on top. He says, "You ain't from around here, are you."

"I'm going down to Camden to see my folks. And I'm betting that they don't have a Christmas tree yet. I thought it would be a nice surprise."

Godfrey nods once. He says, "Camden. That's like down in that horse country, right? Am I right or am I right? Camden. I been down there once a long time ago. My daddy took me down there one time to see a five-legged foal got born."

The woman walks through the medium-priced trees, the expensive ones, all the way to the ten-dollar Leyland cypresses. She says, "To tell you the truth, I kind of need three trees. I need one for my parents' den, and then two more for their help out back. Would it be all right if I placed a couple trees in my passenger seat, just to see if they fit? If they fit, then I'll buy them. And I need to get one of these twenty-dollar trees somehow tied to the roof of my car."

Godfrey says, "I guess you noticed how my sign says GOD'S CHRISTMAS TREES. I'll do my best trying to fit those trees inside. Does your seat fold back? Say, does this car have an engine in the back or in the front?"

The woman points at two of the cheaper trees for Godfrey to put in the car. "Listen, God. Or whatever your name is. I want you to try to put these two trees here in the car, but I don't want them hanging over in a way that they would touch my arm when I shift gears. Maybe you could put one in one way, and the other the opposite way. Kind of like two doorstops, you know."

Godfrey says, "Yes ma'am." Another car drives up. He's down to twenty trees, most of them the higher-end fake spruces. He says, "I'll be right with you."

"Do you have some rope or twine or bungee cord for me to tie the other on the roof?" says the woman.

She holds her palm above her face, as if looking for sailboats on open water. She rests her right foot on the VW's bumper and Godfrey notices her beauty. Hotdamn, this woman has the curves of a brand-new dirt bike track, Godfrey thinks. It's beginning to look a lot like Christmas. "I do, yes ma'am."

"To tell you the truth I don't even know why I'm bothering with all this. My parents haven't bought each other Christmas gifts in about thirty years. They quit when I went off to college. I hate to say it, but I think they don't even believe in the birth of the baby Jesus."

"Well it's up to you to rechange their minds," Godfrey says. "In the Bible it is stated, 'Whatever-whatever-whatever . . . and she brought forth a son.' I think that's in Luke somewhere, like in the first chapter of Luke. Don't quote me on that, though."

Godfrey puts one Leyland cypress in frontways and the other opposite. They fit. He ties a nice near spruce to the front and back bumpers of the VW lengthwise. The woman says, "A five-legged foal. That's a miracle in its own way."

Godfrey says, "Hey, you seem like a woman of worth. You don't have a silver change collection by any chance, do you? Or be interested in buying one for somebody on your Christmas list."

Then he leans to the left for a spit, but nothing comes out.

By December 15 Godfrey Hammett is out of trees. He restudies his maps and realizes that there are no more saplings left, that if he wants to keep up his little scam then he would have to expand his region. I should take this money and pay my doctor, he thinks. I should take this money and buy myself a burial plot over in Gruel Cemetery.

"What you been up to?" Jeff Downer says from behind the bar at Roughhouse Billiards. "Damn, Godfrey, I ain't seen you since then. How you feeling? I heard about your treatments over all this time, and all."

"Not much. Fine," Godfrey says. "Say, you could use a Christmas tree in here. You want a Christmas tree?"

Jeff wipes away an invisible beer spill. Behind him, two men practice trick shots on the pool table. One of them tries to balance two balls atop each other, in the middle of a wooden rack. He's got a twist-off beer top in one hand, and three swizzle sticks that are somehow going to be part of the four-rail spectacle.

Jeff's hair's slicked back and wavy in a way that makes the interstate highway system look simple. He leans on his right arm and says, "Christmas tree? It ain't but December 16. I don't put up a tree until the twenty-fourth, if I even do it then. No one brings me presents to put down beneath it. No one comes by here and gives me an extra tip, like I give the mailman."

"I've been selling trees, that's all," Godfrey says. "People kept calling me God. The sign I had up was kind of hidden in part, and people kept calling me God."

Behind them, one of the trick shooters says, "You didn't call that it was going to double-kiss the ball. You didn't call none of that."

Downer doesn't move or blink. He stares at Godfrey and says, "You remember how your daddy used to ring that bell over there by the Five-and-Dime? Man. He used to follow people down the street heckling them if they didn't put no money in the kettle. You remember that?"

Godfrey says, "I guess I'll take a Bud. If you put a tree up before Christmas Eve I bet people would give you presents. That's your problem, Jeff—you put something up the day before Christmas, no one has any money left."

"All right then." Downer touches his brow. "Go get me one of your trees." He looks up at the ceiling, twelve feet up. "I'll take a big one, I guess. My wife can give up half her ornaments. She's got enough—some guy just come by and sold her a bunch of baby Jesuses inside these glass globes. She's got enough for her tree and another, I'm thinking." He hands a twelve-ounce bottle of beer over to Godfrey. It's nine o'clock in the morning.

"I ain't got no trees," Godfrey says. "I might have some more next week. To tell you the truth, all the ones I sold were stolen. You know." He takes a draw off his beer. "I guess. I mean, I took them off property that I didn't own."

"You been over to the Self property out by Forty-Five? That old boy must have a hundred cedar Christmas trees he's using for a border of his yard. I'm thinking that he's got something to hide, but I don't know for sure."

"My father," Godfrey says. "First there was my father, and then there was my wife. You'd think that a person would get a break every once in a while."

One of the trick pool players puts three balls in a triangle in the middle of the table, and the eight ball next to a side pocket. He says he will hit two balls in the far pockets, that the first ball will end up knocking the eight in. *And* he says he'll use a broomstick instead of a cue stick. The other man says, "You go ahead, Cuz."

"We don't get no breaks in Gruel," Downer says. "Whatever happened to Dora? Is that true what people say about her taking off for Texas?"

"Texas."

"I wonder if they celebrate Christmas in Texas. It's got to be hot down there, you know. You couldn't sell no trees down in Texas, brother. Cactus, maybe. But not trees."

One of the pool players says, "I told you. I told you it wouldn't work. It's a good idea, but it won't work ever."

Godfrey says, "Where does that guy with all the Christmas trees around his house live?"

Godfrey Hammett's wife, Dora, left a half year earlier while her husband sat inside the outpatient waiting room, ready for blood work. She took off. Dora got in her Dodge with two suitcases, a makeup bag, and a trunkful of shoes. Godfrey had to drive some forty miles north to a real hospital, and she figured that she had time. She left a note that read, in part, "All ready I know what the results will be—cancer of the jaw. Jaw, and blood. And you know why? It's because you always chewed with your mouth open. Air got inside there—bad air—and caused the problem. I'm sorry to do it this way, but I can't live with a man with no lower jaw. I guess I'm not the best wife ever, but I don't see myself trying to feed you while you stand on your head, or however people without a bottom jaw have to eat. I'm going to Texas, only because you would never take me to the Gulf of Mexico on our honeymoon."

Dora wrote and wrote about how this decision wasn't spur of the moment—that she no longer cared to live in a loveless marriage, that she couldn't stand Gruel, that she dreaded the days when Godfrey came home early from work, that she was embarrassed when her family asked how things went. Dora blamed Godfrey for their not having children, and said that one of her major disappointments in life had to do with not waking up on Christmas morning and seeing a little boy and girl tear into gift-wrapped toys and games and bicycles and .22 rifles.

When Godfrey got back from the hospital some three hours after he'd left, he wondered if maybe Dora started the letter a couple days earlier. He thought about how she couldn't be more than a few miles down the road.

Then he drove out to Gruel Sand and Gravel, which offered no health benefits anyway, and quit his job driving a dump truck. "I ain't got cancer of the jaw because I eat with my mouth open," he told his boss Freddie Shirley. "If anything, I probably got grit lodged down here," he said, pointing to the side of his throat.

"You can't just up and quit," Freddie Shirley said. "How far are you until Social Security kicks in?"

"Twenty years," Godfrey said.

"Damn. You ain't but forty-five? I thought you were sixty by now."

"See what else that grit will do to a man? I got nothing against you and yours, Freddie. It's time for me to make a change, though. I need to wipe the slate clean and start over."

"What're you going to do, buddy? Does Dora know about all this?"

"I'm going to go home, and sit myself down, and make out a list. After I make out my list, I'm going to let it set for a day, then I'll check it again to make sure."

"You sound like Santa Claus, friend. Hey, you ain't going to start ringing that bell like your daddy did, are you?"

Freddie didn't hear Godfrey's answer. Freddie walked over to a mirror in the office, opened his mouth wide, and peered in. Then he checked his eyes, his pores, the wrinkles on his forehead. When he turned back around, Godfrey was gone.

Godfrey scopes out the Self plantation at three o'clock in the morning. Like Jeff the owner said, there are a good hundred six-to-ten-foot cedars lining the property. Mr. Self and his family ran Forty-Five Cotton, and could afford to have a landscaper come back in and replant the boundaries. But that's not right, Godfrey thinks. You can't cut down a man's trees this close to Christmas.

He pulls into the driveway to turn around, which sets off four motion-detecting spotlights. Old Man Self sits in a cheap, woven, aluminum-frame beach chair, hidden behind a brick springhouse. "Come on back here, boy," he yells. He stands up and raises his right arm. Is that a gun in his hand? Godfrey thinks. "I got you a little Christmas something for delivering my paper on time daily."

Godfrey looks down at his handsaw and ax leaned against the bench seat. In his mind he hears Dora's voice say, "You need to pay your doctor some money. Don't look a horse's gift in the mouth."

Godfrey opens his driver's door. What looked like a gun happens to be an envelope. He says, "I do what I do. I can only do what I do. It's my job."

"Well I appreciate it. You know, I used to deliver newspapers when I was a boy. This was when it used to be an afternoon paper. I'd get home from school, and get out my old canvas bag, and walk down to the *Index-Journal* office, and start to a-folding. I think I had about a hundred people on my route, most of whom didn't pay me on time, and most of whom ended up working for my daddy's mill. And then for me. It's funny how things turn around, isn't it?"

Godfrey says, "Uh-huh. Yessir." He doesn't think about not having any newspapers with him. He doesn't think about how Mr. Self might say, "Hey, so where's today's paper?"

"I hope this helps out for you and yours," Mr. Self says. "Go buy one of your kids something nice."

Godfrey nods and kowtows and takes the envelope. He says, "It's customers like you who make my job a lot easier."

"All right," says Mr. Self. He walks back to his folding chair and carries it toward the house. He doesn't think about not receiving the day's news. A mile down the road Godfrey pulls his pickup over and opens the envelope to find a two-dollar bill, a voice balloon coming from Jefferson's mouth, "Merry Xmas!" written in tiny, tiny block letters.

He forgets everything he considered earlier about it being the holiday season, about not hewing down what one man might consider needful in regards to solace, protection, anonymity, and privacy. Godfrey gathers his courage, turns around, knows that he'll hand over the two-dollar bill should the real carrier plop his rolled cylinder of bad economic news on the shiny, shiny brushed cement path leading toward a brick house built by cough-stricken men and women.

By daybreak Godfrey has only made three trips back and forth between his squatted-upon sales lot and Mr. Self's estate. He carries eight cedars in the bed of his truck each trip, tied down with a series of interlocked bungee cords. On the last trip, he swings by his house, finds some cardboard and a marker, and writes, FREE CHRISTMAS TREES FROM GOD. Because he's hewn more trees than he can carry—or that he would chance poaching in daylight—Godfrey stands his sign up in the Self yard, and hopes it will make a poor local passerby, perhaps an ex-loom fixer or doffer, happy. He thinks, Twenty-four nice trees. Getting close to Christmas, supply and demand.

He stops in at Roughhouse Billiards as the rest of Gruel's retired or unemployed citizens begin their usual day, driving in circles around the square, waiting for anything to happen. "I got you that tree you said you wanted," Godfrey says to Jeff the owner.

"You in here mighty early. If you got the trees, why you in here in the first place?" Jeff sticks his head in the cooler and inhales hard. "It smells like stale beer, but I don't see where anything's leaked or broken."

"I'm going to wait a day or two. I'm going to keep them watered down and all, but wait until tomorrow." He doesn't say anything about not wanting to be near evidence should Mr. Self call the police and so on.

"You went and cut all them trees off Old Man Self's yard, didn't you, Godfrey. I didn't think you'd have it in you. But I know this: You're going to feel guilty as all get-out before it's over. And then when something goes wrong in your life, you're going to look back and think it happened because of what you stole from another man. Like I bet you did when poor Dora up and left. Hey, you want a beer?" The owner reaches in the cooler without looking and pulls out a can. "You better do something awful nice for someone else, so as to even things up. Why, plain *giving* me a free Christmas tree might be a good start."

Godfrey doesn't hear him, though. He tries to think back as to what he could've done wrong in life that would offer such heartache as his wife leaving. He wonders what he did to come down with cancer. "I drove up to the guy's house and he thought I was the paperboy. Look at this." Godfrey extracts the two-dollar bill from his wallet. "It's the tip he was going to give the fellow for delivering his news every morning over a 365-day period. Two dollars! Poor deliverer would probably try to spend it around here and get caught for having phony money."

Downer wipes the bar. He walks around it to turn on his neon OPEN sign. "There's something else you'll pay for— stealing a man's Christmas tip. I swear, Godfrey. I'm believing I better keep an eye on you. Maybe you should stay in bed all day before you accidentally do someone wrong without even knowing it."

"I don't even know what I'm doing half the time, I guess. I promise you that I try to be a good person usually. I don't think of myself as bad. I don't go to church or anything, but I've known way worse people who went twice a week."

Downer sits down beside his friend. "When I was a little boy I used to walk past Wilkie Tolbert's house every morning. I need to explain that I had an unhealthy craving for cheese all the time. Evidently the Tolberts did, too. So twice I walked by and noticed how the milkman had come by and left a quart of milk and cottage cheese and a big old chunk of American cheese there on their front porch. You remember how they used to do, how the milkmen used to do. Both Mr. and Mrs. Tolbert worked second shift at the mill, so they didn't get up sometimes till past the time Wilkie'd already headed off to Gruel Normal."

"It's a shame how Wilkie died. I never heard of anyone falling out of a truck on his *way* to get inducted. That was right about Christmastime, too."

"He probably did something wrong earlier. Which gets me back to my story. I snuck up there twice and stole the cheese they'd ordered, and which got delivered to them. My father found out all about it when, trying to be a good family member, I stuck half of each chunk of cheese down in the dairy section of our own refrigerator. To make a long story short, I worked for an entire year for free doing chores, and had to give what other money I made straight over to my father. When we had enough saved up, he bought a milk cow and made me tie it up to a tree in front of the Tolberts' house on Christmas Eve."

A man comes in and asks where Paula Purgason lives. He says he heard that she was the only real estate agent in town. Godfrey and Downer look the man over, then say she's gone senile and can't work anymore. They say there's no real estate in town for sale, and no agent to sell it in the first place, which isn't true. The man doffs his cap, thanks them, then leaves.

"Did you see that guy's shoes? There wasn't a scuff on them," Godfrey says.

"Last thing we need in Gruel is a clean-shaven man."

"Say," Godfrey says, "I've known you all my life and I never heard of this cow story. I've known Wilkie Tolbert's parents, too. I don't remember them having a milk cow at any time."

Downer lowers his head. He takes his thumbnail and etches into a stain on the counter. "Well, as it ends up, they saw it as a *beef* cow. For about a week."

The cedars completely disappear in two days. Godfrey sells the last stolen trees for twenty dollars each. He puts the cash in a metal ammo bin with the other fourteen hundred plus dollars he took in from the first round of sales. Only one woman had dickered with him whatsoever, and more than a few customers paid money in advance and said they'd come back. The dickering woman—she insisted on writing a check, insisted that it wouldn't bounce, insisted, "If you're living on this planet, then you should know me"—was named Cecilly. She picked up the next-to-last tree, the one blocking the *frey* on Godfrey's sign. "If I'd have known that it really wasn't *God's* Christmas Trees, I probably wouldn't've bought *anything* from you. Next year, *change your sign*, if you want to sell to *me* again."

Godfrey had said, "Have fun bullying Santa Claus, ma'am. Hey, I know a good place where you can buy coal and switches for your husband and kids." Then he disassembled his sign, put it in the back of his truck alongside his last cedar, and drove to the square in Gruel.

Godfrey takes the largest tree to Downer, and Downer sets the tree in an extra hot dog pot, leans it between the men's room and some exposed duct work. He plops a baby aspirin in the water and says, "I read in one them magazines, do this, plants last forever."

"I wouldn't know about that," Godfrey says. "I heard about taking an aspirin a day to thin the blood, but I think the aspirin industry made all that up. What do they know?"

Downer says, "I got me a cousin Morris who's one them hemophiliacs. He eats nothing but sausage and Crisco all the time, trying to thicken his blood. He's coming over for Christmas dinner and I guarantee you he won't touch nothing but dark meat and ham." He looks over at the tree. "You ought to come over, Godfrey. What're you doing for Christmas Day? The wife won't mind. Roughhouse'll be closed. We always have plenty of food, outside of dark meat turkey when Morris comes on down from Slabtown."

"I'll probably stay at home," Godfrey says. "I appreciate the offer, but you wouldn't believe how much I got to do. Plus, I'm on this strange diet due to the cancer. It's too hard to figure out."

"You got to watch what you eat and all. I thought you was in remission. You got to take care of yourself, I'm guessing."

"Shew. You wouldn't believe it. Hey, I think I'll have a bourbon today instead of beer. Unless you've made up some eggnog."

Downer doesn't reach behind him toward the mini-bottle rack. He stares at Godfrey. "You remember what I said about the Tolberts' cow, now, don't you. I feel like I have to invite you over because I feel bad about all that—about stealing the cheese, then having a milk cow get slaughtered accidentally."

"Oh, I remember. They didn't fry out my brain cells when they took out most my neck."

"What're you going to do, then? You can't just sit around all by yourself on Christmas. I bet you didn't even save a tree for yourself. You don't have no kids. What're you going to do?"

Because Roughhouse Billiards serves booze in plastic cups, Godfrey doesn't feel bad about taking his drink to go. He walks out to his empty-bedded truck, cranks it, then swings around the square a few times before heading home. He thinks to himself, I need to think this through.

He knows what will happen: He'll go home, open the Bible haphazardly, and find a verse to fit his needs. He'll spot Jeremiah 6:4, or Deuteronomy 11:5, or 2 Chronicles 1:10. Godfrey will sit at home with his ammo box of money until Christmas Eve, then drive down to a nursery in order to buy seedlings and herbs. He'll plant the seedlings in all the spots where he stole cedars and pines, all the places where other future desperate men might steal trees during economic or personal downturns. He will box up the herbs in festive wrapping paper, open them alone beneath his own tree, and later take the herbs himself, hoping to stave off any possible cancers. On Christmas Day there will be no canned cranberry sauce. No, he'll drive the countryside in and around Gruel, keep himself busy, sort through everything he'd ever done, try to keep tabs on how he needed to change his ways should there be more to this life, or an afterlife.

In the coming year Godfrey will locate old grape arbors—of pergolas and lost lattice—and connive a way to harvest old tangles of vines in order to make holiday wreaths, perhaps. Meanwhile, he knows that he'll only think about that milk cow from now on, and that he'll hold it against Downer for ever telling him such a sad tale in this, the holiday season.

Soldiers in Gruel

AMANDA FUTCH SAVED her three indoor cats' claws for twelve years, not knowing she'd do something spectacular one day. She pried them out of carpet nap, from a variety of scratching posts, off the sides of her couch, out of her aerobics outfits. Amanda dropped each glycerin comma into an empty mayonnaise jar, and with every one she thought and thought. This started right after college, when she got a job waiting tables, when she got her own apartment, and after she visited the Humane Society for the only time. Amanda graduated with a degree in women's studies from Smith, though she took other courses at Hampshire, Amherst, BC, BU, Tufts, Wells, and Emerson. She spent summers those early years anywhere from Ann Arbor to Warsaw, participating in seminars that ranged from Environmental Antiart to A Complete Look at the Feminine Characteristics of Gargoyles.

Amanda moved to New York City, for she knew about postmodern feminism, about glass ceilings. Her bookshelves were lined with everything ever written by or about Susan Sontag, Annie Dillard, Camille Paglia, Georgia O'Keeffe, Frida

Kahlo, Jane Goodall, Joyce Carol Oates, Tom Wolfe, and Margaret Mead. One day, Amanda knew, she wouldn't have to wait tables anymore; Amanda wouldn't have to spit onto pecan-encrusted grouper or yellowtail *crudo*, or poached lobster ordered by men who called her honey, babe, doll, sweetie, sugar, dearheart, sweetcheeks, or bitch. She'd make a difference.

"I don't know how y'all shed so many claw nails," she had said to her cats every morning. "What's up with that? What do y'all do when I'm at work?"

Amanda's three yellow felines, turned to fat, wove around her legs each late morning as she made coffee, prepared to look for jobs, then ended up reading essays about the evolutionary mistake of Man. The cats sat atop the couch as she half listened to CNN. They eased their necks onto the top of her head, made biscuits by her shoulder tops, left claws everywhere. Eve, Gertrude, and Alice attacked any near boyfriend's shins who ever slept over. Amanda didn't know how many claws she'd missed, left in the stretch socks of her seemingly open-minded suitors.

Before two cats died of leukemia and Eve escaped, never to be found, they meowed in unison sometimes. For a dozen years Amanda realized that they said, "Move-south, move-south, move-south." She knew. Amanda tried to conjure reasons not to return to her origins in the Carolinas, but every morning her cats told her otherwise. She dismissed them as the descendants of Flannery O'Connor, maybe Zora Neale Hurston, Truman Capote, Eudora Welty, or Carson McCullers.

Amanda auditioned for off-Broadway plays, applied to teach at experimental schools, and waited tables until she turned thirty-three. Then she surfed the Internet over a long weekend, finally ending up, somehow, on a Web site for strange and oddball festivals attended by a select group of participants.

She scoured over the Red Clay Eaters' Annual Convention and Bluegrass Stomp; the Meeting of Walleyes and their Staggering Fish Fry; a Gathering of Bucktoothed Women. Without much time for reconsideration Amanda sublet her apartment to a performance artist friend of hers named &# who also waited tables, retrieved her collection of shed cats' claws at the last minute for no reason that she could imagine, took off in her 1972 VW Bug, and got on I-95 south.

"You don't need to be a standing member of the club, honey. There's a hundred-dollar registration fee, but that money goes into a big pot so we can pay for the winners. This'll be one plain free-for-all show," Eugene Parker says over the telephone. "There's some people who're renting these houses down in Gruel, and there's people who're staying in their cars. On top of that, there's a KOA campground right down the road. Come on down, dearheart. Me, I'm entering my Cadillac with little army men glued all over it. I call it my Sevillian Soldier. I won't win. But it'll be fun driving it down the parade through the square. They got a square in Gruel the likes of Mayberry."

Amanda Futch sets down her magazine. She hadn't come across the Wild Wheels and Crazy Cars convention while looking up places to visit earlier, but now knows that a higher being directed her to the Clinch River Motor Inn, a room with a Bible on the nightstand and a *Southern Living* magazine atop the small TV, probably left over from the previous tenant. Amanda says, "Do I need to come up with a title for my car? As soon as I saw the ad, I knew what I wanted to do. But I haven't done it yet."

"It don't hurt none to name your car. There's an old boy from Michigan or somewhere puts Kraft macaroni on his hood he calls hisself Pontiac Pasta. This one woman has Barbie doll parts all over her Bonneville. She calls it Ken Backed over Me in the Driveway, you know. She got wrote up in one of the big newspapers one time. I think they going to feature her in some movie somewhere."

"Well," says Amanda. She thinks about the feminist implications of Barbie being violated by Ken. Perfect! she thinks. "Uh-huh."

"Well I guess I'll come down there with my cats' claws. Do you think they'll blow off on the drive down? I mean, I don't want to get all the way down there with nothing. I can glue them on in the way I see them in my mind, but I don't want to have them flake off if I drive over twenty miles an hour."

Amanda calls from a town in western Virginia that is about to succumb to a man-made dam. The festival here—which would be a onetime affair, of course—is called God, Dam This Place Now and Forever. Most of the participants and visitors were brought up in the area and either didn't want to see it submerged or they live there now and can't wait for government checks in the name of eminent domain. The festival features a big barbecue, thanks to the hogs that won't be able to swim anyway, and "the last good water that will come from here ever," namely, moonshine. Plus there will be a retrospective of Doc Watson music performed by a hundred banjo players brought in from as far away as Kentucky.

Eugene Parker says, "We going to have a section blocked off where people can pay a dollar to see art car artists actually work on their cars. That's the category you need to belong to. You got to pay fifty dollars more to be in it, but then you get to split up fifty percent of the money that comes in from the people. The rest of the money goes, you know, to administrative costs, and insurance, and back to one of the four overall winners' prizes. We got first place in wagon, first place in truck, first place in vintage—that would be before 1976—and first place in compact. We got second place, too, but it's half what first place gets. Second place is mostly gift certificates from area businesses."

From her open window Amanda Futch hears what sounds like a gaggle of bagpipers, but it ends up being a herd of sheep bleating toward higher ground. She says, "What's the first-place prize?"

"It matters how many people register, sugarlips. Last year we had the convention up in northern Alabama, so a lot of people didn't show up what with their fear of snake handlers. But I believe first place in each category went for a couple thousand dollars."

Although Amanda Futch never took a course in economics during her college career—she never even crossed paths in the hallways with a business administration professor—she understands that she qualifies for both compact and vintage. Amanda says, "Gruel, South Carolina. I don't even see it on the map."

Eugene Parker laughs. "Well maybe that's why we're having it here." Then he spouts out directions that takes Amanda two pages to write down in the back of her handmade recycled-paper journal bought at the Please Let the Baby Monkeys Live! boutique back in Greenwich Village. And Eugene Parker starts off with, "Can you find your way to Greenville? Gruel's only about forty miles from there, as the bitch copperhead slithers."

Amanda calls her own number back home, gets the answering machine, and finds out that &# changed the outgoing message. &#'s voice now says, "If you have a message for Amanda, please leave it. If you're a woman and have a message for Ampersand Number, please stick two fingers in yourself and groan. If you're a man, stick both fists up your ass and travel elsewhere."

"Hey, Ampersand Number, this is me," Amanda says from Gruel. "I'm in a place down in South Carolina. I just want to call and say that you'll have to get me on the cell phone if you need to get in touch. It's a long story, but I'm in a campground that doesn't have a pay phone. You want something for your conceptual art, you need to come down here, woman. This is the place."

On the way down Amanda bought Superglue in order to adhere her ex-cats' claws all over the VW. In Gruel she stopped in at Victor Dees's Army-Navy Surplus store and bought a sleeping bag, tarp, metal cookware, some Sterno, and a variety of questionable MREs. At the Gruel KOA she's surrounded only by other art car enthusiasts. There's a man from New Orleans who decked out his entire Ford Maverick with Mardi Gras beads. Ex-sergeants Russell and Konetta Threatt—an African American husband-and-wife team camped next to Amanda—covered their Impala in Chocolate Soldier bottle caps, for they met in the military. Ex-Deadheads painted dancing bears and skulls on their hoods, trunks, and roofs, as well as extended tailpipes to look like giant joints. "You and your people might be what I've been looking for ever since I didn't understand those formalists in an Aesthetics 101 course," Amanda says to a group of a dozen people who stop to look at her Volkswagen.

"Man," one of them says. "What are you, some kind of minimalist? I don't get it."

Amanda looks back to her as-yet-undecorated ride. "Oh. Oh, that. No, I came down from New York and I'll be converting the car at the Convert-Your-Car-Now lot. I think it's tomorrow if Eugene Parker told me right."

They nod. One woman says, "What're you going to do?" She hands over a small ceramic pipe.

Amanda partakes, though she's not smoked weed since almost getting a part as a dancing blade of grass in an off-Broadway experimental production based on the life and times of Walt Whitman. "I got these cats' claws I was going to glue all over it. In my mind it'll look like a giant conglomeration of glycerin commas, you know." She hands back the pipe and exhales. She tries not to think about how she has no idea as to her real plans. "What's the story with this town?"

"I'm Jessica. This is my old man, Ted." The rest of their group wanders down the dirt path to admire or scoff at everyone else's cars, trucks, vans, wagons, and one poor fellow with a moped decoupaged in blue DUI tickets.

Ted wears a bicyclist's rearview mirror on his eyeglasses. He says, "That's the way to go if you're just starting. Did Eugene tell you how you'd get some of the door by letting people see you work?" He wears a straw cowboy hat with a kaleidoscope glued lengthwise on top.

"Yeah."

Jessica says, "That's how we got started. We were driving from Santa Fe east to *anywhere*—I won't go into detail as to why we took off with no warning, kind of on the run. Anyway, we came across one of the regional art car festivals being held that year in Asheville. I remember Ted and me looking at each other simultaneously, both of us thinking how it wouldn't be a bad idea to camouflage the Nova."

Ted pulls on his thin beard. He points behind himself. "We're the Pecan Log-mobile. Across country we kept stopping at those Stuckey's places, you know. It seemed appropriate. The statute of limitations is beyond us, now, by the way."

"Only thing we got to worry about is torrential rain-storms. When that happens," Jessica says, "we have to find the nearest Stuckey's and make the repairs. We got to find an overhang of some type, and then another Stuckey's."

"Squirrels and birds, too," Ted says. "Don't forget about the time we spent the night at that rest area not knowing squirrels lived all over the place."

Jessica passes the pipe back to Amanda. She says, "I know it can be scary starting right off. There are a few people who take this whole art car lifestyle a little too seriously. I mean, there've been accusations of bribery and payoffs, you know. We've been to about forty of these congregations over the last eight or nine years. My advice to you is to do the best you can do, try to think up something that no one else has done—*everybody* thinks that covering their cars in pennies is going to be some kind of statement—and have fun. Share any food that you might have with people who look starved. Ted and I've been lucky to win first- or second-prize money for a while now, so we're not hurting."

Amanda says, "I brought some moonshine along that I got in Virginia yesterday."

"We had a big nest egg, too," Ted says. Then he and Jessica start laughing and nudging one another the way only bank robbers act.

"So. You can ask me anything about anything. Do you have any questions?" Jessica says.

Amanda exhales. She actually feels her head lift from her body and hover above the campground. "Yes. The man at the army-navy store in town tried to sell me a gas mask. Should I have bought it? Also, why is it every fucking Republican president thinks that *not* funding our schools will somehow improve America?"

"There are no Republicans in Gruel this weekend," Ted says. "Well, maybe one. We ran across a boy who wants to glue shoe polish canisters all over his Volvo. He'll be in competition with you tomorrow. You'll see him—he's wearing a Nazi uniform."

"I told Ted that it could be he had some kind of knee replacement surgery, but he says doctors have that operation down to a science. Ted says the guy's goose-stepping."

Amanda doesn't give up the pipe. She points that she needs more. Ted fills it, lights it, and Amanda tokes. "I have another question: Do you think I'm unattractive? Should I dye my hair a different color? Am I getting fat in the hips? Why is it that stupid people get glamorous jobs in the United States? My friend Ampersand Number is apartment-sitting for me—well, I mean, she's subletting—and she can't get anyone to take her artwork seriously because she's beautiful. Hey, do people ever dance at these parties?"

Someone walks by offering nitrous oxide balloons. Ted and Jessica distract Amanda. "Moonshine," Ted says.

Amanda wakes up thinking about how she's betrayed her roots. She was born and raised in Myrtle Beach. Her parents owned a gift shop that specialized in puka shell necklaces, an L-shaped motel two streets off the beach that fraternity boys from state colleges inhabited between March and August, a bar called Whitey's Crab Shack that held the largest aquarium wall in South Carolina. She graduated from high school with a near perfect SAT, went north on a full ride, and never returned. When Amanda delved into vegetarianism her sophomore year in college she started off by not eating shellfish as a statement against her father, then eventually eased out of fish, chicken, beef, and pork.

Her head hurts at dawn, but she knows that she must get started on her work, that she'll try to get the VW half done before driving it onto the square and finishing the project in front of paying spectators. Maybe it's the marijuana still coursing through her veins, but she can only think about nine interlocking triangles, of a yantra. She emerges from beneath her tarp and sets to work on the hood of her VW without the aid of a straight edge, yardstick, or protractor. By the time her campground neighbors emerge from their backseats, tents, or pop-ups, Amanda has counted off and carefully placed one thousand shed claws from her dead cats.

"Let me guess: It's a crop circle," says Russell Threatt, the Chocolate Soldier guy. "That's good. That's a statement. Are you from Kansas?"

His wife pours coffee into a speckled ironware cup. "Idiot. It's a spiderweb on the hood. The car's a Bug. The spider's caught the Bug, you know."

Amanda smiles. She nods and shrugs, says, "It's kind of both, I guess." She tries to eradicate one thought from her head: This must be like receiving applause after an off-Broadway production. This is the kind of recognition that I never got while waiting tables, no matter how good the food and service. Amanda says, "Have y'all won awards for your Chocolate Soldier? I like it a lot. I kind of like to think that y'all are making a statement—that you come from a long line of people who were mistreated and held down, that you were forced to serve your country in one way or another, and that no one appreciated your contributions to keeping the United States of America free."

Amanda knows that if it's not the marijuana still bubbling in her system, it's the moonshine she drank with Ted and Jessica while walking around the KOA campground looking at everyone else. She thinks about when she sat in the front row of a Helen Gurley Brown speech back in college. "What are you talking about?" Konetta Threatt says. "Hey, you want some coffee?"

Amanda starts to say, "Workers of the world unite," but doesn't. She says, "Where are y'all going next, after this one?"

The campground comes alive like so many earthworms after a good steady rain. Russell Threatt says, "It doesn't sound right when you say 'y'all' whatsoever. Don't come down here and pretend, girl. You won't get nothing but killed if you try to be one of us, no offense. You and your crop circles."

"It's a spiderweb," Konetta says. "It's a spiderweb, catching the Bug. And I'll make a prediction that if she don't win, it'll be the boy with all the wine corks on his Chrysler. That thing looks cool, but it doesn't have the same philosophical implications."

Cars start up. People drive to town. Amanda calls up &# to check on things, but only gets this new message, in &#'s voice: "What walks on four legs in the morning, two legs in the afternoon, three legs in the evening, and four wheels later on in life? Yes, it's not a pretty sight. Leave a message if you know the answer."

Amanda can't remember if she called her subletter the night before. She can't remember if she paid all the bills, or if she made decisions as to what might be her first big decision since leaving South Carolina fifteen years earlier. She says to the machine, "There are conceptual artists outside of New York City, Ampersand Number. They don't even hide behind fake names, either. You need to get yourself back to being Rachel and take the first flight down this way, believe me."

She mashes the end call button. To Russell Threatt she

says, "I used to say 'y'all' all the time. I guess I've gotten out of practice. I'll get better. I promise that I'll get better."

So the hood ends up a nice nine-interlocking-triangle yantra design, the roof a double helix, and both car doors resemble, somehow, Marcel Duchamp's *Nude Descending a Staircase.* Spectators have their own theories, though: One man thinks the doors look like the Milky Way jammed together. The man with the DUI-ticket moped thinks they either mimic a bag of spilled rice or a large city's streetlights viewed from above. "I've been in an airplane before," he tells Amanda. "I believe it was Birmingham, Alabama, that looks like your doors from the night sky." A husband-and-wife freelance writing team hoping to sell an article to *Art in America* comes by and tut-tuts that the doors are nothing more than a Jackson Pollock rip-off. Then two women stand stunned and begin convulsing orgasmically. One woman says, "Please, *please* let us ride with you to the next convention." Her partner says, "I've not been affected like this since listening to Wagner over and over an entire month."

Amanda glues every available cat claw and tries not to subconsciously count how many visitors she's entertained, calculate the entrance fees, divide by the other dozen art-car-in-progress participants, and divide again by two. She wishes she'd've taken care of a dozen cats in New York, or at least paid more attention to the rugs, carpets, scratching posts, and furniture of her cat-owning friends over the years.

She does not say, "Voilà!" She wipes her brow, looks over at the competition, and waits for someone to tell her when it's time to join the parade of cars around Gruel's square, circling the statue of one hometown Civil War hero named Colonel Dill.

Eugene Parker walks up wearing a shirt adorned with pictures of vintage car lighters. He says, "I bet you're glad you came down, girlie. You the talk of the fair."

Amanda doesn't spit on him as she might if he were a diner at one of her old restaurants. She knows that it's not her expertise in art car decoration, either. Trying to be totally objective, Amanda notices that she might be—physically—the prettiest woman in attendance. She says, "This is kind of like a society within a society. Someone should write a scholarly paper about these people."

"Well maybe you should do that," Eugene says. He sucks on his teeth and scans the other cars. "Maybe you the person who should write about you people."

For a second, still holding her tube of Superglue, Amanda thinks, I'm not one of these people. She feels sick to her stomach, and says, "Excuse me for a second, Mr. Parker."

The grand prize winner for something like six straight festivals was always Ruben Blank, a man who mixed moss and buttermilk in a blender, then slathered the concoction onto his Mercury Comet. He parked it in the woods behind his house near Rutherfordton, North Carolina, and waited for it to come out looking like a Chia Pet. Even the windshield was covered. When Ruben Blank slit out spots so he and any possible passenger could see where they drove, the Comet looked not unlike any green monster invented by Japanese cinematographers. No one involved in art cars—not the man who covered his DeSoto with ceramic Florida tourist knickknacks, not the woman who adorned her Buick in ignitable Joan of Arc bobblehead dolls—could hope for anything but second place when Ruben Blank showed up.

That is, until an as-of-yet unidentified perpetrator snuck up one night with a gallon of Roundup—two art car festivals before Gruel—in Lily, Kentucky.

"Gentlemen and lassies, start your engines!" Eugene Parker finally says, walking around the roped-off vacant acreage on Old Old Greenville Road. "It's time to strut your stuff."

Amanda turns her ignition and gets out of the VW to say to Eugene how he needs to learn how to address women as women, how it shouldn't be "Gentlemen and lassies," "Boys and girls," "Ladies and gentlemen," or even "Gentlemen and gentlewomen." She wants to yell out something about how he should only yell out, "Human beings, start your engines," but her cell phone rings as she gets back in the car.

It's &#. "I don't want to be one of those litigious creeps," &# says, "but I was walking across the den and I cut myself pretty badly, Amanda. I was barefoot—and I've checked into this already, how a person has the right to walk around bare-foot in a landlord's property—and I cut my foot. Or at least I punctured my foot. I hopped down to the free clinic and the doctor there had to get some tweezers and pull out what ended up being one of your cats' claws from the sole of my right foot."

Amanda says, "Ha-ha. Funny joke."

"I'm serious," &# says. "I'm as serious as a splenectomy. It might've been a shard of glass, but the doctor said it looked like a cat's claw, I swear to God."

The cars rev up in a way that might make a chicken row spectator at the Darlington racetrack feel slighted. DUI-ticket moped leads the way out. A man with Adlai Stevenson pictures all over his car comes in second. "Yeah, yeah, yeah," Amanda says. "Listen. Save your bill and I'll pay for it when I get back."

"I'm supposed to premiere a work on the corner of Lexington and Twenty-sixth today, and I don't think I'll be able to do it. The original idea was for me to wear a flesh-tone bodysuit and dance in a giant bowl of pasta."

Amanda pulls off in line. The motorcade proceeds at five miles an hour. "On the street corner? What're you doing, working for people to throw change in a pan?"

"I'll have you know that I got an arts commission matching grant for this, Amanda. I have to keep careful documentation of what I spend, and where I do things, you know."

Amanda honks her horn because everyone in front of her does. She says, "I'll buy you some fucking spaghetti when I get back. Plus your free-clinic doctor bill. Listen, I have to go. I was going to invite you down here, but I don't think you'd be able to handle it."

&# hears all the horns. "What kind of traffic jam could take place in South Carolina? What's all that noise?"

Amanda holds the cell phone out her driver's window. She screams, "It's more than you could handle, Rachel." People stand on the sidewalks as the cars come into town. They hoot and offer war cries and give thumbs-up. "How're y'all doing?" Amanda yells back from her glistening, glistening Volkswagen.

&# says, "What did you say? What was that word you used? Goddamn, Amanda, I didn't know you had changed to one of them, girl."

Amanda looks over at Colonel Dill's statue, then over at Victor Dees in front of his army-navy store, then back to the Gargoyle-mobile in front of her. She says, "Wait a minute. You got *taxpayer money* to dance in a bowl of pasta? How is *that* supposed to further the human condition?" She takes a left-hand turn, then pulls over into the line of parking spots, and awaits the three judges'—one from Mexico, one from New Jersey, and one from Nevada—decisions.

The guy from Mexico kind of gets it, in his own way, in a manner that Amanda hadn't considered. He thinks that Amanda's VW Bug represents the pain and suffering endured by Frida Kahlo after her encounter with a bus, the persistent gnawing question as to whether she should be monogamous with a fat muralist or give herself up totally to a man with communist ideals. The judge from New Jersey thinks that Amanda tried to overlap constellations—Orion over Ursa Major over Little Dipper over Corona Borealis over Camelopardalis, and so on. Amanda nods, as if that's what she meant all along. But the other judge from Nevada thinks that her cats' shed claws look like mere bugs popped on a cross-country drive. He says to Amanda, there in the pulled-over, stalled traffic of Gruel, "You should've just driven your car down here from wherever you're from, and let the gnats and mosquitoes done the work for you, little lady."

And that does it. "Listen, numbnuts," Amanda says. "I could stick a spit in you and turn you over and over, you little shit. You're going to have to learn not to call women 'little ladies' or whatever else you call them. I've about had it with men using these condescending names. Oh, it's not a southern thing, either—I've heard them all the time up in New York."

This particular judge—though he placed Amanda second in the best compact art car category, which would've still given her first place overall—puts the blue ribbon back in his pocket. He says, "What?" as a man unsure of the price of a shot of whiskey might say to a bartender. He says, "I don't think I heard you right."

"You heard me." Gargoyle-car driver and DUI-moped rider and flammable Joan of Arc driver stand nearby, awestruck. Russell Threatt and his wife stand across the way nodding, hoping this will push their car upward in the standings.

DUI man says, "They's people call me Slopehead on a Moped, but I'm smart enough not to back-sass judges, baby."

The judge from Nevada says, "I don't think you want to argue with me. You ever see basketball, girl? You ever watch a baseball game? There's something called a technical foul. There's something called *getting thrown out of the game*."

When Amanda says, "Eat me right now," she realizes that she's never used those words before. She thinks, This feels good. This feels better than ever figuring out what Wittgenstein meant, or getting a fifty-dollar tip on a fifty-dollar meal.

"I'm going to talk to my partners and find a way for you not to win," the judge says. "I can do that, you know."

"Like that will change my life," Amanda says. "Like that's going to make me go back home and slit my wrists."

The Nevada judge only stands five-six, and wears a combover. He doesn't weigh but 130 pounds, and has gotten to where he is by his reputation as an ex-boxer and philosophy major at UNLV. He's worked as a soccer referee, and reaches in his pocket for a red card, out of habit. He reaches and reaches, and then yells out, "Get this woman out of here!"

"That's right," Amanda says. "*Woman.*" She feels her blood pressure rise. She thinks, I'm going to change everything wrong in America—that's my lot in life. She thinks, God, there has to be more in life than wondering why people can't figure out ways to better the human condition. A man driving his art car covered in broken pieces of tile, so that mosaics of the Virgin Mary appear, burns rubber out of control, veering through the square. Amanda thinks, There has to be more in life than simply spinning wheels. She says, "Are you a judge at every competition? I hope you're not a judge at every competition we have in the future."

And then she attacks him in a way that no one's seen in Gruel since old, retired, and decorated Colonel Dill took on a carpetbagger back in 1880 or thereabouts, thus gaining his reputation as statueworthy on a square. Later on, after Amanda gets escorted out of her KOA campground site, people say that they heard "We aren't stuck on this planet for no particular reason. And we aren't stuck here to put up with the likes of you" over and over from her mouth—the same thing Colonel Dill supposedly said.

She yells out lines owned by Tennessee Williams's plays, too, though no one recognizes the allusions. Amanda Futch crumples down on the pavement, and shoos everyone away, and almost thinks about driving south to see where her parents are buried.

In years to come the cats' claws will fly off in the wind. Amanda will drive west, then north to Seattle, then east to Michigan. She will drive back south to Gruel in a naked VW adorned only with the memories of what projects she had installed at various shows in small towns anxious for attention. She'll think about the slight money she took during her first competition, when onlookers examined her glued-on masterpiece. Back in Gruel, she will walk into Roughhouse Billiards and say, "I think I still have a dozen hot dogs coming my way for second-place finish in last year's art car competition. Hey, let me get a couple hot dogs all the way, while I go over to Gruel Pharmacy for my Goody's powders, Band-Aids, gauze, Neosporin, hydrogen peroxide, vitamins, Pepto-Bismol, Maalox, Geritol, eyedrops, and milk thistle." She'll say, "I have a great idea. It's about healing."

Jeff the owner will say, "How you want your hot dogs?"

"Mustard, ketchup, onions, and relish. That's all. No chili."

Jeff will look over at two men playing eight ball, then say to Amanda, "You don't want no buns?"

She won't take his comment as some kind of antifeminist slight. She won't think that he said "buns" in some kind of double-entendre kind of way. Amanda will lean over the bar, pull back the draft beer dispenser, and hang her head upside down. She won't think of what statues might be erected in her name. She won't think of her previous life, of the cell phone she quit answering, of any scholarly tracts she once considered meaningful.

Assurance

MY FATHER DEFLATED the tires of his Plymouth down to about ten PSI, he said, so that the car would grip the road better. There was no road, as far as I could tell, only four inches of snow—BLIZZARD IN CAROLINA! the weekly paper would read in its next issue—and my father said we needed to drive some twenty miles away to buy an air compressor for when he felt it safe to reinflate the Goodyears. I was too young to say something like, "Why don't you get chains instead?" or "Why don't you keep a set of spiked snow tires in the shed out back?" or "Where is it, exactly, that we might have to visit that's so far away we'll have to drive?" My mom said something, though. She followed us right to the end of the driveway, screaming, using the two-foot indented tracks for better footing that the Plymouth's more-than-half-flat tires left. My father stepped on the accelerator and we roared out on Old Old Greenville Road at a blazing five miles an hour. Unfortunately, I *was* old enough to say, "Why don't we walk? We'll get there faster." My father took off his high school, Masonic, wedding, and Insurer of the Year rings—all of which he kept on his right hand for some reason—and punched my left arm, the arm I *wouldn't* use when I pelted the back of his head with snowballs later in the day.

"Hey, you want to stop by and pick up Watt or Louis or Andy? We can all squeeze in. The air compressor will fit in the trunk when we get it. We can keep the chain saw set up here between you and me."

I didn't slink down in the car seat like I normally did when Dad made me ride around town with him, blowing his horn at current and future life insurance policyholders. I said, "I doubt they'd be awake this early, seeing as we don't have school. Even if we did have school, I doubt they'd be awake at six thirty in the morning."

This was late January, and when the electricity went off the night before, my father held up a finger and said, "I guess y'all aren't going to argue with me about trading out that stop sign I found for three transistor radios with Mr. Dawes, are you?" He didn't say much when only one of the radios had a battery that wasn't fully dead. He found an AM station out of Graywood that reported statewide school closings. The announcer said that absolutely no one should go out driving, and that a number of trees had fallen on secondary roads.

"I know of a great ice cream store up where we're going. I'll get y'all ice cream, son."

I didn't say, "It's snowing. People drink shots of whiskey, like I know you'll do later, when it's snowing." I said, "Shouldn't you turn on your headlights? It's dark."

My father drove in the middle of the road. He took his hands from the steering wheel and asked that I pound against my door should we lean too much to the left, that he'd do the same should we lean toward the ditch on my side. "Don't need no headlights. The moon's leading us on. Look at that snow glowing! It's like the Yellow Brick Road. Except white. If I turned on the lights there's no telling how many deer we might hit." He pulled his coat sleeve down below his palm and wiped a circle on the windshield, then asked me to do the same.

I said, "Double negative. 'Don't need no headlights' means that you actually need headlights."

My father quit defogging the windshield. He punched me and said, "Maybe you should hold my rings in your hands so it'll make you remember what might be coming your way. Here." He handed them to me. "Don't never say I never gave you nothing."

I put the Masonic, Insurer of the Year, and high school rings on my left thumb and the wedding band on my right, not thinking about how—when I would later pelt the back of his head—the wedding ring would fly off obliquely, somewhere, in virginal snow unperturbed by traffic.

"I can't believe that I was looking at the want ads not last week and saw this air compressor for sale. At the time I only thought how nice it would be to blow up your bike tires, your basketball and football, and maybe the spare in your momma's car."

I banged my door and the car righted itself, somehow. "It's not that far down to Gruel Gas. Mr. Bratcher doesn't charge for air or water."

The windshield wipers stopped. My father turned on his headlights. "Mark my words, boy. They'll start charging for air and water before long. Back when your grandfather—well, maybe your *great*-grandfather—was a boy, they didn't even charge for *gas*. Now look at it. You know how come they didn't charge money for gasoline when your great-grandfather was a boy, Bane?"

I'd heard this one before. My father'd either forgotten or tested me as to whether I listened to his stories. "Because there were no *cars* back then. Horses didn't need gas."

He nodded. At the top of a hill he stopped the car, got out, retrieved a bottle of bourbon from the trunk, and poured some of it out on the windshield and the wiper motors. They came back to life. "Damn it to hell, I hate having to do that," he said as we continued up Old Old Greenville Road. "Say, did you hear that disc jockey list off anything about the liquor stores being closed today?"

I was too young—and sore—to say that I did.

Earlier in the week, before the official blizzard, it had been my turn to give morning prayer over Gruel Normal's intercom system. This was supposed to be a sixth grader's perk—and since there weren't but fifteen of us in total, we pretty much got to do it once a month, taking into account holidays, teacher workdays, and so on. We were supposed to give a standard recitation made up by the principal that started off something like, "Our Father, who art in Heaven, please bless all of Gruel, and may we have a safe journey into the day's events." It went on and on. Then the Pledge of Allegiance came next, followed by an instructional verse from Psalms. Most of my classmates practiced what they would preach, but me, I normally opened the Bible, closed my eyes, and read wherever my finger landed. To say that I already didn't cotton to the fire and brimstone of the Good Book would be an understatement. My father wouldn't allow us to attend church. Any Gruel church had such small congregations that it would take at least a hundred dollars' worth of tithings each month to pay for the preacher and keep up summer league softball uniforms. To attend a church with a respectable membership would mean driving way past where he and I went to get an air compressor. Being in the insurance business, he knew that chances for a wreck multiplied with each foray down a two-lane stretch of asphalt.

"If anyone in the house feels the need for religious counseling, you can come to me," he said more than once. "I'm in insurance. God's in *assurance*. They're practically the same word."

This is not to say that my father saw himself as God's right-hand man, or that he scoffed anyone's personal beliefs. He'd taken a variety of seminars over the years all the way down in Jacksonville, Florida, and felt like, somewhere along the line, he probably got the same kind of education as a middle-of-the-road seminarian.

My mother, though, found it necessary to put out the fire when asked to meet with Mr. Haddon, the principal, after my little slip of the tongue during morning prayer. First off—in order to prove my innocence—I'd like to point out how none of us at Gruel Normal even thought to call the guy Mr. Hardon. We didn't know.

"Bane was a touch-me-not baby at birth, Mr. Haddon," my mother started off. We sat in his office. I still wasn't sure what went on. "Any time another human being came to pick him up or stroke his cheek he'd start to crying. He wouldn't stop until he got put back in the crib. I couldn't even *b-r-e-a-s-t* feed him until he was about four years old."

I said, "I can spell, Mom."

She held up her hand. "That didn't come out right—I didn't breast-feed him when he was four years old. But that would have been about the time I could have, if it would have been morally acceptable and doctor-approved. It's not and wasn't, and I didn't. By then he ate regular food, like every other child, and he let me stroke his head every once in a while. But what I'm saying, as a touch-me-not baby, he might not have gotten some of the social graces that the rest of us have."

Mr. Haddon wore a lot of Brylcreem in his hair, making the top of his head look similar to a roller coaster. He said, "What? I don't think anyone tried to touch Bane when he gave his prayer. Did anyone come up and poke you in the ribs, boy?"

I said, "No, sir."

I'd given the requisite part of the morning prayer about God looking after us through the day, but then unlike my classmates I plain popped open the Bible and stuck my finger down to what I knew, somehow, would be a pertinent passage. Each verse is pertinent, in its way, if stretched enough. I hit Psalm 77, verse 10, which reads, "And I said, This *is* my infirmity: *but I will remember* the years of the right hand of the Most High."

First off, the print in a regular Bible is small enough, but this was out of one of those tiny pocket-sized green ones given out by one of those do-gooder organizations at the beginning of each school year. And secondly, maybe I suffered from a variety of dyslexia. I know this: I said, "I will remember the right hand of the Most High on my rear." I'm sure I could've gotten away with it—perhaps even commended—at a parochial school.

My mother said, "Who's to say that God didn't come down and touch his little bottom while he was still in the womb? Maybe that's why Bane was such a touch-me-not. Maybe he didn't like anyone else's hand, after feeling God's. Say, while we're on the subject, do you believe that Jesus is everywhere?"

Mr. Haddon stared at my mother for a good five-beat. Looking back on it all I bet he either thought about obtaining state funding or asking me to leave his office in order to screw her on the desk. He said, "I certainly do."

"Do you believe that God resides with the downtrodden, the sick, the poor, and even the evil sinners of the past?"

Get this: Mr. Haddon said, "Indubitably."

"I guess he's in hell, then. Jesus is in hell. Jesus lives in hell. All these people think He's up there in heaven, Bane, but according to Mr. Haddon, Jesus lives in hell. Come on." She grabbed my arm—which I didn't like, of course—and drug me out of Gruel Normal. If there had been another country school within, say, a hundred miles, I'm sure I would have registered there presently.

In the car on the way home my mother said, "Please tell me you didn't turn that Bible verse around on purpose. Making fun of the Bible will get you a one-way ticket to Hades, Bane, that's one of the laws of the universe."

I was old enough to say, "Maybe I want to go live with Jesus."

My mother began taking off her rings and setting them atop the dashboard.

My father didn't fully understand supply and demand. For some reason he thought he could wrangle a snowy day air compressor deal. I guess he thought umbrella salesmen sold their wares for less on big city street corners during thunderstorms, too. But as soon as the guy selling an air compressor noticed my father's tires, he jacked up the price. This was in downtown Ware Shoals, a cotton mill town with a couple traffic lights, a place that—ten years later—would fold completely into a ghost town. My father complained, but forked over the money. I helped him get it in the backseat of the Plymouth. We drove off after my father told the man, "I would normally try to sell you some life insurance, but with the way you conduct business I can understand how you won't live very much longer and thus it would be unwise for me and my company. I try not to sell cancer insurance to a man who's coughing up lung, you know."

The man said, "Is that a threat you making me?" His eyes were sunken in, his chin jutted, but he looked as though he'd been sitting out in the sun for a good couple decades. He wore a plaid shirt and striped pants.

My father kept his window rolled down and said, "Don't slip on the ice and bust your head, boy. Don't go off to work and get your fingers stuck in a machine, unless that's the kind of thing you do to make money off the mill."

We drove to the first stoplight and pulled up next to a woman driving a Fairlane. The snow wasn't as bad in Ware Shoals, and people drove to and from the mill. I didn't notice the woman staring at us until my father said, "Watch this." He stepped on the accelerator and lurched four feet toward the intersection. The woman turned her head and drove straight across, running the red light. A driver crossing the intersection through his own green light hit his brakes, fishtailed, and barely missed the Fairlane. He honked his horn, and gave the woman a finger. My father said, "Now we wouldn't have been able to see none of this had we not gone out, could we have?"

The light turned green and we proceeded. About a half mile down the road my father spied the Fairlane parked at the Piggly Wiggly. He said, "Let's you and me go in there and get us some them three-for-a-dollar barbecue sandwiches. We'll get six."

I might've been a touch-me-not baby who grew up to feign dyslexia when reading Bible passages, but I knew enough to know that my father would go inside the grocery store, seek out the staring woman, and try to sell her insurance of one sort or another. I said, "I'll just sit here."

He pulled in right up front and parked next to her. I waited until I saw him veer toward the back of the store. Then I got out, started making snowballs, and lined them up on the hood of our car. For some reason I remembered Ricky Timmerman giving his selected verse earlier in the year. It went, "Oh that I had wings like a dove! *for then* would I fly away and be at rest." We all made cooing noises at him when he returned to class. Ricky also was the first person to tell me that *bane* wasn't a good word. He told me how one time his own father said, "Ricky, you are the bane of my existence," which got him all confused. For a while he thought that we were brothers, or at least half brothers.

I had a good hardpacked twenty-four snowballs lined up when my father emerged from the Piggly Wiggly, toting his sack of barbecue. He turned around, I assumed, to say something to the Fairlane woman. Did he apologize for revving his engine and pretending to drive forward? Did he remind her of his hours of operation should she want to come in and get some health/life/fire/auto?

The first snowball hit the back of his head in a way that I couldn't have drawn up on paper. I couldn't have gotten a potato gun and aimed a better shot. This is probably when his wedding band flew off my thumb. Snowballs two through ten hit his head, back, butt, and right ear. He dropped the sack. I missed a few times, nailing the ice machine, a stray buggy, a picture of the Piggly Wiggly mascot Scotch-taped to the window.

But my father laughed—he laughed and ducked and grabbed our barbecue before running at me all wide-armed, smiling, acting like some kind of B-movie monster confronting his tormentors. For a split second I thought he might try to hug me. I ran.

"You don't want these things getting cold, Bane," my father yelled. He circled behind the car and opened the driver's-side door. I watched him stamp his feet first. "Come on, son. I ain't going to show you no affection in public or nothing, I promise."

I stopped in the middle of the street, not knowing if it was a trick. He got in the car and turned the ignition. The woman in the Fairlane came out with two paper bags. She set them on top of her car and gave my father a wave. Was she flirting? I wondered. What had my father said to her?—maybe in the cereal aisle, or over near the picnic supplies, or in the dog food section.

When he pulled around and reached over and opened the passenger door, I got in. He said, "Boy, that woman's boobs are so big I'd *never* sell her insurance. She's going to fall over one day unbalanced and kill herself like a turtle fallen over on its back." He said, "Hey, let's take some *really* back roads on the way home and see if there are any fallen trees. I'll let you use the chain saw! Mom will be happy if we come home with some free firewood."

I got in. He said something about my arm being major league. I took a bite out of a thirty-three-cent barbecue sandwich and watched the white, white landscape slide by slowly. The snow stopped, but a full gray cloud hung not ten feet above any irrational traveler.

So we filled up half of the trunk and all of the backseat with scrub pine sawed in three-foot lengths. My father was obsessed with bringing firewood home. I know this, because a couple of the trees weren't blocking back roads—my father pulled into the overgrown dirt driveways of more than a few abandoned houses, and cut down trees that might've been bent from the snow but weren't blocking the road whatsoever. The snow halted, but the temperature still hovered at thirty degrees, so we didn't pull the air compressor out immediately. No, we gathered my last complete and uneaten barbecue sandwich, and a half of my father's, put them back in the sack, and offered them to my mother as some kind of hunter-gatherer prize.

"I figured we wouldn't have electricity left yet, so we brought you some supper," my father said. "And on top of that, Bane and me got some logs so we can cook in the fireplace. I'll do it all! I learned to cook over an open fire a long time ago, in the Boy Scouts. You go get out some pots and pans, and I'll make us some good eggs and grits for breakfast. Hey, seeing as the refrigerator's out, let's you and me pull out everything and pack it in the snow, Bane. Outside's colder than inside, you know."

My mother held her head tilted upward and didn't blink. She stared at my father. "You been drinking? Tell me you didn't take our only son out in this weather so you could drink the whole time."

I shook my head no. "We had to use the bourbon to unstick the windshield wipers," I said.

My mother looked at the wood. "Pine causes too much sap and soot to gather in the chimney. You don't want to burn pine in a fireplace, Buck. I read it somewhere in one of my magazines." My mother crossed her arms in a way that would've made any TV sitcom actress look like an amateur.

"That's a myth!" my father bellowed. He turned to me, almost touched my shoulder, and said, "Bring that wood in, son. Stack it up on the hearth."

Even out in the driveway I could hear my mother say, "Where are all your rings? Where's your wedding band?"

I heard my father say, "Oh." I imagined him looking down to his own hands. "Bane's got them all."

Right before I picked up three pine logs I looked down at my hands and noticed the Masonic ring, the high school ring, the Insurer of the Year ring. Where was Dad's wedding band? I checked my pockets, looked on the floorboard of the Plymouth, even felt inside my ear seeing as sometimes I thought about getting an ear pierced, even back then. Then I remembered a *ping* sound on the Piggly Wiggly plate glass window right after I threw my first snowball.

I came inside with my logs and Mom said, "Hey. You got your daddy's wedding ring?"

I shook my head no. I started to cry, I think. "It's at the Piggly Wiggly in Ware Shoals. It fell off when Dad assured her about everything."

"What woman?" My dad had gone to the bathroom.

"He said he was going to try to give her assurance, but then he said her boobies were so big he decided against it. I guess he didn't want her calling him up when she stretched out on her back like a turtle one more time."

My mother stared at me, then looked back at the bathroom, then looked back at me. I had never seen her eyes so big, not blinking. She pushed her hand through what used to be a permanent hairdo, then began shoving that pine into the fireplace. It might've been thirty degrees in our house, both literally and figuratively now that I look back on it all. Dad came out of the bathroom still all hunter-gatherer, hoping to be commended, whistling a sound-track song, smiling. He said, "Them sandwiches should still be warm enough. If they ain't, I'll show you how to put a stick in them and hold them over the fire."

My mom said, "I can't believe that you would take our boy

with you while you're out scalawagging around looking for loose women."

My father stared at me and turned his mouth in a way that looked like a dog playing tug-of-war with rope. He said, "What lies you told, Bane?"

I said, "I didn't say anything. I ain't said nothing."

"Buck, I want to know why you threw your ring down to meet a woman at the Piggly Wiggly. Why would you throw away all we've done in our lives? We were talking about a *lake house*, for God's sake!"

I said, "I think it fell off when I threw that snowball at you, Dad. Please don't touch me, please don't touch me, please don't touch me."

"Bane!" my father yelled. And then I ran out the door wearing his Masonic, high school, and Insurer of the Year rings still on my fingers.

Outside I heard my parents yelling at each other for a good five minutes. Then it sounded more like cooing, like all of us performed when Ricky Timmerman got through with his dove verse that one morning. I don't know what happened inside. Me, I had damn near scooped up every granule of snow from our front yard and piled up a snowball arsenal should either of my parents emerge from the front door or garage, or sneak from around the back, in order to grab me from behind, drag me down to the ground, and hold me in place. I had other things in mind. There were chunks of our gravel driveway in most of them.

My parents seemed to know better than follow me, though. I'm not sure what they did inside. My friends Watt, Louis, and Andy trudged over at dusk and Watt said, "Where you been? We went over to the old sand pit and slid down with our cardboard. My daddy says this kind of day won't happen again for fifty years. Are you still in trouble for making fun of God touching your ass?"

I said, "Uh-huh."

"Y'all have wood in your fireplace?" Louis said. He pointed up. I looked back behind me. I said, "I guess."

"Man. You're lucky," Andy said. "We just keep looking for more sweaters. My mom says she knows she didn't sell all the sweaters at the last yard sale. We already burned up all our extra *Forty-Five Platter* newspapers, plus some unused rolls of toilet paper and what branches fell in the yard."

I looked up at the smoke billowing out. At the time I felt proud, seeing as I had something to do with the chain saw operation. But I also felt bad that I didn't invite my friends inside to warm up, maybe drink some hot chocolate. I feared we might find my parents either coupled up, or punching one another out, nothing in between.

All three of my friends said, "How come you don't have any snow in your yard?" in unison, like they practiced, as if they were the Three Wise Men at Gruel Normal's yearly Christmas pageant.

Andy said, "My mom says your dad's one with Satan. She says y'all don't go to church and you'll all fry in hell." Watt and Louis stood there. They didn't add on to what Andy said, but they didn't take up for me, a boy who already had to slump down in the Plymouth most days embarrassed. Andy said, "That's why you ain't got no snow in your yard. The ground's too hot from hell's nearby flames."

I don't know if my parents still cooed, or argued, in the house or not. I shook my head, said nothing, and fired my now ice-covered snowballs until my only three friends ran home crying.

———

I helped my father take the air compressor out of the trunk. He filled the Plymouth's tires almost to normal PSI, though he wouldn't go all out, in case. We waited for the worst snowfall in upstate South Carolina's memory to melt down—which meant by one o'clock in the afternoon the next day when it reached about sixty-five degrees outside—and then got in the car in order to go find Dad's wedding band. My mom had said earlier in the morning, "If you don't find it, that's all right. I believe there's a little motel in Ware Shoals where y'all can spend the rest of your lives."

Halfway down Old Old Greenville Road my father said, "Whatever goes bad for you in the rest of your life, Bane, I want you to think back to this day. Or to the day before this day. Anything wrong or immoral or unjust that happens to you, I want you to think back to the time you threw a snowball at your daddy and lost his wedding band."

I watched him say his little speech and didn't see his lips part once. Unfortunately for me, I said, "You look like a dummy talking like that."

My father threw his Masonic, high school, and Insurer of the Year rings out his open window, into a slight two-inch drift on the roadside. He said, "Will you never learn? Will you never learn?" but didn't punch my arm.

I wasn't old enough to say, "Maybe when something bad happens to me I'll think about how my father hit me on the arm all the time." In actuality I was old enough to think that, but back in the early 1970s it wasn't considered child abuse or endangerment. I said, "I didn't mean to say that Bible verse wrong."

My father looked in his side-view mirror, as if memorizing the location of his three cherished rings. He said, "I think there's one in there about how a guy saddled his ass to a tree and walked three miles into town. Something like that. You should've read that one. It's funny. Mr. Hard-on wouldn't think so, but the rest of the world outside of Gruel would."

We turned onto Main Street in Ware Shoals, and pulled into the Piggly Wiggly parking lot. For some reason I found it necessary to say, "Dad, if that woman's here you made run the red light, I promise I won't tell Mom."

We searched the parking lot for ten minutes, and looked down a grated drain hole as much as possible. My father leaned back a soda machine and I got down on my hands and knees. We waited for two cars to move, and checked beneath their tires. Somehow the sun blazed, and would've glinted anything this side of sandstone. I said, "Maybe someone turned it in. Maybe they got a lost and found inside."

My father stood up from the asphalt. He had an impression on the side of his head. "Who would keep a wedding band?!" he said. "Hotdamn, that's the kind of Bane I've been looking for all these years. No married man wants another, and no single man in his right mind wants even *one*."

We went inside and walked to the lone cashier, a girl who had "technical college aspirant" written on her blank forehead. She wore a Piggly Wiggly pink and white striped smock. Her nametag read MAUREEN HUFF.

I said, "Hey, More Enough." That's how it came out.

My father said, "Don't mind the boy. Say, did anyone turn in a wedding band from outside in the parking lot? Do y'all have some kind of lost and found?"

Maureen Huff didn't smack gum. She turned the sides of her lips up and stared at my father with her large, round blue eyes. She said, "You ain't from around here."

My father said, "Bane, go down to the end of aisle six and see if you see anything. I'm betting we need something."

I looked up to scan the signs. "In the automotive repair section?"

"Yeah, uh-huh. Go on down there and get us some oil or something."

I slinked away just as More Enough said, "You think it's going to snow anymore?" Later on in life I would realize that Maureen Huff's parents screwed up by not enrolling her in one of those scam modeling agencies.

I heard my father say, "Little snow bunny like you don't need to worry about no more bad weather," and then her giggling. My father said, "I sell assurance, Maureen, but I can tell that you have more to spare."

What else could I pick up on aisle six but can after can of Fix-A-Flat? I loaded up. I found an abandoned shopping cart parked against the frozen chicken section, brought it back, and put a good fifty canisters of tire goo in. I turned around, looked at my father, then backed out toward aisle three. There, I loaded up on feminine napkins and diapers. My father was about halfway down on one knee proposing when I returned. I yelled out, "Mom says you're about out of denture cream, Dad, but I couldn't find it." I wasn't old enough to bring up suppositories, my father not old enough to need them.

More Enough walked from behind her island to the lost and found, picked up a wedding ring, and rolled it on the linoleum counter to my father. She said, "I'm assuming you been hit in the head too many times to know any better what you just done."

I raised my hand and smiled. I pushed my cart up to the register. In years to come I would remember our drive back home, how my father passed his three other rings on the road-side with only a sideways glance, how he transferred his wedding band from right to left ring finger as we hit the square in downtown Gruel. I would think about how I needed to move far away, where men weren't automatically infatuated with women at intersections or cashiers who gave out trading stamps, where odd weather didn't throw everything out of balance in regards to rational behavior. I vowed to study harder, apply to colleges, and move away from my parents'—and every other Gruelite's—unhealthy, awkward, and skewed influences to a place where more was never enough.

I opened my father's glove compartment, pulled out the map, and blindly stuck my finger down to West Virginia. I shook my head, did it again, and hit Kentucky. Two out of three, I thought. I tried to visualize New York or California, maybe somewhere near the Canadian border. My finger landed in the middle of Louisiana.

"What the hell are you doing, Bane?" my father asked. He took his hands off the steering wheel and banged against his door.

I didn't say anything about how I needed to start taking French classes in order to communicate with Cajuns. I said, "Mom will be happy."

He said, "Your mother. I don't know why she doesn't trust me. Never marry a jealous woman, Bane. I wish the preacher had given us some kind of test beforehand."

I refolded the map and set it back in the glove compartment. In a weird way I wished that my finger had landed right on Gruel proper. In a way I wanted to be able to stick it out, and change some things later—maybe become principal of Gruel Normal. When we pulled in the driveway my mother sat in a cheap woven fold-out aluminum chair right in front of the carport. She wore cheap pointy sunglasses and lifted a martini glass our way. My father rolled down his window and held his ringed hand out like a five-legged octopus, like a starfish. I got out of the car and looked up at a blue, blue cloudless sky, but realized that other storms might come. I knew that, thirty years later, I would hear about the house of my upbringing burning down, that the pine tar soot and all of its dormant qualities finally ignited.

The Novels of Raymond Carver

ONCE I FINALLY got to explain the family dynamics of my childhood homelife back thirty years earlier—I'm talking I started with my first memory of tracking sand into a Myrtle Beach motel room on summer vacation, and ended with my waving an invention covered in flypaper for my father in order to clear dust motes and imaginary speckles from the air the day before I left for good—the magistrate only sentenced me to 180 hours of community service for attempted grave desecration. The security guard and subsequent sheriff's deputy believed wrongly that I wanted to steal my dead father's rings, watch, or lucky change he insisted fill his postmortem pants pocket. They didn't notice my recently deceased mother's crematory ashes balanced atop the headstone. This was two in the morning on the outer edge of Gruel Cemetery on the first day of spring—a day, traditionally, that my father made Mom and me scrub the entire house with ammonia, then Clorox, then Texize pine cleaner: walls, furniture, appliances, floors, even ceiling. Back when I had an indoor dog named Slick, it was my job to vacuum him every morning before school, every afternoon at feeding time. Slick took to watching the front door endlessly, and finally escaped through the legs of two Mormons one summer day. He never returned.

"What you're saying is, your father had a phobia against germs," Judge Cowart said as I stood before him without a lawyer two weeks after the incident. "There's a name for that kind of behavior now." Judge Cowart wasn't a real judge seeing as magistrates got voted into office, either Democrat or Republican. In real life he owned Gruel Modern Men's Wear, one of the last businesses on the square to evaporate.

I said, "Yessir. And he was plain mean, too."

The deputy and graveyard security guard had stood at the other desk to recount their version of events. There was no jury, but the magistrate's courtroom was packed. My arrest made the weekly *Forty-Five Platter* newspaper, the next town over. The deputy, a boy I grew up with named Les Miles, pretty much went over everything that happened in his life on up to taking me to the Graywood County Detention Center. I think Les liked having such a large audience.

Say "Les Miles" real fast. It's one of those names like Mike Weir. Or Derrick Rapp. Ben Dover. Mike Hunt. I hadn't noticed growing up that maybe it built up inside him so much that his only options in life appeared to be cop, professional gambler, or sad mime.

Judge Cowart said to the deputy and security guard, "What you're saying is, he only got a good two feet down in one spot. It wasn't like he popped chalk down and dug up the entire site."

"We measured it out to be a two-foot-by-two-foot piece of sod," said the security guard, an older man named Niblock who moved down to Gruel from somewhere in Pennsylvania with his wife in order to semiretire. I couldn't imagine how bad his life must've been up there to make such a drastic choice. "I keep a measuring tape on my belt at all times," he said. "Sometimes I get time to build bluebird houses up in the office during my shift."

I remained seated until the magistrate asked if I would like to question either man. I stood up and said, "Everything they've said is true," which brought about a massive gasp from the pewed spectators, followed by accusations of my being a Satan worshipper and ungrateful son. I said, "All of that is true, but it was for a good, moral, spiritual, ethical, bighearted reason." I had practiced my speech ever since posting bail.

Judge Cowart said, "Let's hear your side of things. Go ahead and loosen that 100 percent silk tie bought over at Gruel Modern Men's Wear on the historic square, unbutton your Botany 500 sport jacket, and let all us in on what's of a higher purpose."

Of course I wasn't about to say that I wanted to pour my mother's ashes into my father's grave so that he would have to live forever covered in a fine dust. No, I went through my daddy's stories of germ-free insistence, how he one time covered the entire exterior of our brick house in Saran Wrap. I told the judge, cop, guard, and seated guests about the times my father installed window fans in every room, *blowing out*, until our electric bill from Duke Power came in at over four hundred in 1968 dollars. None of these stories were false or exaggerated. I offered midstream to take a lie detector. Some time after I left Gruel for good my father got it in his mind that Mom's skin peeled off microscopically in their bed, and he bought a neoprene diver's suit for her to either wear at night with him or sleep in the guest bedroom with the door closed. He'd gone so far as hanging transom-to-floor thick clear plastic flaps at every entranceway in the house—the kind usually found in warehouses, drive-through car washes, and between where a butcher cuts his loins and meets the public—in case he needed to hole up by himself.

Judge Cowart finally said, "This is all very interesting in a woe-is-me kind of way, Mr. Cary. I'll give you exactly two minutes to find a point."

In retrospect I think I should've requested a jury. Swaying the gawkers wouldn't matter, I supposed, but I followed through with my plan. "My father got electrocuted while trying to rewire a central heat and air system backwards so it sucked dust out of his living space. That happened some fifteen years ago. My mother believed that caskets and funeral plots cost too much money, and she requested to be cremated. I followed through with her desire. On the night that I got arrested in Gruel Cemetery, I only wanted to pour her ashes on top of my father's final resting place. I knew that they needed and wanted to be together. Nothing else. She had already sold the plot directly next to Dad. That's it."

Luckily no one called me on the lie detector test; the final section of my defense—and I got my voice to crack a few times—was not quite as sentimental or melodramatic as the truth, like I said. I really only wanted to envelop my father so he'd be bothered and distracted for eternity.

I'm pretty sure that I heard more than a few women behind me go *"Aahhh,"* like that. Judge Cowart wrinkled his brow and looked at Les Miles and Mr. Niblock. They shrugged in unison. "Well. I got to say I have no precedent to work with. I believe you, Mr. Cary. But we, as a democratic society, can't allow people to take up shovels at their whim." He went on and on, said something about both King Tut and the remains of Confederate soldiers trapped inside the Hunley submarine, banged his gavel, and gave me community service.

I should mention that I came back to Gruel completely alone, that no woman will ever marry me. My first name's Ellis, so it comes out one of those names like Les Miles, Mike Hunt, all the rest. It's an old-fashioned South, and exactly zero women want to be called Mrs. Ellis Cary, wife of a desecrater. I'd have a worse chance in a land of Cockney women. At least that's what I've always told everyone.

It took my English department chairman four semesters to completely understand my great scam, a series of sophomore-level courses approved by a six-person curriculum committee, then approved by the stupid dean, a clutch of hands-on busy-body trustees, and the president of the college. For all I know our state legislators and governor, too, thought it utterly fantastic and unselfish of me to teach five classes per semester while my colleagues took on only four.

"I don't know how you do it," Donna Mickel, a Faulkner scholar who got a master's degree from Clemson and doctorate from the University of Alabama, said to me more than once. She'd been at Anders College since its 1975 inception as a state institution. "Some of us kind of wish you'd slack up, Ellis. You're making us look bad." Donna Mickel liked to tell a story about how she *almost* had a paper accepted one time in *College Writing, College Reading!* It was a section of her dissertation entitled "William Faulkner, Closet Merchant Seaman: The Feminist and Oceanic Politics in the Collected Stories." Then Donna Mickel gave up altogether, and took up the clarinet.

What else could I ever say to her but, "These first-generation students need to know"? "Call me obsessed, but there are works of literature that I think will only make them stronger citizens, no matter what fields of expertise they choose later on in life."

My ex-department chairman once said—I swear to God—"One of the best classes I took in graduate school was the novels of O. Henry. I wouldn't mind teaching it myself if anyone else could take over my Hardy Boys and Postmodernism course." Dr. Blocker went to one of those Ph.D.-by-mail outfits. "I got to tell you, Ellis, we're happy and proud to have you on the faculty here. Keep up the good work."

The first-generation students got it, though: They knew that my made-up course in the nonexistent novels of Raymond Carver meant that they would have nothing to read, that they would have no major papers. They showed up faster than Eskimos at a handwarmer giveaway. What started out as my teaching only one Ray Carver's novels class and four sections of English 101 ended up being five identical courses, each jammed with thirty students. I handed out blank sheets of typing paper for my syllabus.

"Your students really love the Raymond Carver novels class," every one of my colleagues told me during the course of each semester. "I wouldn't mind sitting in on it myself."

I didn't fear that ever happening as much as I feared some pinhead real scholar finding a Raymond Carver novel locked up inside a Syracuse, Iowa City, and/or Port Angeles basement, of the treasure being reported in *USA Today* or on *Entertainment Tonight*—how *the very first novel ever* of Raymond Carver was found by a snooping grad student, and a bidding war continued between publishing houses up in New York. Then I'd have to admit how I met with my students during their Monday-Wednesday-Friday or Tuesday-Thursday sessions and we basically talked about real-life problems concerning love and hate, conformity and rebellion, innocence and experience—the regular themes in all of Carver's short stories. I'd have to admit that although I urged my students to read all of the writer's stories, I never tested them, or offered up themes, or graded a paper over a two-year period. Everyone made an A as long as they showed up for class. It had been my contention long before that grades didn't matter in the history of the universe.

"It has come to my attention that you haven't actually taught *any* of Raymond Carver's novels since developing the course," Dr. Blocker finally said. "Could you explain this to me?"

We sat in my office. I turned off my computer so he couldn't read the screen where I was writing up another set of fake courses on the novels of Ring Lardner. I looked out the window at two of my students trying to catch a Frisbee in their mouths. One of them, I knew, would grow up to be an administrator. I said, "What are you talking about?"

"I think you know what I'm talking about. I was going over our majors' exit questionnaires, and more than a few of them mentioned how they learned more about life in your class than any other, even though there was nothing to read."

I should mention that I already knew that my mother was dying, that her oncologist's prognosis was for her to be gone in three months tops, and that I would probably have to ask for a leave of absence in order to tend to her limited estate. So it wasn't like I was brave or anything when I said, "You fucking idiot—Raymond Carver wrote *zero* novels. If you people here knew anything whatsoever, you'd know that when I made up the course it was only a joke. I thought for sure somebody would say, 'Hey, that's funny, Ellis Cary—that would be like teaching a course called The Poetry of Ronald Reagan.'"

Dr. Blocker sat forward. "Well, as a matter of fact, I brought this up with Dr. Mickel and she said that it would be like teaching the poetry of William Faulkner."

I didn't say, "You bunch of fucking morons, Faulkner's first book was poetry." No, I said, "Listen. Let me tell you about my father." I went into everything, exactly as I would have to do soon thereafter with Judge Cowart, from Myrtle Beach motel sand in the carpet to the giant flypaper swatter catching microbes in the air. Then I said, "In some kind of genetic bad luck, I am highly allergic and fearful to chalk dust. Y'all are lucky that I haven't sued the college for workmen's comp, or for not establishing a safe workplace for the handicapped. Anyway, I made up the Carver course because I knew it would keep me from having to write on the chalkboard, thus saving my life."

Dr. Blocker leaned back in his chair. "I'm going to have to fire you for insubordination. There's an insubordination clause in your contract. I can only classify you as being insubordinate."

I said, "Nancy Drew wouldn't have had anything to do with the Hardy Boys, in case you're interested. Now *she* was postmodern."

I trashed everything in my computer, outside of a little song I'd written about the English department, and boxed up my books, and left town. My mother died within the week, but not before telling me that she wished to be cremated and scattered in places that I thought she'd be most beneficial.

My community service involved literally painting the town red: fire hydrants on the square, two brick alleyways, the base of Colonel Dill's statue across from Victor Dees's Army-Navy Surplus, a wooden house on Old Old Greenville Road where, supposedly, Jefferson Davis slept while his troops got massacred in a variety of fields to the northeast. Get this: My parole officer was a kid named Buck Hammond who underwent my first Novels of Raymond Carver class two years earlier. I met with young Buck and said, "I take it you're familiar with what went on in court."

He said, "No one's ever mentioned where your mother is now. Where's your mother now? I mean, if you didn't finish the deed of pouring her onto your father's grave site, then what happened to her?"

I taught him well, I thought. "She's still in the little snapshut plastic container that they gave me at Harley Funeral Home over in Forty-Five. She's on the mantel back home."

Buck said, "I know I didn't take any psychology courses over at Anders. I majored in sociology. But I learned enough in your Raymond Carver class to know that you still want to spread her ashes on your daddy's grave. Am I right?" He wore a suit that came from Gruel Modern Men's Wear, I could tell. The lapels could've been torn off and used for curtains. "Understand that I have to tell you what you have to do, and what's right, and all that. I have to tell you not to return to your daddy's grave armed with a dead mother, you know. I got to tell you never to dig up any ground in a graveyard, no matter what you think's for the best in the long run."

I said, "Hey, Buck, if I finish everything y'all tell me to do before 180 hours is up, do I get to leave? Or will y'all find more things for me to do? Should I spread out my time, or work my butt off?"

Buck Hammond had a photograph of the president behind his desk, beside a framed miniature reproduction of the Bill of Rights. Off to the side was a needlepoint Lord's Prayer. "I trust that you would know what to do. Do the same thing any of those characters in a Raymond Carver novel would do."

I said, "I got it," and winked without winking. I smiled, but then wondered if it was all some kind of trick. Did I accidentally give Buck a B? I wondered.

"I think we have us something like two or three other men and women doing community service here in Gruel right now. Picking up trash on the roadside. Talking to teenagers about the dangers of smoking pot—that's the easiest community service there is right now seeing as there aren't but about two teenagers left in all of Gruel. Next time you decide to confront the law, you might want to get caught for smoking dope, Mr. Cary—you can get done with your community service in about thirty minutes."

I said I'd keep that in mind. I said, "What do I do, check in with you or someone every morning? I'm staying over at my parents' old place while all of this is going on. Hell, I guess I'll be staying there after it's done, too, seeing as I don't have a job."

My ex-student the parole officer said, "*Ellis Cary*. That kind of comes out like a complete sentence, don't it? Noun, verb, adjective. Is *scary* an adjective or an adverb? I was always taught that adverbs come right after verbs."

I shook my head. I wondered where my father's specter drifted at the moment, whether he spooked a germ-free lab or hovered above the crystalline air of Mount Whitney. Did my mother feel trapped within her plastic confines? I said, "There are too many rules in language, and there aren't enough at the same time, Buck. It's one of those things. I can't explain it all."

He handed me a can of paint and a four-inch brush. "You might as well start with the hydrants, I guess." He said, "Listen, I can bring in Les Miles and that graveyard guard on the pretense of asking them questions, if you want. I'll let you know. I'll call them in, and then you can go spread your momma anywhere you want without them putting you in jail."

I told Buck Hammond that I should've given him an A plus.

I walked off from the office like Michelangelo, thinking but one thing: Raymond Carver could've written a novel if he'd only given the main male character the same name throughout every story. Sure, the guy would've had a different wife every chapter, and a different job or lack thereof, but pretty much it would have held the same voice. I walked to the first hydrant, right in front of Roughhouse Billiards, and set down my can. It wasn't eight thirty in the morning. Some fellow came out and bet me a dollar he could put a cue ball on the sidewalk, strike it hard with his eighteen-ounce stick, and get it to bounce off my can of paint and balance, finally, on the fire hydrant. He said he was training to be the best trick shot player in history, and that people were out there already writing novels about him. I suggested that he talk to a man or woman somewhere in the vicinity doing community service lectures about the evils of drug usage.

I worked diligently until noon and had all of Gruel's fire hydrants sparkling red. I thought to myself, 176 hours to go. I walked back to Buck Hammond's office for another can of paint to say that I would start the alleyways, but he was at lunch. One of my community service comrades sat in Buck's office—the woman—and I said, "I'm betting you have to talk to people about pot." She wore a tie-dyed skirt and matching bandanna, a torn tank-top shirt that exposed her belly button ring, and a tattoo on her left bicep that looked like a bull's-eye, like a target.

"That's the other guy. I'm doing community service for throwing an apple core out the car window. The judge didn't believe me that an apple core will disintegrate into roadside compost. He got me for littering. Either a month in jail and a thousand-dollar fine, or two hundred hours of cleaning up the town." She slid her index and middle fingers beneath her nose and I thought for a second that she'd give me the secret Phi Beta Kappa handshake presently, but she didn't. "Are you the guy painting? I'm supposed to follow around behind you and clean up any drips you leave."

I introduced myself quite clearly: "My . . . name . . . is . . . Ellis . . . Cary," so she wouldn't hear "Hell-is-scary."

She stuck out her hand. She looked about the age of some of the first students I ever taught at Anders College, maybe thirty years old. She said, "Wow. Weird. I'm Cashion," She stuck out her hand. She didn't say her last name. And it was Cashion who said, "Hey, if I married you my name would be Cashion Cary. Like some kind of grocery store."

I don't know if it was because I was the kind of man who could figure out ways to get paid in full to teach textless classes, but I was way ahead of her. As soon as she said "Cashion," I had spelled it correctly in my mind, figured out what people would call her if we became betrothed, and in my mind's eye foresaw how we'd decorate my inherited house in Gruel. I said, "Yeah. Yeah. I get it. Is Cashion some kind of family name? I get it."

She nodded. "I wonder what time this guy's coming back. I need to see if I can take tomorrow off. I think I have the town pretty cleaned up. You haven't dripped a bunch of paint, have you?"

Ding-ding-ding! I thought. I thought, I will from now on. I said, "What's going on tomorrow?"

"For some reason I decided to go back to college after all these years. It's a long story that involves wanting to follow the Dead around straight out of high school, you know, but then Jerry died. I followed some other bands around, but it wasn't the same. I made enough money selling ginseng I probably wasn't supposed to dig up up in Tennessee, but nothing felt right. So I came back home here and enrolled in a couple classes over at Anders. I either want to become a nurse or a financial planner. I want to help people."

Please never come back, Buck Hammond, please never come back, Buck Hammond, I thought. I said, "You're having to take all those general education requirement courses, I'm guessing. I used to teach there."

Get this: Cashion Cary-to-be said, "The dean said I could come in as a sophomore due to life experiences. I mean, I'm having to pay for everything myself—I didn't get any scholarship money—but I'm not having to take English comp and all that. Maybe I should have. I'm kind of having trouble in this course called the Novels of Raymond Carver. Dr. Blocker said we're supposed to find out what we're supposed to find. Every day he sends us to the library to do research, but I have no clue what he really wants."

The Novels of Raymond Carver! I thought, setting down my new paint can. "You have to believe me when I say that I can help you immeasurably," I said. "I haven't been this serious since I told my father that it wasn't healthy to take a bath every hour. But that's another story. Listen, if you want help on the novels of Raymond Carver, then I'm your man. I'm the idiot who *designed* that class. You either have to hand him twenty blank pages stapled together at the top left or you and I can come up with a fake paper that'll make him scurry around trying to check your citations for the rest of his life.

I'm willing to write the fake paper for you, if you want. I can do it in a second. We just have to come up with one or two made-up titles. This'll be fun. This'll be easy."

I waited for Cashion to say, "You're my hero, Ellis Cary. How can I ever repay you?" She didn't.

Buck Hammond walked back from lunch and I yelled out, "Tell this woman how much I taught you in my Raymond Carver novels class. Tell her. Tell her this very instant! Tell her now."

I took the paint can home and poured half my mother inside. Listen, I stirred her in. I whipped those ashes, no matter what. At one point my paint stick popped the sides of the can in a way that sounded like "Froggy went a-courtin' and he did ride, uh-huh" over and over. I pureed. As I figured it, my mother would infiltrate and dust up Gruel full-time should my mean weird father decide to revisit his homeplace.

"He seemed to write a bunch of short stories," Cashion said from the dining room table where she spread out a slew of blank pages. "I read, I think, all his stories—some of them seemed to be the same, with only different endings or beginnings. And he wrote some poems, too."

"You damn right," I said. I wore a pair of goggles in case my mother's ashes flew up in my face. I'd read and taught Sophocles enough to know better. "Listen, tomorrow when I go to paint, I promise you I won't spill anything if you promise not to leave me alone. Litterbug."

"Grave robber."

"Weird hippie who can't predict a band member's death."

"Loser."

Oh, we went on and on. I got all giddy and found myself daydreaming about discovered lost manuscripts of Raymond

Carver, or of taking the time to write an entire novel about a wife who leaves her husband for smoking too much dope, and the blind man the husband brings in as a boarder. Or maybe a novel about a man who runs a drying-out facility and all of the funny-sad stories he hears from clients and visitors alike. I thought of a novel told from the point of view of a scared, scared divorced man who takes to carrying a gun at all times, eating rat poison on purpose, or maybe a guy whose wife leaves so he puts all their furniture out on the front lawn, arranged perfectly.

And so on. I fantasized about a life with Cashion, one where we would travel far from Gruel to live out our days. I would come back yearly, at night, to visit my parents' remains.

"You're not really going to paint your mother in town, are you?"

I said, "My mother became attached to the town after Dad died. Her neighbors slowly accepted her when they found out she wasn't afflicted with verminophobia. It seems logical to me. As a matter of fact, that should be a law—that every dead person get painted to a storefront or alleyway. Make kids think they're being watched all the time. Kind of like animism."

Cashion continued to sit at my mother's dining room table and printed her name in the dust. She said, "I was only kidding earlier about being a nurse. I'm not freaked out by molecules, but—still—there's no way I could see people dying all the time."

I finished sieving Mom thoroughly. Would I keep the other half of her remains in a glazed clay vessel for the rest of my life? Would I come back in a year and risk getting caught by Les Miles and Mr. Niblock again? Cashion picked up one of Raymond Carver's collections and opened it up in the middle. Fifteen minutes later she said that the characters came across a dead woman in the river, but did nothing. She didn't think it right. I said it was only a story, it was only made up.

We stared at the paint can for too long, then walked over to the pool hall an hour before it unofficially closed. Our parole officer never said we couldn't offer toasts to one another and to those surrounding us. I didn't say anything like, "Here's to my spending more than my allotted time cleaning up this town." I didn't say, "Here's to a woman destined to clean up after my mistakes." The bartender slid two shots our way. He said that he'd met more desperate people in Gruel, that we shouldn't get optimistic.

Bluffs

EIGHTEEN MONTHS AFTER the accident I've almost regained feeling from the neck up. My speech improves daily, but not enough to keep cops from pulling me out of the car, making me walk a straight line, touch my nose, recite the alphabet. For a year and a half I've dealt with people patting me on the head, talking to me slowly, smiling as if I were slow-minded, retarded, the kind of grown-up who served as a high school football team's lucky charm mascot. I don't mind. I understand. It has occurred to me that I've been destined to undergo near death and numbness in order to make other people feel better about themselves. It isn't beneath my station in life to gather up whatever free beer and dollar bills everyone offers. And I pretend not to hear people tell my story.

Listen, if I'd not retreated to Gruel, South Carolina, in the late 1990s, much worse might've happened in West Memphis. I'd've bet all my money on the wrong dog, found its owner, made threats, and gotten killed. I'd've gone into Memphis proper and gotten run over by a trolley or horse-drawn carriage, drunk myself silly down on Beale Street, wondered why

I couldn't get a steady job playing piano at one of the hotel bars so that I wouldn't gamble professionally. Before I moved to Gruel, the only thing my future held was a weeklong stint as some kind of brunt-of-a-joke banter between the hosts of *Alive at Nine!* each morning, them saying, "Well it's miserable outside again today, but probably not as miserable as poor Scurry Hodgins sitting in his hospital room for what he did last week," et cetera, et cetera, et cetera.

Or I might've done something wrong in Little Rock, Fayetteville, even Calico Rock, trout fishing on the White River. Hot Springs. Oxford on down to Jackson. Somehow I would've pissed off someone and gotten a vital organ punctured at best, if not killed altogether.

"Scurry Hodgins there used to be a world-class poker player," I hear men say at Roughhouse Billiards on the square in Gruel. "He come here hiding out, you know, trying to kick the habit. I seen him on ESPN2 one time playing that game no one knows how to play, and bluffing his way to a million-dollar prize. Nowadays I doubt he'd know a deuce from a king of diamonds."

Oh, I hear them. I sit on the barstool, watch Jeff the owner make hot dogs. I pretend I don't know what's going on when someone pulls out a deck of Bicycles and shuffles them loudly right behind my head.

"What happened was, there was this art car show come through here having their convention two years ago or thereabouts. Scurry gone over there—hey, Jeff, did he go over there with you?—and the next thing you know this old girl driving a Dodge Dart—hey, Jeff, was it a Dodge Dart or a Comet Caliente?—covered in little Jesus and Mary figurines ain't looking where she's going, and veers off the parade route, and knocks poor old Scurry right up against Colonel Dill's statue right over there. He hits his head, you know, and this is what happened."

I don't need to turn around to see the guy pointing his thumb toward the middle of the town square where Colonel Dill, Civil War hero, stands proudly in granite. I don't need to see the man turn his thumb my way afterward.

I think, Full house beats a flush. Flush beats a straight. Straight beats three of a kind.

"Word is he only had a pair of sevens, nothing else, in that last hand he won. What Scurry Hodgins won."

"Lucky sevens."

"I'd ask him, but he might only say something like, 'Mississippi River.' One time I asked him how he was doing, and I swear what he said came out, 'Best for all wick lighters.' Man, he has no clue what's going on around him these days. And with all that money sitting in the Bank of America."

I drink what Jeff slides my way. I nod at whoever buys it. One day I'll stand up and recite everything I've heard said about me, buy drinks for a month, and leave tiny Gruel. I'll return to the flat, flat expanse of western Tennessee, or farther.

I like to think that the art car woman craned her neck to check me out. It wasn't a Dodge Dart or Comet Caliente, either—she drove a Fairlane. And it wasn't covered in Jesus and Mary figurines. No, this woman had converted a Ford Galaxie—about a 1965—into a shrine for Buddha. I don't know for sure, but I can only imagine that she saw some kind of connection between Buddha and the universe. Me, I stood there all by my lonesome watching the other art cars sidle by. To be honest I focused on this woman in a VW Bug covered in what ended up being her cats' claws. Man, that car glistened. I have no clue what she wanted to espouse philosophically, or morally, but she looked like some kind of movie star, or at least a woman who offered melodramatic dialogue on a Broadway stage.

Then I found myself knocked up against Colonel Dill's rock feet, not that I remember the incident, really. And who knows how the human central nervous system operates? I didn't break a bone, but something bruised deep on my brain caused a reaction not unlike a stroke. Oh, I pulled one leg behind the other for a good six months, and got that weird curled hand for a while, and spoke to people as if I juggled three bowling balls with my tongue.

I didn't sue the woman, if that matters. Everyone's insurance paid off.

"I guess Jesus and Mary didn't like the way he held his mouth," a man says behind me at Roughhouse Billiards. "The real Jesus directed that lady's Dodge Dart right to him, you know. Like destiny."

Two men practice trick shots on the pool table, making bets with each other. I want to go over there and slap down a few pictures of Ben Franklin that they'll never get out of Gruel, but don't. Jeff the owner says to me, slowly, "Hey, Scurry, would you like a ham sandwich? You need to eat something."

I shake my head no. He slicks back his slick hair, then plops a can of PBR in front of me. I palm the counter three times.

Back in Memphis my ex-wife once bet me a thousand dollars that I couldn't go a week without gambling. I took her on. She said, "I win." Then she left.

"He gets up every morning and takes a shower, evidently. You can't smell him or nothing. His clothes seem clean enough.

And then he walks over here and drinks till two o'clock. Then I guess he goes home and takes a nap. Then he comes back for happy hour and stays until closing. That's it. He don't read the paper or nothing. He just sits there."

"What a pitiful life. Say, you want to play rock-paper-scissors, see who pays the next round?"

I keep a journal in my head that I'm thinking about putting down in a notebook. One time a man came in here from Forty-Five, trying to sell Jeff flashing stick-on buttons that looked more firefly than advertisement. He said he could make them go ROUGHHOUSE BILLIARDS! like that, and everyone could wear them.

Jeff said, "Wouldn't my customers already know where they are, outside of Scurry here?"

The salesman said, "Well, yeah, but they could wear them outside, on the streets, to show people where they've been."

I sat on my barstool, feigning nonchalance to the salesman and retardation to anyone who'd been in Roughhouse Billiards more than twice. Jeff said, "I don't know about life in a big town like Forty-Five, but most of my customers try to hide the fact that they hang out in a bar. They don't like to admit it, you know." He turned to me and said, "What do you think about that, Scurry?"

I said, of course, "Aaaaagh. Aaaaagh. Aaaaagh. Aaaaagh," and nodded my head up and down like a Hot Springs racehorse.

The salesman left after giving over two samples. Jeff's lit up HARD ROCK CAFE. I'm pretty sure that mine was broken. It read BAR AND G ILL.

When the salesman left, Jeff said to me, "If it's not one thing, Scurry. Say, do you remember the time before your head injury when we drove out to look at that old boy's new herd of llamas? That was fun, wasn't it?"

I had lost that bet: Jeff said that he could make me feel like we all lived in Peru right here in Gruel. I said he couldn't. He did. I paid up.

With the right smirk, an ace, king, queen, jack of spades plus a two of hearts in the hole beats four eights showing any day, nothing wild. Unfortunately, there are men in Arkansas who will pull pistols out and say, "Show me what you had. Show me that royal flush. Show me you weren't bluffing." There are men in Arkansas, living in dry counties, who don't give a damn about protocol.

There are men from Memphis, with or without wives, who keep a ten of spades up their sleeves.

"They say he's got a concubine living up there in the house with him. She don't get to go out none in the daylight, but she drives up to Greenville and gets his groceries and whatnot. His new clothes. Look at that shirt. You can't buy no shirt like that in Gruel. They ain't even no store. She's supposedly part Mexican. They say her name's something like Who-letta."

"Who let a man like Scurry Hodgins move to Gruel, more like it. One us ought to go over there and check things out. Say, you stick around here, and I'll go look around his house. That Mexican woman asks any questions, I'll say I'm with the department of health come check out levels."

My door's unlocked. I don't care. My big house has one single bed and twelve hardback chairs. My sock drawer's filled with nothing more, and the dining room table's got a sheen on it unlike anything else in Gruel. One time the meter reader walked in all nosy thinking I was gone and found himself staring at his reflection in my sink. When I tapped him on the shoulder he turned and said, "We got a 911 call. We got a 911 call from this address, and I'm here to check things out."

I pulled a piece of paper from my back pocket, a pen. I wrote, "Nice try, amigo," and pointed toward the door. After he left I drove up to Greenville to buy new shirts, pants, some soap, and skin conditioner. On the way back I got pulled over by highway patrolmen and sheriff's deputies every mile on Highway 25.

Here's why it all went downhill: I'd been invited to participate in a clandestine poker tournament over in Pine Bluff. Six of us threw in ten grand each. Spectators and invited guests put down money as to who they thought would win. These poker players, I knew, spent more time raising gamecocks and pit bulls than they did figuring out odds in a nonrigged poker game.

I should mention that all of this took place before I won the big game in Las Vegas, before my wife left, before I moved to South Carolina in hopes of rehabilitation. This old boy Dale Ray called some kind of dead kings/one-eyed jacks/deuces wild game. I anted up. I got dealt two twos, a king with a sword in his head, and a one-eyed jack. I set down my cards and shoved all my chips to the center of the table.

"Two-hundred-dollar limit," Dale Ray said. "You can't just go and bet everything you got. Good God, man, everyone here would be trying to bluff out everyone else."

I said, "Okay," and put out twenty ten-dollar chips.

Dale Ray called. "How many cards you want?"

So I had four wild cards and a nine. I thought, Well, if I

get a ten or face card I at least have a royal flush. I have five of a kind no matter.

But I couldn't remember if five of a kind beat a royal flush. Who plays poker hands where five of a kind is a possibility? Who doesn't play high-low games with this many people at the table? I said, "I'll take one card."

Two men folded. One big red-haired fellow got up and looked for a bag of potato chips, then he said he didn't want to ever play poker again—which, in retrospect, might've been smart. Dale Ray took two cards. "Up to you, cowboy," he said.

I looked at my draw card and saw that it was the four of clubs. So I either had an eight-high straight flush or five fours. Who could lose on a hand like that? I bet two hundred, Dale Ray matched and raised, I called and raised, he called and raised—no one ever said anything about a limit to all of this—and so on.

I finally called. Dale Ray had four natural queens and the ace of hearts. I flipped over my trash and said, "You shouldn't call a game with so many wild cards, Bubba," and raked the chips my way. "Hotdamn, you would've won that hand anywhere else."

When I left Pine Bluff later that night, I drove toward Fort Smith, then back toward Jonesboro, before turning south. I imagine that somehow I missed lynching that night only because I foresaw Dale Ray's roadblock.

When I got home my ex-wife said, "Did you have any luck?"

I said, "I broke even, counting gas money. Say, what did you do yesterday?"

My ex-wife crinkled her forehead, and shrunk her entire face before saying, "Have you not noticed the new drapes?"

"Well I'm sorry that I haven't, dear. I guess I'll either go to hell or have some kind of horrendous life-changing tragedy happen to me for not seeing them." I looked at the drapes in our den. "What's that called, paisley?"

My first real word must mean something. I can't say "hot dog" or "beer" or "Excuse me, I think you've accidentally mistaken my umbrella for yours." My next word or words has to be right up there with Schopenhauer, or Wittgenstein, or Hoyle.

It doesn't matter that my house has been ransacked. It doesn't matter that ESPN2 shows the 1997 World Poker Championship every afternoon at least once a week.

"After he hit his head and got all fucked-up, he started liking boys," Victor Dees, the owner of V.D.'s Army-Navy Surplus, says. He's eating boiled peanuts and throwing shells down on the floor. "Luckily for us, we ain't got no men in Gruel who like other men."

"Shit," says Compton Lane. "Luckily in Gruel there aren't any women who would understand that Scurry's faking it all along." I turn around and hold my hands up. I think, How does he know? "Ain't that right, Scurry? I'm on to you, man. I know."

I turn back around and shrug at Jeff. He says, "If you are faking, I want to make it clear that I've been keeping tabs on you for what you owe me. I know you have money. We all know you got the money, Scur. We all know that, sooner or later, Jesus hitting you shinbone to forehead will make you speak the truth."

Let me say that I didn't undergo this kind of stress while playing Native American Indian poker with a group of Green Berets who holed up in a hunting lodge weekly outside Blytheville, back in the old days.

Compton Lane says, "I used to put dogs asleep daily when I was a veterinarian. I know that look, Scurry."

I hold on. I look at myself in the mirror and pretend not to hear anything. Someone else yells from the other side of the pool table, "That woman wouldn't have hit him with her Jesus-mobile if God didn't want it that way. If it weren't preordained and whatnot."

I bend my half-drunk can of beer and want bourbon next. I point behind Jeff, pull a wad of one-dollar bills from my pocket. "It was Buddha that hit me, you fools. It wasn't Jesus. There were about a thousand little one-inch Buddhas glued onto her hood and fender and roof. Get it straight before you go tell a story. Jesus isn't behind everything, believe it or not. Jesus might be the reason y'all are stuck here day in, day out, gossiping about nothing that matters, goddamn it. If there's any kind of retribution going on in the world—if there's any kind of payback for what you did in a previous life—everyone I've ever met in Gruel has done something really, really bad."

I slug down a straight bourbon, neat, from a coffee mug that advertises Hawley-Cooke bookstores, an item that Jeff either got in the mail by accident or bought at a yard sale, seeing as no one in Gruel reads books. Lookit: One time I brought a hardback dictionary into Roughhouse Billiards and everyone asked me why I carried a doorstop around.

"None us got knocked over into Colonel Dill's knee," someone says. "You can talk and talk and talk about Jesus, but none us got struck by a car out of nowhere, like lightning."

I walk out of Roughhouse Billiards knowing that I can only return to my homeland, that I have no other choice but to look up my ex-wife in Memphis to tell some lies, find my old poker-night friends, and start anew. Already I know that I'll put my house up for sale, never get an offer, and give it up as a rental—that I won't care if my monthly money comes in on time. What kind of loser would move to Gruel, anyway, unless he or she hid from passions or obsessions beyond rational thought? Jeff the owner yells out how I owe him two thousand dollars. I wave my arm. It's not two grand, I think. It's only about eighteen hundred dollars.

I wish that I'd've said something better, and know I will think of the right response once I reach those bluffs above the big, big, slow, mighty river. It's always that way, no matter where, no matter what brand of cards.

The Opposite of Zero

IT TOOK UNTIL SEVENTH GRADE before I had—what I thought of initially as—an idiotic teacher call my name wrong on the roll at the first of the year. She got through Adams, Bobo, Davis, Dill, Farley—the easy ones: There were only easy last names in Gruel, no foreign names like Abdelnabi, Gutierrez, Haughey, Narasimhamurdhy, Napolitano, Nguyen, Papadopoulos, Xu, Yablonsky, Yamashita, Zhang, Zheng, Zhong—Goforth, James, Knox, LaRue, before she came upon my last name. Me, I came from a long line of utopians who pronounced our last name like the opposite of silence. Noyes, like *noise.* My great-great-great-great something was John Humphrey Noyes, leader of the Oneida community, a man who believed that God spoke to him, et cetera. Mrs. Latham went through her junior high class roll and when she came to me she said, "Gary No Yes?"

I said, "Maybe."

Of course I'd been in school with my classmates from kindergarten on, and they all yelled out, "No, Yes!" like that.

"No, Yes! No, Yes!" They had never noticed the possible mispronunciation, but then again I hadn't either.

"Gary No Yes?" Mrs. Latham said. "Well. I bet you'll do quite well on true-false tests."

And that was it for me. No one ever called me Gary Noyes again. I took shit from that point on until my comrades started having sex, started telling me about how their dates kind of yelled out part of my name during intercourse—either "No, no, no, no," or "Yes, yes, yes, yes." Some of them—debutantes-to-be—went ahead and said my name in full, over and over.

It didn't matter that all of my other teachers pronounced my last name correctly from eighth grade onward, that even some of my philosophy, religion, and literature professors in college up in Chapel Hill had studied up on, and written about, my great-great-great-great whatever. Every one of my classmates called me Gary No Yes for the remainder of my time in Gruel. In French class they called me Non Oui. I changed over to Spanish and became No Sí. Gruel Normal didn't teach Greek or Latin or German. These days I blame my lack of globe-trotting on the fact that I only took two first-year introductory courses in separate foreign languages.

Right after the original incident I came home and said to my mother, "There's a new teacher at Gruel Normal and she may or may not be stupid, Mom. She can't say our last name. She calls me No Yes. She thinks my name's Gary No Yes."

My mother's maiden name was Godshell, but that's another story.

"You must take *farts* and turn them into *rafts* to float away on, Gary," my mother said. "Your father will tell you the same thing. He once told me that your great-great-great-grandfather—or maybe your aunt—underwent a similar problem because of his ancestry. It makes us all stronger people. You must take *shit* and turn it into *hits*."

My mother never said anything about turning lemons into lemonade, oddly. I could count on her to stay away from the clichés, and always wanted her to turn dirty words into aphorisms. After I became No Yes I would come home sometimes and say, "Patty Goforth said to me, 'Eat me now,'" only so I could see my mother drop her vacuum cleaner and rewire her brain to figure out what *Eat me now* could turn into.

"Meant woe!" she would yell. "Patty Goforth is in some pain, Gary. What she's saying is, she's hurting. Probably from her home life. You need to be a lot nicer to her, what with the situation she's in."

My father said, more often than not, "I wish someone had called me No Yes when I was a kid. That's all right. *No Yes.* Ha! I think you're lucky to have Mrs. Latham for a teacher." Then he made us hold hands at the dinner table while he prayed for something like eighty minutes. My father had trickled down from being an Oneida plate maker into a man who sold specialized venetian blinds to people living in mobile homes. My mother—a Godshell—hailed from people in eastern Kentucky who thought anyone without a toolbox might as well be standing next to Satan.

Should anyone come up to me now and ask—let's reach way out and pretend, a psychologist—"Do you think you come from a fine, fine, hardworking and moral family?" I'd say, without thinking twice, "No, Yes."

Mrs. Latham confused me daily. She claimed to use the Socratic method of teaching—which none of us figured out, seeing as she never explained anything about Socrates—and later on I realized that she kind of misrepresented, or stretched, pedagogical terms. Maybe my memory's off, but I remember her saying more than once a week, "If Sparky walked ten miles north at five miles an hour, and Rufus walked five miles south at ten miles an hour, would they meet halfway in between?"

Lookit: My name might've been No Yes, but I fucking knew that it mattered where they started. Let's say if little Sparky began his wayward and unlikely hike in the Yukon Territory, and Rufus started in Pensacola, then Sparky'd be frozen and Rufus would drown. Who were Sparky and Rufus, anyway? I thought. Was this the beginning of some kind of off-color, racist joke? Sometimes my father came home from a highly productive day of selling six-inch-wide venetian blinds and tell my sister and me a joke about little Johnny ingesting BBs and later shooting the pet dog. "No? Yes?" Mrs. Latham would prompt.

I wouldn't even raise my hand, thinking she called on me. I said "Maybe" every time, without divulging my keen geographic knowledge.

"Miz Latham, I have a dog named Sparky," Alan Farley always said. "He's fast. He can go a lot faster than ten miles an hour, I know. He can chase a car all the way down to Old Old Greenville Road. My daddy dropped him off in Forty-Five one time and he found his way home in less than an hour. Forty-Five's something like twenty miles away."

"No? Yes?"

Becky Herndon said, "I have an uncle named Rufus but he keeps saying he's going to change his name so no one doesn't think he's black."

I thought each day, You idiot, Becky. I said, finally, "Sparky and Rufus need to find other ways to entertain themselves, ma'am. As many times as they walk north and south, they'll hit foreheads too many times."

"Exactly! Pretty soon they'll learn to walk east to west, right?"

I didn't get it. I wanted out. Every time Mrs. Latham asked us about Sparky and Rufus—and she was supposed to be teaching us English and U.S. history, not math—I came home and told my mother. I said, "Mom, Mrs. Latham keeps asking us about two guys walking toward each other. In the real world do people walk toward each other at different speeds every day? Is this something I need to know about? Yes or no."

My mom always put down her dust mop, or can of Pledge, or Lysol, or prescription bottle of "special pills," or spatula, or can of Raid, or feather duster, or putty knife, or bottle of vodka "your father doesn't need to know about," or box of jig-saw puzzle pieces, and said, "There are many, many words that you can come up with for *Yes or No*, son. As in, *Rosy One*. You can figure out the others. Right? Can't you?" Then, usually, she'd say, "Here comes your dad. Hey, don't say anything about the bottle of rubbing alcohol."

I would nod, then find my way to the push mower, even at dusk, even in winter. Usually I'd find my sister somewhere out in the backyard, either gnawing bark off a sweet gum tree or burning insects with a magnifying glass. Judith was in the fifth grade, in my old elementary school wing at Gruel Normal, when I sat in Mrs. Latham's class. Judith had a destructive streak no one in our family could trace back in the gene pool, seeing as we came from those utopians.

Mrs. Latham must've really enjoyed her woodburning kit at home. Each year she made little personalized signs to go on her students' desks, kind of like nameplates used by CEOs, or professors who needed to remind colleagues that there was a Ph.D. at the end of their family names. Mrs. Latham handed these nameplates out on the last day before Christmas vacation— Mr. Adams, Miss Bobo, Misters Davis, Dill, and Farley, Miss

Goforth, Miss James, Mr. Knox, Miss LaRue, Mr. Pendarvis, Mr. Pinson, Miss Seymour, and so on. They were perfect, on thin oak, and slid into specialized metal stand-up frames balanced at the front of our desks. Everyone else's was perfect—she didn't write out in cursive *Pin son* or *Go forth*—except for mine. There, in quarter-inch-deep brown letters, stood my name as she pronounced it.

When the three o'clock bell rang Mrs. Latham said, "Gary, I need to speak to you for a moment before you go." Everyone else ran out the door with their empty book bags, half of them thinking it was the end of the school year.

I said, "What did I do? I didn't do anything," which wasn't quite true. Earlier that day I intentionally wrote down every wrong answer on a true-false test because I knew that John B. Dill—that's what he insisted on being called—copied from my paper. At the bottom of my test I wrote "Opposites" so Mrs. Latham would get it. Because it was Christmas Mrs. Latham lobbed up some softballs, too: "Antarctica is the most populated continent," "The capital of the United States is Gruel," "Abraham Lincoln is best known for his tales of the Mississippi River."

"You let me know who's cheating on tests, and I want to thank you for it," Mrs. Latham said. "When you get your paper back after the break, I'll put a big fat zero at the top in case John B. Dill looks over your shoulder at it, but write 'Opposite' above it. That's not what I want to talk to you about, though, Mr. No Yes."

Already I knew it was a trick. I tried to think of the opposite of zero. Was it one? Was it a hundred? Was it infinity? I said, "I need to get home pretty soon because my mom wants to go shopping up in Greenville," which wasn't true either.

Mrs. Latham sat down behind her desk. She shoved aside the gifts our parents had bought, wrapped, and handed over for us to give. Ten kids out of our class moaned, at eight thirty that morning, when the first present happened to be a pencil holder. Mrs. Latham got so many wooden block pencil holders she could've built a cabin, as it ended up. John B. Dill's parents gave her a tie, for some reason. My father—bless his heart—gave her a gift certificate for specialized miniblinds, should she ever move out of her regular house into a trailer.

"The opposite of zero is Yes, by the way—I can tell by the look on your face that you're trying to figure it all out. But that's not what I want to talk to you about, specifically, either. I want to talk to you about the two most powerful words in the English language. You might go to church and hear that those words are Good and Evil, or Love and God, or—around here—Cotton and Gun. But the real answer happens to be Yes and No. More has happened in the history of our land because of someone answering Yes or No than any other two words, Gary. That's why I like to call you Mr. No Yes. I don't like to advertise it here in Gruel, but I took a bunch of philosophy courses in college—a load of courses about the existentialists. Yes and No were major themes in all of their treatises, which you—I hope and feel sure—will come to understand later on in life. Do you understand what I'm talking about?"

Another trick, I thought. Was I supposed to offer up one of the two most powerful words in the English language? I had no choice but to nod. I didn't want to let Mrs. Latham down, here in the holiday season, by saying, "Maybe."

"I would also like to tell you that sometimes in March or April the farmers have put their gardens in. They've planted tomatoes, beans, okra, squash, watermelon, and cucumbers to take over to the Forty-Five Farmers Market. And out of nowhere a giant frost comes in for just one night. A lot of people think that it'll kill the plants, but a good gardener knows better. His plants become what is called 'frost-hardened' and they somehow become stronger. No one knows why, but frost-hardened plants can later withstand bugs and drought and too much rain. Even hail."

I said, "Yes ma'am," like I knew where this was going. I didn't.

"And that's what I'm doing for you, Gary No Yes. I'm frost-hardening you. After you get out of my classroom, you're going to be so strong you'll be able to withstand anything that comes your way. I made a promise to someone years ago to act thusly. Do you understand what I'm talking about?"

I didn't nod this time. I said, slightly, "Yesnomaybe, uh-huh."

Mrs. Latham said, "Good." She said, "All right," and clapped her hands together. She wore a sweater with a Christmas tree on it, with two ornaments right about where her nipples would be, I thought. I tried not to look. I tried not to think about how I hadn't noticed this earlier in the day, maybe when we had to stand up and do jumping jacks beside our desks. "Now. For more important things: What's Santa Claus going to bring you? Your ma tells you all about Satan Claus, doesn't she? Oh—that's called a Freudian slip. I mean *Santa* Claus."

I stood up to go. "Well. I don't know. We don't make a big thing out of Christmas. Dad says we should celebrate the birth of Jesus more and the birth of Sears, Roebuck less. I'd kind of like to get a new globe, a telescope, and maybe a set of encyclopedias."

Where did that come from? I even thought right then.

In my eyes Mrs. Latham's Christmas ornaments shook up and down, though she didn't appear to laugh. She said, "I want to give you an extra credit question for your test. Yes or No: Mrs. Latham is stupid to believe in Santa Claus."

I looked behind her at the clock. Could it be that only ten minutes had passed, or had I been there for *twenty-four hours and ten minutes*? I thought. I imagined my friends already playing basketball down on the square—or our version of basketball, which meant hitting Colonel Dill's statue straight on the nose for two points—and my mother circling the den with a drink in one hand and a box of rat poison in the other, worrying that I had run away from home. I said, "Please don't do this to me. I can't take it anymore. I don't mean to be disrespectful, ma'am."

Mrs. Latham got up from behind her desk and clicked her way toward me standing there. Her hair stood up on end in a way that spaghetti might look infused with static electricity. She put her right hand on the crown of my head. I might be wrong here—maybe she told me to scoot on off and have a wonderful holiday—but what I heard came out, "Wait till we get to Easter, No Yes."

I ran home without looking back, scared that a life-threatening disease had happened upon me. This was seventh grade, but it was the early 1970s, understand, and I had no prior reason to ever get an erection in Gruel, South Carolina.

My father wanted to invite my seventh-grade teacher over for day-after-Christmas leftovers. He said, "We can straighten all of this out." He said, "We'll invite Mr. and Mrs. Latham over, and we can have turkey hash. We should've invited them over four months ago, as a matter of fact. Town like Gruel, we invite newcomers over. Did we bring them a pie or cake when they moved in? Hey, if there's one thing that I can understand from my ancestor John Humphrey Noyes, it's that forgiveness is next to godliness."

My mother, tilting in the den, said, "My dictionary has some words in between, which start with *f* or end with *damn*. But that's just me. That's just my personal dictionary. Listen. Like I said before, you can turn *Latham* into *halt Ma*. That's all I have to say. I can't believe that it didn't hit my brain earlier. That's all I need to say! That woman is damaging our son, I can tell. When have I been wrong?"

This occurred on Christmas Eve. My sister Judith huddled in the bathroom with a watercolor kit, as usual. Mom had encouraged her artwork, though only on the shower curtain where it would come off four times a day. Because I always woke up earliest, I discovered such dictums as "We shall never repent from our immoral ways!" or "It's a straight line between boredom and death!" or "May the Prince of Darkness teach us forever!" or "Roses are red / violets are blue / I've got a secret: / may the Prince of Darkness come out of nowhere in the middle of the day and select you for one of his minions." Judith wasn't right in the head, I figured out early on. This was before any of those scary movies, too. She'd get straightened out two years later, I thought, when Mrs. Latham called her Judith No Yes.

"Maybe you were wrong when we got married," I almost heard my father say. He looked up at my mother's secret cabinet, above the refrigerator. I do know that he said, "You thought I'd only be selling venetian blinds to convicts, ex-cons, runaways, and ne'er-do-wells. Look how that ended up. I seem to be putting food on the table. I don't hear you wanting for want."

My mother stomped around a bit, between running into various pieces of furniture in our den, living room, and kitchen. She asked me for a syllabus, kind of—she said, "Hey Gary No Yes, get me that long sheet of paper that has y'all's day-to-day activities typed up on it mimeographed with the goddamn teacher's name and address on the top of it"—and found Mrs. Latham's home phone number.

And she called. Only later in life did I find it sad that Mrs. Latham answered the phone, considering. Here it was, Christmas Eve, and she should've been either visiting her folks or her in-laws, like every other American with any sense of duty. I hung out by the stolen Christmas tree my father bought from a man on the side of Highway 25, and I pretended to be enamored with a couple gifts wrapped for Judith and me that were obviously either socks or underwear. My mother said, "Hello, Mrs. Latham?"

I assumed that my teacher said something other than "Get lost, it's Christmas Eve."

"Hey, this is Gary No Yes's mother, and I would like to invite you and Mr. Latham over for some day-after-Christmas turkey hash. I have this recipe I got from my mother's mother, and she got it from my husband's father's father's father's mother." I looked beneath the tree and saw a box that might've actually been a set of encyclopedias. "Yes, that *is* odd how my family could know my husband's family, but that's the way it goes. Anyway, we want you and Mr. Latham to come over on December 26—it's so much trouble for people to take care of everything the day after Christmas, we understand."

I picked up a package and shook it. The card said FROM MOM/TO GARY. This is no lie: glug, glug, glug emanated beneath the box. Booze, I thought. It wasn't hard to figure out how my mother made it sound that she would bear the brunt of taking on all day-after-Christmas eaters. I listened to my mother listen to Mrs. Latham.

My mother said, "Uh-huh. Uh-huh. Okay. Uh-huh. Well that would be great, then," like that.

To me she said, "Well that's settled. She seems to love you, Gary No Yes." Back in the bedroom later I heard her tell my father, "She has no right to call herself Mrs. Latham. Halt Ma! She's not even married. What kind of a woman would pretend to have a husband? Most sane women walk around town with their husbands, but pretend like they're strangers who happen to walk in the same direction at the same pace."

The next thing I knew, my father got me out of bed, told me to put on some tennis shoes but stay in my pajamas, and we were off in his Dodge to place surprise Christmas gifts on the miniature porches of house trailers. He gave out extra-thin feather dusters, made especially for the Galloway micro-miniblind. Somewhere halfway to Forty-Five he said to me, "Gary No Yes, it's important to make people feel like their homes are first-rate. Remember that. Even if the homeowners aren't clean, it's important for them to feel that their trailers are first-rate. Am I clear on this?"

I thought, We must turn *first-rate* into *rat strife*. We must turn *first-rate* into *tar fister*. I said, "Yes," got out of the car, wove my way through about twenty curs, and propped micro-miniblind dusters against aluminum doors. I imaged my sister inside the bathroom, painting a picture of Satan Claus with horns and fangs.

The glug-glug-glug gift ended up being a quart of aftershave, something I would use in about five years. Judith got a new shower curtain, some more watercolors, a white leather Bible, and a slew of knee socks. Me, I got underwear, some knee socks that were probably meant for Judith and mispackaged, and one of those miniature black Magic 8 Balls that you shook to get a Yes or No answer. I'm ashamed to admit it now, but when my father said, "Ask it a question and see what comes up," I secretly asked myself, "What does the future hold for me, in regards to Gruel?"

I hadn't quite gotten the hang of how to ask it questions, obviously. The answer came up, "It's in your future." I kind of thought how maybe Mrs. Latham came from the family that manufactured these things.

So we sat around the table for a few hours seeing as my father needed to pull off a two-hour grace, he couldn't carve the turkey right, and my mother kept throwing away entire cans of congealed cranberry sauce when they didn't slide out unmarred. "It's bad luck to have dented cranberry sauce," she said. "We must turn *dented* into *tended*."

Fa la la la la, la la, la la.

My mother shaved, honed, scraped, and pulled what turkey carcass scraps she found soon thereafter, chopped the meat into dust mote–sized bits, set them in a pot of boiling turkey broth she'd saved, added enough jalapeños to cure the world of head colds. The next day she got up earlier than usual, took the lid off her turkey hash, sampled a wooden spoonful, and declared, "One day I might open up a diner here in Gruel. What this town needs is a good diner."

I waited for my mother to turn one of her words into another, but she didn't. No, she seemed happy and confident and optimistic.

When Mrs. Latham came over at noon, my mother took off her apron, answered the door, and performed a perfect sweeping arm gesture for my seventh-grade teacher to follow into the den. Mrs. Latham said, "Merry belated Christmas, Mr. Noyes," to either my father or me, I couldn't tell. She didn't use the normal No Yes form of salutation.

"Judith, come on in here and meet Gary No Yes's teacher," my mother yelled out, though. I prayed that Mrs. Latham wouldn't have to go to the bathroom during her visit. Sure enough, Judith had taken her new watercolors and painted a nice representation of Grant Wood's *American Gothic*, but instead of a pitchfork the farmer only held up his middle finger, and the farmer's wife had blood running down both sides of her mouth.

Judith came out all smudged and said, "I guess you'll be my teacher in two years, if I don't fail on purpose. My last name's Noyes, not No Yes, by the way. You have from now until then to memorize it."

I said, "Ha ha ha ha ha ha ha. Judith got a new Bible for Christmas."

Mrs. Latham said, "If I'm here in two years you can go ahead and shoot me in the brain, Judith," as my father pulled the dining room chair out for her. "Did Santa bring you that set of encyclopedias you wanted, Gary No Yes?"

My mother pulled out her own chair and sat down. "How come you insist on people calling you *Mrs.* Latham when you don't even have a husband?"

My father said, "Dorothy Marie." I never knew my mother's middle name up to this point.

Judith said, "Marie? Marie?!" and ran back into the bathroom to paint something else.

I said, "We are humbled by your presence here, Mrs. Latham," because I'd seen it in a movie.

My teacher scooted up. She looked at my mother and didn't blink. "My husband was in Special Forces. He was killed in 1968, somewhere in a Vietnamese jungle. I don't know about you, but where I come from we keep our deceased husband's name. We'd met in college up in Chapel Hill, and I asked him not to volunteer, but he was too patriotic. His father and two uncles all died in France and Pearl Harbor. My husband had straight As right up until he left college his junior year. He studied philosophy and religion, and minored in literature. He had hopes of one day teaching elementary school either in an inner city or way out in the country—kind of like here in Gruel—so kids could have some kind of future. My husband didn't so much believe in the war in Vietnam, though, let me make it clear. He thought that he'd studied enough Buddhism to talk the enemy into giving up altogether. He's buried down in Florence, at the national cemetery there, should y'all wish to ever visit and place a small American flag on his grave. The one I placed yesterday should be faded by the end of January or thereabouts."

My father stuck out his palms to hold Mrs. Latham's hand and mine before he said grace. I looked at my mother and noticed how I could've taken every available linen napkin, wadded them up, and still not filled the space her open mouth created. My father only said, "Let us remember our heroes and victims. Amen."

Judith shouted from the bathroom, "Amen."

My mother let the canned cranberry sauce fall out at will, on a silver-plated stick-butter plate. She served the turkey hash atop cheese grits, with homemade bread to the side. Mrs. Latham finally said, "My husband had straight As, just like Gary does. That's maybe why I'm a little hard on your son."

My parents said nothing. Even Judith knew not to say anything about how she wanted to be a tattoo artist later on in life. We ate, Mrs. Latham left, and my father and I spent the next week visiting his micro-miniblind customers to see if they'd tried out their surprise feather dusters. When I went back to school for the second semester, Mrs. Latham took me aside on the first day right before we filed off for a lunch of cling peaches, black-eyed peas, corn bread, steamed cabbage, and sloppy joes. She said, "Yes or No—that story I told your parents could've gotten me a movie award."

I looked into my teacher's eyes and realized that I would be getting such questions for the entirety of my life. I wore my sister's knee socks that day, though no one could tell seeing as we didn't have a PE class at Gruel Normal. But I felt the smile coming on, and let it go before laughing out loud. I said, "Christmas." Mrs. Latham put her hand on the top of my head and walked with me toward the cafeteria. She said, "Every day."

Polish

NELLIE SIZEMORE TAKES every bottle of her dead mother's fingernail polish out on the front porch, props her bare legs up, and spots each chigger bite a different color right there in full view of anyone passing by a half block off the town square. Later she will rummage through the bathroom cabinets looking for rubbing alcohol to wash her blackened fingers, the result of blackberry picking. As a girl Nellie harvested the surrounding land's patches with her mother each July. They made tarts together, pies, ate the berries cold with whole milk. If anyone had asked Nellie to imagine the blackberry patches of her youth she would've guessed that they'd been plowed under by now, lost to retail drugstores, subdivisions, maybe a cleared horse pasture. But in Gruel, South Carolina, the blackberries thrive more so, it seems to her. Whereas most adults look back and notice how something that seemed so large in earlier days ends up minuscule, Nellie finds her old thorny acreage at least doubled in size. She swabs her ankles in Pink Arctic Ice, and wonders if her mother might've gotten lost back there in the blackberries in future years, should she have lived longer. Nellie knows that she cannot move back, no matter what the financial benefits, the lack of temptations.

Sammy Koon spies Nellie's exposed legs as soon as he turns the corner at Roughhouse Billiards. He knows that there's an estate sale tomorrow and hopes to get a look inside first. He changes street sides and uses trees for camouflage, his eyes on her legs.

Nellie doesn't change positions when Sammy shuffles through her mother's side yard. She holds the applicator in her right hand. "Sammy Koon," she says.

He wears khaki pants ironed the wrong way, and a short-sleeved white shirt. Two pens pop out of his cigarette pocket. Nellie thinks, One thing about Gruel: The men all keep their hair in the same style as twenty years earlier. Sammy says, "I heard you come back, Nellie. Hey, remember that time we was driving to school together because your daddy's car broke down, and we seen that bloated cow? Goddamn. Hey, what you doing?"

"I got some bad chiggers. I'm killing them with fingernail polish." Between her ankles and knees she's used Purple Passion and Jasmine Jubilee. Sammy stands in front of Nellie and pretends not to look up her sundress.

"Peanut butter works, too. Vaseline. You can use lighter fluid to kill them off. One time I fell asleep out in the woods one night and woke up with over three hundred bites. I thought about writing them people at that world record place, but I never did. I had chigger bites on my eyelids."

Nellie drops her feet to the porch floor. "You still living here in Gruel, Sammy?"

"I'm thinking about opening up an odds and ends store, you know. I can get a storefront on the square for just about nothing, seeing as the square's gone dead."

Nellie uncaps and sniffs Red Dynamite Flare for her upper arms. "You never know what might take off in Gruel."

Sammy shades his eyes. "K-Y jelly works for chiggers, too. Whatever can keep them from getting air through your skin. They got to suffocate, you know."

"Yeah, well, I don't think I have any K-Y jelly in the house."

"You gonna come back here and help run the pharmacy? We hear you got all the way up to being a pharmacist somewheres."

Nellie pats each bite three times, then goes on to the next. She'll have to go inside and use a full-length mirror for her backside. "Nashville. But I'm not a pharmacist anymore. Let's just say I got a little too close to my work."

Sammy Koon lights a cigarette. "Well it's good to have you back home, no matter. I was sorry to hear about your momma. I was sorry to hear about your daddy when he died. How long ago was that?"

"I have no clue." Nellie looks at her collection of bottles lined up on the railing. When did my mother ever get the chance to wear these colors? she thinks. Where could she go all dolled up? "He died, and that was that." Nellie chooses Daffodil Delight for her left forearm.

"Say, you know if they's any Tupperware in there?" Sammy points to the dining room window. "Tupperware, or maybe some Case knives? I believe I could resell those kinds of things if I had my odds and ends store."

Nellie turns around toward the house and opens her legs accidentally. She says, "Only thing I know is that I'm keeping a sideboard, the single iron bed that was mine, and the yellow ware. There are a bunch of my father's Shriners hats. Those fezzes. Come back tomorrow and you can grab those up. They're odd, and it's the end—so I'm sure they'd sell at an odds and ends place."

"Say, let's you and me go over to Roughhouse tonight and have us a beer or two. You know the whole town's going to be by here tomorrow morning. You might need someone with you tonight to explain all those spots on your body. People around here, they talk. They might start saying you got that disease."

Nellie thinks, I'm not supposed to have booze, either. She thinks, I'm not supposed to ingest anything that would further damage my liver. "I'll meet you there at eight o'clock if and only if you don't talk anything about my living in Gruel in the past, ever."

Sammy Koon grins, doffs an imaginary cap, and walks backward.

When speckled Nellie Sizemore walks into Roughhouse Billiards, the regulars turn her way. Two trick shot specialists quit setting up their balls for impossible combinations. Nellie orders a double bourbon and a bottle of Pabst.

She sits on the barstool closest to the door. Her chigger bites don't itch as much as they vibrate; there's a certain amount of electricity surging beneath my skin, Nellie thinks.

By nine o'clock she realizes that Sammy Koon's inside her house, either stealing wares or waiting for her return. She hadn't locked the front door. No one ever locks doors in Gruel. Everything—*always*—remains open here. Nellie Sizemore stares at her fingernails, knowing that she'll drink until it's safe, again.

Snipers

ON VALENTINE'S DAY Victor Dees pushed gas masks. Twelve months earlier he convinced the citizenry of Gruel that mess kits were all the rage, not chocolates, flowers, or tennis bracelets. In previous years Victor Dees talked sweethearts into buying each other tarps for romantic nights beneath the stars; ammo boxes, as a joke, to envelop really sentimental gifts bought in towns with actual stores; peacoats, wool blankets, ponchos, Seward Trunks, and pith helmets. Victor's owned V.D.'s Army-Navy Surplus on the square since 1976. He had no competition in Gruel, South Carolina.

"There's never been a time in the history of the United States when infiltrators from American-hating countries—on top of crazy madmen anarchists of our own—want to come in with their nerve gas and whatnot. What, in this time of high anxiety and mental strife, could prove your love more than a gas mask?" Victor asked every Gruel resident who walked in.

And we were all there, daily. Roughhouse Billiards, Gruel Drugs, Gruel Home Medical Supply, and a diner that specialized in twelve different types of oatmeal were the only storefronts remaining. The statue of Colonel Dill still stood in the square's center, but not much else prospered. My one friend Chink Larue took antique furniture and knickknacks out of his own house and displayed them inside old Gruel Business Supply twice a year—when lost Floridians went to Asheville summers or back home winters. That's it.

I said, "A bomb shelter. That'd prove my love for Lynette." My wife's birthday fell on February 14, too. For fifteen years I gave her a variety of presents on this date, and let her guess which stood for which occasion. On her fortieth birthday I gave her a first-aid kit, a bottle of wine, and a piece of Beatrice Wood's pottery that I bought elsewhere. Lynette got drunk, then asked me if I wagered to put her ashes in the urn should the first-aid kit not be sufficient. I told her that I'd've bought land mines from the army-navy store had I such plans.

"Gas masks this year," Victor Dees told me. This was February 13. I'd driven nearly to Charlotte the day before on business and chosen for Lynette a box of French chocolate and a handful of mums. I'd stopped at an antique joint in view of the giant peach water tower on I-85 and bought a pocket of genuine Cherokee arrowheads—which I thought could be translated into a Cupid-like love—and an ancient, silver, hand-forged watch. "I've almost sold out. Hey, Sim, you don't want to be known as the only man in Gruel who don't love his wife enough to save her from biological warfare, do you?"

Victor Dees seemed to know what bad things would occur on this planet. He predicted correctly droughts, tax hikes, ice storms, the construction of interstates that redirected traffic farther away from downtown Gruel, and the birth of little retarded Clarence Brown. I said, "Did she get one of these things for me?"

As much as Lynette hated her birthday falling on Valentine's Day, I felt guilty for taking gifts from her. I always prayed that she'd forget February 14 so I wouldn't undergo the embarrassment of handing over flowers, candy, and a bayonet sponsored by Victor Dees, only to find a new riding lawn mower or table saw out in the garage from her.

"Lynette hasn't been in my store for months," Dees said. "I understand, though. I haven't seen her since the hand grenade clearance sale."

All of the hand grenades sold were disengaged, of course, except for the one I bought Lynette. As a joke she pulled the pin, flung the thing into our backyard, and ruined any chances of planting tomatoes in a new patch two months later. We also lost bird feeders, a row of Leyland cypresses, and—maybe—a couple of the neighbor's twenty stray cats. I liked to think that the cats merely ran away to safer environs, like a back alley behind the new Jin-Jin Chinese restaurant over in Forty-Five.

I took the gas mask and put it on, then walked around the store. The smell of pup tent, as always, both overwhelmed me and caused a series of teenage backyard flashbacks that had me asking for God's forgiveness. Surrounded by camouflaged helmets and photographs of Stonewall Jackson, I said, "I guess I'll take two of these things. I'm thinking Lynette wouldn't want to survive nerve gas without me."

"It's exactly what my wife told me, Sim." Then he wrapped both masks in special jungle-print paper.

This won't end up like that O. Henry story wherein a guy sells his watch to buy a comb and the wife sells her hair to buy a fob. I awoke on Valentine's Day early, got up, and started the coffee. I let the dogs outside and told them not to chase cats or fall in the crater out back, then changed all the clocks to the wrong times. When Lynette opened her watch, I figured, I could say something about how I knew she needed it, et cetera, in order to be certain.

My wife got up all smiles and sat down at the kitchen table. "You fell for Victor Dees's weirdo pitch again, I see." She tapped the wrapping paper. Then she opened the gas masks.

I said, "I guess it's kind of cheating to buy two. One of them's mine."

My wife got up, poured her own coffee, then threw the cup at me. Luckily I wore insulated long johns I'd bought at the army-navy store. "Hey, hey!"

"I know that joke—you wear a bag on your own head in case mine falls off. How could you do this to me on my birthday, Sim? On Valentine's Day."

"No, no, no," I said, then explained the threat of crazy anarchist madmen, of American-hating world leaders, the high anxiety and strife that could infiltrate Gruel. I about went into how I knew she couldn't live without me, but thought otherwise. Lynette poured another cup of coffee, said that she wanted to be alone, and went upstairs.

When I went to the end of our driveway to retrieve the newspaper, Victor Dees's wife stood there, her dachshund lifting his leg on my mailbox. Mrs. Dees drawled out a hello, then waved haphazardly a diamond ring she'd only put on her hand an hour earlier. "These things start out as coal," she said. "Diamonds withstand heat, cold, and war, says Victor."

I unfolded the paper and looked at the headlines. I wouldn't mention the diamond later, but I would point out how troops amassed on all kinds of borders. I would say something to my wife about how we could use our backyard to advantage should the world close in.

Lickers

THE MAN SAID he found his dog on the front porch one November, right before Thanksgiving. He said it was the truth, and that if he wanted to tell lies he'd've said Christmas, or Easter, or one of the other healing holidays. It caught me off guard, certainly, understand. While he went into a description of his dog's capabilities I stood there sockless at my front door trying to capture "healing holidays." Ash Wednesday, maybe? Independence Day probably made people feel better, especially recent immigrants. What about Valentine's Day? Me, I always felt ultimately worthless and destroyed on Valentine's Day— not healed in any human conception. I couldn't pay attention right off. The dog appeared to be part shepherd, part beagle, part Lab. Nothing special. She had long black and brown hair, flopped ears, legs a little too short for her body. The dog made decent eye contact, panted, and let her fat tongue loll out long to one side or the other.

"If you'd like to see some snapshots, I got them. And official documentation," the man said. "I have witnesses and phone numbers."

This was a Saturday morning. I'd lived in Gruel for a good year, trying to fit in. No one seemed anxious to make my acquaintance. The woman I bought bread from down at Gruel Bakery one time said, "You should try my special bread with Jesus crust," and two locals trying to perform trick shots down at Roughhouse Billiards once said, "Thanks" when I picked up their errant cue ball. But that was about it.

"I got a picture of a guy who says he zipped his pants up funny on his testicles. Oh it cut him to pieces. Personally I think he had something else happen to him, like maybe he tried to cross a bob-wire fence one night drunk and cut himself something awful. But that's neither here or otherwise. What matters is I got a picture of his things sliced, and a other of good old Pam licking the sore, and then a other of it healed." He lowered his head and said quietly, "I don't show that picture to the women, by the way."

The man had an old-fashioned army knapsack with him that he pulled off his right shoulder. His hair stood up wild and funny gray on his head, wiry. He dug in and started pulling out three-by-fives. I said, "Your dog's named Pam? Pam?"

"This is Pam. Say hey, Pam."

Pam sat down and stuck out her right paw. I waved, and looked out in the front yard to see if some kind of hidden camera posse stood nearby, like on one of those TV shows. I bent down and shook Pam's paw. "Good dog. Sorry I don't have any kind of sore," I said.

"Here's a picture of a boil, before and after," the man said. He handed me Polaroids of a giant neck pimple and then of smooth skin. I didn't say, "Anyone could take a picture of a giant dermatological abrasion, and then another of someone else's smooth skin." I said, "Huh. How about that."

"Here's some more." He handed over photographs of cuts, scrapes, possible leprosy, oozing sores of one variety or another. Then he had the supposed cured areas in vivid color. He said, "Five dollars. You can't beat that. Try going down to a doctor in Forty-Five. It's thirty-five dollars just to walk into the door. And then you got drugs, salves, and ointments to pay for later. Try going to the Graywood Memorial Emergency Room. You ever noticed how if you turn GMER around it comes out GERM? There's a reason for that."

He wore a T-shirt that read MIRACLES HAPPEN, but no picture of Jesus underneath the statement. I sat down on my steps and pet the dog. I said, "What do you do, travel from town to town, healing people with Pam here? That's kind of cool. Someone should make a documentary."

"It don't matter none my name," the man said out of nowhere. He stood stiff, and had a look on him mostly captured by Confederate soldiers posed brave and defiant. "Let's just say my name's Seth. If I were a real doctor I'd have me a Seth-a-scope, you know what I'm talking?"

I didn't. If I were a doctor named Seth I'd probably try to pick up women by saying, "You want a little of the Seth-a-scope," like an idiot, poking my groin back and forth.

I stuck out my hand and said, "I'm Curt." It's the first time I'd had the opportunity to introduce myself since moving to Gruel, I thought. "I'm Curt." My parents might as well have named me Angry or Short-tempered.

Seth shook my hand and Pam the healing dog stuck out her paw, all reflexes.

"You trying to tell me, Curt, that you ain't got a bruise, some joint pain, a blister, skin rash? Pam the healing dog can fix it all. Hey, I tell you what—you look honest enough—I can have her lick your needs, and then I'll come back the next day for the five dollars. I'll come back tomorrow. All's I'm asking is that you be honest with me."

Please understand that I'm not a sick man, physically or mentally, but for some reason I thought about this: What if I had some bad and persistent hemorrhoids? Would this Seth fellow allow his dog to lick a man's butt? I said, "Not a twinge, as far as I'm concerned. Hell, I'll give you five dollars if you're hurting for money, man."

Seth said, "I got pictures of Pam's work on sprained ankles. Tendonitis. This one old boy over in Forty-Five had a nervous tic she licked away, though it can't be documented very well on photographic paper. I needed to get me one them cameras with a fast shutter speed, so maybe the before picture would come out a blur what from the tic. Pam will lick away about anything, except hemorrhoids. I draw the line there. I won't let her lick some stranger's ass, excuse my language."

Can he read minds? I thought. "Okay. Now that you mention it. I was just trying you out, seeing how persistent you were. A long time ago I was a distance runner. This was maybe twenty-five years ago. Right into my freshman year in college. Anyway, I ran and ran, and I'm starting to think that the cartilage in my knees is pretty much worn away. Especially on wet fall days, my knees ache and throb."

"I've seen it before," Seth said. Pam the dog pricked up her ears. "Roll up your pants leg, son. Ready yourself for a miracle."

I have to admit that Pam's healing session was more than pleasant. Not that I've ever spent money on a massage therapist of any kind, but I imagined that my experience with the dog was similar in a "non-deep tissue" kind of way. That dog licked and licked for a good hour. Seth walked around my front yard smoking cigarettes. I pet Pam's head and said things like, "You a good girl, aren't you?" Every once in a while she pulled back her lips and kneaded my knees for fleas in that way that only dogs can maneuver.

I said to Seth, "How can y'all live off five bucks a session? There's no way."

He said, "Well, it's five bucks for fifteen minutes, officially. I guess I should've mentioned that. Technically, you owe twenty dollars. But it's up to you. So far, Pam ain't had to take no more than fifteen minutes to heal a wound, you know."

I kind of felt the way I did when I first said, "Oh, hell, yeah—go ahead and give me some cable TV," not knowing that every little religious station added on at Charter Communications' whim would cost me more monthly. I said, "Yeah, you probably should've said something about that."

"But it don't matter. It's up to you. Tomorrow I'll come by, and you'll be honest, and you'll tell me whether or not your knees feel better. And then you'll either pay me what Pam deserves or you won't."

I stood up and rolled my pants legs down. I looked at the dog and said, "Thanks." To Seth I said, "It's been a known fact for years that a dog licking an open wound makes it heal quicker. I mean, when I was growing up and had a scab, my dog Dooley'd lick it."

Seth lit another cigarette. He looked out toward the Gruel skyline, which meant the back sides of four one-story brick buildings. "That's true, Curt. But I've had Pam's salivary glands tested. And I have documentation right here," he patted his wallet, "that states her spit—for some unknown reason—contains higher levels of stearic acid, sodium borate, allantoin, and methyl paraben. The doctor up at Duke who conducted all the tests said she also has a way of secreting acetaminophen that he'd never seen before. Oh Pam's a medical mystery."

I'm no idiot. I understood that it didn't take much for a man like Seth to memorize the ingredients of any burn cream, plus an extra-strength headache powder. I thought to myself, In a way that's my job, in a way. I said, "Well. Whatever. I'd like to talk to that Duke boy. He might've gone to too many basketball games."

"Here you go," Seth said. "Goddamn it. It's true. Most people I run into haven't even heard of medical research, man. I'm glad to talk to someone who's been around. What're you doing in Gruel, of all places?"

I didn't go into how my wife left me for another man—a high school *guidance* fucking counselor she worked with up in Greenville where she taught social studies to tenth graders who couldn't pass the class in seventh, eighth, or ninth. I didn't say how I threw a goddamn dart hoping to hit Montana or Maine, that I'd made a promise to myself to go wherever it landed, and how the stupid thing landed only fifty miles south. I didn't say how there weren't many places in America where you could buy an antebellum house in need of slight repair for ten thousand dollars. I didn't say, "Fuck, if my dart had landed in the Bermuda Triangle I would've moved there." I said to Seth, "I could live anywhere. I work as a freelance indexer."

Pam sniffed my crotch. I tried not to view this as a sign.

"A freelance indexer. That has something to do with fingers?"

"Nope. Well, I guess in a way it does. Somebody writes a book with a lot of notes. A lot of citations. It's my job to read the book, and then have everything in alphabetical order at the back of the book. You've seen books like this, I swear. I do

mostly biographies. Publishers call me up and send me manuscripts, and I filter everything out. You've seen it before. At
the back of books."

I didn't go into where I'd made major contributions: books
by or about Kissinger, Nixon, Bush, Reagan, Lucifer, and Satan.

"The backs of books. And now you're here."

I said, "With a dog licking my knees."

Seth looked left and right, pulled out his cigarette twice,
and exhaled. He said, "Bubba, this ain't much of a town. What
do you do in a town like this? What can I do for my dog here?"

I looked across the way. I lived on Old Old Greenville
Road, in a Victorian house that . . . sure, the ceilings fell down
throughout, and the roof looked like some giant sat on it; the
gutters hung like weird incisors; the floor sagged in a way that
made it impossible to walk from den to dining room—but
otherwise it seemed a perfect place to freelance indices. I said,
"I don't know. Here I am. But by goddamn I don't have a sore
on my leg."

"Well."

Pam the dog cocked her head. I thought about doing a
couple deep knee bends, but didn't. I knew that I'd perform
such things the next morning. I said, "It's been good meeting
you, Seth. Pam."

Seth said, "Uh-huh," and looked at me like I was out of
my mind. Index freelancer, you know. He said, "Tomorrow,
Bubba. Tomorrow's Sunday." And then he gave me a look that
might've said, I'll kill you if you don't come up with the
money. Or maybe he gave me a look of You and me could drink
some beer together. Sometimes I get those looks confused. I do
know that my knees didn't have a hair on either one of them,
if that matters, after Pam got done.

―――――――

I perform my job the old-fashioned way: I keep a notebook open, I read, and I take notes with a pencil. Normally I place twenty-six little tabs at the top of the pages, A through Z. As I read, I place asterisks in the margins, and go to my notebook to jot down what I've found.

Let's pretend that I'm indexing a biography of, I don't know, Pavlov. I might have to turn to the S's under "Salivation" and write pages 1, 2, 4, 6–120, 122, 124–400, and so on. Under "Temper tantrum" I might only have to place down "—with dog, 98," "—with wife, 360," or whatever. It's a meticulous job that I never mind, but one that a spouse might find both all-encompassing and anally retentive. As a matter of fact, if my ex-wife indexed my biography she'd probably have pages one to the end marked for obsessive-compulsive behavior. I don't care.

Since I had moved to Gruel my job as a freelance indexer was more or less at a standstill. I wouldn't call it a self-imposed hiatus, seeing as the publishing houses teamed together and quit sending me work. Evidently I'd gone too far on three successive books in a row from three separate presses—one on George Wallace, one on Jesse Helms, and another involving the 1994 Republican "Contract with America." Each one had pretty much the same section that began with the letter I. Under "Idiotic behavior" I listed every page of each book. The same went for "Idiotic thought." Then I listed my own name under "Rational thought."

Hell, who knew that someone actually read those indices back at the publishing house? I'd never had a copy editor chosen for my own work. As far as I was concerned, I *was* the copy editor, in a way. But then some newly graduated do-gooder from Smith or Sarah Lawrence or Vassar who got a job somewhere between intern and courier decided to take a look at my work, told on me, and so on. I think she's probably senior editor now, at age twenty-three.

But I'm not pouting. You'd think, seeing as Marissa left me soon thereafter and I moved to a town named after the worst breakfast ever invented, that I'd've gone to cutting myself or holding my hands too close to a flame (bad indexer, bad, bad indexer) in such a way that would give Pam the healing dog a challenge. I didn't.

I woke up the next day at four A.M. as normal, and did my routine. In the old days I got out the book at hand and got to work. I know I've always told myself that I'd never be like my father, but I woke up two hours before dawn, got to work, and prided myself on being finished for the day before *The Today Show* finished. Then I could take a nap, watch the noon news, maybe practice horseshoes, most likely play about four thousand games of solitaire, wait for Marissa to get home from her job as a teacher of at-risk teens, listen to her stories about some nineteen-year-old tenth grader confused at there being a Washington, D.C., and an entire state with the same name, prepare supper for us, then go to bed. This occurred in Raleigh, Charlotte, Greensboro, Charleston, and Savannah. Let me make it clear that I could work anywhere, so we always moved only because my wife either "had" to move or "had a better offer." I don't want to start rumors, but I have a funny feeling now that she got "asked" to leave some of those jobs, that maybe she belittled students and colleagues alike. Who knows.

So I got up at four, and walked around the kitchen drinking coffee, putting everything in alphabetical order. I don't want to come off as some kind of seer, but I could feel someone standing on my front porch, so I went out there and turned on the outside lights to find Seth and Pam the dog. I opened the door and said, "What did y'all do, sleep in my front yard?"

"How're those knees feeling, friend?" Seth said. He wore the same thing as the day before. "Do a couple deep knee bends right now and tell me you don't feel better. I'm serious. If you can honestly say you don't, I'm on my way. If you do, then it's twenty dollars."

I said, "Now I can see how you make a living. If you're waking people up at four in the morning and working till midnight, that makes sense." Pam sat down and wagged her tail, sweeping a couple leaves and a ton of dust around.

I did the knee bends, and sure enough I didn't feel the tendonitis/arthritis/effects of being thirty pounds overweight that I normally felt. My ligaments didn't feel as though they stretched to the bursting point, is what I'm saying. "Come on in," I said, like a fool.

Seth and Pam ambled into the empty den—or probably the "parlor"—and stood five feet into my house. I went upstairs to find my wallet. When I came back down Seth said, "They's a bunch of gurus living out at the old Gruel Inn. Did you know that? Pam and me went by there hoping to do some healing, and this one yoga fellow bent way over and licked the back side of his knee. It's people like that might put us out of business."

I handed over one of those new twenty-dollar bills that look more like French money than American. I said, "I pretty much keep to myself," but didn't go into the whole I-might've-gone-crazy-for-a-little-while explanation.

Seth said, "We appreciate it." He bent down to Pam and said, "Dog food for a month, baby!" and showed her the money. Then he walked backward to the door and opened it.

He said, "You don't know how much this means. Hey, tell your friends about Pam the healing lick dog."

I said, "I will," and didn't go into an explanation about how I knew no one in Gruel outside of the woman with the Jesus crust bread and the trick shot players who said, "Thanks." I said, "Good luck to you and yours," for some reason.

On the porch Seth said, "You know, on our way up here— on our way through your yard—I thought I saw some kind of snake hole you might want to be aware of. It's right out here."

He pointed. I wasn't afraid of snakes, but I'd overheard some people at Roughhouse Billiards talk about how there seemed to be a preponderance of snakes that infiltrated the town lately. I said, "Where?" and followed him out in the yard.

I might've made it five or six steps barefoot before I felt what ended up being broken glass and tacks in the soles of my feet. I yelled out a couple damn-it-to-hells and made it back to the steps on my heels. Because, again, the porch lights were on I could see the blood flowing from the balls of my feet, from in between my toes, et cetera. I said, "Ow-ow-ow."

"Uh-oh," Seth said. "Hey Pam, get to work on this old boy's sores."

The dog approached me on cue.

Of course I knew that Seth spread broken Coke bottles and tacks in my front yard and lured me out there to step on them early morning barefoot. And I didn't hold it against him! He'd probably seen me go out every morning without shoes to pick up my newspapers—the paperboy drove a step van and delivered the local *Forty-Five Platter*, the *State*, and the *Greenville News* in three long swoops as he drove by in a way that made me walk from gravel driveway to property edge to retrieve them all. I figured that I'd only been cased, just like in crime drama movies.

We sat down in the kitchen and Seth said, "That coffee smells good."

I said, "You can have some for twenty dollars a cup, peckerhead," like that. Maybe I wasn't as amused as I pretended.

Pam the dog licked and licked my bare feet in a way that reminded me of my honeymoon, in a way that reminded me of a woman I'd worked with on an early biography of Rasputin. Seth said, "You look like the kind of man who might hold some bourbon around the house. You got any bourbon around the house? I like bourbon in my coffee."

I didn't say "Here we go" aloud, I don't think, but I thought it. If I were indexing this scene for a book I'd've written "here we go" under "Bourbon request." "Yeah, there's some bourbon in the cabinet over there. By the way, I'm not paying you five bucks a quarter hour for this. I'm on to you, man." I looked at the dog lapping my soles. "I'm on to you, too, Fido," I said.

Seth retrieved a quart of Old Crow and sat down across from me. He got back up, found two jelly jars, and placed them on the table. "To be honest, it's not good for you to drink while Pam's at work. Drinking thins the blood. It's the same with tattoos, you know. My dog can't lick and lick if the blood's going to keep spewing."

I looked over at Seth and noticed how one eye wandered off funny. I'd known people with this affliction before, men and women who were tired, or got drunk, and then that one eye rolled around loose. I said, "Are you all right, buddy?"

"I'm you," he said. "I don't know anything about your personal life, but I'm betting that we're one in the same, if you know what I mean."

I looked down at Pam and said, "Hey, that kind of tickles."

"Don't think that I've always wandered around with a dog licking sores. I've not always been this way."

I nodded. I waited for him to tell me how he once worked on Wall Street or as a lawyer, maybe a lobbyist. I said, "Go on."

"You ain't from around here, are you?"

I said, "No sir. I'm not." Come on, I thought, tell me how you used to be a real doctor.

"People from around here will tell you about how I coached high school football. That's what I did until I couldn't take it no more. And maybe I wasn't the best coach in the world, but by God I could tape an ankle. I could put a halfback back out onto the playing field with a broke foot and he wouldn't even know it. He wouldn't feel the pain. I could talk a broken ankle into feeling like it only got a slight sprain, you know what I mean?" Seth took a drink of his jelly jar bourbon. The sun rose outside. A dog licked my feet nonstop.

I said, "Huh. That's weird."

"I taught history, and driver's ed, and PE. And I coached football down in Gig. Then I found Pam. Then I got fired for beating a kid on the sidelines during a game, and some parents didn't like that. It was only a placekicker."

What else could I say but, "Everybody's gotten politically correct about those kinds of things."

My knees felt invigorated. My feet immediately felt better. Seth said, "I'm telling you. I was out of there on a rail. A placekicker! That boy couldn't kick his sister's butt, much less a football through goalposts."

I drank from my own jelly jar and felt good. Not that I'm proud to admit it, but sometimes in the old days I got up at four A.M. and poured bourbon while doing my index work. I'm pretty sure it shows in that one biography I did of Truman Capote. There were things under "Q" that didn't need to be there.

"Do you know what it's like to pull off a perfect end sweep?" Seth said. "Do you know what it feels like to pull off a flea flicker when the defense has no idea it's about to happen?"

I said, "No sir."

"You ain't much of an athlete, are you? No offense, but you have no clue what I'm talking about, do you?"

I said, "Yes, I do. Fucker. I do. I'd go outside and challenge you in one-on-one basketball or a game of horseshoes, if my feet weren't all screwed up from your little game."

"You got any cards? While we're here we might as well play some poker." Seth threw down the twenty-dollar bill I'd given him earlier.

I had cards right there in the kitchen drawer, next to the couple spoons, couple knives, couple forks. I said, "No."

"You don't seem to be the kind of man who can take it," Seth said. "I've known men like you."

His demeanor certainly had changed since the afternoon before, of course. And I thought about saying, "Hey, buddy, I don't know where you come off giving me life lessons, seeing as you travel around with a licking dog." But I didn't. I said, "I've taken more than you could imagine."

"You got any dice? Hey, let's play rock-paper-scissors-dynamite!" Pam the dog kept licking. "Hey, you want to see a picture I got of a woman who lost her eye, and how Pam licked it back into seeing? This might be the scariest thing ever."

Pam the dog withdrew from my bleeding feet. She hacked a couple of times. And then she got up, wobbled away from us, fell over, and died.

Seth said, "If Jesus had a dog hanging around him, those stigmata wouldn't even be mentioned. We wouldn't even have no religion if a dog like Pam were around at that time."

We stood there in my kitchen with a big dead dog. What could I do? I never got trained to deal with such a situation. I said, "Jesus."

"I ain't got no land to bury her. Do you mind putting her in your backyard? I ain't got no land to bury her, outside of the old football field back in Gig. Right on the fifty-yard line. That would be kind of funny. And fitting."

I said, "Let's just put her down here in my backyard. I would be honored to have Pam in my yard." What else could I say? I didn't mean it whatsoever, but Seth seemed to want to hear such.

I creaked around on my swollen and defective feet, sidestepping the dog. Pam's tongue stuck out funny and her open brown eyes clouded over minute by minute. I said, "Well. There's a shovel outside. We can find a couple sticks of wood for a cross, if you want. Hotdamn." I got the bottle of bourbon and brought it back to the table.

"You're walking better," Seth said. "The least you could do is give me twenty more dollars for your feet."

I looked at him as if he were insane. What did he mean? This big dead dog lay or lied or laid out in my kitchen. "I'm sorry, buddy. I'm sorry that you lost your job as a high school coach. But this ain't my problem. I have enough problems right now."

Seth knelt down to his dog and pet it. He said, "Pam, Pam, Pam," and I have to say that I almost cried right there and then.

I said, "This is weird, man."

"I don't even know you," he said, crying. "I don't even know who you are, Curt. And here I am crying in front of you." His hair flowed around like an old sea anemone. "That's my dog," he said, pointing.

Pam almost looked like she only slept. The dog didn't move, of course.

"Come on," I said. In my mind I thought about how I could index such a scene—Seth crying, Seth weeping, Seth in disbelief—all in alphabetical order.

"What do I do now? What do I do now?" Seth said.

I circled the dog a couple of times, and then approached Seth. "I'm not so sure I can lift her up what with my feet all mangled."

Seth said, "Do you have any *good* liquor? I don't like this stuff. You got any smooth liquor?"

I heard "Licker" more than anything else. I didn't say it, though. That's what kind of got me in trouble with Marissa—saying what came into my mind at inopportune moments. Somebody should write a book about it—I could do the index. I said, "This is all I got," and pointed toward my bottle of what, by the way, I considered great bourbon.

Seth pointed at my legs, halfway down. He said, "Well, come on."

We grabbed Pam. I took the shoulders and Seth took her haunches. He walked backward out of the house, and down the steps, and into the backyard. We set her down at the foot of a wild fig. I said, "Figs are supposed to be recuperative," just like that. Recuperative! I hadn't used the word in my entire life, even in indexing.

"Well," Seth said. He looked over at an old shed on the back of the property, an eight-by-sixteen tongue-and-groove structure I'd not even figured out what to do with. Up to this point I only kept a shovel and a rake inside. "Hey, there's another house there."

I said, "If I ever get a riding lawn mower that'll be its resting place."

Seth said, "I ain't got a place to live."

I walked over and got the shovel from inside. When I opened the swinging door, though, I envisioned Seth inside, sitting there atop an empty and upside-down drywall bucket. I foresaw myself going to pick him up at night, walking with him to Roughhouse Billiards. We'd get inside and wait out the trick shot players, then spend hours trying not to knock the eight ball in at wrong moments. Whenever I bent over hurting he'd say, "We need Pam about right now."

I said, "Here's the shovel."

He didn't scoop into the earth daintily. I tried not to think of what a healing dog couldn't do with the rest of us treading ground in an uncertain manner.

Seth said, "Good dog. Good dog. I'm sorry. Good dog."

On his way off my property—and I don't know how to convince anyone that I knew how he'd never come back—he let out a low howl. He turned his head to the rising sun and let one loose, not unlike what a bloodhound emits when a fire engine's siren's far, far away. I hobbled my way back inside. Later that day I turned on one of those business channels and stared at what happened with the major indexes, elsewhere.

Scotch and Dr Pepper

WHEN I FOUND MYSELF believing that the entire town of Gruel was after me for accidentally misrepresenting myself as some kind of historian and memoirist, I had no choice but to answer an ad in Tryon, North Carolina, that read, in part, "Choose your hours." The rest of the job description seemed similarly vague: creative person needed, salary negotiable, ex-convicts welcome to apply, and so on. I'd chosen Tryon because I remembered from my old days as a speechwriter for the lieutenant governor that the average age here stood at something like eighty. Who would look for a runaway masquerader amid retirees? I figured. If my former acquaintances in Gruel wanted to find me, they'd probably send out envoys to Las Vegas, Atlantic City, Gulfport, or any of those Native American casino towns where ex-speechwriters and faux memoirists hole up.

I won't go into detail about my escape from Gruel here, but let me say that I left town with only the clothes I wore and a sock filled with cash money stuffed into my underwear. That last detail might explain why it wasn't hard to hitch a ride up

Highway 25 the 120 miles between Gruel and Tryon from a woman named Cynthia in an old Chevy LUV pickup truck, even though she only planned on going as far as Greenville. She looked as though she'd spent about six years doing aerobics daily, and wore a modified blond pageboy haircut not normally found on southern women.

I was a gentleman the entire way, and when she dropped me off in front of Preston's Bar, she seemed to let me know how much she didn't appreciate my self-control and valor. I showed her where this copperhead had snagged me twice earlier in the day, but she seemed unimpressed. Cynthia peeled down the main drag before I could offer her gas money, before I even had two feet on the macadam.

I went in the bar, ordered a bourbon, went to the men's room, and pulled the sock out of my drawers. I placed ten thousand dollars in each shoe and four grand in my wallet. I put the sock back in its place.

"Did you say bourbon and Coke, or scotch and Dr Pepper?" the woman behind the bar asked me when I returned. "That's a bad scrape on your elbow."

I said, of course, "Scotch and Dr Pepper? Who drinks that?"

"We host a slew of retirees," she said. "People drink such stuff." She made my bourbon and Coke, though I noticed how the dispenser had Pepsi.

I looked at my elbow and slid my sleeve back down. I knew, also, that I had similar abrasions on both knees and shoulder blades.

Maybe when I jumped out of the step van as my ex-wife drove me to Graywood Emergency Regional Memorial Hospital I should've tried to run instead of opting for the roll-in-the-field approach. "You should see my foot. I got bitten by a copperhead twice earlier today. Or yesterday. I couldn't get any antivenin."

"You mean antivenom?" She set my drink in front of me. She said, "My name's Cynthia, in case you need me again," and then she walked over to the end of the bar where two men wearing plaid sat, drinking, I supposed, scotch and Dr Pepper. I thought, of course, *Cynthia?* Well this isn't going to be good if I ever tried to really write an autobiography—two Cynthias in the same day.

The *Tryon Bulletin*—a little tabloid-sized daily news-paper—set in front of me and I read all about the upcoming steeplechase; the upcoming barbecue festival; the upcoming blood drive; the upcoming Meals-on-Wheels benefit; and a human interest item about Junior Miss Tryon, a sixteen-year-old girl whose parents died the previous year at ages eighty-four and fifty in a tragic automobile accident. It was the father's second marriage, after he retired as the vice president of Exxon, the article read, for some reason. The wife had origi-nally hailed from Atlanta, and graduated cum laude from Agnes Scott College. The Junior Miss's talent involved turkey calling and clog dancing.

I said, "Hey, Cynthia, is there a hotel or motel nearby?"

She said something to one of the retirees about me, I could tell, then turned to say, "They's a bunch of bed-and-breakfasts. They's a Days Inn between here and Columbus, off I-26." She turned back to the retirees, listened to what one of them said, then said back to me, "They's a bunch of little rock cabins over that way you can rent by the night, week, or month." She pointed south.

One of the retirees said, "Or hour."

I said, "Thanks," and turned to the last pages of the news-paper, where I saw the classified ad for a creative, ex-convict, negotiable person. I reached in my pocket and pulled out a pen.

"As long as I shoot less than my IQ, I'm happy," one of the men at the bar said. "My IQ's 128."

"Are we talking nine or eighteen holes?" the other guy asked.

Cynthia came back to me and said, "Another scotch and Dr Pepper?"

I said, "Oh, okay, what the hell." She made it. The two retirees, for some reason, got up from their seats and came down my way. One guy had a pince-nez! The other one's splotched bald head looked a lot like those islands coming off of Alaska. I said, "Hey, fellows," to them, for I was trained to be polite to the elderly.

"I noticed you circled one of the classifieds," the guy with the pince-nez said. "I got an ad in there for a claw-foot tub. That's not what you want, is it?"

I said, "No. No, not a claw-foot tub. I'd *like* to have a claw-foot tub, but right now I have to worry about a place to live and a job worth working." I looked back down to the want ads and searched for his claw-foot tub, just to see what he asked for it. Remember, I had twenty-four grand packed around my body in places.

Pince-nez and Melanoma got back up and went to their original seats. Cynthia handed me some kind of booze drink. On the television there was an infomercial about weight loss through eating nothing but fatback. Over behind the pool tables a mechanical-voiced video game yelled out, "Are you ready? Are you ready? Are you ready?"

I took one of those stone cabins—a quaint place right outside of Tryon—for a month. This only cost me six hundred bucks.

I got a mini-refrigerator, a hot plate, and a mirror above the dresser, which I thought was a deal. The woman in charge didn't ask for me to show my driver's license. I never had to say, "My name's Novel Akers," is what I'm saying. I said, "Victor Dees," because I thought Victor, owner of Victor Dees's Army-Navy Surplus store back in Gruel, would be the most likely to hunt me down.

But that's another story. That's an entire novel that someone should write.

I didn't need to get out a calculator to figure out that I didn't have but two years to live off the money I had, minus what it would cost me for food and drink, minus clothes, minus shoes and the probable cigarettes I'd start smoking since it was North Carolina again. I could put twenty thousand in the bank and get .0109 percent interest, I thought, which meant about thirty dollars a month, more or less.

Two years wasn't enough for me to write what I needed to write about all the collusion and forgery and graft I'd seen in Gruel while I ran my ex-wife's weird inherited twelve-room motel and interacted with her childhood buddies who ran Roughhouse Billiards, the Gruel Bakery, and Gruel Normal School, among other places. Again, that's another story.

Anyway, I called the guy up with the opaque want ad and he met me at Tryon Stone Cabins—Day/Week/Month. Please suspend disbelief, as they say, at this point. I opened the door and the guy—which from now on will be called "The Guy" seeing as I never learned his name at my threshold, but figured out later through either deductive or inductive reasoning—said, "Oh, yeah. Seersucker's perfect for what I have in mind for you and me."

Looking back on it now, he kind of sounded like he made a pass at me, I guess. I had gone down to one of the three stores in town and bought up every pair of thirty-four waist, thirty-two length pants available, and luckily, some old widow must've cleaned out her dead husband's closet the week before. That's one thing about a retirement community, you can find all the seersucker you want, and this old fellow must've worn nothing but. I'm talking regular light blue stripes, but also a pale gray and a brown. There were matching coats, too, and seersucker shirts. I came out of there with enough outfits to wear over two weeks without ever doing laundry or dry cleaning.

To The Guy I said, "Your ad sounded interesting to me."

He came in and said, "It's a small town. I own a business, and I have no competition. But business is slow. People are counting pennies and cutting back on more frivolous needs. So. I got a feeling about you. I don't want to know your name, and I don't want you to know mine. You'll probably see me from time to time in Preston's Bar or Sidestreet Pizza. Pretend we never met. Trust me on this one, buddy. I don't want to know about your past. I don't want to see a résumé."

The Guy couldn't take me if we got in a fight, even if I did wear seersucker. He stood about five-five and appeared to have spent years bending over. His carriage looked like cement blocks hung from his wrists. I said, "I don't want to be involved in anything illegal. This job doesn't entail transporting an attaché case from one place to another, does it?"

"Not unless you carry your wine in a briefcase, man." He laughed. "Listen. I'll know when you're doing your job. And I'll pay you ten percent of my net. I'm figuring you can make upwards of a hundred dollars a day, working as little as two hours."

He opened my screen door and backed out. I said, "That sounds like a deal. What is it, again, that I'll be doing?" I looked out the door and noticed his car, a late model Land Rover.

"You go into any business or restaurant in the Tryon area. You can go as far south as Campobello and Gowensville, and as far northeast as Lake Lure. Make sure there's a carpet. Get yourself invited to parties. Order wine, and spill it on the carpet. When you spill the glass, make sure the stain comes out looking like the letter . . ." The Guy paused. "What's your favorite letter?"

I said, "X, I guess."

"X might be hard. Do a G. Then I'll know it was you. I'll come by at the end of the week and hand you cash money in an envelope. Enough said."

I didn't have time to think about, then say, "What about my expenses? Wine's going to cost some money, per glass." I said, "Okay. It looks like we're partners, in an odd way."

We didn't shake hands.

It didn't take an interior decorator to understand how my new boss ran the only carpet cleaning outfit in the county. I got out the slight telephone directory, looked at the Yellow Pages, and noticed under "Steam Cleaning—Carpet" only one entry, namely "Kirkland's Carpet Care, Ronald Kirkland, Proprietor."

I was glad that he didn't get all cutesy and call his business Kirkland's Karpet Kare, what with the three Ks in a row. He must've not hailed from Alabama originally.

I'm not proud to say that I took to my job like ants to sugar water. Oh I ordered the house wine at Sidestreet Pizza, the Brick Oven, El Jalisco, the Vineyard, Lake Lanier Tea Room, and Dewel's Seafood. I showed up at the Tryon Arts Center when they had gallery openings, and sloshed my red wine right down in front of overpriced watercolors depicting mountain vistas. I soaked the town. I invested money in an old-timey fountain pen and leaked out my Gs in nursing homes, the lobby of the Days Inn, Town Hall, Jack's Lingerie and Orchid Nursery, the balcony of the Tryon Movie House, A. L. Watson's Everything Country Kitchen, and so on.

I slept until eleven in the morning, got up, and stared at blank sheets of paper for hours on end, still intending to write my autobiography—the highs and lows of being a lieutenant governor's speechwriter, the highs and lows of running an unsuccessful writers retreat in Gruel, the lows of learning that my wife liked women more than she liked me. Hell, I couldn't even come up with a title worth picking up out of curiosity at a local independent bookstore, much less get placed on that Discover New Writers display at Barnes & Noble.

My salary showed up every Friday afternoon around six o'clock. Ronald Kirkland never knocked, never honked his horn. He placed the Manila envelope between my screen and front door, and drove away, probably on his way to work at places that closed early—like the pathetic tanning salon—and then restaurants where he cleaned carpets in the middle of the night.

I made some money, that's all I have to say. In that first month I earned more than three grand, tax free. I finally went into Sidestreet Pizza and said to the manager, "What does it cost you to get the carpet cleaned here?"

"Quarter a square foot. Plus extra for deep stains."

I looked around the restaurant and figured that he had about four thousand square feet. I said, "Good goddamn, man. Twenty-five cents a foot. How often do you get it steam-cleaned?"

"Used to be only once every couple months. Lately, though. Man. It seems like that Kirkland fellow's over here every other day. I ain't been having to get the entire place cleaned, but that son of a bitch charges per stain, and it adds up after a while. I guess that's the price you got to pay for having an older clientele. Parkinson's, you know. The palsy. They spill a lot."

Let me say right now that I didn't feel good about myself. Not that I've ever been a capitalist, but I could tell that this fellow just tried to do the best he could with what he got. I said, "Have you ever thought about putting down hardwood floors? Maybe it's time to rip out this carpet and put down some good tongue and groove."

I don't want to come across as a genius or anything, but already my mind raced ahead and I foresaw my starting up a business, then hiring out some runaway outlaw to wear golf spikes in restaurants so as to scratch and scuff and mar the premises in a way that would cause me to get hired out more so in order to trowel in a special mixture of fine sawdust and glue.

"I've thought about it more than once, but it costs so much. You mean like Pergo?"

"I mean like southern yellow pine that comes in eight-inch widths." I said, "I'd give you my card, but I left them at the office."

This special, untaught motif is called the "blowing notes in an empty bottle until a recognizable tune emanates" approach to bullshitting. I learned it early on, at about the age of twenty-eight, when I got the lieutenant governor to convince eastern North Carolina constituents that farm taxes would drop once someone developed the four-teated sow.

"I never thought about a wood floor, for some reason. When I bought this place back in the sixties, we had shag carpet throughout. You know how hard it was to get a good thick marinara sauce out of shag?"

I said, "The only thing I can think would be better to clean up than a hardwood floor would be a glass floor. But that might confuse your customers. They might think they were on some kind of boat ride down in the Okefenokee Swamp, you know, or one of those clear springs in Florida."

That seemed to stump him. I shouldn't have asked a restaurant manager to visualize.

Of course, in addition to not wanting my name advertised and my whereabouts known, I was too lazy and unskilled to really open up a flooring business. I didn't want to blow all my savings on real business cards, or on offering unskilled laborers insurance. No, wait—I didn't want to hire out unskilled laborers and *not* be able to offer them insurance, as most businesses in both Carolinas got away with, what with the lack of unions. And I couldn't afford it, anyway.

So I spilled my Gs less and less, and talked to a man named Hut Baxter who worked as a semiretired handyman of sorts, but mostly spent his afternoons drinking champagne cocktails down at Preston's Bar. Hut made his money down in Texas back in the 1970s as a master carpenter during one of the oil booms and after being a star high school quarterback in Midlands but blowing out both knees the summer before entering either the University of Oklahoma, Texas, Nebraska, or A&M—depending on how much he'd drank and with whom he spoke.

I said, "Hut. I know you're getting up there in age and whatnot, but I think I have a deal you might be interested in."

He said, probably because he was from Texas, "Old hell."

"Yeah, okay. Anyway—and I know you'll respect me enough not to ask how I know what I know—I think I can talk about every business owner in Tryon to rip out his or her carpet and replace it with either high-priced Pergo or regular tongue and groove. I'm only asking that I get 10 percent of the net. You can charge an ungodly sum of money to make up for the 10 percent. Don't ask me how I know these people will go for it."

Hut held his champagne cocktail to his lips and spoke in a whisper. "I won't do parquet. You have to promise me that there'll be no parquet involved. I got a thing about parquet. And as you asked me not to ask you about everything, I ask you not to ask me about everything."

I couldn't quite follow him—and I'd met other Texans who spoke in non sequiturs back when I was a speechwriter but kept eye contact that made them look like they almost knew what they talked about—but stuck out my hand to shake as if we had a deal.

We did.

I said, "This is a little bit like spraying Raid and hoping the bugs travel off course and fly into it by accident, but I think it'll work. I can meet you here and tell you what's up."

Hut nodded slowly. He took a sip from his flute. "My goddamn mutual fund ain't what it used to be," he said. "Salmon going *down*river these days. Sunflowers turning backwards at dawn. Prairie tornadoes don't know which way to turn. My last wife got it in her mind that little kids in South America were worth more than our own. She might've been right."

I held up my finger to Pam and said, "One Jim Beam and Coke. One champagne cocktail, whatever that might be."

I thought, I have made yet another big mistake in my life.

Hut said, "Cynthia," and looked off into the distance.

I've never been one for believing in signs, but something about his wife being named Cynthia didn't set well with me. I held up my glass, though, and said something about bigger and better things. Or at least something about things.

Hut clinked my glass and said, "I can't afford another wife, I'll tell you that much. There toward the end of the marriage she only wanted to go by Cyn. Like *Sin*, you know."

I said I knew. But I didn't go into detail how my ex-wife, Rebekah, went from that, to Bekah, to plain old Kah, like a crow.

Now I could've moved out of my one-room stone cabin rental. I could've more than likely called in the retirement money I had never touched, and bought a house in one of the developments: Horse Trail Acres, Steeplechase Acres, the Links of Tryon, Tryon Falls, Tryon this and Tryon that. There weren't apartments per se nearby, outside of assisted living sprawls. But I liked the anonymity, and kind of relished my life as one in need of hiding out. A qualified psychologist might call it "delusional" or "paranoid." I didn't care.

So months went by, and I bought my groceries over at the IGA and cooked what I needed on a hot plate. I left my windows open in the summer and listened to frogs in a nearby mountain pond. Occasionally I chatted it up with the owner of Tryon Stone Cabins—Day/Week/Month, a woman named Dora Sizemore who said to me one morning, out of nowhere, "We've had some desperadoes stay here in the past. We believe that Eric Rudolph stayed here for two nights right after they charged him with those abortion clinic bombings. I didn't pay attention at the time, and he signed in as Steve, but without a last name. He said he was like Cher, or those other one-named stars. He even pulled out an ID card that only read 'Steve.' I wished I'd've known then what I know now. Because I *know*, now."

Dora might've been sixty, or forty. I stood there to pay my upcoming month. I said, "You might could've gotten a reward."

"Before I owned this place they say that F. Scott Fitzgerald stayed here. He was either supposed to be up in Asheville or someplace with his wife, but he'd gotten drunk and couldn't make it that far. That's what they say. You might not know who I'm talking about."

I thought, Rub it in. Make fun of me. How did you know I've been meaning to write down my life story? I said, "His name rings a tiny handbell."

"Some of Nixon's people stayed here in the early seventies when they said they were up at that camp, but really they met here in order to get some privacy and plan some things out."

I didn't believe that one, but didn't respond to it. I said, "All right. Well, Dora, here's my money. I plan on staying at least another month."

"You know that it's customary to tip the chambermaid, don't you? I've been meaning to tell you that. The chambermaid's mentioned how you don't put out a dollar or three when she comes by."

I said, "Oh, man. I didn't even know. It's been a long time since I've seen one of those etiquette books."

"I'm the chambermaid, by the way," Dora said, winking.

I went back to my room, got out a clean sheet of paper, and wrote down,

After everything I'd done over forty-plus years, or had happen to me—the parents who made me sell shrimp on the side of the road up in the mountains; the parents who made me pan for gold; the high school drama teacher who made me practice my lines while speaking directly into her uncovered breasts; the lieutenant governors who didn't know when I toyed with them when they gave speeches to Optimist clubs, 4-H clubs, the DAR, the DWBS, the Tobacco Farmers of the South, or Re-

publicans for No Environmental Laws; the wife I married who
came from a long line of forgers; the job I held at the Nor-
mal School as a fake historian-in-residence; the snakes I handled
in a teaching capacity and the copperhead that finally bit my
ankle twice—I believed that my latter years in Gruel would
prove to be either the apex or nadir of my time on this planet,
with nothing in between. And then I moved into a 256-square-
foot room and pitted the carpet believers against the hardwood
floor zealots.

It might've taken me two hours to get all that down on
paper. I read it and reread it, and said aloud to myself, "That
first sentence probably needs more appeal."

Yes, I talked to myself. And it just so happened that Dora
Sizemore showed up to change my sheets and refill my toilet
paper dispenser. She knocked and said, "We had a man stay
here one time killed four, five men and stuffed them beneath
his floorboards. His sentence got an appeal, and the next thing
you know he's wanting to move back here for good."

I jumped. I grabbed a towel and put it around my waist—
somewhere along the line I'd read where one had to be completely naked when writing one's history. I don't think it was
F. Scott Fitzgerald, though.

Within a month I went out and spilled more wine, ink, or
found ways to traipse red clay into an establishment and grind
it into the carpet. Meanwhile I found ways to set up impromptu
meetings with owners and managers alike, never admitted that
I was the cause of their carpet-cleaning worries, and talked up
the wonderful benefits of hardwood floors. More than one person said to me, "You get a population of elderly people, though,

they come in here on a rainy or snowy day, track water in, and the next group of people falls down and breaks their hips."

Would this endless circle ever cease? I thought. I thought, *Now* I need to find someone who installs sandpaper-covered duct tape.

Needless to say Mr. Kirkland's business dwindled. I gave out Hut Baxter's phone number to those merchants who seemed most interested, and maybe a month into this entire double-agent fiasco, Hut met me in Preston's Bar and said, "You got to ease up a little, son. I'm an old man and they ain't but so many day laborers around here." He handed me a Manila envelope similar to the same ones that Ronald Kirkland left at my door. Ten percent of a half-million dollars ain't chump change, I thought.

But that didn't matter: Let me say right now that Hut didn't quite use the word "day laborers." He didn't use "migrant workers" or "unemployed citizens crushed by the myopic and ill-conceived economic policies of the current Republican administration," either. He kind of sat there with his champagne cocktail—who drinks booze with a sugar cube, anyway?—and spouted out some politically incorrect racial slurs that I never even heard in a place as seemingly backward as Gruel. I'll admit that Gruel hadn't gotten to the point of attracting any Mexican or Central American workers, seeing as there was no industry or farming left—and perhaps I never heard a negative word about African Americans because most of Gruel thrived on a preslavery mind-set—but for the first time since I'd run away from my previous troubles I felt nostalgic to return.

And I thought, also, Jesus Christ, now I have to find a way for Hut Baxter to go under, just like I'm trying to do to the inadequate and conniving Ronald Kirkland. What could a small man, in a tiny town, inside a picayune stone cabin do? I said, "Well. I'll try to slow down, Hut. I thought I was doing you a favor."

He turned to me there at the bar and said, "Well, you're not, goddamn it. If anything you're giving me more headaches."

Right before I punched him in the nose—and I'm not proud to say that I hit a guy who was more than twenty years my senior—I said, "You know that champagne cocktails are the preferred drinks of gay men, don't you? Did you know that in San Francisco, the champagne cocktail is the official city drink?"

In my defense, Hut clenched his fist and made for me first. And no one in the bar—the men dressed in plaid, the bar-tendress attired in a low-cut blouse and miniskirt—came to Hut's aid when he hit the linoleum floor.

I got an envelope with no money, even though I deserved some. No, I got an envelope with a note that read, "I'm in the car."

I opened my door, and it fell from behind the screen. I looked up and saw Mr. Ronald Kirkland sitting there in his Land Rover, wearing the kind of cheap wraparound blue-tinted sunglasses that I'd admired at the IGA. What else could I do but approach him with a framing hammer hidden behind my back? It's kind of like how I walked around most of Tryon and Gruel, and before that both Charlotte and Chapel Hill. I said, "Hey, Mr. Kirkland," as if I were a paperboy waiting for payment. I said, "What's up?"

He said, "How'd you know my name?" Remember that I was supposed to be doing all of this on the down-and-down. We'd made some kind of pact, remember, even though I never shook hands over it.

I said, "Goddamn, man, it's a small town. I heard your name when you bought some lingerie over at Tryon Panties. I walked by the front door and heard the saleslady say your name." I looked at him square in the face. That's one thing I learned to do while being a speechwriter, back in the day.

"I have a feeling that you're double-crossing me. First off, I'm not getting any of the same carpet cleaning accounts receivable." Who talked like that? Who said, *I'm not getting any of the same accounts receivable*? "Second, people are talking about some new guy talking them into ditching my carpet cleaning opportunities and going to wood. That wouldn't be you, would it? Would it?"

I said, "I'm just a small man in a small town, man. I don't know what you're talking 'bout," even though I knew. I kind of thought about the movie *Deliverance*, but not the novel. I don't know why. I said, "There's no way you'd know what I've gone through over the last couple years. The last couple decades." I figured that would get me by, saying that.

It didn't. Mr. Kirkland pulled out a pistol and pointed it at my forehead.

I packed up. Give me a break: What else could I do? I had an entire town ready to find and persecute me seeing as I'd faked being a historian and memoirist—which is another story— and another town that would end up walking on dirt floors. I left. I skedaddled. That's the way things go.

Who do you think picked me up on Highway 108 between Tryon and Rutherfordton, on my way to West Virginia? The same Cynthia who brought me in, of course. She said, "I've driven through here a few times thinking I'd see you. Wha'chew been up to? I take it you didn't die of the snakebite."

I looked behind me. I said, "Nothing in this town. What a dead town!"

She said, "Before I go wherever we're headed, would you

mind if we stopped in this bar up here? I got a hankering for a Scotch and Dr Pepper." She pointed at Preston's.

Now, I knew that it wasn't a good idea, but because I had become used to inviting uncomfortable situations into my life I nodded. I said, "I don't mean to get personal, Cynthia, but how old are you, anyway?"

She performed half a U-turn in the Chevy LUV, and parked in a space. She said, "You never did tell me your name back when I brought you here. Is it, by any chance, Novel Akers?"

I didn't know how to suavely change the subject. I said, "You don't appear to be much more than thirty."

Cynthia didn't get out of the cab. If this scene were in a movie we wouldn't have been in a Chevy LUV pickup. We would've been in a car with automatic locks, so that Cynthia could keep me inside until I confessed. I said, "That's me."

She laughed and laughed and opened her door. She said, "I bet you're on the run, aren't you. I bet you think you have people looking for you all over South Carolina." Then she started laughing again, whipping her head around, slapping her knee out on the street.

I got out and said, "What?"

She said, "I'm thirty-three. And I know your ex-wife. Hell, I know everyone you used to know back in Gruel."

I trotted across the two-lane main drag to catch up with her. I opened the door to Preston's, and immediately saw Hut Baxter seated at the bar, his head wrapped in gauze. He held his hands up and said, I think, "You'll be hearing from my lawyer." I couldn't tell. His lips bloated out like a Hollywood starlet gone obsessive.

I said to him, "I'm sorry. I should've learned a long time ago not to lose my temper on a racist. I'm sorry."

I pointed to Cynthia the bartendress to get him another

drink on my tab. Cynthia my savior ordered her own Scotch and Dr Pepper. She said to me, "You've got it all wrong. I didn't move to Gruel until 2000 after entering their art car festival. Everyone there still talks about you, though, Novel. You're legendary. Down at Roughhouse Billiards they say your ideas helped revitalize the town. Believe it or not they're talking about holding a Novel Day down there, right after that yearly thing for Colonel Dill."

"Dill Days." I said to the other Cynthia, "I'll have whatever they're having."

I think Hut mumbled, "I wish you'd've tried all this twenty years ago. Ten years ago. I'd've beat your ass." He said, "Thanks for the drink."

My Cynthia said, "Yeah. Dill Days."

We didn't drive toward West Virginia three hours later. No, she backed out of the parking space, and we passed Tryon Stone Cabins—Day/Week/Month, and kept going south, back to Gruel where I could walk on the square the returning hero. Cynthia promised that she wasn't a detective or private eye. She promised that she wasn't some kind of bounty hunter. She must've said it twenty times between Tryon and Spartanburg—a thirty-minute drive. I'd long before learned that anyone who insisted on her benevolence probably didn't deserve such. Then, finally, I opened the door and jumped out, leaving my suitcase in the bed of the truck. I rolled and rolled in a fallow field. In the end I had only traveled some eighty miles from one place I needed to leave, forty from the other.

Shirts Against Skins

LET'S PRETEND THAT I felt positive about building a wood-fire kiln out back of our two-story house, that I took care when stacking soft brick on the inside and hard kiln brick outwardly. Let's pretend that I didn't mind taking a chain saw to hew what oak and maple stood on my old family land, then splitting said logs into quarters. I tried my best to keep an appearance of wanting to continue my life in clay, but knew that I'd never create vessels similar to the ones I sold to museums' permanent collections across the country. My signature multi-nippled archetypal man would vanish, back in the town of my training, as soon as someone there got overcome with nostalgia.

I set up my old-fashioned kick wheel beneath one shed on the property, and an electric Brent—attached to a long, long extension cord coming out of the ex-mudroom—beneath another shed nearby. That first week in the house of my upbringing, I called up Highwater Clay in Asheville and got two tons of stoneware delivered at twenty-one cents a pound. Me, I stacked it all in a root cellar I'd been scared to enter as a child. The six or eight little kids still being brought up in Gruel ran to our driveway, screaming as to how they'd never seen a real truck in town.

I didn't say, "I hope you're happy," to Charlotte. I didn't have time. Hell, I didn't even see her much! She took one of those home repair books into the attic, got on the cell phone, and ordered two-by-twelves for beams, two-by-fours for studs, more Sheetrock, shingles, and double-paned windows. Somehow Charlotte found contractors, who hired subcontractors, who paid off day laborers to fix up what no longer seemed standard living.

I didn't pay attention. I foresaw what would, inevitably, happen.

"I've talked to Dr. Bobba Lollis at Gruel Drug, and Jeff, the owner of Roughhouse Billiards. Let me say that they've been positive about my ideas," Charlotte told me about a month into living back in my hometown. At this time I'd not ventured out onto the square. Me, I couldn't figure out how to direct our satellite dish toward a regular channel, outside of a scary Japanese station and what seemed to be twenty-four-hour Mexican soap operas.

I said, "I don't know how to say this, Charlotte. I'm sure you've gone into great detail as to what you're about to do, and I apologize. I'll be the first to admit that I'm a little on the self-absorbed side. I've been that way for as long as I can remember." Oh, I went on and on, but to tell the truth I only wanted to stall what I knew my wife would bring up. "What, again, is your moneymaking idea?"

"Did you have, like, four nipples at some point in your life?" Charlotte asked me. "I saw a picture of you, and some hairy guy, and these fellows with freckles all over their legs and chest. Y'all were on some kind of church basketball team that hadn't lost a game in the entire season."

I said, "Those were moles. On those two boys, not me. On me, there must've been some kind of smudge or blot of ink on my chest." But I didn't make eye contact, and I felt my face redden. Charlotte knew when I lied. We stood in the backyard, between house and my work spaces. Two full fig trees looked as though they needed to drop fruit soon or bow to the ground. In a weird way they appeared to have massive brownish nipples poking out.

Charlotte said, "I couldn't tell. The newspaper had turned kind of yellow. But on you?"

I said, "I told you it wouldn't be good if we came back here. I told you that you wouldn't want to know my background better."

Most good wives, I would think, would say something like, "Ohhhh, you poor thing. I bet you got teased to no end," and then kiss their husbands on the cheek, et cetera. My wife said, "Those were really *nipples*? Goddamn, it looked like you could've nursed a litter of kittens. Those things were in perfect alignment down your chest. Let me see the scars. I've never even noticed the scars."

I walked to the front window when I heard a dump truck back into the driveway. When the driver unloaded what ended up being a six-foot-high mound of gravel, I said, "Uh-oh," thinking maybe the guy meant to go to one of our neighbors.

Charlotte jumped up and down somewhat and said, "All right! I can get to work now!"

At least it took her mind off my past. I went in the bathroom, closed the door, and searched for two scars that, up to this point, I thought had disappeared years earlier.

Our point guard sported matching port-wine birthmarks, chest and back, that looked like either the continents of Africa or South America. For some reason God decided to sear that stain right through little Cleve Haulbrook's torso, and although I never said anything in the locker room, I wondered if an X-ray might point out that all of his organs got purpled in the process, too. Ray Sanders, our six-foot center, underwent an odd puberty that caused the worst case of acne I'd ever seen from sternum to navel, and a mat of wild hair on his back that stood straight out three inches when he got excited. Our forwards—the Dickey brothers—had more precancerous moles than someone brought up inside the Savannah River Nuclear Station. Whereas Cleve Haulbrook had the two continents, these two boys had entire star-filled galaxies spread around their bodies. Even our benchwarmers had their visible flaws: warts, rashes, oozing sores, and misstitched scars. We had an albino named Half-blind Kenny squinting at the lights.

Me, I played shooting guard with four nipples.

These were tough times for junior church league basketball teams, what with the oil shortage, gas prices skyrocketing, and people asked not to drive and/or fill up their cars on certain days of the week. From what I understand, a lot of people quit going to church regularly and used the "Oh, I forgot what day I could drive" excuse. Preachers complained every Sunday and Wednesday about not enough money coming in on the passed plates, and talk was that congregations would have to undergo sermons in the dark to save energy and electric bills, or not meet altogether.

"We can't even afford to print up new jerseys for our basketball team," preachers said on miserably hot Wednesday nights in August.

No one, trying his or her best not to slip off the pew in a pool of sweat, groaned all empathetic.

At least that's how I imagined it. The year before, the

team had gone 0 and 72 between September and January—there were a lot of churches in Forty-Five County, and even the church league commissioner had gone so far as dividing it up into North, South, East, West, Northeast, Northwest, Southeast, and Southwest regions before the top two teams in each division played a round-robin tournament held at the First Baptist Church gymnasium.

The year before—and I'd not played for two reasons: I'd not been asked, and my father made me drive around with him after school on his job teaching people how to plant Christmas trees for the Clemson University Agricultural Extension Service—our team lost to four Pentecostal teams who spent their halftime handling snakes, and twice to Jehovah's Witnesses who left in midgame to hand out pamphlets. For some reason the referees never found a reason to call a foul on the other team, and the coach actually heard one of the men say, "Aren't y'all of the belief that you've been persecuted over the years anyway?"

Let me say right now that I didn't play for a synagogue. No temple existed in all of Forty-Five County. I played basketball for Saint Francis Catholic—even though I wasn't Catholic, or even Christian, or allowed to attend church services by my father the agnostic—because of my buddy Cleve-of-the-birthmark, who said, "Hey, Phil, we need a shooting guard. We need someone who can at least make a shot from the free throw stripe."

I didn't know that old Francis was the patron saint of animals—like dogs and beasts of burden—at the time. No, I showed off my eighteen-inch vertical leap there in my front yard and shot an imaginary jumper. I said, "When's practice?"

Cleve said, "We don't really have practice. There's a game about every night, so we don't have time."

I said, "I might have to talk to my father. If there's a game every night, how can you do homework?"

"Father Nick says God will take care of that for us."

Again, let me point out that I wasn't Catholic or Christian. I said, "I thought your daddy's name was Leroy."

I don't want to get into any of that priests-as-pedophiles argument, but it was Father Nick who approached the church league commissioner and suggested that, to save money, maybe the teams could play Shirts against Skins. He said that one team could wear plain T-shirts of any color, and the other team would go topless. Father Nick said that Saint Francis would be more than happy, in the name of good sportsmanship, to always be Skins. I can only assume now that the commissioner went around the league, that he talked to Baptists, Methodists, Presbyterians, and the like, and offered up Father Nick's suggestion. And I can only assume that the more conservative, right-thinking, modest denominations said, "Okay, good thinking, this'll save us thirty dollars."

I don't like to think about how Father Nick already perceived what would happen—how he knew ahead of time about the two continents, all the galaxies, the rashes, warts, oozing sores, and so on. I don't know what they teach in good Jesuit schools, but I have to figure that Logic 101 must've been a requirement, and that Father Nick foresaw what an opposing team would do, or not do, when a near blind albino drove the lane for an easy layup.

I don't want to re-create the entire season on up to the play-offs against Forty-Five First Baptist, Forty-Five First Methodist, Forty-Five First Presbyterian, Forty-Five First A.M.E., Forty-Five First Lutheran, Gruel Interdenominational, and Ninety-Six Quaker, but let me make it clear that we didn't lose a game. No one would guard any of us. I could drive from the top of the key right on down for an easy two-pointer without anyone touching the four-nippled boy. Cleve could do the same. The Dickey brothers never took a bank shot beyond six feet without opposing players scattering, shielding their faces, afraid that a mole might jump off of them. If a member of the other team looked like he could handle Ray Sanders's acne, Ray swung around and ran backward with his hairy back in order to make the other guy dribble off his foot, or throw an errant pass into the stands. When we were up something like 38 to 6 midway through the second half Coach Father Nick would put in Kenny the Half-blind Albino, and even the refs wouldn't call double dribbling on the guy or out-of-bounds when he veered off the court accidentally.

We were Skins. All opposing teams' coaches agreed that good, modest Protestants would not feel comfortable taking their shirts off, so there we stood at midcourt each game, stripping, standing there embarrassed. I don't know about my teammates, but I could hear girls and adults alike screaming, gagging, going, "Ugghhh!" like that. And no opposing player came near us. It might've been the highlight for all of our lives.

But then came our downfall. One of the players for Ninety-Six Quaker had a fucking do-gooder dermatologist father. That family moved down from Pennsylvania, of course, because Daddy signed some kind of med school document saying he'd work in an impoverished area in order to forgo his student loans. Dr. Guilford scouted our team—that's the way with dermatologists, I suppose; they have time to do things at night without fear of being called in on an emergency boil—and saw where our strength emanated from no one being willing to get within five feet of us.

"I can freeze off your boy's extra nipples," the doctor said to my father in the stands. "It's painless. Those aren't really nipples—they're just abnormally large skin tags. Bring him over to the office tomorrow. It'll take about ten minutes, tops. And I won't even charge you a fee. I only want to see kids feel good about themselves, and feel good about the world. That's the way we Quakers are."

He said about the same thing to the Dickey brothers' father, evidently. And the doctor had a new pill for acne, plus an on-call electrolysis specialist for Ray Sanders. Of course he couldn't do anything for Cleve's port-wine birthmark, outside of Avon face powder, or for the half-blind albino. But I know this: I found myself in the waiting room of Dr. Larry Guilford, surrounded by most of my teammates, the day after our final regular season win. There was a week off for Christmas holidays, then the eight-team tournament began.

I would like to go on record as saying that Dr. Guilford wasn't so smart for a doctor. First off, freezing off my two extra nipples hurt like hell. Second, he could've saved himself some money by finding a way for us to wear shirts.

When I left the office, the doctor and his wife-receptionist told me to eat more oatmeal.

For two reasons my wife, Charlotte, made us move back to Gruel some twenty-five years after I'd emigrated elsewhere, gotten an education, and found a woman who enjoyed winemaking, day-trading, home improvement projects, and intercollegiate sports. That fucking pinhead in the White House talked enough of my state legislators into believing all that No Child Left Behind crap, and the next thing you know I either had to go back to college and take education courses such as How to Use an Over-

head Projector in order to gain "certification," or quit altogether. I chose the latter option, out of principle.

Listen—and I don't want to brag any—but I had gone off to the Kansas City Art Institute in 1977, received an MFA in ceramics from Alfred University, taught a little at the college level, and had a number of one-man shows in New York City, Santa Fe, Atlanta, and Chicago, plus about everywhere in between. I'd received grants, awards, and recognition. I could've worked at any university in America, pretty much, or chanced living solely off my sales. I don't know if a Higher Being came down and spoke to me in my sleep or what, but out of nowhere it became increasingly apparent that I needed to go out and help other kids learn the intricacies of clay, fire, and glaze. Because my signature works all displayed four-nippled male figures, I thought that it was my duty to go out in the hinterlands, find a school that contained students similar to those on the Saint Francis Catholic basketball team, and teach said students how to throw pots on a wheel. Not every multiply warted, acne-ridden, unwanted-haired, albinotic boy in South Carolina had the opportunity to happen upon a kindly Quaker dermatologist, I knew. A potter worked alone. He could have his physical flaws and still live the meaningful, prosperous, and happy life of a solid taxpaying citizen.

I don't want to sound the martyr or moralist, but I found out pretty quickly that I could've stood anywhere in the state, thrown a rock, and hit a high school populated with such male students. I got hired on in Darlington County, and traveled between four public high schools five days per week. My freakish students won more scholarships and awards over a three-year period than had been garnered in the history of the school district.

And then the governor sent a letter to my principals, saying that I wasn't qualified. The principals said I could apply to a number of state colleges and universities, undergo the required education courses, and be back teaching ceramics within two years. I don't remember my exact words, but "good" and "luck" might've been included in there somewhere between the cussing.

Charlotte said, "This might be a blessing. I can *not* work anywhere, you know." Did I mention that she used to be in advertising, and that when the economy showed signs of a bust most of her clients quit advertising? Charlotte said, "I've been hoping to find the best time to tell you this, Phil, but what we should do is move to your hometown and take over your father's house. No rent or mortgage. We can build a kiln in the backyard. And I have some advertising ideas that won't work anyplace else, or at least not in a place that has regular newspaper delivery."

When I originally left Gruel I promised myself never to return. When my father died in a tragic accident that involved a neighbor's favorite bull, a series of groundhog holes, a swarm of yellow jackets, and some unskilled emergency room attendants at Graywood Emergency Regional Memorial Hospital, I told myself that anything I inherited in Gruel could fall to the ground for all I cared.

I said to my wife, "What idea? What idea could work only in my near vacant hometown that wouldn't work in a town where people know that the Civil War ended?"

Charlotte said she only needed a computer, printer, Ziploc bags, and small irregular chunks of gravel. She said, "And I love you, Phil. Why would you not want me to even know you better? I never even met your dad. Why won't you let me in on your past, so that I can love the whole you?"

That sounded all nice and lovey-dovey, I knew. I didn't say anything to Charlotte about how, to love the entire me, she might have to visit a drain hole inside Dr. Guilford's office.

When we had no real afflictions it didn't matter that we went shirtless, of course. After Dr. Guilford got done with us, we showed up on court, our heads hung low, and to a team player it didn't matter what happened next. Before, the referees would come up and say something like, "Do y'all want to be Shirts or Skins?" and Coach Father Nick always shot his arm up and yelled out "We'll be Skins!" as if he worked on the floor of the New York Stock Exchange. Against the Ninety-Six Quakers, though, he only shrugged.

We got to be Skins again, but it didn't matter. No moles, boils, or nipples caused those peaceful basketball opponents of ours to recoil. Cleve wasn't even there with his matching birthmarks, for he readied himself homebound for some kind of skin graft operation.

At the tip-off I stood with my back to our goal, but I saw the Ninety-Six Quaker center offer his hand toward clear-skinned and electrolyzed Ray Sanders and knew it would be a long, bad game. The Quaker said, "Peace be with you," or something like that. He said something about good sportsmanship, and love for humanity, and may the better team win, and what goes around comes around, and whatever happens is God's will, and big buckles atop hats are cool no matter what anyone in Graywood County says, I swear.

The Quaker took the tip-off. It went to this little guy guard of theirs who flew down the sidelines, and veered toward the lane, then made an easy layup. One of the Dickey boys threw it in to me, but I was used to no one being within ten yards of my four nipples, and this other Quaker flew right in and stole it. He, too, got a layup. The other Dickey brother took the ball out of bounds, tossed it lazily toward my friend Slick Koon—who used to be covered in a few weird warts but no long held them—another six-foot center who had to take the place of Ray.

You might wonder why we didn't play Kenny the Albino. Well, with everyone else looking kind of okay, he dropped right off the team before the play-offs. He met us in the locker room and bandied his head around like a blind man, then announced that he didn't care to be made fun of, to be the only weirdo on what *used* to be a team of freaks. Kenny the Albino said, "If y'all win the church league championship trophy, I hope you let me touch it, but I understand if you don't, seeing I am what I am."

Let me say right now that I almost cried for poor Kenny the Albino.

But it didn't matter seeing as we all knew that we couldn't win anymore—more than likely not if we got picked Skins, and certainly if we got picked Shirts.

The Quakers ran all over us. I'm prone to think that those boys were so fucking nice that they wouldn't have been affected should we have still played them when we still owned all our weird and ugly defects.

I threw a ball up right before halftime from midcourt that somehow went in, and that gave us two points—this was a time before the three-point line. Then I tried a weird hook shot at the end of the game, but it went somewhere in the stands. We lost 82 to 2, no lie.

None of us wanted to shake hands with our opponents— who ended up losing 62 to 36 to Forty-Five First Baptist in the finals, thus proving that they weren't all that great from the beginning—but we did. We couldn't believe that anyone would want to touch us!

I hate to say that it kind of felt good. I have no sociological or psychological or homophobic studies to back up my losing team's slight newfound self-confidence in regards to appearance, but there's something to that theory that human touch heals. We shook hands, got patted on the shoulder and back, and left for the locker room probably feeling better about ourselves than we ever did after a still-physically blemished victory.

I hung up my invisible jersey after the one church league season and never played basketball again. Oh sure, Coach Father Nick tried to make all of us sport fake warts, moles, and nipples made out of Play-Doh the next year, but none of us agreed to his little scheme. Me, I studied hard, and got the hell out of Gruel.

My wife visited every business establishment in the county, signed them up for special ads, came home, designed and printed the ads on colored paper, shoved said advertisements and two pieces of gravel inside generic-brand Ziploc bags. Then she drove around and threw the bags onto people's driveways. The rocks kept her bag and advertisement from blowing away.

Get this: Businessmen and -women alike paid upwards of a hundred bucks for one week's—which meant one day's—worth of advertising. The army-navy guy ran a special on fleece-lined boots; Jeff Downer ran a buy-five-get-one-free hot dog special over at Roughhouse Billiards. Some guy who started up a housecleaning service offered free window washing with four steam-cleaned rooms of carpet. The man who ran Gruel BBQ and Pig-Petting Zoo advertised free All-U-Can-Eat pigs in a blanket for children under the age of twelve when accompanied by two parents ordering buffet. And so on. Dr. Bobba Lollis at Gruel Drug ran a 10 percent off coupon for Whitman's and Russell Stover Valentine's Day candy boxes, seeing as it was mid-June. Paula Purgason, amateur real estate agent, said she would throw in the first lawn mowing and gutter cleaning for any house sold. Maura-Lee Snipes offered a free crescent roll with every Jesus crust Jewish rye loaf sold out of Gruel Bakery.

"Four nipples," Charlotte said. "Goddamn. That explains why all your pots, bowls, vases, and wall hangings had that little guy on it with tits falling all over the place. Am I right or am I right? How come you never mentioned this before? I bet it's been bearing down on you subconsciously forever."

We drove down Old Old Augusta Road, past fallen-down houses, and fallow land that couldn't sell for a hundred bucks an acre. On the passenger-side floorboard set a good two hundred plastic bags, each filled with ads and gravel. I said, "Did you figure fuel costs into this little business venture? Man, it seems like it's hardly worth it to drive this far. You never had to deliver papers as a child, did you?"

My wife put our car into fourth gear and said, "The Gruel Inn's up here and we'll have to throw out thirteen bags, Phil. Get ready."

The twelve-room Gruel Inn now housed a dozen real-life imported gurus who waited for aimless, rich, bored, last-strawed, wit's-ended, born-into-wealth, trust-funded, restless women to show up from New York, Connecticut, and Massachusetts. The thirteenth woman was named Bekah Akers, a crazy woman who tried to transform the town of Gruel into some kind of New Age mecca. Word was she killed her husband Novel Akers, took on baker and lover Maura-Lee, and they went off twice a year to San Francisco.

We approached the place from Charlotte's side. Me, I had to lob hook shots over the car roof. The first one I threw barely made it into the parking lot. My wife said, "Give it some testosterone, Phil. You can do better than that."

Oh I had some flashbacks as to when I threw that last two-nippled hook shot against the Quakers at the end of my last game. I threw the next one better, but it landed on the roof. About this time a Chinese man wearing what looked no more than a fancy diaper came out of room 3 and yelled out, "Hey, we're trying to meditate in here, motherfucker!" like that.

Charlotte pulled off to the side and I got out. She said, "Phil. Goddamn it, Phil, get back in the car."

I don't know what happened but I approached the half-naked guru and screamed out, "You dumb fuck. I'm one of the top ceramic artists in America. I'll kill you, shithead."

Right before the guru slapped me upside the head with the back of his heel I noticed that he had two weird birthmarks right below his nipples. I'm talking I was just about to say, "Hey, I used to have four nipples," but then he went into some kind of kung fu stance, then waylaid me hard.

I wasn't sure if I dreamed it or not, but I'm pretty certain that Charlotte threw a bag of advertisements his way, trying to stop the occasion. And in between his wild side kicks to my temple and karate chops to my neck, I'm pretty sure that this half-naked man took the time to open up Charlotte's Ziploc, pull out the advertisements, and read out loud, "Hey, a free crescent roll with Jesus crust bread! I like that Jesus crust bread!"

We got into the locker room and Coach Father Nick pulled down his pants. He took down his white underwear. He said,

"Well boys, it could be worse. Y'all had the marks of Satan before this game, and now you don't. Think about what I've had to live with. People always wonder why priests become priests. Look at this thing. Look at it! In Luke it is said, 'And thou shalt have joy and gladness; and many shall rejoice at his birth.' But that's not true, always, is it? We shalt not have rejoice at our birth. And in Ecclesiastes it is said, 'For he shall not much remember the days of his life,' blah blah blah. Do y'all know what that means?"

I said, "Please don't tell us that we have to play baseball."

"Look at this!" Coach Father Nick said, wiggling his one-inch pecker. "Not only is it little, I got a mole on the end of it, which makes me pee sideways! At a urinal I have to stand facing anyone who's beside me, as if I'm about to pee on his leg."

Well of course it was more than I could handle. I came home, but didn't tell my parents what happened. My father said, "You had a good season." He said, "Not that I'm all that religious, but I think that it's in Ecclesiastes where they go, 'To everything there is a season, and a time to every purpose under heaven,' or whatever. Well that's what you had, Phil."

I said, "Can I go down by the creek and pull out some of that gray clay in order to make a bowl for art class?"

My mother said, "You can do anything you want, son."

I went behind our house a hundred yards and scooped out what I would later learn to be a good Edgefield clay used by Dave the Slave to fashion his stoneware back in 1850.

Back in the basement I made what my art teacher Mrs. Cathcart would call a pinch pot, though I didn't know it at the time. Later on she taught me how to coil clay, and even later she tried to make me paint replicas of religious paintings first done by Girolamo Savoldo, but that's another story.

I finished my pinch pot and squeezed it on two sides,

turned it a quarter way, and did the same. It looked like it had four flattened nipples. When I took it into class Mrs. Cathcart said, "You should glaze a figure around those little outcroppings you got there on each side."

I said, "Yes, ma'am," not knowing how I'd use this advice for my entire career. I said, "Yes, ma'am."

She said, "What are those things?"

I said—this was tenth or eleventh grade—"I call this bowl 'Portrait of Dr. Naismith, Inventor of Basketball.'" I'd been reading American history. Hell, it looked like one of those peach baskets he set up.

Mrs. Cathcart said, "You're a different kind of student, aren't you, Phillip."

Some of my classmates at Gruel Normal tittered at this remark; some of them rubbed their open wounds beneath their shirts, and tried, like me, I'm sure, to figure out if it's better to be a star with flaws or a physically flawless nobody.

I never thought about it again until, back in my hometown, I saw a mailbox with SANDERS neatly spelled out, at the mouth of a pine straw–strewn driveway. Through the trees I spied a white clapboard cottage with perfect green shutters. I asked my wife to pull over before I threw out advertisements. There in the front yard sat Ray Sanders, reading the weekly *Forty-Five Platter* newspaper, in a makeshift Adirondack chair, a normal-looking auburn-haired wife to his side, a beautiful hound dog at his feet. He wore khakis, but no shirt; she wore a lime green pantsuit that I'd seen in one of the catalogs. Were they sipping lemonade, iced tea, mint juleps? It appeared so.

"You want to go down and see them?" my wife asked.

I held the plastic bag outside my passenger window, but didn't want to throw it and break their tranquillity. I asked my wife to drive on.

Soles in Gruel

THE MOST IGNORANT MAN in the state legislature, Howard Purgason, banged his hand on the desk and yelled out how he wanted all elementary schools in the state to take the N, A, C, and P out of their classroom alphabet borders, seeing as the NAACP boycotted South Carolina. Representative Purgason represented all of Gruel and a part of Forty-Five. He almost knocked his tobacco juice cup onto the floor, but none of his fellow legislators noticed. The second most ignorant state representative—a lay preacher from northern Greenville County who went by Brother Fain—always tried to introduce a bill that would cause schoolchildren to say the Pledge of Allegiance, the Lord's Prayer, then sing the National Anthem and "Dixie" each morning. This day, though, Fain balanced atop his swivel chair and yelled out how all foreigners in the state should have to wear a parachute on their backs at all times, so that they could understand how the government could send them back to their homelands at any moment. No legislator mentioned education. There were no motions concerning health care, the environment, jobless rates, state taxes, infant mortality rates, or unsafe roads.

"I'll agree with my brother from Greenville if he'll include the singing of the alphabet the way I want it to go," Howard Purgason yelled. "It ain't gone be that hard—B, D, E, F, G, H, you know. It'll be shorter to sing in school, then there'll be more time left for prayer and patriotic hymns."

The Speaker of the House banged and banged his gavel. He'd come from family money, gone to law school, been a prosecutor, a district attorney, and rose within the ranks of the Republican Party. He yelled, "Order, order," and after a pause said, "We supposed to be talking about how we need to protect our state's water supply from all the terrorist cult cells thriving in Georgia, Tennessee, and North Carolina. I read it on the Internet just last night." He banged his gavel again, then asked every journalist to leave the chamber. He dismissed pages, secretaries, and the casual capitol visitor wanting to view government in action.

He stared at Purgason, then Brother Fain. "We can't have no chaos. We already getting too much bad press in those other forty-nine states."

The third dumbest member of the state legislature, a man named Case—who once introduced a bill saying that all boys should take at least three years of shop in high school, all girls three years of home ec—stood up and reminded everyone that it was their ancestors who fired the first shots on Fort Sumter. He said, "Look how far that got us, now."

Then he fell over dead from a massive heart attack. The connection between his utterance of "first shots fired" and his subsequent collapse caused half of the state legislators to dive under their desks. All of them said they swore they heard gunfire, that they thought Eugene Case succumbed to snipers.

As all of this occurred, I read a couple of days later on page D4 of *USA Today*, my wife and I readied ourselves for a trip to Gruel, South Carolina, so that she could look into buying as many vacant, crumbling, dilapidated Victorian houses that weren't burned by Sherman. Evidently, according to some of the lesser-known Civil War history books, he'd been a classmate and friend at West Point with a boy who grew up to be Confederate minor hero Colonel Dill, and Sherman enjoyed hearing Dill's stories. So he crooked his troops over somewhat and aimed for Columbia instead. I liked to believe that Sherman missed Gruel only because of its name—that he figured any people who would name their town after lackluster porridge didn't need extra problems in their lives.

"I still think there have to be other near ghost towns that we can go reconstruct, Mayann. Moving back to my original hometown will make me feel like I've wasted life, given up, and lost altogether."

Mayann said, "Go get your tennis shoes. You're not packing your tennis shoes, are you? Go fetch them so I can put them in the refrigerator." Already she'd ditched milk, eggs, sour cream, and every other item with an expiration date past Saint Patrick's Day, the earliest that she foresaw our return. Mayann took every fresh vegetable out of the lower bin and tossed them outside for our near pet rabbits. What remained, as I remember, was yogurt and cheese shoved off to the side of the top shelf. Then she placed about a dozen pair of black Dansko clogs on the shelves. My one pair of favorite Converse high-tops—the only other footwear I owned outside of some rubber-soled Nunn Bush almost-dress shoes—went where celery once took up space. Mayann placed a box of baking powder in the vegetable bin, too. "It's for good luck, you know," she said. "We're going to need good luck, especially being outsiders."

I rolled her suitcase to the edge of the kitchen. "I'm not an outsider of Gruel. I lived there until sixth grade. There are memories of Gruel branded in my mind that I wouldn't wish on anyone. Hell, about South Carolina."

My wife had undergone a vivid dream a month earlier. She felt certain that she and I needed to leave Knoxville for good after finding a town that seemed to be on the verge of implosion, both financially and spiritually. Mayann said that ex-president Jimmy Carter offered this vision, and handed her a hammer, handsaw, and a child's coloring book that didn't have page folios. Nevertheless, the president kept saying, "The answer's on page twelve. Look at page twelve," and so on.

Mayann, up to this point, had been a shrewd, compassionate, and successful ACLU lawyer. Over the dozen years of our marriage—to Mayann, Jimmy Carter's "twelve" reference and our length of betrothal meant something—she'd garnered millions of dollars for injured workers and discrimination sufferers. Then she thought that there had to be more to life than helping people who may or may not have fallen down on purpose, or led a boss on to calling his secretary "sweetheart" or "honey."

I couldn't argue with Mayann, for I had left teaching college English in midsemester when I realized that my older colleagues were spineless, the younger ones idiots. Luckily, I'd inherited all of my father's woodworking tools, his crude hand-drawn blueprints, and enough handheld turkey calls left over to use as templates. I went back into the family business, though, in retrospect, I never really left it. I still constructed about a dozen turkey calls a year in my spare time, and kept them boxed up in the carport for whenever one of my father's favorite longtime customers called up with some sad story about how he sat on his call, or stepped on it, or got it stolen by an avid and jealous fellow turkey hunter. Each time I tested a handheld paddle box turkey call, made from the finest maple and poplar, the yelps, squawks, clucks, and purrs that emanated within my work shed sounded exactly like any responses my English 101 classes made as I called the roll.

Mayann placed her flip-flops, two pairs of pumps, and special shoes worn only for aerobics workouts on the refrigerator shelves below the Danskos. She said that her mother did the same thing whenever they went to Myrtle Beach on vacation. "My mother read somewhere that one of the ancient tribes always hid their shoes before leaving on a hunt or pilgrimage, because the afterlife didn't accept people without footwear. So, according to my mom's story, if you got in a bad wreck, you might get mangled and maimed, but you wouldn't die, because your soul couldn't go to heaven without shoes."

I said, "Did y'all go to Myrtle Beach barefoot? That doesn't make sense. Wouldn't you wear shoes in your car?"

Mayann slammed the side door of my van—she thought we should enter Gruel without showing off. She thought it best we not take her VW Rabbit. "Huh," she said. "I never thought about that. I guess maybe Mom thought we'd be barefoot a lot because we were at the beach. Maybe she feared us getting killed by sharks."

Going back to Gruel, ultimately, could only be blamed on me. Mayann had the dream, then got out a Rand McNally to look up odd-named towns that could only be in states of disrepair. She started in Tennessee—Gassaway, Hanging Limb,

Hohenwald—and ended up in the south Georgia town of Needmore. Mayann took notes. I said, "Tell me what, again, you have in mind?"

Mayann set down her highlighter. "I was thinking that it might be neat if I applied for some grants, hired out local help, and got to work renovating old homes. I could either start up a series of retirement homes for, say, indigent textile employees. Or I could bring the arts to such a downtrodden community, you know. Like start up an artist colony. Don't worry about any of that. It'll come to me sooner or later. An artist colony. Sooner or later. That's it."

I didn't say, "Maybe you should take a nap and see if Jimmy Carter has some better answers." I said, "In the early 1970s there was exactly nothing in the town of Gruel, South Carolina. My mother and I lived there for a couple years. There was a pool hall and diner. An army-navy store. I think maybe there was a pharmacy. All of this was on a square with some kind of Civil War hero standing in the middle."

My wife opened her atlas to South Carolina. Then she looked in the back matter for all towns listed with a population over six hundred. "It's not in here," she said. "What do you mean, your mother and you lived there for two years? Where was your father? You're making this up. How come you've never told me about this Gruel place?"

I shrugged. I opened up her atlas and pointed out where Gruel would be if it were big enough to mention on a map. I didn't say anything about the prison farm located farther south, toward the Savannah River nuclear facility, or how Mom and I went down there on Saturdays to visit my father.

Mayann said, "Gruel. Gruel. Grewwww-ullll. Grewwww-ullll. I like the sound of that. Listen. I'm not going to quit my job, or let anyone there know about my plans. But I've got a few weeks' vacation time saved up. Let's you and me drive on down there and check things out."

For the next two days my wife kept a list of things we'd need to take along. She packed my van meticulously, including tax statements, paycheck stubs, and the like, should she need to meet with a local banker in regards to a mortgage loan. She emptied her closet, for she wanted an ensemble appropriate for any possible occasion, from pool party to soiree.

I packed our dome tent and sleeping bags. My wife didn't understand that there would be no Hyatt, Omni, Hilton, Marriott Renaissance, or Gruel Inn located on the square or down an alley where locals probably still hitched their palominos.

I also shimmied six sample turkey calls into the van, knowing it would be a surefire way for me to make instant friends and stay out of fistfights. My wife would come off as a carpetbagger, certainly, but I planned to blend right in—something I didn't pull off in the fifth and sixth grades as my father served a two-year sentence for operating without a business license, tax evasion, and failing to respect Tennessee fire codes, which is what I told friends.

Mayann drove. Near the North Carolina border on I-40 she asked me if I might be interested in starting up some kind of Montessori school wherein I could impart knowledge that involved composition and manual labor. I held the map and stared forward.

Listen, parents and students had two educational choices if they lived on the square in Gruel or one of its four offshooting side streets: either get bused an hour's ride to Forty-Five to attend their elementary, junior, and high schools, or enroll in Gruel Normal, a private school run by an intelligent, multiple-divorced couple who hailed from the old Black Mountain College community. Gruel Normal wasn't a K through 12 white flight school. Parents paid a few hundred dollars a year to send their children there. More than a handful of bake sales, car washes, and raffles took place in order to pay the school's unaccredited teachers—mostly other disenfranchised adult runaways with penchants for history and literature, plus near nuns who knew Latin and a little biology—enough to live in their run-down mansions.

When I was in the fifth and sixth grades there weren't more than two dozen students altogether. I don't know how many Gruel schoolchildren took the bus to Forty-Five—there couldn't have been another twenty-four—because their parents distrusted the moral or intellectual abilities of the disenfranchised. I'm sure that some of my mother's neighbors believed that their children were better off listening to some southern belle say "I before E, except after C," like a mantra, over and over.

Gruel Normal's teachers weren't like that. Our classrooms were housed in two cement block buildings donated by a defunct sand and gravel company, which provided a great playground, and each day began with our teachers saying something optimistic like, "What do you think would happen if we no longer had food?" Then they listened for an hour, and told us to read the book of Job, *The Grapes of Wrath*, maybe some poems by T. S. Eliot.

"Why are people mean to each other?" "Why's it impossible for there to be another planet Earth somewhere in the universe?" "Do you think that the floral and candy industries invent holidays?" These were our daily questions. And every day we were told to read something, something else, and the book of Job. In between we learned multiplication tables, long division, and a skewed version of geography wherein the rest of America was the United States, and Gruel was Gruel.

Here's health class:

Right before my father got paroled and moved us back to Jonesboro, Tennessee, where he had originally started up the Wiggins Palm Clucker Turkey Call Company, all of us in sixth grade—which would mean *both* of us, Dwight Tollison and me—sat in the old sand and gravel company's break room. The principal, Mr. Lupo, brought in four men to talk to us, but not about sexual education or condoms or venereal disease. The special guests didn't mention exercise or hygiene.

The first man was blind. He said, "I wasn't borned like this. Back when I was about y'all'ses age we had a full solar eclipse, and I looked straight at it for only about three seconds. The next thing you know, I was completely blind." He left the room tapping his white cane. He also had the aid of a German shepherd that both Dwight and I knew guarded the army-navy store at night seeing as it was Victor Dees's pet.

I thought the second man was blind, too, but he took off his glasses and had the worst cross-eyes ever. Then he went off to tell a story about how his mother warned him not to cross his eyes or they might stick like that. Sure enough, they did. Mr. Lupo said, "I see you boys crossing your eyes all the time when I turn my back. Let this be a lesson to you. Job was cross-eyed, by the way."

Dwight and I nodded. I'm not sure if I even breathed during this supposed health class. The third man said, "I'm glad you boys are able to sit down on those nice chairs. I wish I could do the same. But I can't. No sir. If I did, I might pop and bleed to death. Let me tell you about sitting down on cold cement and the history of lowly polyps."

I thought he said something about lollipops.

I was about to ask if he had any extras, but Dwight nudged my ribs and started giggling. He wasn't making fun of this poor soul, though. Already he'd caught a glimpse of the hair growing off the final guy's palms.

Mr. Lupo dismissed us. He said nothing about how a frog set on his nose at one time, thus causing the wart, or how his own knuckles were the size of jawbreakers due to popping them in his early years. He said to me, "I understand your daddy's about to be released on good behavior, Charlie. Is this true?"

Dwight ran off to one of the sand dunes to shoo one of the stray, wild cats that always lurked on the edge of Gruel Normal's boundaries. I said, "My momma says he was never guilty in the first place. She says he got caught up in a trap between people who were plain jealous that a man could invent a better turkey call and people who were plain jealous that a turkey call maker could have a pretty wife. That's what she says."

Mr. Lupo said, "The same could be said of Job, son. Don't you worry any about all that. Don't feel embarrassed about your father's shortcomings. You are you."

"He's getting out, and I think we're moving back to Tennessee. My father says if he'd not been so stubborn, he could've gotten out of the fire code charge. The only thing he had to do was burn up his wood scraps instead of letting them pile up in the backyard." That was my story in Gruel. I never mentioned how my father was really sent upriver on an indirect murder charge.

My principal and I walked back toward the other building where one of the other teachers would ask, "If it's true that American livestock lay down before a storm, what happens to cattle south of the equator?"

When Mayann and I hit such a small state road that its number went something like 108801, a mile from Gruel's square, I said, "I'll never teach again, honey. I might expand to duck calls or silent dog whistles, but I have no ambition to bring kids in to view a man's fake hairy palms."

My wife veered from an animal I never saw lurch out onto the macadam.

The amateur real estate agent, in charge of many of Gruel's falling and bleak-storied mansions for sale, happened to be state representative Howard Purgason's wife. Paula Purgason grew up in nearby Forty-Five, but her father owned and operated Gruel's once-thriving pet store. I didn't remember a pet shop on the square, but with my father in prison I doubt my mom would've walked me past a place that advertised other mouths to feed. "My father was the first man in South Carolina to import chinchillas," Ms. Purgason said to Mayann and me as we sat down on fur-covered wingback chairs in the den. "My uncle had a pet store over in Ware Shoals. He was the first to import Siamese fighting fish and spread the rumor that all chinchillas had rabies."

Mayann said, "We saw some of the houses for sale. Boy, they sure do need work, don't they?" which I thought was pretty smart. She didn't want to seem eager.

I thought about my shoes in the refrigerator back home. I wanted to be wearing tennis shoes at this particular moment, should I decide to take off running. At the moment, a horrendous scream emanated from upstairs. "That's just Howard," Ms. Purgason said. She shoved a *USA Today* in my direction and directed me to page D4—that's where I learned about what I concluded had to be the three stupidest members of the

South Carolina state legislature. I read the item and said, "I'll be damned," then handed the paper to my wife.

"Howard's got a theory, but I don't know if it's right. He keeps thinking he's got a bleeding ulcer or internal bleeding of some type. I keep telling him it's plain old hemorrhoids. I told him to wipe hisself with rubbing alcohol, and that'd tell him which was which."

I said, "I guess if he had a bleeding ulcer, it wouldn't burn, right?"

"Not lest he drank it," Ms. Purgason said. She wore a hairdo that could've doubled as a termite mound on the Brazilian pampas. Tom Waits and Lucinda Williams could've collaborated and written an opera about the woman's large, loud dress—which was punctuated with a bow the size of a barn owl in midflight. "Y'all want some iced tea or anything before I take y'all over to look at what they got me selling? I want to make sure Howard comes down okay, you know."

Mayann had originally called Ms. Purgason when she finished a few good hours of investigation. I'd told my wife that there was no remaining Chamber of Commerce, that anyone calling information would get no Realtors' listings, and so on. I'd said, "Why don't you get on the computer and punch 'Gruel, South Carolina' in. See what happens. I'd be willing to bet no one there has a computer yet, so there won't be any Web pages or whatever."

I never did understand how Mayann got ahold of anyone, amateur Realtor or not.

We declined the iced tea. Mayann said, "Charlie here says there's no motel nearby. Is that true?"

"Not a one. Used to be the Gruel Inn way off on Old Old Augusta Road, but that's a sad story. It became some kind of weight-loss clinic, and then a writers colony. Some crazy fellow named Novel lived there for about a year, but then he took off and no one heard from him again. Now we got a bunch of guru types living in there, doing yoga all the time."

I said, "What?"

"But the other people who've come down looking I've let stay in the houses they was interested in. All the houses still have all they furniture. I've been good about washing and changing linens."

"Did these people just die off with no next of kin?" Mayann asked. She shifted in her seat and a plume of chinchilla hair floated upward.

"Oh they got kin. Kin just don't care. Some of them so old they can't get back down here to sell what they inherited rightly."

Howard Purgason eased down the stairs directly, leaning heavily on its banister. He wore suspenders and a straw hat with the brim flattened straight up. "Well I guess my screaming and moaning came out loud and clear. I forgot Paula said y'all was coming. Good news for me; bad news for me, too."

He stuck out his hand to shake. I'd like to say that I didn't want to shake hands with a racist, first off, but to be honest I didn't want to shake hands with a man so stupid he'd wipe his ass with toilet paper soaked in isopropyl alcohol. I stood up, but said, "I have a bad case of poison ivy."

"Well. Okay, then. That's mighty considerate of you." He nodded at Mayann, but didn't take off his hat. Who sits on a toilet wearing a hat? I thought. "Listen. I just come up with one more way to solve the South's problems. Listen, you know how buckets and pails and barrels of water fill up with mosquito larvae in the summer? Well, what we should do is keep those buckets of rainwater filled with minnows. Then they'd eat the larvae. In times of drought, you'd just have to keep filling up said buckets, pails, and barrels with tap water so's to keep the minnows from frying."

I thought about being in elementary school and singing the alphabet song without an N, A, C, or P. My wife said, "Back home, we go out after big summer rainstorms and simply dump the water out so mosquitoes don't lay their eggs."

Howard Purgason looked at my wife as though she spoke in tongues. He squinted, raised his eyebrows, and shifted his weight from one foot to the other. Paula Purgason said, "They don't drink iced tea, either."

"Why your parents name you after the most northern state?" Howard Purgason asked my wife.

Evidently my wife didn't possess mind-reading skills. She didn't turn her head their way and blurt out, "Help, help, Charlie's going to kill me as soon as we're alone in the car. That's what he's thinking, that's what he's thinking."

My wife and I camped out inside 101 Old Old Greenville Road. This particular house held some thirty-six hundred square feet, and might've been painted white back in the 1920s or thereabouts. The original owners, according to Ms. Purgason, lived through the Civil War and ran a gristmill. Their final kin left Gruel in the early 1960s for job opportunities on the coast, after having inherited grocery stores, train depot cafés, textile supply companies, and car dealerships.

We spread out sleeping bags atop metal springed iron beds in one of the two downstairs bedrooms. There were two others upstairs. The house also included an old-fashioned parlor, a den, living room, dining room, added-on kitchen and mudroom and bathroom downstairs. Upstairs, outside of the two bedrooms, was another bathroom in what probably used to be a closet.

The wraparound porch slanted downward in a way that might've made wheelchair victims feel as though they were unwanted.

Outside stood a summer kitchen, springhouse, and outbuilding of indeterminate use. Scuppernong vines encased an ancient wooden pergola of sorts that must've run twenty yards in length, five feet above the ground. Muscadines hung from another such structure, perpendicular. Fig trees clumped sporadically beneath hundred-year-old magnolias. A stand of twelve pecan trees ran up the pea gravel drive.

Any sane human being in the middle of the day would've said the place exuded flat-out aristocratic Old South charm.

I was inside the place for about ten minutes before I saw specters flying around, fifteen minutes before I had a tent pitched in the front yard and my flashing lights blinking on the van next to it. Mayann came out and said, "What's your problem?"

I said, "Listen. If you want to move to this place, you go right ahead. But don't include me. What I'm saying is, I can make my turkey calls about anywhere, but not here. And I'd rather go back to teaching four hundred students English 101 per semester than make turkey calls here, even if the University of Hell had a branch campus. Did you or did you not see those ghosts flying around in there?" I pointed at the house. Me, I saw lights flashing and buzzing about.

"It only smells a little mildewy," my wife said. "It stinks in there, but that's it. Kind of like stale bread."

I pointed at the house's facade. It looked to me as if ten whirling dervishes spun flashlights around inside. "If you're nuts enough to stay in there, you go ahead. I'm going to sleep in the van. And I might sleep in the van about two counties away. I'm serious, Mayann. *Maine.* I don't know if I can become one with this community."

My wife wore a white nightgown down to her shins. She stood barefoot in the front yard of a house she thought had possibilities. "I think it would be kind of cool living in a place where the smartest man thinks putting minnows in rain barrels will keep the mosquitoes from reproducing. We could take over." She spanned her arms outward toward the other houses she planned to check out and make bids on.

I didn't say anything about her "shoes in the refrigerator" theory. I said, "I need a drink."

"Go on down there to Roughhouse Billiards. Maybe you'll see one of your old friends from sixth grade. Stay as long as you want."

She pointed in the direction of Gruel's sad square. I told her my memory was better than she thought. Mayann said she'd be all right alone. I disengaged one of my turkey calls and slid the top into my back pocket.

I walked the two blocks into downtown slowly, trying to remember any good feeling I might've had as a child. I heard Mayann close the door to her new house about the time I noticed Roughhouse Billiards' broken neon sign advertising "old Bee."

"You want a hot dog?" Jeff Downer asked when I entered the pool hall. He owned the place twenty-five years earlier. Back then he looked seventy, also, I thought. "We got the best hot dog in town. And coldest beer." He didn't wear a shirt and his belly hung half inflated over his belt. "We're also the only topless bar in the area."

I said, "Hey, Jeff. I'm Charlie Wiggins. I doubt you remember me from way back when, but I used to live here for a couple years."

"Charlie Wiggins. Your momma and you come down here to be close to your daddy. He'd gone to prison over on the

Farm for some kind of near felony. I remember you. You come in here one day and ran a table during Junior Pool Championship Week."

I said, "Yessir."

"Well let me give you a hot dog in appreciation of your return. You look good, boy. You look normal. Wha'chew been up to all these years? Where you been? How you want it?"

I said, "Oh, I guess mustard, onions, and chili."

"That's all? You don't want no bun or nothing?"

Three grown men played a game of cutthroat. I pulled my turkey call out and squeaked it out of habit. "No sir. No bun," I said, like I knew what I was doing.

"Now I remember. Your daddy made a turkey call so lifelike that some old boy was in the woods working one, and another old boy shot him. So your daddy got hit up on some kind of involuntary manslaughter charge seeing as if he'd've made a turkey call not so realistic, no one would've got killed."

One of the three men yelled out, "You don't have to call your shots in cutthroat, Bo. Hell, you can knock your own balls in just to keep shooting."

I squeaked my turkey box. No one looked. I realized that I didn't have my father's skills.

We slept in eight different houses. Mayann soon wielded her I-have-good-credit power and bought up each of them for less than a hundred grand total. By night five I didn't fear Gruel, her people, or the ghost-ridden dilapidated houses any longer. I went to Roughhouse Billiards each night until closing, then crawled back to wherever my wife set up our sleeping bags. She always said, "I need you now more than ever, Charlie. Do you know anything about plumbing?" Or termites, Sheetrock, flooring, pump houses, roofing, French drains, blight, weight-bearing walls, sump pumps, and wiring.

I had relearned that it only took staring at the cue ball and using bottom left or right English to make most shots. I said, "Yes," to my wife. Each of her houses had an outbuilding where I could reinvent and relocate the Wiggins Palm Clucker Turkey Call Company. It would be a better life than trying to convince first-year college students that Ice-T, T-Bone, Bone-Afide, Fi-Dough, Dough-Boy, Boy-Man, Man-a-Fest, Fest-Er, Ergo-Sum, Sum-Atra, and Jewel weren't really poets. It would be better than waiting for tourists in Jonesboro, Tennessee, to show up and tell me how they didn't really hunt turkeys, but only wanted to nail my work on the walls of their "country kitchens."

"I can figure out about everything," I told Mayann, "outside of how to get that Jeff guy down at Roughhouse to quit asking me if I don't want a bun. You do what you have to do. Me, I'll figure out what I'm supposed to do."

"Are you sure? This is a big, big change in our lives. Or it could be."

We had no children. Our parents were all dead. "We could make history here," I said, all hyperbolic. "One day—if Gruel ever gets town fathers—maybe they'll erect a statue of you in place of the one of Colonel Dill in the square."

I think my wife said, *"Or town mothers"* as she walked into house number six's sagging kitchen. I couldn't hear her. I was on my way out, wearing my only shoes.

Howard and Paula Purgason entered Roughhouse Billiards as if everyone should've kowtowed to them. She wore a thin whitish stole. The state rep wore a gray vest that didn't match his tan leisure suit. I said, "So I guess you're pretty happy with the commission," to Ms. Purgason.

Jeff said, "How y'all want your hot dogs?"

Howard Purgason said, "All the way. Buns and everything. I'm feeling prosperous." He had on the same hat I saw him wear coming out of his upstairs bathroom. To me he said, "Wiggins," and half nodded.

I said, "Congressman," because—although I had no respect whatsoever for him or his cohorts—I'd had two PBRs and a mini-bottle of Jim Beam. "Ms. Purgason."

She held out her lank arm for me to kiss the back of her hand. I did, what the hell.

Jeff said, "Something good must've happened. Y'all don't come down here to us lowlifes unless something good happened. I guess every two years when you win the election."

When I sat down at the bar, the turkey call in my back pocket clucked. The congressman said, "Say 'Excuse me' in front of my wife."

I stood up, pulled the turkey call from my back pocket, and showed it to them. "That noise was this. That sound came out of my turkey call."

Howard Purgason said, "I might not be the most polished man in the world, but I don't deserve being in a place that allows men to make such noises." Jeff handed over two hot dogs. "We going down to Pawleys Island for the weekend, and I don't want to start it this way. You want to start it this way, sugar?"

Ms. Purgason said, "No."

I held my turkey call box above my head and squeaked it, squawked it, peeped it, purred it. "You've got it all wrong," I said.

A man at the pool table yelled out, "I didn't need to call bank shot. You better figure out cutthroat rules."

I looked at Jeff. He didn't seem to care one way or the other. I looked down and noticed that Howard and Paula were barefoot. Now, in the real world I would've said something about why he wore a suit, she a stole, in a pool hall. But this was Gruel—a place where my own wife challenged our bank account, a sad town where right might've been construed as wrong. I said, "As we speak your shoes are in a refrigerator, aren't they?" To Jeff I said, "I want three beers and three shots."

Howard and Paula Purgason stood stuck, as if we all played a game of freeze tag. Jeff reached down and popped beer tops off, then twisted my mini-bottles. I didn't look at myself in the mirror behind him. How would my life end up in a town called Gruel? I thought. What would it be like in five years after Mayann gave up everything, packed her bags, and left me here? Would I spend all of my time setting quarters on a pool table's edge? Would I argue with Jeff over hot dogs until the first of us died?

That night, as the state legislator and his wife walked out, both probably considering a world without public education, I understood that Mayann and I would end up serving three meals per day to people who would never understand the value of nourishment, that we—my wife and I—would pretend to care about strangers who pretended to care about the ways of the world. We would start up the artist colony, view our lodgers' new canvases and sculptures, and know that something was missing. Everything in our world would appear to lack something essential, like a magnolia without blooms, a dog without a collar, fish without gills, a bulldozer without its scoop, or the perfect runway model without shoes.

But I wouldn't turn back. There had to be more turkey hunters in South Carolina, I figured. More turkey hunters, more turkey hunters, more turkey hunters, I said to myself like a mantra, as Mayann decided that each house she bought didn't really need closets should she find a deal on chifforobes.

Recovery

I AWOKE FROM ANESTHESIA maybe one minute before Evelyn, long enough to remember my burst appendix. I'd dated Evelyn in high school fifteen years earlier, had mostly forgotten her, and in those sixty seconds inside recovery could only understand this coincidence as some kind of omen. Here we were at Graywood Memorial, three states away from our northern Mississippi upbringing, in a town that—for me at least—only stood as a midway point between Atlanta and Charlotte, between Savannah and Asheville, where I showed off hand-blown figurines, Christmas tree ornaments, the nameless bauble for a company called Kicking Glass and Taking Names! fifty-some-odd weeks out of the year. I almost remembered passing out inside a Main Street boutique, the owner of which is the wife of an internist. She evidently called an ambulance and her husband. Somebody called my ex-wife, who gladly agreed to emergency surgery, I imagined. My story's one of near fatal poisoning, of a thirty-three-year-old fish- and vegetable-eating man with inexplicably weak organs that fizzled like ancient

matchbooks. Somewhere down the line, I knew, a religious person would explain it all to me.

A hovering nurse said, "How many fingers am I holding up?"

Evelyn's father ran a bait shop, then later a catfish farm like everyone else. Her mother taught seventh grade over in Oxford. I asked Evelyn to junior and senior prom even though she dated star quarterback Quint Stubbs, and she politely declined. But right before graduation she called me at home and said, "Listen, Jamie. I've been thinking about higher places. Who knows when a log truck going to Memphis might run my car off the road and splatter me down an embankment? I've been thinking about heaven. You've been asking me out since ninth grade. Maybe I should say yes, in case God says I've been mean. So I'll give you one date."

I said, "Who is this? Is this you, Slade?" It was a time before caller ID. "You ain't funny. I know it's you, man."

Evelyn had said, "They're having a festival on the square. You can take me, from eight o'clock until about nine thirty. It'll be dark by then."

We went, she wouldn't let me hold her hand, I won her a giant stuffed animal crawfish, and she made me drop her off at the end of her parents' driveway without a kiss. I moved on to Tennessee three months later. Evelyn, from what I understood, continued her cheerleading career at Ole Miss.

To the nurse I said, "Eleven. I see eleven fingers." But I kept my head turned toward Evelyn, still under, a sheet up to her neck. Weren't there some kind of privacy laws concerning recovery rooms? I thought.

"Whoa. You might not be ready to go to your room."

Exactly, I thought. I wanted the nurse out of there. I

wanted to crawl off my gurney and scoot next to Evelyn, even if she had a hysterectomy, double mastectomy, hemorrhoid surgery, or cesarean. I felt like I needed to kiss her cheek, her eyebrows, the tip of her nose, the back of her knees.

The nurse said, "We had a man come in here one time with web toes? He had this surgery for his web toes? And then he needed, too, his gallbladder taken out? And the doctor took out his appendix? So when he woke up I asked him how many fingers he saw? And I held up three like I am to you now, right in front of his face? And he said, 'Duck.' I don't know why. I guess because he had them web toes. Say, how many fingers do you see now?"

She kept three fingers in my face. I said, "Frog."

The nurse lifted my sheet up and looked at my feet. Evelyn awoke and moaned. I said, "Good morning, Evelyn. It's me, Jamie Hinson. From back in Water Valley, Mississippi. Do you remember me? My daddy and your daddy used to be friends, before my daddy fell into your daddy's catfish pond and drowned when he supposedly hit his head. Now it all makes sense, though: I'm thinking he had a burst appendix like I did, and he only passed out face-first from the pain. Oh, I started to go to law school, but changed my mind. I took the LSAT and everything, but didn't want to feel confined to either Tennessee or Mississippi, you know. For about four years I worked in Nashville for a company called Braid Electric. I got married, and that lasted almost nine and a half years. She ended up getting drunk every day, then went to rehab, and from what I understand is still in recovery. We didn't have kids, which might be good. Anyway, out of nowhere I met this man who corralled a bunch of glassblowers together and got them to work on some knickknacks to be sold nationwide. There's a catalog and everything. I drive a van around showing off samples. The one thing I have to worry about is not hitting potholes in the road. Handblown glass Christmas tree ornaments are fragile fragile. I got pretty good shock absorbers. So, what brings you all the way out here to South Carolina? Why're you in the hospital? I like your hat. I got one just like it, right now."

The nurse walked over to her and did the how-many-fingers test. Evelyn didn't turn her head. She said, "I can't stand tacos."

I could only smile. There was a lone Mexican fellow at the festival in Oxford who told us that we should one day celebrate Cinco de Mayo in Juárez or Tijuana. He said, in broken English, that Evelyn's stuffed crawfish looked like a piñata, and offered her three tacos for it.

Her answer to the nurse was like a code, I believed.

I said, "Yeah, it's me. Jamie."

The nurse said to Evelyn, "You don't worry, honey. Your hair will grow back and your scar won't show." To me the nurse said, "Say. Are you Frank Gunnells, the man who had to have penis reconstruction?"

I said, "No, ma'am. No. I only had an appendicitis."

"That's right. You're awake enough to go to your room, then."

Evelyn blurted out, "Hammond organs." I tried to make some kind of meaningful correlation as I got wheeled to my room on the fifth floor, but couldn't.

I pray for late December earthquakes daily. This isn't something to brag about, but sometimes I wish for massive Christmas tree fires so that people have to buy more handblown glass ornaments. One time I got on the Internet and tried to figure out what kind of barometric pressure would blow my product to bits. I've talked the glassblowers into making their products more fragile at our annual meetings. They—all of them with shaved heads in order to prevent sudden combustible hair—said they'd do their best.

But they don't, evidently.

I spend my time at places called Antiques and Things, Collectibles and Things, Knickknacks and Things, This and That, Wicker and Things, This and Suche, Everything and Else, Arts and Crafts, Crafts and Things, and plain flat-out Things. I walk in with samples. I offer order forms. Owners choose and customers buy. Our most popular Christmas ornament involves a tiny glass baby Jesus swinging on a glass tree bough inside a clear, softball-sized orb. $79.95. Available at your favorite boutique, plus Belk, Rich's, Montgomery Ward, and Service Merchandise. Our worst seller involves Gandhi, in glass diapers. My boss, Leland Dees, tries to be both politically correct and religion-encompassing. I like him fine, and respect his tenacity. We sell a fair amount of big fat glass Buddhas.

We could have our products carried at every Bloomingdale's in the country, but some woman named Sheralee, their head buyer, doesn't like the cover of our catalog. Leland Dees sent her one of the glass Buddhas one time and said if she attached a battery to it she might find it useful for her midnight needs. I didn't blame him, though it might've kept me out of about a quarter-million dollars' worth of yearly commission.

"I'm in a hospital outside Forty-Five, South Carolina," I said to Leland over the phone right after I figured out how to use it, the channel changer, the bed-height control, the nurse call button. What I'm saying is, I called Leland Dees two hours after I returned to my room, maybe fifteen minutes after a good shot of Demerol.

Leland said, "Please tell me you didn't wreck the van, Jamie."

Somewhere down the hall a man moaned for a bedpan. "They thought I had a heart attack or stroke. I *didn't*, but they didn't know. I guess it's my fault I haven't seen a doctor sooner. I've been blacking out sporadically for the last year or so, from pain in my side. I finally exploded."

Leland Dees said, "My wayward brother lives in Gruel. It's right next door to Forty-Five. You want me to send him over?" He said, "Wait a minute—so you blacked out and they automatically decided to operate? That doesn't sound likely."

I reached down and felt a bandage on my lower torso. "Don't ask me. I'm alive, that's all I know. Who would operate on a person who doesn't need an operation?"

"Watch one of those TV shows one time, Jamison. *60 Minutes. 20/20. Dateline.* Those others on the other channel."

I wanted to call the patient information person downstairs and get Evelyn's room number, then find a way to wheel myself her way. To Leland Dees I said, "It doesn't matter. My body probably needed a shock. Maybe this explains why my sales went down over the last year or so. I spent too much time not taking care of myself."

"What do you need?" Leland said.

"I can't drive for a while. I'm calling to say that orders might be coming in a little slower." The Demerol kicked in. I said, "The capital of Missouri's not St. Louis. Missouri's the Show Me state. Pi equals 3.1416, but it goes on forever. My ex-wife Patina could drink bourbon and vodka and beer, but not scotch or gin or wine. Maybe Evelyn only hit her head—it might not've been a tumor."

Leland said, "What's your doctor's name? I want to talk to your doctor. What's your room number, so we can send flowers."

I said, "Man, I'm feeling good all of a sudden. This is nice. I could use a milk shake and a baseball game. And an umbrella.

I told the guy I didn't want a catheter. I didn't get a catheter, and that's good."

At least this is how Leland Dees said the conversation went. Me, I don't remember. Evelyn says I called her up in 519 and tried to run down the periodic table of elements, that I was intent on getting through it all. She said I professed love not only to her, but to her older sister and parents back in Water Valley.

I got her room number and said, "That *was* you in the recovery room, right? Evelyn. This is Jamie Hinson. So you remember me?"

Evelyn might've said, "I want to take my life much like a martyr." Later on I realized that her words came out as such. I heard at the time, though, "I want to be your wife and birth your daughter."

I said, "Yes, yes. From back home. I can't believe we both ended up here, in a hospital. Not far from my boss's wayward brother's store."

I couldn't make out what "I give up, come on down to 519, it doesn't matter, obviously," could've meant otherwise. I couldn't. I thought, at the time, that she could mean it without sarcasm. I made sure my IV bag hung on a rolling tree. I made sure that my hospital gown almost attached in back.

For safe measure I punched the nurse call button in order to keep anyone from entering my room for another thirty minutes.

"Excuse me if I don't get up," Evelyn said. She wore one of those fife-and-drum head bandages. "I'm taking it that you've stalked me forever. I guess the last time I saw you was the Ole Miss–Tennessee game. I stood on top of the pyramid. You had a sign that read MARRY ME, EVELYN. Don't think I didn't notice. I pretended not to notice, but couldn't help it. How'd you do that? Was it a neon sign? Did you have sparkles attached to it or what? I've always wondered."

I rolled past a hardback chair and a Naugahyde lounger built for overnight guests in ICU. I said, "That wasn't me, Evelyn. Lord, think about all of your admirers. When I left for college I pretty much left Water Valley for good. For what it's worth. For better or worse. I didn't think I could go back and hear our classmates speak in clichés for the rest of my life. To each his own, I guess."

"It wasn't malignant," Evelyn said. She pointed toward her scalp. "The size of an orange, they're saying, but not malignant. You have to believe me."

"That's good. Oh, that's lucky. I mean, I've heard about people with lumps the size of lemons, limes, grapefruit, and kumquats. It doesn't matter the size. If it's malignant, it's trouble. I saw a woman on either *60 Minutes*, *20/20*, or *Dateline* one time with a tumor the size of a cantaloupe. She's fine, because it was benign. Rhyme—ha, ha! Maybe it was on that other channel."

My side hurt and my mouth could've held a convention for bedouins and their dromedaries. Evelyn said, "Nothing right's happened since I moved to South Carolina. I came here only to be close to my niece and nephew. That's why I'm here. Does that make any sense?"

Outside of the weird headband, Evelyn looked the same as I'd seen her at Oxford's crawfish festival. She picked up the television remote and turned it on to one of those entertainment news channels. A host talked about upcoming situation comedies, PG-13 movies, what fashions the stars had been spotted wearing lately. I said, "I remember your sister. Why is she here?"

"Her husband," Evelyn said. "He's upper management at Fujifilm. They got a big factory here. Treesa and he moved here ten years ago when he got a job. Normally I hate him, but he's the first person who noticed I might've had a problem. I mean, a lump. I got to give him that."

I rolled two inches closer. My IV stretched. "I bet he's in the optics division. They notice everything. There was probably a reason why you moved here. If you stayed home, I'm betting no one would've noticed your lump until it got bigger than a watermelon. They say that when a tumor gets to the point where it can't be compared to a fruit, then you're in trouble."

What was I saying? Evelyn smiled, lifted her knees beneath the sheets. She said, "My head doesn't hurt like I thought it would. I wonder where my sister is."

I told Evelyn I knew how to use the telephone. I rolled over to the nightstand, pretended to mash in the numbers she called out, then said it was busy. "Were you working here? God, I hate to bother you, Evelyn, but I can't get over running into you under these circumstances."

A nurse walked in and said, "How you feeling, hon?" To me she said, "I can tell by your skin color that you're not supposed to be getting up and about. Or bothering this lady."

After I'd gotten back to my room, after it took the nurse ten minutes to get me back in bed, and long after she left, I thought to say, "Oh, don't worry—I'm an albino." It never failed. One time on the road I had stopped in at a little Asheville boutique run by the Greenspoon family. They said that they weren't Orthodox, but that they didn't see a need to test Yahweh's patience. Twenty miles down the road I thought how I should've promised some as-yet-unblown glass dreidels, yarmulkes, candleholders.

I thought about how a glassblowing salesman without an appendix wasn't probably the most enticing prospect for a Mississippi ex-cheerleading woman with nieces and nephews who loved her. I turned on CNN. Our soldiers lured in more American-hating, probable terrorists by offering them a bag of flour, a bottle of water, a handful of kernel corn.

Why was it so easy elsewhere? I wondered in my Demerol haze.

The first sign of my first wife's deterioration occurred when, for the fiftieth time, she insisted that swans, cranes, hawks, and geese wiped her after each bathroom visit she took. "A tiny gander visited me this morning, and took care of everything," she would say. This happened while we tried to conceive children, when we took her temperature, vitamins, ate Chinese herbs, and kept me off the booze. I understood my ex-wife's behavior as pre-postpartum depression—hell, I'd read about the syndrome in more than a few women's magazines, usually two or three columns across from post-premenstrual syndrome items.

We separated soon thereafter. From what I understand, she's applied for jobs at Kicking Glass and Taking Names! more than once, wanting to work in an advisory capacity.

My own nurse walked in and handed me a photocopied sheet of everything that would occur post-op, everything that I had already done whether I knew it or not—most of which involved shaving—and what I could expect in years to come should I make the right choices that involved the urge to defy a dentist's orders involving extractions or crowns, eating un-processed meat, riding motorcycles, smoking cigarettes, drink-ing booze, not wearing a seat belt, and so on. I was told that I shouldn't live in a town with smog or undue violence, that I should drink purified water always, and that I should wear a condom. There would be problems should I overuse a cellular phone, visit countries south of the United States, shoot up heroin, drive a riding lawn mower barefoot, golf during lightning storms, handle venomous snakes, or forget to check out open sores on my feet. I wasn't to own a firearm over a BB gun or eat fish hatched near a paper mill. There may or may not have been something about operating heavy machinery while under the influence of drugs and/or booze.

I looked over the document and wondered what it would be like to reach two hundred years old. "Thanks," I said.

My nurse stared at the television. Men and women alike wore gas masks. "They need to add more warnings," she said. "But this'll be a start."

Leland Dees's brother Victor—owner of V.D.'s Army-Navy Surplus store in nearby Gruel—popped in wearing camouflage. I'd forgotten and thought about Evelyn at least three times. In and out of sleep I couldn't recall what was real, what was odd hope. My boss's brother said, "I brought along a couple few MREs in case you didn't take to the hospital food. I got a connection down at Fort Jackson. Over at Fort Benning. Fort Stewart. Everywhere. Lookie here." Victor Dees opened his shirt to show off a hand grenade duct-taped to his chest. "It's real, baby. I like testing out all these public places to see how security's working. It ain't, here, obviously. I got a fake permit and all, should I ever get stopped on the other side of a metal detector."

Peripherally I noticed that my nurse call button wasn't within a sneaky, imperceptible reach. I said, "They told me I couldn't eat solids for a while."

"They know *right at nothing*," Dees said. He looked exactly like my boss: broad-faced, happy, strawberry blond, and fidgety. He looked like the love child of Alfred E. Neuman and David Letterman.

I groaned but didn't mean it yet. "Leland told me he had a brother. I guess I don't see him that much, really. I'm on the road about fifty-two weeks a year."

Victor Dees walked to the window, opened the blinds, then closed them. "I wouldn't have come visit if you were on the third floor. That's where they keep the nutcases. You wouldn't believe all the boys I've sold bayonets and Don't Tread on Me flags to who ended up on the third floor of this hospital. Canteens. Helmets. Military police armbands. Decals. Gas masks, especially gas masks. Bayonets—did I already say that?"

I actually thought about saying, "There weren't any rooms left on the third floor," but didn't. I said, "Were you in the military, sir?"

"My brother asked me to go fetch your van. He said there might be upwards of five thousand dollars' worth of samples inside. I said I'd do it. So what I'm doing is, I've driven over here and left my Humvee. Then I'm going to get a cab over to wherever you left the van. Where'd you leave the van?"

On the television, a throng of Arabs burned photographs of Nixon, Reagan, the first Bush, and George Washington. The commentator said, "I don't know if it's fortunate or unfortunate that these people don't know America's current president." I said to Victor Dees, "Bric-a-Brac and Things. Over on Main Street between Slide Rule City and the Afro-Sheen Outlet."

"I got you," Victor Dees said. "I know the area. Across from that carbon paper joint and map shop."

The map place had atlases that still portrayed a forty-eight-state America. I went in there one time trying to push the Kicking Glass and Taking Names! solar system series—I'd sold this glorious chandelier to about every middle school science class in the southeast—only to have the store's manager ask what those balls were past Saturn. I would've been better off bringing in a flat windowpane and saying it stood for Earth.

"That's right," I said to Victor Dees.

"I'll need about twenty dollars and the keys to the van," he said. "You can get the money back from my brother. Or I'll get you a receipt if you want, for tax purposes. Either one. This or that."

My innards panged, throbbed, and seared. I told Leland Dees's brother that I needed more painkiller, and reached for the nurse call button. About the time my hand got six inches from it, though, he stopped me, reached into his flak jacket, and pulled out a syringe.

At the time it seemed like a good idea. I said, "Okay. But could you get me in a wheelchair right after, then push me down to 519? It's a long story that involves a woman I need to know again."

I woke up hopelessly shoved into Evelyn's room closet. Who knew that my keys were gone, that my samples were on their way to being sold at an army-navy store, that my van would never be found again? I yelled for help. I heard people running down the hallway, the squawk of walkie-talkies, someone yelling, "He looked like some kind of survivalist."

There's a museum of sorts in the lobby of Graywood Memorial, flanked by the old white smoking and black smoking areas. Visitors come through the wide automatic doors, ask a receptionist for patient information, maybe veer behind her to the gift shop where, sadly, no Kicking Glass and Taking Names! products line the shelves. Off to the left of patient information, though, is a conglomeration of ancient bone saws, tongs, knives, and nurse's caps. There are electrical devices once used only on the third floor. It's like a torture chamber. The best display, four three-by-three-foot pedestals covered only with Plexiglas bonnets, follows the career of one Dr. Holloway and his personal history of odd extractions. Written out in perfect cursive on three-by-five note cards, there's "Sewing Needle in Child's Esophagus," "Buttons in Child's Esophagus," "Locust in Child's Esophagus," and so on. "Bullets Extracted from Feet" seemed a major theme in the 1930s through the late 1950s. Many children of the area, for one reason or another, found it necessary to snort peas into their lungs.

And there were silver dimes and quarters. *"Were,"* said the security guard who dislodged me from Evelyn's hospital room closet. "Somebody just stole all the change. They ain't cataloged everything yet. There was some Civil War surgical devices down there they think are missing. A collection of sharp sticks, mostly. Somebody said there was a rare penny down there worth ten thousand dollars."

I said, "I don't know how I got here. I must've been delirious with pain. You can check me out, though. I didn't go downstairs and steal anything."

Evelyn slept. Renoir couldn't have made her look more glorious. "If you can't remember nothing from the pain, who's to say you don't remember stealing all them Mercury heads?" The guard read my wristband. He said, "I'mo push you back to your room. Then we're going to get a male nurse to check you out. I used to work in the prison system, Bubba. I can direct him to all the hiding places."

"Evelyn!" I yelled out. "Evelyn, I'm in 592. When you get back on your feet, come on down there." About halfway back I looked up and behind me. I said, "Do y'all have one of those Crime Stoppers phone numbers around here? I got an idea. As a matter of fact, I'd make some bets as to your perpetrator downstairs."

The guard pulled up outside of the laundry room. He rechecked my bracelet. "If you was on the third floor I'd give it to you for schizophrenia. I don't know what your defense is going to be now."

After I convinced the security guard that I would sue anyone outside of a proctologist for examining me for polyps, and seeing how I had good, full insurance, why didn't they merely take X-rays and/or an MRI?—I called Leland Dees collect. "I have reason to believe that your brother tried to kill me, then went downstairs to steal a large amount of silver coins plucked from the inner organs of small children originally."

My boss said, "So they're giving you the good stuff, huh? They're giving you the morphine. Maybe I should get me one of those appendiciti."

In the background I heard the thrum and roar of an open furnace. "He took the keys to the van, and I'd be willing to bet we'll never see it again. I'm serious, Mr. Dees. I have reason to believe that your brother—and you called him 'wayward' yourself—shoved me inside Evelyn's closet, then went downstairs to the museum they got here in the hospital, and stole a bunch of silver. The guard thinks he might've taken some sharpened sticks from the Civil War, too."

My boss might've said something about how it was time for me to take an extended vacation. He might've said that I should consider a career change. I didn't listen. Evelyn walked in. I hung up.

"A long time ago you and I went out only because God might be watching me, I thought," Evelyn said. "And I'll be the first person to admit how maybe I led boys on back then.

There's only one way to explain how we ended up all the way out here. God. You know, the words *God* and *Good* aren't so close for no reason. There's a reason why *God* and *Good* are almost spelled the same with just an *o* in between. It's not my idea, though. I read it in Dear Abby back when I took a religion course in college. Our professor had us read Dear Abby and grade her decisions."

I said, "I'm a good person, I promise."

Evelyn shuffled farther into my room and sat down on the edge of my bed. She wore a veil of gauze still wrapped around her scalp. I turned the television channel from the sad, sad news to one of those situation comedies that involved diverse teenage characters living under the same roof. An actress held her hands to her face and drawled out in a fake southern accent, "Please tell me you didn't *drink* with him," like an idiot, to another actress who must've been twenty-five but played a sophomore in high school. Evelyn said, "I'm beginning to think that my sister and her husband, and my niece and nephew, don't really care about me. How long have I been here? I might need to go back to Mississippi. At least Daddy's catfish will surface up and look at me."

I tried not to think of my father facedown dead in that same pond while catfish aired their whiskers. No, I only lifted my right hand and stroked Evelyn's shaved head. "I always thought I'd be a public defender," I said. "I thought I'd work for the Department of Social Services, or run a United Way, or get a permanent position with the Red Cross. I meant to do something that helped people. I didn't."

Evelyn said, "It might be malignant. Don't touch my head." She leaned down and hugged my neck. "Does this hurt?"

I scooted over. It hurt like hell. "No, not a bit," I said. "Crawl under these covers."

Evelyn got off the bed. "Maybe you were meant to be a preacher. Maybe you were destined for politics. No—a *psychologist*."

My surgeon came in the room for the first time. He said, "Mr. Hinson, how're you feeling?"

I said, "I'm sore, but fine. I'm alive. I don't feel up to robbing banks or anything, but I'm fine."

The doctor nodded to Evelyn. He said, "Do y'all know each other?"

I wanted to go into vivid detail about karma and fate, long-lost love, catfish farms, and pity dates. I said, "We haven't seen each other in fifteen years. We're from the same town all the way over in Mississippi."

Dr. Stevenson hit the nurse call button. I figured he only wanted to order me up more painkiller or a blood pressure test, maybe my temperature. He said to Evelyn, "You put quite a scare into us yesterday. I talked to Dr. Amick a little while ago. He thinks you'll be ready to go back down to your regular room later this afternoon." To me, Dr. Stevenson said, "Have they had you up and walking around yet?"

I said, "Hey, hold on. What's he talking about, Evelyn?" Like I didn't know, what with my luck.

Evelyn slid her feet across the floor. She held a finger to her lips, then pointed at her head. She took her other hand, shaped it like a pistol, and pretend-shot me. "All men," she said. "Every man on the planet."

When Evelyn left the room Dr. Stevenson said, "You might want to run, son. To heck with walking. You might need to run for your life." He looked at my incision, smiled, and left.

I didn't need to ask any hospital employee if my old friend Evelyn resided on the third floor. I didn't ask anyone about possible self-inflicted gunshot wounds or how long the waiting list stood for people destined for the state asylum. Already I foresaw my leaving the hospital alone, maybe taking a taxi over to Gruel, looking up my boss's misguided brother, and stealing back my empty van. I would return it to the company. Then, scarred and not fully healed ever, I would move on, probably to my place of early training, in order to ask questions and recover what history I'd somehow missed.

Slow Drink

It started off with a simple need to deposit some money, not even a paycheck but a one-dollar rebate from Marty Mallo. I didn't ask her how much she spent on Mallo Cups in order to receive a dollar, not to mention how it cost probably a thirty-seven-cent and a twenty-three-cent stamp to mail off five hundred cardboard points. Some of the candy packages only offered up five points, some ten, the rarer ones twenty-five or fifty. If, somehow, a person were lucky enough to find a fifty-point Mallo Cup coupon ten times in a row, that would be something like ten bucks of candy, for a dollar rebate minus the sixty cents in postage. Then there's the cost of gasoline to get to the drive-through bank, and so on. But I didn't say anything. I sat in the passenger seat and pretended that she'd almost won the lottery.

"Open up the glove compartment and hand me a pen," she said. "I need to sign the check and fill out my deposit slip."

I didn't say anything about how maybe she should wait until she had a regular paycheck, or some kind of stock dividend, maybe birthday money from a great-aunt who still sent five-dollar bills inside a bad greeting card. I had a great-aunt like that. For my thirtieth birthday she sent me a coupon she'd cut out of the paper for ten dollars off toward the purchase of a hearing aid at a place called Hear Ye, Hear Ye in Youngstown, Ohio, where she lived, some thousand-whatever miles from me in South Carolina.

I didn't say, "You know, sending off an envelope full of Marty Mallo Cup points, and writing out a deposit slip for only a dollar—that's environmentally bad, seeing as you're helping kill trees for no real financial gain." To my own great-aunt, of course, I wrote a thank-you note and said that, should I ever go deaf, it wouldn't be rational to drive for two days and only save ten bucks, but thanks just the same.

Maybe my aunt thought it was a joke—like to tell me that being thirty was the beginning of the end, you know, like I gave a fuck.

Anyway, I opened the glove compartment and shuffled through a series of old quarterly paid car insurance registrations, oil change and tune-up receipts, paper-covered straws from fast-food restaurants, a box of Kleenex, cellophane-wrapped flavored toothpicks, and yellow napkins. I found some unopened mail, a photograph of what appeared to be immigrants, a Phillips head screwdriver, and a Swiss Army knife.

Then there was a roach clip, jammed right beside a giant bottle of Valium. I didn't say, "Who takes Valium anymore? Why aren't you on Prozac or Xanax or Zoloft?"

I found a push-top pen that advertised Venlafaxine HCI Effexor XR extended release capsules, and handed it to her. But I have to admit that I kept my eyes on the slightly amber

Valium vial, and noticed that the "date filled" section wasn't even a week earlier.

In a weird way this was all serendipitous, seeing as I had forgotten her name. Right there on the pill bottle below the Rx number was "Kristin Pack." I handed her the pen and said, "Hey, Kristin, if my last name were Pack and I had a child, I'd name him or her Rat. Or Back. Battery."

She scrawled her name on the back of the rebate check. She said, "What?" and lodged the plastic cylinder in the pneumatic tube. Her Ford Taurus wagon vibrated. My old Jeep remained in the shop while John and Johnny—two great mechanics—awaited a rebuilt water pump. I vowed to never listen to my friend Connie again, a coworker and boss who said that my house was on Kristin's way, et cetera, and she'd arrange my pickup on this Friday afternoon, so we could join Connie and about ten other couples at her inaugural slow-food dinner party.

The bank teller sent back a receipt and told us to have a great weekend. Kristin said, "Thanks!" told me to put the receipt in her glove compartment, and honked her horn on the way out. "A free dollar!" she said. "Another day, another dollar."

I didn't say anything about how it wasn't really a dollar, et cetera. I didn't say anything about how the most attractive human being in the world, male or female, became nothing but hideous once he or she resorted to clichés.

I opened the glove compartment and looked at the Valium again. Then I used the opportunity to rifle through what I had not spied earlier, pulled out an old Polaroid, and looked at it to find three preteen girls—one of whom was obviously Kristin—standing in what appeared to be a 1970s living room.

The three girls all wore monogrammed pullover sweaters, each adorned with the letter *K*.

This isn't a good sign, I thought. KKK. I said, "Is this a picture of you and your sisters?"

"Me and Karla and Karen," Kristin said. "They don't live here anymore. They moved up north. Karla's in Virginia, and Karen's in Kentucky."

I wanted to ask if her father kept a sheet hung up in the closet, but didn't. I knew. My mother always accused one of our neighbors of being in the Klan because, as she said, "He never would let anyone look in the trunk of his car." She thought that's where he kept his hood and robe, et cetera.

I put the picture back in Kristin's makeshift photo album, then the pen. I closed the door and said, "So, this slow-food thing Connie's having—is it supposed to last a long time, or is it, you know, like food that took hours to cook but we can eat it in a normal amount of time?"

Kristin turned onto Highway 72 and drove toward Gruel. She said, "I've known Connie a coon's age. I'm surprised me and you've never met." She pulled into the parking lot of Forty-Five Wine and Cheese, a new store that never had a car out front until nightfall seeing as none of the locals wanted anyone to know that they drank, I figured. Or ate cheese other than Kraft American slices. "We should bring a bottle of wine. Connie says she's making both fish and beef, so I guess we should bring both red and white."

I thought, This is a good idea. I thought, In a weird way it's probably good that Kristin picked me up, seeing as I hadn't read any etiquette books in a while.

I walked in behind Kristin and noticed for the first time that she might've had the same figure as any of those women who perform aerobic exercises on cable TV at dawn. Kristin might've stood five-eleven, too, which I couldn't tell when we sat scrunched up in her car at the teller window.

Again, though, none of this mattered, seeing as she unwittingly advertised the KKK in her childhood.

I'm not quite sure how I got stuck buying two bottles of wine that came to $120. Who buys wine that costs over seven bucks a bottle? Kristin had said, "Slow food deserves wine that's fermented more than a couple days."

I said, of course, "I agree a hundred percent. Indubitably," and opened the driver's door for Kristin. I got in with my double-bagged brown paper sack and said, "Do you know who else is going to be at this little dinner?"

Kristin drove out of the parking lot. "Are you Connie's boss, or is she yours? I still can't believe that we've never met. Me and Connie used to be sorority sisters down in Charleston. And then we both got jobs down there working for Merry Maids, after we graduated."

I didn't want to know any of this. What kind of bad degree only offered up opportunities as a housecleaner for time-share condominiums? And because I admired and enjoyed Connie's friendship, I didn't want to know that she once lived in a sorority house, singing stupid songs. I said, "What do you do now?"

Kristin said, "What's your name, again? I'm kind of embarrassed about this, but I can't remember your name."

We drove down 72, which had recently been turned into a four-lane for reasons unknown to anyone, seeing as people didn't go to Gruel very often, and Gruelites tended to be an uncurious, nontraveling citizenry. I said, "I can't believe that you don't know my name. Hey, if my last name were Pack I'd name my boy Ice. Ice Pack." I said, "My name's Bernard, but everyone calls me Charlie," which was true. As a child I kind of owned a big round head and large ears. "Connie probably told you that my name was Charlie."

She said, "Charlie." Kristin slowed down and took a right on Old Old Augusta Road. We passed the Gruel Inn, rounded by Gruel Mountain, and headed toward the square. Kristin said, "I'm thinking about writing a trilogy of novels. The first one will be called *Me*. The second one's *Now*. The third one will be called *Eat*. Then when they're all on a bookshelf in the library, in alphabetical order, you'll read *Eat Me Now* on the spines. What do you think about that? In the meantime I'm selling real estate. Even though everyone talks about how Graywood County's growing, I ain't sold a house or lot in something like two years."

She turned into Connie's long gravel driveway and approached the gingerbread-laden, turn-of-the-century clapboard house. Everyone else invited seemed to be there already. I counted three Volvos, four BMWs, one of those Cadillac SUVs, and a fancy Mazda.

I couldn't say anything about how Kristin hadn't sold a piece of land. Me, I taught geography at little Anders College, as did Connie. We traded off chairpersonships every other year, and this was her year. I guess after she got through with that job cleaning houses and apartments she went off and got an advanced degree, I don't know. We didn't talk about our pasts. Connie got hired on before I did. Her specialty, oddly enough, happened to be Peru, the Sudan, and northern India. She taught a course every other year called "Inca, Dinka, Urdu."

Me, I concentrated on the Native American Cherokee nation and its changes due to the casino industry. My favorite course, which none of the students cared about, either, though they should have—until ESPN started airing poker matches—was called Indian Poker. Luckily no one in Forty-Five, South Carolina, or its environs knew about political correctness, because Native American Poker wouldn't have the same draw, so to speak.

"Give me one of those bottles so it looks like I didn't forget to bring a gift," Kristin said. She held out her hand. I gave her the Chianti. She stood up on her toes and hovered above me by a good six inches. I thought to myself, Remember the KKK photograph. I thought, Whatever you do, don't fall for this woman even though you haven't found a relationship since moving to South Carolina.

We walked to the door and Kristin said, "Well, here we are. I need to make it clear that you'll need to get a ride home with someone else if I should meet a man or woman with whom I want to sleep."

Kristin rang Connie's doorbell. I thought nothing else but Damn, that was pretty good grammar. I thought, Could I have misjudged this woman? and wondered, also, if maybe I should pop the proverbial brakes a couple times in regards to her mother and father's name—and sartorial photographic attire. I said, "I understand. Yes. Maybe I'll meet someone, too. I hope not everyone here's married."

I didn't believe myself, though, for I saw the cars, knew about the guest list, and so on. There would be Connie, ten married couples I didn't know, Kristin, and me. Connie'd already told me that she didn't invite anyone from Anders College, which was okay by me seeing as I didn't want to spend an evening talking about rainfall, the difference between Porter and Sherwin-Williams house paints, the benefits of milk thistle and vitamin B for human livers, why corduroy sports coats should come back in fashion, mold, why the government knows how to keep milk from spoiling but won't let on, the history of billed ball caps, how the founding people of America spoke with English accents, bagpipes, allergies to old books, the wonders of Faulkner, and dry rot. But what did these people want to talk about? Me, I could only talk about casino gambling on the Cherokee reservation, or maybe how scared I was to find three children dressed in KKK paraphernalia.

Slow food, I thought. Kristin rang the doorbell again, then turned the doorknob and let herself in. I scuffed my shoes a couple times on the off-brown, hard-bristled welcome mat, then followed her inside going, "Hey, hey, hey," holding a bottle of expensive white wine like a pussy, to people I didn't know waiting for their fucking simmered food.

Connie came up first and said, "Y'all need to walk softly. I'm baking some almond-encrusted Mediterranean sole in a butter-and-rosemary compost for the first entrée. I don't want the fish to fall. Come on in and meet everyone." I think that's what she said. I hate to say it, but I was transfixed on Kristin's butt in front of me. I thought, What blue jean company hasn't discovered her yet, sweet-toothed child of KKK member or not? I thought, I don't think *compost* is the right word.

I looked at the clock in the dining room and saw that it was only 5:20. Connie had told me we would begin eating around six, and the last dessert wouldn't be served until nearly eleven. She had it all planned out. I said, "I probably need to open this red wine and let it breathe," and found Connie's corkscrew in the kitchen.

She followed me in and whispered, "So what do you think of Kristin?" all smiles.

I said what I could only say, namely, "You were in a sorority? Good God, woman, were you out of your mind in college, or what?"

"Kristin's always been hot. I guess she told you about how we were Merry Maids, too. You should've seen her in the outfit. She looked like one of those French maids in the movies."

I opened the bottle and put its cork on top of the refrigerator. In the den I heard a man tell a story about how he needed a new real estate agent—that he'd cashed in all of his stocks and planned to buy nothing but "land, land, land." He said, "Graywood County's growing. It's a good place to raise children." For a split second I had a vision of fifty kids grazing in a field, but then kind of got stuck imagining Connie and Kristin in their French maid outfits, bending over to dust the legs of an ottoman.

Connie looked through her oven window. I said, "I need some bourbon before this all gets started."

"On the table in there," she said, pointing backward.

I went to join the party, introduced myself, and tried to remember names: Victor, Jeff, Paula, Bekah, Maura-Lee, Barry, Larry, Nellie, Sammy. Half of the people only nodded, smiled, and didn't say their own name, which I thought was kind of rude but made it easier. "Slow food," one of the women said, "is taking over the nation, you know. Everyone's tired of fast-food joints. I'm glad we can just relax like this every couple weeks or so."

Let me make it clear that there were no fast-food restaurants in Gruel. I'd been here a few times to see Connie, and we always wandered over to Roughhouse Billiards, a place that prided itself on hot dogs, which I guess counted as fast food. Thirty minutes away, Forty-Five had a Hardee's, but the Mc-Donald's and Krystal closed down within a year back in the late 1990s, partly because they didn't offer up plastic drink cups with stock-car racers emblazoned on the sides, I always believed.

Kristin said to me loudly, "Charlie's real name is Bernard. Let's play a game wherein everyone chooses an alias. I'll start. From now on out I want y'all to call me Odile."

I went to the table and poured four fingers of Knob Creek, no ice. I thought about setting my glass on the table for everyone else to share, then carrying the bottle around with me. I said, "I have a hard enough time remembering people's real names. And I failed recess in third grade 'cause I told the teacher I don't play."

"Booooooo! Booooooo!" Kristin yelled at me. She pointed. Everyone looked my way.

"Y'all hold it down in there. I'm afraid this sole's going to fall," my colleague said from the kitchen. I didn't ask anyone if the sole had been stuffed with yeast.

Victor wore regular knit pants, but a camouflaged T-shirt. "Y'all can call me Rommel."

Uh-oh, I thought. If Odile and Rommel get together there might be a lynching before the night's over. Jeff stood up and said, "I need a smoke. Do you smoke, Charlie? Come on out on the porch and have a cigarette with me."

I had quit some ten years earlier. I said, "Yes."

Outside, Jeff said, "Is Odile your wife, man? How long y'all been married?"

I took a cigarette from his pack—an unfiltered *Picayune*, of all things, which I don't think had been made in two decades— and lit up. "I just met her today. She eats a lot of Mallo Cups, saves the points, and sends them off for rebate checks. That's about all I know about her. She supposedly sells real estate. There's a picture of her in the car with two sisters named

Karla and Karen, and they're all wearing monogrammed sweaters so it reads *KKK* in a row. That's it. No, I'm not married to her."

Jeff squinted and blew out smoke that he had held in as if lighting up a joint. "I'll be damned." He inhaled once more, then dropped the cigarette on the ground, stepped on it, and went back inside without as much saying good-bye to me. I stood alone, like an idiot. It would've been a good time to break into some houses, I thought, seeing as the entire town seemed to be at Connie's house.

I took about eight more drags, coughed, remembered why I quit, and went back inside. Kristin stood up in the middle of everyone and tugged on her ear. Fucking charades.

After the sole we ate a dish called "Duck and Cover," a mostly southwestern dish with habaneros, sage, and paprika, all slathered with orange marmalade. Then Connie brought out a sourdough bread–covered pork shoulder she called "Pig in a Comforter." It was beautiful, I'll admit. We all sat on the floor, or in chairs, plates balanced on our thighs. Each entrée came with two tablespoons of a vegetable: wild rice, glazed baby carrots, yams and such. At ten o'clock she served up a leg of lamb. "I got this recipe in a cookbook called *Slaughterhouse Eight*. It's all about cooking cow, pig, lamb, turtle, fish, buffalo, turkey, and deer. I bought it last year when I had that fellowship to go to India. It kind of surprised me that they'd have cow in there."

We drank and drank, and no one cottoned to the "red wine with meat" rule. I sat between Kristin and Connie, and more than once felt it necessary to keep a leg glued to one of theirs. Nobody talked about politics or religion or baseball. The Maura-Lee woman across from me talked nonstop about her new yoga class taught by honest-to-goodness gurus. The Bekah woman told someone that she'd not heard from her ex-husband, a guy named Novel, in more than four years, and that she checked Amazon.com every day to see if he ever published his memoir. Kristin thought it necessary to tell everyone about her trilogy, *Eat*, *Me*, and *Now*. Either Barry or Larry—they looked alike and I assumed that they were brothers, if not twins—said, "I've always thought about writing a book. It'll be a picture book of pool trick shots."

Connie tilted her head for me to follow her back in the kitchen. I got up pretending to need ice. She said, "It's a mousse, pretty much," quieter than a cockroach pissing on cotton.

I said, "What?"

"I've made a mousse for the dessert. But that's not what I brought you back here for. For which I brought you back." Her eyes went funny, kind of cockeyed, then crossed. I was reminded of that old Pong video game, and started thinking about if it was the very first video game ever. Connie's eyes sliced back and forth like windshield wipers. I didn't think it was the lamb causing all of this.

"Okay," I said. "Mousse would be good. If it's not too rich. I've never been much of a dessert person, you know. Booze gives me the sugar."

"These people are going to leave right after dessert, I'm hoping," Connie said. She bent her head forward and swayed in a way that suggested she might wish to break the traditional and unspoken colleague-on-colleague rule of interoffice romance.

I said, "Go in there and tell everyone that the dessert didn't come out right. We've had enough to eat anyway. Hey, do you have any toothpicks?" I thought about how I couldn't undergo another slow-food session for at least another year, what with my distended stomach and horrendous guilt for eating more food over a five-hour period than most pottery-making Native Americans on the Pueblo reservation in Taos might eat in a week.

And then I kissed Connie hard. Not that I'm any kind of Romeo, but I felt her knees slip, which made me hold her up harder. In the den I heard Kristin say too loudly, "I'm so *wasted*," which she probably said about every Wednesday through Saturday in the sorority house.

I took my face off of Connie and yelled out, "The dessert didn't come out right. We all have to go home now," which caused my boss to grab my rib cage and tickle me hard. She laughed and kind of slurred out, "The Sudanese have a word for what you just did, Charlie. I forget it right now, but it has to do with getting guests to leave when the hosts have something important to do. Like milk the cow. Or build a fence."

I heard Victor say, "You shouldn't drive. Hey, I got a spare bedroom."

I looked at Connie and noticed that she'd unbuttoned her blouse a couple notches somewhere along the line, right down to the clasp of her brassiere. I said to her, "I feel like I'm undergoing a propaedeutic experiment. This is a trick you're playing on me."

Connie said, "What?"

I'd been reading the dictionary. There wasn't much else to do in Forty-Five, or Gruel, or all of Graywood County. Or South Carolina. I said, "Let's you and me just lay or lie down in bed until the morning," because it had worked for me one time when I met this woman in France while doing a North Carolina State geography department–sponsored semester abroad called European on the Land. My buddy Dan Murray and I took it half seriously, and tried to piss about everywhere publicly, though more often than not we found ourselves riverside. In between we met French women and told lies about our upbringings in the United States, both of us saying that we were children from ghettos seeing as no real French woman cared about men born to wealth or power.

Kristin screamed out, "I forget who I am. Am I Odile? Is that the name I chose for myself? I forget. Wait, I want to be Marilyn from now on out. But not like Marilyn Monroe. I want to be a different Marilyn. I want to be a Marilyn all my own. None of you people ever played along and changed your names."

I thought, I'm Marty Mallo.

I think either Barry or Larry said, "Call me Bubba. I'm pretty sure I chose Bubba."

I released myself from Connie and tried to subdue any erection that might have emanated—another dictionary word—then went into the den. "Connie says it's time to go. Y'all have to go. Slow food or not, it's not called 'slow leaving.'"

Kristin said, "How're you getting home? What if I decide not to leave? Then how're you getting home? You have to get home, right?"

People filed out, offering thanks to Connie, who had emerged from the kitchen apologizing about the ruined final dish. She said, "The next one of these things we have, I'll be responsible for the dessert, I promise. I'll go on record right now as saying I'm responsible for the next dessert. If Charlie has it next . . . Charlie, I got the dessert."

I thought two things and two things only: First off, I would not be participating in another one of these goddamn slow-food extravaganzas. Life was too short to spend six hours on a meal. And, of course, I thought *three-way* between Connie, me, and either Kristin, Odile, or Marilyn.

"Good night," everyone said. Victor, again, offered Kristin his spare bedroom, but she said that she wanted to drink a cup of coffee and sober up a little before taking me home.

When Connie closed the door she said, "That was a close one," for reasons I didn't understand.

Kristin said, "Not one of them sons of bitches will ever buy real estate. Oh they'll talk a big game, but—no offense to your Gruel friends, Connie—they're the kind of people who play it safe. They'll put all their money in a savings account getting point naught one interest."

If this were a movie scene Kristin would've pulled a condom out of her pocketbook right when she said, "Play it safe." Hollywood, evidently, hadn't come to Gruel. I said, "I don't know why anyone would want to buy land around here, unless they planned on living about another hundred years. Investing in wasteland doesn't seem all that smart a thing to do."

Connie stood behind Kristin. She put her finger to her lips for me to shut up, and unnotched the next button on her blouse. She backed toward the bedroom. Kristin said, "What we need around here is a myth. We need a big mass murder. There for a while the girl named Bekah who was here, she had a husband named Novel who was supposed to bring this place a claim to fame. But he disappeared before making any kind of mark, you know. He ended up being a fake novelist, I guess you could say."

I listened to Kristin, but peripherally watched Connie backing toward the threshold of her bedroom. I said, "Crop circles. Aliens landing. A Civil War reenactment. I can think of a bunch of things y'all could do. Nudist colony."

And then, for some reason, I kissed Kristin on the forehead, took her hand, and tried to pull her in the general direction of Connie's bed. She said, rightly, "What're you doing? I know you teach geography and all, but this road map ain't going to work."

Connie said, "Oh come on, Odile. You weren't this way before." She said, "Are you having a sugar low? Go into the kitchen and get a Mallo Cup out of the pantry."

Connie went into her bedroom and came back out wearing a sweatshirt over her blouse. Kristin sat on the couch, watching CNN, eating a Mallo Cup that only offered up five points in play money. The president said that we lived in a dangerous world, and that, as a Christian, he understood that no one else deserved to have weapons of mass destruction besides America. Connie said, "A real gentleman would offer to do the dishes."

I unscrewed the bourbon's cap and poured two jiggers' worth into an unused wineglass, stared at it for a minute, then poured it back in the bottle. Connie sat down on the couch next to Kristin and said, "Do you remember that time we were having to clean up all those time-shares at Seabrook Estates? This would've been in about March, right before the tourists came in."

Kristin said, "I need to go find a palm reader and see if I'm ever going to sell another piece of land. This is ridiculous. There has to be some kind of career line on your palm."

Connie looked at me. "This wasn't a giant place. As a matter of fact it used to be just a regular-sized apartment building, but as the old people died off, the owners transformed the place into condos, kind of. Anyway, Kristin and I went in there with all our cleaning supplies and a list of which rooms needed what. We had a passkey, you know."

I poured two more jiggers in the glass and watched it. I thought, There's no way any kind of sexual entanglement's going to take place here. I thought, What am I doing teaching geography to a bunch of undergraduates who mostly hailed from Graywood County and would never leave the area?

Kristin kept her eyes on the television. She said, "I thought about having that key copied. There was a man for a while down at the Slave Market market who made keys."

Connie punched Kristin with a throw pillow and said, "Listen to me. Do you remember?" She looked at me and said, "We'd done about three apartments—most of this was only vacuuming, and spraying down the bathrooms with mold and mildew remover—and then we went up to the top floor. I think this was a four-story apartment. Anyway, Kristin opened the door and a man sat in the den, behind a rolltop desk. He wore a suit, too."

Kristin said, "I hadn't thought about that in years. We jumped, and I think you yelled, Connie."

"I yelled like crazy."

"At first we thought we'd gone into the wrong apartment, but our boss had made it clear that no one rented out in February, and that was the month when they brought in repairmen and painters, and us," Kristin said.

I poured the bourbon back in the bottle. I thought, I have wasted my entire life up to this point. I'll never make more than thirty or forty grand a year, I'll never fall in love with a woman in Graywood County, I'll never have kids who'll grow up to hate the world as much as I. On the news, the president joked about his days in college and kept talking about "turning the corner." I thought, There is no real justice, and tried to think about what Cherokee Chief Skyuka said right before he secretly gave up his people's land and secrets to the U.S. government in order to escape death.

I poured bourbon back out.

Connie said, "Kristin asked what he was doing there. We couldn't see his torso what with the rolltop desk. At the time I thought he wrote something meaningful, you know, like he was handwriting a novel."

"Later on we figured it was a suicide note. Somewhere in between we figured that he somehow got in his family's time-share, and he wanted to hang himself or something so that when they got there during the peak season they'd find him all dead and whatnot, and ruin their vacation." Kristin got up from the couch, took all the silverware off of the plates in the den, and set them up on what used to be the sole platter. "It would make a good movie scene."

I tried to think back if I'd thought about prospective movie scenes over the day. It's what I did, always. Sometimes when I saw poor men on the side of the road collecting aluminum cans, wearing VOTE FOR BUSH T-shirts, I thought about movie scenes and irony.

"But he didn't seem to want to kill himself," Connie said. "He stood up and bowed, of all things, then walked right past us. Kristin and I walked over behind the desk to see what he was doing, but you know what was there?"

I said, "What?" I took my wineglass and poured two ounces of bourbon back in its bottle. "A battlefield map of how the South should've acted once Sherman went to town. Went to *towns*."

Connie said, "No."

"That would've been worth some money," Kristin said. She picked up the channel changer and pointed it at the television, but didn't mash a button. The president mispronounced two words in one sentence.

"He'd been etching a recipe in the wood. He printed out 'Shrimp, sausage, rice, okra, corn, bay leaves.'"

I said, "Frogmore stew. That's good stuff. It takes a long time to make." I poured out about three jiggers, some of it by accident. "Who was he?"

Connie took her sweatshirt off. Kristin looked at her funny, and for a second I thought she'd take off her clothes, or at least grab me by the neck and kiss me as if I were a Mallo Cup with a fifty-point cardboard prize. Kristin said, "Who was he?"

"Somebody's unhappy grandfather. Somebody's unhappy and neglected grandfather. I never told you this, Kristin, but afterwards I went down to the Francis Marion Hotel bar and saw the same guy, just sitting there by himself. I think he was drinking brandy. That's what it looked like. One of those drinks in a big old goblet."

"It was weird," Kristin said. "He had all his hair. He had this great white hair that stood straight up. He could've dyed it and looked like a real punk."

"I wanted to go up and talk to him, you know, but I was waiting for some people. Why weren't you there?" Connie said to Kristin. "I guess you had a date with that boy from the Citadel. Anyway, I sat there, and waited. He drank and drank and drank, but not like a drunk. More like he *reduced* that brandy."

I slugged down my bourbon. For some reason I felt like I had been tricked throughout the entire evening.

Kristin shoved off her shoes. "I couldn't tell if he was a college professor or a CIA agent. He kind of looked like both."

"Anyway, he was something," my boss Connie said. "He was amazing. You should've seen him. Right before I left the hotel bar and walked up to him and said, 'You seem to be the kind of man who works on making people afraid over a long period of time. Do you know that?' And he said to me, 'I've seen some things I'm not proud of seeing. I worked down in

Nicaragua during the Reagan administration.' That's what he said! Then he turned around before I could say how part of me wanted to—later on in life, after I finished being a maid—teach Incan culture. He walked off before I could say any of that. He wore a nice gray wool suit."

Kristin said, "Yeah. Yeah," in a tone of voice that suggested that all men in power did those sorts of things—they walked off before people could explain their lifelong dreams.

Me, I picked up the bottle of bourbon and went outside. I said, "I'm going out to smoke." But I didn't, of course, seeing as I'd quit and didn't have another person around to hand me a Picayune. I walked out, and looked at the slight streetlights of Gruel. There were no sounds outside of crickets, tree frogs, or the occasional barking dog.

Inside the house I heard Connie and Kristin stomp up and down playing patty-cake or whatever. I thought, I need to save additional points for valuable prizes or send for a prize catalog. Then I looked back to the house, knew that there was no taxi service outside of Gruel, and started walking south out of town, slowly.

What Attracts
Us to Gruel

EACH DIVORCED PARENT with child in tow claims that Gruel BBQ stands at the midway point of their new lives. Any psychologist, though, might factor embarrassment into the equation, and point out that Gruel BBQ—with its slight pig-petting zoo/slaughterhouse off to the side—could only traumatize children more so. Parents would counter that no McDonald's, Chuck E. Cheeses, or city parks exist within fifty miles of Gruel, South Carolina. Parents might contend that psychologists were the downfall of the original marriages in the first place. Any worthwhile documentarian would agree with the parents and nod behind his or her camera, then cut to three-year-old boys and girls kissing the snouts of piglets, of hogs lured into tin-roofed, cement-floored buildings, of ex-spouses saying, "Now don't be late on Sunday like last time. I don't want to miss Darlington," or Talladega or Rockingham or Daytona.

Jerry McCrary is the only father here with custody of his son. On a normal Friday afternoon, up to thirty different women drive into the gravel parking lot of Gruel BBQ with their kids, and wait for ex-husbands who possess weekend/holiday/summer privileges. On Sundays all of those men and Jerry's ex-wife Terry wait around to relinquish custody of their children. The slight town of Gruel indeed stands about halfway between Greenville and Augusta, Columbia and Atlanta, Asheville and Savannah. It's halfway between New York City and Miami, should any two parents need to make that drive.

"Does your ex have a drug problem?" one of the divorcées usually asks Jerry, waiting on late Friday afternoons. "Normally a child needs to be with its mother, if you ask me. That's what almost every judge in the country thinks, too. Hell, I could be hooked on about everything outside of heroin and still deserve to have custody of my little girl. Does your ex have a prison record or something?"

Jerry diverts his focus to the petting zoo portion of Gruel BBQ, shades his eyes, yells out to his Henry, "Don't get too close to that piggy, son." He's smart enough to mean it both ways—not to get nipped and not to get emotionally attached. To the women he says, "My ex-wife's a good mother. I don't know."

Henry always yells back, "Where's the one I liked last week? I want to pet the one from last week. Daddy, you remember that one from last week? He had freckles."

Smoke emits from an added-on back room stovepipe of the restaurant, a clapboard building with picnic tables and three varieties of chopped barbecue, two of sauce, one of coleslaw. Regular customers drive up, brown bagging.

On Fridays the fathers arrive, and for the most part the children transfer from nearly new Japanese cars to pickup trucks. Most of the kids run toward their daddies, open-armed, and the fathers flick half-smoked cigarettes into the parking lot before lifting their children high into the air. On Sundays the children walk back to their mothers, get a pat on the head, and ready themselves for a week of sensible rules.

Jerry notices all of this. Any documentarian would.

"Where you coming from all these times?" Wanda Styles says to Jerry one autumn day. The piglets chase fallen leaves in their sty. Good children throw more leaves in; taciturn kids find rocks.

"I come from Atlanta. My boy and I live in Atlanta." Jerry points toward Henry, who's staring at the stovepipe.

"Where's your wife living? I mean your ex-wife."

"She lives in a town a little east of Charlotte. She got a job up there after our divorce."

When Wanda Styles turned thirty she went and got a tribal tattoo around her ankle. She makes a point to wear shorts or leggings, the occasional dress. "I guess I've been noticing you for a year coming out here. Rhyme! Ha-ha."

"It's been about a year."

"You're the only man with custody, I guess."

"I guess," Jerry says. He thinks about how his name rhymes, how this might be something to bring up. Wanda sports a hairstyle that isn't twenty years out of style. She doesn't wear a mouthpiece of teeth whitener in public. "Be careful over there, Henry," he calls out, even though Henry still stares at the stovepipe.

Wanda sticks her right hand out and introduces herself. "I live in Athens, and my ex-husband lives in Columbia. He's the one who doesn't drive a pickup truck. My ex always says he's a little uncomfortable with everyone waiting around. He feels like he doesn't belong. Last week I told him to think about how *you* must feel."

Jerry shakes her hand and says, "My name's Jerry Mc-Crary. It rhymes."

Wanda points to a first grader doing cartwheels near Henry. "That's my Flannery. She's named after Flannery O'Connor, who was this great southern writer who died too early."

Jerry unfolds, then refolds his arms. He says, "I know Flannery O'Connor." He's amazed that anyone in the parking lot would know the writer. "I'll be damned. My boy Henry's named after O. Henry. I mean, I know that O. Henry wasn't the writer's real name. That's how much I know. But it's better. It's better that I named my son what I named my son."

Wanda stretches her back. She wears a loose-weaved blue-gray sweater. "I'm betting that we're the only literati here in Gruel."

Jerry looks at the horizon. He thinks, When's the last time I heard a person use the term *literati*? He says, "Flannery."

"I confess to teaching college English," Wanda says. "My ex-husband used to, too. Now he doesn't. That's that. What do you do that's so great you get custody?"

Jerry McCrary sticks his hands in his pocket. He looks over to find his ex-wife entering Gruel BBQ's parking lot. "Henry, here's your mother!" he yells out. "Get your bag out of the car."

Henry stops staring at the stovepipe. He says, "I forgot to bring my book."

"Your mother will buy you a book, I bet."

Jerry walks in the direction of Terry's car, then leans down into her open window. He retrieves his wallet, hands her a twenty, and says, "Take him to that Borders, or there's a Little Professor closer to where you live. He forgot his book."

Terry says, "Don't think I don't have books for Henry at home."

Henry gets in the car, and Terry leaves without saying good-bye.

Jerry walks back to Wanda. He says, "I make documentaries."

Wanda's ex-husband takes Flannery away soon after Terry takes Henry back to North Carolina. The cars and trucks streaming into Gruel BBQ now come only for food, not children of divorce. Jerry and Wanda both have found ways to stick around: Jerry pretends to check his oil, a fan belt, his windshield wiper fluid. Wanda fiddles with her sunroof. They finally emerge from their cars, parked three spots apart. Jerry says, "So, you teach at the University of Georgia?"

"I wish. No. I *went* there, but I teach at the community college. I teach football players who couldn't get in to the university because of their scores."

Jerry says, "Huh."

"What kinds of documentaries do you make?" Wanda scratches her left ankle with her right big toe.

Jerry says, "How long have you had that tattoo? I got a tattoo once. It's a chameleon." He pulls up his shirtsleeve to show nothing but bare skin. "Damn, it must've camouflaged itself again."

Wanda says, "I'm not exactly a vegetarian, but I can't eat a pig I might've pet. There's a great little pool hall in downtown Gruel called Roughhouse Billiards. You want to go over there for a beer or something before driving back?"

Jerry thinks about meeting Terry for the first time, in Atlanta. She had helped him gain access to Ted Turner's list of employees, from lawn maintenance man to manicurist to mechanic. Jerry wanted to film a documentary on the men and women behind Turner called *Behind Every Successful Man There's a Debtor*. It won a prize at the Gulf Coast Film Festival. Terry came to Jerry's rented office in Buckhead one morning, then they drank beer at a Virginia Highlands joint from lunch onward. Terry had graduated the year before with a degree in communications. She wanted to work for the networks eventually, unless it meant doing weather. She had a friend who was developing the Obituary Channel for cable, and she wanted to sit in a chair and read aloud everyone's funeral plans for the upcoming week.

She said she didn't have time to ever have children.

Jerry says, "I'm starving," to Wanda. She reaches down and unsmudges the ashy spot on her tattoo where she's been scratching. Her breasts hang out like two filled pastry bags. Jerry says, "I'll follow you over there," and tries to remember the rules of eight ball.

"You're not some kind of mass murderer or anything, right?" Wanda says. She doesn't smile. "What kinds of documentaries have you ever made? You don't spend all your time in prisons talking to mass murderers, do you?"

Jerry shakes his head. "I've made three that have been shown on the Weather Channel. One about Hurricane Hugo's effects on the lowcountry of South Carolina, and one about a tornado that hit Commerce, Georgia. Another one's about drought in the southeast, but it's pretty dry. Get it?"

Wanda says, "My ex-husband is obsessed with mass murderers, that's why I ask. Back when he taught college, he'd find a way to stick *In Cold Blood* into the syllabus. When I said I wanted to name our daughter Flannery, the only reason he agreed was because of that Misfit character in her story."

Two men get out of a blue Ford short bed and yell over,

"Is today the two-for-one day?" Jerry shrugs his shoulders. He says to Wanda, "I did a documentary one time where I asked people on the street to tell me everything they knew about Henry Kissinger, but that's as close as it comes. Oh. And I did this other one about men and women who kind of worked as character actors."

They play two games of pool. Jerry wins both games only because Wanda scratches on the eight ball. They order hot dogs. Jeff, the owner of Roughhouse Billiards, says each time, "I'm Jeff, the owner. How do y'all want those? I'm Jeff, the owner."

"Mustard, ketchup, and relish for her, mustard and onions for me. No chili," Jerry says.

"Y'all don't want no buns?" says Jeff.

"You should do a documentary on this place," Wanda says. "I didn't see any camcorders or anything in the backseat of your car. I'm surprised you don't carry one around with you at all times."

Jerry racks the balls for a third game. He plans on missing as many shots as possible only to watch Wanda bend down and show off her boobs.

"Y'all ain't from around here, are you?" Jeff the owner asks. "Let me guess: Y'all are some them people come up to Gruel BBQ to let off kids. I know. I can tell. Two, three year ago the same thing happened—people hooking up, only thing they got in common is one bad marriage and a Rand McNally. They married now together—living over on Old Old Greenville Road."

"Jerry, if you're a filmmaker, why don't you wear clothes that are a little more artsy?" Wanda says right before banking the one ball in the side pocket. "I thought all filmmakers wore paisley shirts with big collars, you know." She's drinking Pabst Blue Ribbon from longneck bottles, which Jerry admires.

"I wear blue jeans. So what? I'm not interested in the camera turning toward me, Wanda."

She says, "What is it, exactly, that your wife does now? And tell me again why you got custody of Henry." Wanda bends down and shoots the six ball into a corner pocket.

"She's the PR director of a big zoo. That's true. She didn't get custody, because she doesn't like children. That's that, plain and simple."

"It can't be only that. I don't want to contradict you or anything, Jerry, but it has to be something more than that." Wanda circles the table. She looks over at the jukebox and frowns when a Merle Haggard song comes on. "It has to be more than that." She shoots at the three and misses. It careens around the table, then knocks in the eight ball. "Goddamn. I'm too drunk to play anymore." She throws her stick onto the table and opens her arms wide. "Whoooo. I might just lay out here until Sunday when I have to pick Flannery up again."

Jerry looks at the owner of Roughhouse. Jeff shakes his head sideways. There is no motel nearby.

Wanda says, "I don't know how your bladder can handle all of this. I got to take myself a pee."

Jerry bends his face down, and in a lowered voice says to the owner, "There's not a motel or hotel nearby?"

"The best thing you can do is pretend to be married. Old Paula Purgason runs a so-called real estate office, and she'll let prospective buyers stay in one of her houses for sale. I can call her up if you want, and then she'll come over here and take you to one of the antebellum places she has. Oh, they're furnished and everything. People died off in Gruel and left their estates to loved ones, but loved ones don't seem to care about either moving back here or selling off what they now own. You can get a good two-story Victorian for ten grand, I swear to God. Furniture and all included."

Jerry slides a ten-dollar bill across the marble-top bar. He says, "Give her a call when you get the chance."

Wanda looks through her purse in the one-toilet stall. She looks for a prophylactic, her old diaphragm, a sponge, anything. She looks for a dental dam, in case Jerry's of that persuasion. She doesn't think of Flannery, or Henry, her students, or ex-husband. Wanda flushes the toilet and checks her teeth in the mirror for hot dog remnants.

"I have a student in my English 101 class who thinks he wants to make movies. He's older than I, something like forty years old, and used to play in one of those Athens bands that didn't make it as big as REM or the B-52s. I believe he said his band was called the Jungsters. Anyway, he wants to follow bands around and film what they do first thing in the morning."

Jerry looks at the restroom door. He holds the cue stick's handle against his toe. "It takes some luck, more than anything, to become a filmmaker. You got to find people who'll invest money. They have to be stupid enough to only want to break even, or maybe make a dollar over a two-year period. Say, would you like to do some shots of bourbon or tequila or rum or schnapps, or all of the above?"

"You're trying to get me drunk," Wanda says, coming out of the restroom. "You're trying to get me all fucked-up so I can't leave Gruel. There's no hotel in this town, you know. We'd have to sleep in our cars."

Jerry looks at Jeff the owner, who stares at a ten-gallon pickle jar. The television's turned to a documentary on Hollywood's fallen women. Jerry says to Wanda, "You have beautiful legs." He wants to know exactly what would be the best thing to say. "You have legs that could be used for two sides of a sturdy kiosk."

More men walk into Roughhouse Billiards. They nod at the owner, order Budweiser, and head toward the other tables. They look at Wanda and know that she's an outsider. "Climpson'll beat shit outta Florida State," they say. "Climpson gotta defense kill them boys." They wear orange. They say things about what life was like when they went to Clemson: frat parties that drifted to Tigertown Tavern or Nick's, the Esso Club or Sloan Street Bar.

Wanda says, "I don't want to sound easy, but I think I can't drive back to Athens tonight. There's got to be a motel in this area."

Jerry racks more balls. "If you don't mind," he says. "If you don't mind, this woman is going to show up. We only have to pretend like we're married. We have to pretend like we want to buy one of her houses. And then we can stay there." Jerry points to the owner. "He promises."

Wanda says, "This is some kind of joke."

"No. Nuh-uh. It's not a joke. Believe me when I say that I'm honest, more than anything else. It's the truth." Jerry doesn't mention how he wants to make a documentary on headwaiters working fancy restaurants located inside airport restaurants. He fails to bring up his latest project: a six-part made-for-A&E documentary that concerns southern primitive artists who claim that God tells them secrets.

Paula Purgason, amateur real estate agent, walks into Roughhouse Billiards wearing a muumuu, a headband, bare feet. She says, "Who's it wants to buy 103 Old Old Greenville?" The owner points at Jerry. "This your wife? You think you can handle Gruel, honey? I care, I really do. It's tough living here unless you hiding out from something. Or someone. And if you planning on selling houses and land, forget it."

Wanda places her cue stick on the table and takes two steps in Paula Purgason's direction. She says, "What?"

Jerry sticks out his hand and takes a set of keys from Paula. "Yeah. Well, we're just normal people looking for a place to get away from the big city, you know. We can't take the traffic anymore. We can't take the tension."

"Well we ain't got no racial problems here if that's what you mean. Everybody gets along fine. Look at them boys there." Paula points at the other pool table. Both men stare down, as if mesmerized by the arrangement of balls.

Wanda shifts her weight from one foot to the other twice. She says, "What?"

"Well that's exactly what we're looking for," Jerry says. "We'll get back to you in the morning and talk money. But I can tell you right now that we're pretty interested in moving here."

"There are clean sheets and all." Paula juts her chin at the owner of Roughhouse and says, "I guess he told you that I plain let people stay in the house to get a feel for it and all. Trust is number one with me. It's location, location, location, and then trust."

"Okay. Hey, do you want another hot dog, Wanda?" Jerry says.

"She *appears* to be vegetarian," Paula says. "I can't believe you'd eat hot dogs. Welcome to Gruel! You'll do fine here. Unless, like I said, you want to sell land or houses."

Wanda lifts the left side of her mouth in a slight smile. "We have two children. That's what concerns me most. What're the schools like here? I know you're going to say that they're perfect, seeing as that's your job. But honestly. We have a couple kids who might be worthy of skipping ahead a few grades. What're the public schools like here?"

"Gruel Normal's the best. It's private, but it's not white flight, I promise. Otherwise, the public schools are thirty miles away over in Forty-Five. You probably don't want your kids going over there." Paula Purgason sticks her pinkie into her left nostril and flicks it. Jerry wonders if it's some kind of local sign.

Wanda curls her toes and says, "Well that sounds about perfect." She looks at Jerry. "That sounds about perfect, doesn't it, sweetie pie?"

He says, "Perfect."

"There you go," Jeff the owner says. "Take the keys, figure out the room, buy the house. Hey, who wants a hot dog?"

Paula Purgason says, "Give me four to go."

"How you want them?"

She shrugs. "I know that trick. I want all of them on buns, first off. And then mustard, onions, chili. What else? Hey, put some ketchup on those things, too. I wish you'd cave in to sauerkraut."

Jerry says, "How do I get in touch with you tomorrow?"

Paula Purgason reaches in her pocket and extracts a business card. She says, "Don't think I don't know what's going on. This ain't the first time this has happened." She puts the card back in her pocket. "Leave me some money on the nightstand. You look like a respectable couple, generally speaking."

Wanda smiles. She curtsies. "We're freaks," she says.

They leave their cars parked, walk to 103 Old Old Greenville Road, a half block up, then a half block over from the poolroom.

They don't hold hands. Jerry brings along a six-pack of Pabst. "I've never heard of a place where people will let you stay in their abandoned houses. It seems like there would've been some kind of background check," Wanda says. "I feel like I'm on *Candid Camera* or something. Did you arrange this little situation some time ago?"

Jerry shakes his head. He hopes that the sheets weren't washed in too much bleach. He's gotten a sty at every hotel he's ever stayed in. "You and I should move here and not tell our ex-spouses. Then we'd only have, what, a two-mile drive every weekend?"

Wanda takes his hand. "Maybe my ex-husband and your ex-wife are doing the same thing. Maybe they've hooked up and stay across the street." She points at a two-story house, the porch sagging, a pergola off to the side in disrepair. "This could end up one of those towns. Wouldn't that be weird?"

Jerry thinks, Someone should make a movie, but says nothing. He creaks open an iron gate for Wanda, then follows closely behind her. "This could be some kind of setup. I mean, we didn't bring a change of clothes, or toothbrushes, or anything. Tomorrow morning we'll have to go back to the square and find a place that sells such. They kind of have a monopoly on everything, I'd imagine."

He turns the key and walks in. Wanda turns on the lights. Both of them feel as though they've stepped onto the set of a 1950s movie or sitcom. In the kitchen, there's a squat refrigerator, a metal table with four yellow cushioned chairs, even a turquoise hand-cranked ice crusher the size of a napkin dispenser. Jerry sets the beer in the fridge. Wanda says, "If there's no toilet paper in here we'll know it's a setup."

There's no television set or radio. But everything's perfect. The beds are turned down. Fresh towels hang from heavy racks in the bathroom. There's even a scale that works, and all three guest bedrooms have single iron beds.

The master bedroom's got a canopy, of all things.

In the parlor there's a table, two hardback wooden chairs, and a game of Monopoly set up. Jerry says, "Monopoly! I haven't played this game in a hundred years."

Wanda sits down. "There's a theory about two strangers sitting down to play Monopoly. It's kind of like the zodiac, you know. Like how two people with different zodiac signs will either work out or not."

Jerry says, "You lie."

She says, "I'll write it all down if you want. I've memorized it. That student of mine who used to play in the Jungsters told me all about it. It makes sense to me."

Jerry sits across from her. He says how she doesn't have to write anything down. He does say, "It's hard to play Monopoly with two people, though. Neither player wants to sell off one piece of property when the other player has the other two or three."

Wanda picks up the shoe. Jerry shuffles the Chance cards, then the Community Chest cards. He sets them down, and picks up the dog. Wanda smiles, and takes off her sweater.

At two o'clock in the morning, with the game at a standstill because, of course, Jerry owns two railroads, one utility, Park Place, and Tennessee Avenue—while Wanda owns Oriental Avenue, two railroads, Boardwalk, et cetera—Jerry says, "Let's go back and get our cars. Let's see what they look like parked beside one another in the driveway."

They sit naked. At midnight Wanda suggested that if one player makes an offer and the other player refuses to sell or buy, then the refusee must take off an article of clothing. By a quarter past midnight they both sat naked on Paula Purgason's owners' claw-footed chairs. Wanda says, "I'm not walking down to the square naked. I'm willing to bet that there's a camera on that statue's head, scoping out the whole place."

"No, we'll get dressed. Come on." Jerry takes the six empty bottles and lines them up on the kitchen counter. From in there he calls out, "I'm being forward. I'm sorry."

Wanda walks in fully dressed. "Okay. As long as you admit it, I'll go get the cars. It might not be a great idea keeping them there overnight anyway. Who knows what hubcap-stealing gang members roam Gruel at night?"

They leave 103 Old Old Greenville Road, and clutch each other. Jerry kisses the top of Wanda's head three times and says, "That theory about the game pieces. What would've been wrong?"

"Car and dog. Car and shoe. Car and wheelbarrow. Car and iron are okay, but weird. Car and lighter's the perfect one, really."

"There's no lighter. What're you talking about? There's no lighter."

"And nothing's perfect," Wanda says.

Two six-packs of Pabst Blue Ribbon sit atop Jerry's hood. There's a note from Jeff the owner that reads, "We took bets. I say it's two in the morning. Let us know tomorrow. We open at ten. I cook more than hot dogs."

Jerry says, "Wanda. I don't even know your last name."

She gets in her car and turns the ignition. Wanda cranks her sunroof closed. She doesn't say, "It'll be McCrary one day." She says, "See if you can drive home with those beers on your hood. That'll be a sign, too. If you can, it'll be a good sign, you know. If you can't, then we'll change your flat tire together. I know how to change a flat tire. I know how to change a flat tire."

Jerry looks at the cartons. He doesn't say, "This is a strange, strange love story that couldn't be filmed ever."

When they drive back home—when they arrive with unbroken beer knowing that they'll stay another night not feigning prospective-buyer status so much—Jerry gets out of his car and says, "Do you ever listen to Tom Waits? I wish there was a stereo in this house."

Wanda nods. She doesn't say, "There will be." Wanda doesn't say, "Oh, this isn't the time to get all maudlin, you drunk, drunk documentary filmmaker." Inside, she takes her sweater off again, goes to the Monopoly table, and asks if Jerry wants to sell off North Carolina.

What doesn't matter is this: Jerry and Wanda go to bed at dawn, they don't make love, they only spoon, they don't hear Paula Purgason let herself in to check on them. What doesn't matter is that Gruel BBQ holds a three-for-one special on Saturday wherein any person can get enough chopped barbecue to feed a family of four for eight dollars, slaw, buns, and potato salad included. It doesn't matter that Victor Dees gets in an allotment of World War II canteens Saturday morning via Federal Express at his army-navy store on the square that, later, he would have to donate to the three boys left in Gruel's only Boy Scout troop.

It doesn't matter, ultimately, that dogwood blossoms finally bloom at 103 Old Old Greenville Road, that azaleas emerge, that potholes in the gravel driveway dry up.

Jerry and Wanda awake at noon and both of them realize that they don't need to brush their teeth. They aren't hungry, either. They walk around the house naked as chicklings and shade their eyes in sun-filled rooms. "We might be dead," Wanda says. "This is something I've never felt in my life."

Jerry says, "Last night I had a dream. You were in it. You could jump over everything. We were standing on a curb, and these cars kept flying by, and you'd jump over them. My boy Henry was always on the other side, holding on to this freckled pig."

Wanda puts on her panties and brassiere. She steps into her blue jeans and fingers her front teeth. "Man. Man. I had a dream that my daughter kept running toward a dog that ran away from her. But she had to stop and tie her shoes. Have you ever had one of those dreams where you could see yourself? I could see myself pointing at Flannery, telling her where to go."

Jerry says, "I'm glad we didn't have sex last night." He thinks, That might sound like I'm an idiot. He says, "We might as well stay one more night. We could start that Monopoly game over. And over. And over."

It doesn't matter that half of Gruel knows about their tryst, that they want new people moving in just so they have something to talk about. It doesn't matter that Jeff the owner plans on offering his version of self-esteem lectures for men who can't play eight ball. It doesn't matter that, even now a day early, so many men think about how they only have twenty-four hours to take their sons or daughters back to Gruel.

Wanda says, "I have about two hundred English 101 papers to grade. Would you mind? If you can talk the real estate woman into believing that we really want to buy this place, maybe we can stay." She approaches Jerry and kisses his lower chin. "We can do that, can't we?"

What matters is this: Jerry doesn't say, "You know, my camcorder's in the trunk. Let me make a short-short involving you running out of red ink." He says, "Wanda, Wanda, Wanda. Have you always been this beautiful and smart? I mean it. I mean it. I mean it, I swear to God. Do you believe me? Do you believe me? Please say that you believe me."

Jerry and Wanda wait in two separate cars for their respective ex-spouses to show up at Gruel BBQ. They're parked two spots away from each other. Jerry tries to find an NPR station on his radio; Wanda looks into the backseat for a book. Terry shows up first, parks to Jerry's right, and Henry leaves the car carrying his slight duffel bag. He drops it and runs toward the pigsty/petting zoo.

"Everything okay?" Jerry says to his ex-wife.

She slides a pair of sunglasses above her forehead. "Henry got to see a giraffe birth a foal. He might have nightmares. How're you? How's the porn industry?"

Jerry rolls up his window and looks peripherally toward Wanda. "There's a difference between talking to those people and filming them in the act. Could you please get over it? *That's Not My Finger* won best documentary at the Western Delaware Film Festival."

Henry reaches over the wooden fence and tries to pick up a piglet. He yells back to his parents, "I bet it's easier falling from a pig than it is falling out of a giraffe."

Wanda starts her car.

"I've fallen in love with a man," Terry says. "I hope you can take it if I show up with another man. Henry met him and he loves him. It shouldn't be that big a thing." She squints. "Are you wearing the same clothes you wore on Friday?"

Wanda's husband drives up in his car and lets Flannery out. He parks between Jerry and Wanda. Jerry rolls his window back down. Although he looks at his ex-wife, his attention's toward Wanda. He hears Wanda's ex-husband say, "I promise. I promise. I swear to God. Say that you believe me. Say that you believe me, Wanda. I'm a changed man."

Jerry says to his ex-wife, "That's good. I'm sure Henry will be fine," though he's not listening. Terry goes on and on about how her new boyfriend used to work at zoos in Cincinnati, San Diego, and Nashville. He has degrees from North Carolina State and Cornell. Jerry sticks his head out the car window and yells to Wanda, "I wrote out an earnest money check to Paula Purgason, by the way. That's how much *I'm* a changed man, Wanda."

Jerry isn't sure if he really hears Wanda say to her ex-husband, "Don't tell this guy about what *we* like to do on weekends. He'll want to make a movie about it."

Henry gets in the backseat of Jerry's car. Other cars and trucks turn into Gruel BBQ, the ex-spouses ready to deliver or pick up. Terry looks over at Wanda's ex-husband's car, eyes Wanda. She says, "You're wearing the same outfit as on Friday, too. Hey. I notice what everyone wears around here. I've seen things and remembered them." Back down to Jerry, Terry says, "Maybe you rubbed off on me. Filmmakers can only watch and remember, right?"

When Wanda drives off with Flannery, her ex-husband follows, but not in a threatening way. More than likely they'll both drive to Highway 25 before splitting off, Jerry thinks. He turns to his son and says, "You saw a giraffe get born? Was it gross?" Henry nods, squinches his nose.

Terry gets in her car and says, "I'll see you next weekend," then leaves.

Jerry wonders if he should ask his son if he'd like to leave Atlanta and move here. Should I promise him his own pet piglet? Should they drive home via Athens, in hopes of finding Wanda stopped at a convenience store in Elberton, the granite capital of the world? Jerry says, "Let's you and me go get a hot dog and shoot some pool. You're about old enough to learn how to play pool. I was about six years old when my father taught me how to hold a cue stick."

On the way back into downtown Gruel, Jerry remembers that it wasn't pool. No, his father taught him how to bluff in straight poker. Striking balls took an understanding of angles, of geometry. No one ever taught him that game, officially. In five days he'll park elsewhere in the barbecue joint's parking lot intentionally, as a test.

What If We Leave?

IT WOULD BE EASIER to explain past Breathalyzer tests, and littering, and obstructing justice charges to the local television station than it would be for me to admit what we did to sad, blind—though beautiful and tanned—Mrs. Swift. I wouldn't even tell a therapist, the first time around. Mrs. Swift lived behind my parents' house, and thus my house, in the late 1970s, and she and her childless husband built a swimming pool back there. Every afternoon, between about one and five o'clock from mid-March until late October, she toddled her long white cane out to one of those green woven and aluminum lounge chairs, stretched out, and sunbathed. She wore those extra-large sunglasses, like regular blind people always sport. What blind person cared about a suntan? I thought even back then at the age of thirteen. Who told her that a white woman needed to have some color to her skin in order to stand out at a dinner party? Wasn't being blind enough? Mrs. Swift, I'm sure, stood out from everyone else when she showed up clanking her cane against end tables and lamp stands, half of her face covered in a way that suggested ophthalmological dilation, or the rare afternoon of witnessing a solar eclipse.

Mrs. Swift didn't keep a windup alarm clock beside her chair. More than once, though, I took note of when she flipped over from stomach to back, then back to stomach. She had one of those internal clocks, I guessed, that told her when thirty minutes was up. Not that I was ever a perfectionist, but I used a stopwatch to make sure that she, indeed, turned better than barbecued rotisserie chicken at the local Piggly Wiggly.

Anyway, I watched her endlessly through the largest crack in our cedar plank fence. Later on I figured that my father kicked himself for going to such an expense for privacy, only to have a blind woman move in behind us. Mrs. Swift stood five-ten at least, wore a pink rubber bathing cap at all times outdoors, and had the body of one of those large-chested beauties on *Hee-Haw*. My father never talked about her, but more than once I noticed how, on Saturdays and Sundays, he found ways to slowly pull crabgrass and weeds back there at the base of our fence. Me, I possessed Mrs. Swift all summer long while my mother and father worked their respective first-shift jobs—Mom at the hospital as a nurse and Dad at Graywood Mills trying to come up with new and better fabrics.

She wore a flesh-colored one-piece bathing suit every day. I wondered if Mr. Swift knew how naked she could appear from a half acre away, viewed through a one-inch crack between eight-foot-high one-by-sixes. He wasn't blind at all. He was a barrel-chested man who owned a sand and gravel company. Word was that he used to own a lye-making factory, that Mrs. Swift worked for him, and that's where she got blinded. Word also was she got her tits stuck in a steering wheel one time, and wrecked, and that windshield glass punctured her eyeballs in a way that made her a walking kaleidoscope.

"We're trying to come up with a fabric that'll never stretch or shrink at all, and we're trying to come up with a cotton fiber that'll easily expand or contract up to six sizes on men's pants," my father said at one time or another during every dinner conversation. "It's a lot harder than it sounds. Rubber—if we made *rubber* fabric—we could do that. But what would rubber clothes do to a normal human being, I ask you."

My mother never looked up from her chicken *Buenos Noches!*, a dish that she made up herself and served about five nights a week. She always said, "For women, it would give them yeast infections. For scuba divers it'd be perfect."

"You goddamn right," my father would say. "And not everyone's a woman or a scuba diver. Or lady scuba diver."

Then we'd look back down. I'd drink my milk and pretend that spicy food didn't bother my esophagus. I was an only child who spent his day thinking up what excuses I could use when my father or mother asked how I spent my day. As far as they were concerned, I pretty much read all of O. Henry's stories before I went to eighth grade, and kept a collection of model airplanes hidden beneath my bed. My best friend Andy Agardy—the only Hungarian in Graywood County, and of course in tiny Gruel—and I spent all day perfecting our chess acumen, from what my parents knew.

"We can't seem to get a decent phlebotomist from the technical college," my mother said inevitably. "I'm having to show girls veins once, twice an hour. It's as if the only thing they're teaching in schools these days is sponge baths."

Sometimes at dinner I would think that I felt a splinter stuck in my eyebrow from staring at Mrs. Swift so long. Sometimes when a twitch took off in my eyelid I daydreamed about winking at Mrs. Swift, and that she winked back even though she couldn't see.

"Next year you need to go get a job," my father said this particular summer toward the end of every meal. "I don't know what the legal age is for Social Security cards, but it's time. Fourteen's when I got my first job. Well, hell, actually I was *five* when I got my first job, but it wasn't for real, you know. My father had me out there selling his cantaloupes and watermelons. We went door-to-door down to the rich people in Columbia, people who didn't have to keep gardens or know directions to the farmers market."

Chicken *Buenos Noches!* wasn't anything more than boiled breasts, thighs, and legs slathered with paprika and jalapeños. It went well, my mother always contended, with rice, mashed potatoes, macaroni and cheese, turnip greens, brussels sprouts, beets, stewed tomatoes, or—on special occasions—jellied cranberry sauce. I always said that I thought so, too.

"I shouldn't complain," my father ended every dinner conversation. "If no one lost or gained weight they wouldn't have to go buy new clothes to cover their bodies. At least I'm not trying to work up new fabric out there in those nudist colony places. Hell, the only thing those people would need would be flesh-colored, I guess."

At this point I should've told myself, "Uh-oh. Get that thought out of your head, get that thought out of your head." It was as if my father wanted me to think up a trick on Mrs. Swift.

Dad wore a crew cut his entire life. He wore seersucker shirts and khaki pants when we went on vacations to Myrtle Beach. Both of my parents believed that anything in the house out of place might tilt the Earth one way or the other. My mother's spice shelf always stayed in alphabetical order, as did my father's tools. Melvil Dewey himself would've been ashamed of his decimal system had he met my folks.

Unfortunately, I'm now able to admit, they never took the time to make sure I hadn't misplaced any of the various Magic Markers that they bought me as a set, after I made an A in seventh-grade art class. I don't want to sound the victim, but I'm sure that if my parents cataloged my possessions and kept track of what I actually did with them, I wouldn't be the mean, guilt-ridden, ex-pervert that I am today.

Andy Agardy came over one mid-June day at five after nine in the morning. My mother and father had left for work thirty minutes earlier, as had Mr. Swift. I had already taken to my spot in the backyard, even though it would be another four hours before Mrs. Swift appeared. This occurred daily for the rest of the summer. It seemed logically possible to me that, for some unknown reason, she might decide to change her routine, and I didn't want to miss it. What did she do in the mornings anyway? I wondered. What could be so important? Maybe she painted her toenails, or listened to the TV set. Maybe she had Braille books in her house, and read about skin cancer.

"Hey, Louis," Andy Agardy said after he snuck up. "What're you doing out here?"

I jumped. I hadn't told Andy about Mrs. Swift's routine, and up until this point in the summer had told him that I couldn't leave the house from one until five because my parents expected some phone calls. "Keep it down," I said, and stuck my index finger to my lips.

Andy looked through the second-best crack in the fencing. He said, "What're you looking at?" I sat down on the ground and told him everything about Mrs. Swift's daily sunbath. Andy said, "Word is she lost her eyesight when she found her first husband doing it to her own sister. This was back when she lived in California. She used to work as a stewardess, after she quit being a movie star."

I looked back through my crack and said, "That's not the truth. She was never a movie star. When she lived in California she worked for Walt Disney himself, as some kind of adviser."

Andy looked through his crack and said, "Is that the bathing suit she wears?" He pointed. I'd been so enamored with the sliding glass door from which she always appeared that I'd not noticed the clothesline, and that her bathing suit dried there amid blouses, Mr. Swift's blue pants, and some T-shirts.

I shifted to Andy's crack and looked. "Yeah, that's it. That's what she wears. I swear to God she looks almost naked if you squint your eyes enough."

We must've stared at her limp one-piece for fifteen minutes in silence. Andy said, "She doesn't walk out here naked and put it on, does she?"

"No," I said. "No. I've never seen her even walk past the pool. She just lies out in the sun, and turns over. That's it."

Andy said, "Hey, I got this idea." He stood up. "You're sure she's blind, right?"

I said, "Uh-huh."

"Watch this," he said, and took off out of the side gate. I looked through the crack in the fence and saw him tiptoe into Mrs. Swift's backyard. He didn't turn and look at her house until he reached the clothesline. Then, slowly, he uneased the wooden clothespins to her bathing suit, draped it across his left forearm, and began running back over. I watched the sliding glass door most of the last part of this escapade, certain that Mrs. Swift would regain her eyesight and nab him.

I took off running for the inside of my own house, as a matter of fact. When Andy Agardy came in, he laughed and said, "Maybe she'll go out there and accidentally put on one of those T-shirts, and be naked down on the bottom." He sniffed her one-piece, then placed it on my parents' kitchen table, where we ate our chicken *Buenos Noches!*

I said, "You have to take it back. This is too mean. She's a blind woman."

Andy shook his head. "*You* have to take it back. I got it, Louis. If you want to be in the club, *you* take it back. Hey, do y'all have a camera? We should take pictures of us doing crazy things like this. That'll be funny. I could take a picture of you putting it back."

I didn't ask what club. And I had a camera of my own that my father won for saving his company something like a million dollars with an idea he had for saving the company money. The previous year, he got a pocket watch, but he gave that to my mother.

I don't think he won that set of Magic Markers, but for some reason I found it necessary to go unearth the cardboard box in which they came, bring them to the kitchen table, and draw perfectly circular brown nipples and V-shaped black pubic hair on Mrs. Swift's flesh-colored one-piece bathing suit.

I did. And when I was done I said to Andy Agardy, "Oh, I'm in the club. Let's see what you can do to top that."

I don't think he ever closed his mouth. He shook his head, and didn't blink. "You're going to hell, Louis," he said. "I won't tell anyone. Unless they ask." And then he took off running for home.

If I'd've thought things through I would've gotten on my bicycle with Mrs. Swift's bathing suit and thrown it in a Dempsey Dumpster behind the Quik-Way convenience store.

Or I would've buried it in the woods back behind our subdivision. But I panicked. Before my Magic Marker pornography had time to dry well I carried it back over to the Swifts' house, and stuck it back on the line. I averted my eyes from their back porch. If caught, I planned on saying how our dog must've drug it over. We didn't have a dog at the time, but I figured that Mrs. Swift wouldn't know the difference.

It wouldn't be long before I howled at night anyway.

The few times I've told this story—outside of when I had to explain it to my parents, Mr. and Mrs. Swift, and this over-eager child psychologist—every damn person thought I would be stupid enough to take photographs of blind Mrs. Swift, fake nude, then run the roll of film over to a Jack Rabbit, Eckerd's One Hour, or wherever. Then, upon development, the processor there would call the authorities, and when I came in to get my three-by-five glossies a cop would jump out from behind the counter and arrest me. I wasn't stupid. I went to the library and checked out a number of books on photography and so on. I planned on making straight As in eighth grade, then asking my parents for film trays, chemicals, an enlarger, and paper. I planned on promising my father straight As and a washed car weekly for the rest of my life if he would convert our basement into a personal darkroom. Meanwhile I stored the completed rolls in my hollowed-out O. Henry book.

Mrs. Swift, indeed, went outside and gathered her dry clothes that first day. She went back inside and returned wearing her graffitied one-piece, and looked as naked as any celebrity photographed from afar on a French nude beach. I took pictures through the crack in the fence for a while. Then I got out my father's stepladder, stood on the last step before the DANGER! sign, and took unobstructed shots. I turned the camera sideways, then off-kilter. I changed the shutter speed to get ghostly effects. I saved up my allowance, and bought both color and black-and-white rolls of 35 millimeter film.

If I didn't get the darkroom I wanted, I figured, I could hold off until my junior year in high school, where I could volunteer for the yearbook, and get free use of the tiny art department's darkroom. Then I could go in there after hours, develop Mrs. Swift, and somehow get a commendation for the hardest working yearbook staff member of all time.

I never thought about how Mrs. Swift might go check the mailbox. What blind person worries over mail? I never thought about how she might wander into the front yard, and how every housewife up and down Calhoun Lane might look out their front windows daily—either expecting or dreading salesmen and Jehovah's Witnesses—and see her fake naked self slowly edging down the driveway. I'm sure that, being tolerant folks that surrounded us, they gave her three chances before finally calling the sheriff's department to report indecent exposure from a blind woman. And I'm sure the sheriff's deputies gave Mrs. Swift about three times, and that they, too, took photographs for evidence.

Listen, if you put dark glasses on Eve herself, then took away the fig leaf—that's how beautiful Mrs. Swift looked. I don't want to brag any about the drawn-on figures on her suit, but it proved that I deserved that A in art class, plus another in geometry.

"Our neighbor got arrested today," my mother said to my father right before the Fourth of July. "June Chandler called me up at work to see if I left the iron on. She said that fire trucks and county cops came by."

My father took off his clip-on tie. "Which neighbor? That peckerhead who runs the sand and gravel joint?"

"His wife," my mother said. "His blind wife. She was walking around naked in the front yard, from what I heard. June Chandler said that she was drunk, and not wearing a stitch of clothes. Word is she's been senile for more than a few years. Word is she might be the youngest woman in the history of medicine to go senile, and that Hollywood's thinking about doing a movie about her life, just like *The Three Faces of Eve*. And she was doing cartwheels."

My father went to the cupboard and pulled down a bottle of Jim Beam. He said, "Why would a blind woman do cartwheels? Turn on Walter Cronkite, Louis. Maybe scientists have found a cure for blindness." I raised my shoulders high to see if my hair touched them yet. I raised my eyebrows.

I said, "I didn't see anything. I don't know anything about Mrs. Swift walking around her backyard naked. Y'all know her better than I do. I don't know anything about it." I felt like I might cry, and I could feel my face turn red—a sure sign of when I lied to my parents.

My father looked out the den window and said, "I thought you said she was in the front yard. Hey, why is the ladder set up against the fence?"

I wouldn't have known exactly how things turned out with the Graywood County sheriff's department deputies had my father not, finally, gone over to Mr. Swift's house to say that he had a good lawyer friend in case the Swifts needed one. I'm not sure what conversation took place between those two men, but the next thing you know here come the Swifts over for cocktails. These people had been living behind us without either party ever making an attempt to act neighborly. Now, because of me, my mother got out her fancy crystal glasses and a blender. She made up some concoction called tequila *Buenos*

Noches!, which involved limes, salt, and everything else required for what most sane people called a plain margarita.

Mrs. Swift came over wearing a backless sundress. She didn't have her cane with her, and relied solely on her husband's elbow. He wore a bow tie.

I watched all of this from the cracked hallway door. I'd told my parents that I needed to work on a model airplane that night because my tube of glue was about to expire. A half hour into their visit I heard Mr. Swift say, "It was the damnedest thing, Lou," to my father. "Evidently I left a pen in my pocket from work, and the way the ink washed out in the machine it came out looking just like nipples and pubic hair. How could Evelyn know? She's blind as a bat."

My father, who never cussed in the house, said, "Shit. Damn it to hell. Nipples and a wedge."

"I'm so sorry that we didn't meet earlier," Mrs. Swift said. "I've just found that I make people too uncomfortable. No one knows how to act around the blind. When I go into town I can hear people in *wheelchairs* trying to roll away from me." She laughed in two short spurts, like a tugboat leaving the harbor.

My father and Mr. Swift went out in the backyard to smoke cigars. My mother said, "You know, I guess if we could educate people at an early age, they wouldn't be scared of people with limitations. *Louis! Louis, come in here, please, and meet Mrs. Swift.*"

I waited for what would be a normal time for me to get from my bedroom to the hallway door, then entered. Mrs. Swift had her naked back to me. She wore those big sunglasses. I said, "Yes ma'am?" to my mom.

Mrs. Swift held up her left hand. "I've already met your son indirectly," she said. My mother looked at Mrs. Swift, then back to me. It took seventy-five minutes for all of this to occur, it seemed. "In the afternoons when I take my sun, I am always aware of a cologne coming across the breeze. I believe it's British Sterling. One time I was at Belk's walking through the men's cologne section, and I smelled this particular brand and asked the saleslady what it was. British Sterling."

I didn't shave yet, of course. But I was known to fog up a room with British Sterling, Brut, and/or Old Spice. Aqua Velva. Williams Lectric Shave. I said, "Hello."

My mother made the proper introductions. Mrs. Swift said, "Yes, that's the smell. Have you been spying on me when I take sun, Louis? If you have, I must commend you on your stealth. Usually I can hear the slightest movement within a hundred yards." She cocked her head. "Did you hear that lady-bug fly by just now over on the other side of our lot?"

I looked out the window, like an idiot. This time my mother joined Mrs. Swift in two short pulls from their tugboat-horn laughs. Seals from the zoo in Columbia probably perked up. Geese probably U-turned going north.

My father and Mr. Swift came inside. "This is my boy, Louis," my father said. He pointed at me. "Louis, shake hands with Mr. Swift."

I started to do so—and was glad that the subject got changed—when Mrs. Swift said, "On weekends I smell that cigar wafting over our way, too."

The doorbell rang, my mother went to get it, and then Andy Agardy came slumping in as if he'd carried a bag of rocks over. He said, "Hey, Louis, you want to go catch some bats tonight?" He looked over at Mrs. Swift and pulled the tendons in his neck tight. My mother, I think, started making introductions again, I don't know.

Maybe I had seen too many *Candid Camera* episodes as a child. That program can make an entire nation wary, I'll go on record as saying. With the Swifts over all of a sudden, and Andy showing up—with Mrs. Swift recognizing my aftershave and my father's brand of cigar—I knew that a giant practical joke was being played on me. So I went ahead and blurted out, "You didn't have an ink pen go through the washing machine. I painted those things on Mrs. Swift's bathing suit, and y'all know it. Y'all know I know it, and I know y'all know it. So the joke's on you. Ha-ha." I did a good impression of Mrs. Swift's laugh. "Ha-ha."

Andy Agardy left when my father said it was time for him to go home. Mr. Swift stared at me in a way that could make wet cement flow back up a truck's trough. My mother went into the kitchen, and Mrs. Swift said, "I bet *I* know what Louis was doing on the other side of that fence every afternoon. That'll make you go blind, you know."

I didn't laugh. A noise came out of my throat, but it could never have been taken for laughter.

My second wife doesn't believe this entire story. She says that a book came out about that same time wherein parents were encouraged to test their children, to out-and-out play tricks on them. "It was called *What If We Leave?*, Louis. My parents had the same book. They used to fake splitting up all the time. The next day, they'd be giving each other shoulder rubs and asking me which babysitter I liked most so they could go out on a date."

Claudia and I sat in Tryon's new Korean restaurant, waiting for our friends, Drayton and Louise. Dray and I used to work together for a fund-raising organization. He quit when he got diagnosed with diabetes, and when he couldn't get workmen's comp. Dray felt sure that he'd contracted the disease as a result of eating too many pecan logs, World Famous Chocolate bars, and Blow Pops that we sold to high school glee clubs, pep clubs, PTAs, church youth groups, and Shriners.

I said to Claudia, "This kimchi stuff isn't so bad with the right beer. What is it again?"

The eighteen-year-old white waitress had brought it out and said, "Now this is kind of like salsa in a Mexican restaurant, but you don't eat it with chips." She leaned down and said, "From what I understand, this is really the only real Korean food here. It's complimentary." She put down tear-apart chopsticks. "So are the fortune cookies."

"Pickled cabbage," my wife said. "I don't think you want to eat much anymore. It'll kill you."

We'd been there a good hour. Claudia asked to change seats right away so she could look out of the plate glass window to see if Dray and Louise passed the restaurant by accident. She said, "Sometimes with diabetes in the advanced stages, a person will lose his eyesight." That's what got the whole Mrs. Swift-and-her-special-bathing-suit story started. Claudia and I hadn't been married six months yet. We had both thrown up our hands and gone to a justice of the peace before knowing each other, more than likely, as well as we should've. Claudia's first husband left her one day when he decided that he wanted to live off of the land. On a houseboat with his secretary. I'd been divorced for six years. Claudia worked as a cheerleading coach at Polk County High, they needed giant lollipops, I came in at lunch time, and we married four months later.

The waitress came up and said, "Y'all still waiting on your friends?" She wore a high school graduation ring on her index finger and another one on a chain around her neck.

I said, "They'll be here." We sat at a four-top and, because it was a new restaurant, prospective diners waited in the small, Pier 1 Imports–inspired lobby.

"Would y'all like to order an appetizer? We got boneless spare ribs on special. We got crab rangoons and shrimp toast."

I pointed at the kimchi and said, "I like this slimy stuff. Bring us more of this cabbage. I'll tip you well, I promise."

My wife closed her eyes, and I thought about how, in most real-life stories, the Swifts would have never come back to our house. And they wouldn't offer any invitations to theirs, either. They would either move out of town presently or construct a privacy fence of their own—maybe out of brick, or cement block, and eight feet high. Maybe my parents and they decided to go from conservative, upstanding members of the community to free-for-all, live-and-let-live swinger types in the matter of one evening's batch of tequila *Buenos Noches!* I know this: No one ever brought up the incident again directly. The Swifts and my parents took to visiting one another once or twice a week. My mother called Mrs. Swift almost nightly, and took her to doctor's appointments, grocery shopping, and the movies. My father and Mr. Swift went fishing and bowling. They played poker with some other men twice a month.

One time Mrs. Swift said to me, "Hey, Louis. Come on over here and feel my face. I don't have one wrinkle. Do you know why?" I walked over and stuck my hand on her forehead. "Because I don't squint, and I don't laugh or smile very often. Now quit looking down my shirt. Ha-ha."

Claudia said, "Drayton and Louise are having marital trouble. I can feel it. That's why they're late. Why wouldn't they call? They have your cell number, don't they?"

I said, "It affected me, sure. You can count on that, believe me. No one involved acted like anything was wrong—not my parents, and not even Mrs. Swift. She got to where she'd tap on over to our house in the middle of the day when she knew my parents were at work. And she'd say how she just wanted to know how I was doing. Nothing else. I wouldn't ask her if she wanted to sit down or have some iced tea or whatever, but she'd just come right on in and get her own iced tea and sit down."

Claudia kept her eyes closed. "Did you tell this story to your first wife? What did Patti think about all this?"

I picked up my chopsticks by the wrong end, pretended to know what I was doing, and pulled more kimchi from the white ceramic bowl. "Andy Agardy quit coming over to my house altogether. I can't even remember his talking to me again all the way until we graduated from high school."

"He might've been in on the trick. Maybe your parents paid him money to prod you toward drawing those nipples and pubic hair. I'm promising you that these kinds of tricks and guises are in that book I mentioned. That book my parents had. I finished it, too. I'm thinking about making it required summer reading for my cheerleaders."

When I graduated from high school Mr. and Mrs. Swift gave me a check for a hundred dollars and told me that I had to use the money to buy books in college. Mrs. Swift handed over a horrendously wrapped box and said, "This might help you out in college, too. With the coeds." When I opened the package—it was a pair of fake X-ray glasses, like the kind ordered out of a comic book—Mrs. Swift laughed and laughed and said she had no idea if they worked or not. "I don't know if they're as good as my X-ray glasses," she said. "I hope so."

The waitress came back. "Our manager said y'all need to probably go ahead and order. We have some reservations for people coming in later." She set down two margaritas and said,

"These are from some people over there." She pointed at the bar. I looked, expecting to see Dray and Louise. Hell, I imagined to see Mr. and Mrs. Swift, even though I knew that they still lived in Graywood, that they had retired, that they spent most of their time down on Kiawah Island.

I said, "Who? Who sent these over?"

No one from the bar looked toward us. "That man. That man right there wearing the hat." She pointed again. I'd never seen him before, but he turned and lifted his own drink our way.

"He comes in here all the time. Well, he's come in here for two weeks, seeing as we ain't been open but that long," our waitress said. "He's my little brother's psychologist. I forget his name. He's supposed to be good, though."

I lifted my margarita. I told myself over and over that he must've heard me tell the story to Claudia, that he overheard the word "margarita." I wished that I had a box of fund-raiser candy out in the car to give him. My second wife ordered the Happy Family. I pointed at the menu, for I couldn't pronounce anything that looked good, and knew that I would slaughter anything I wanted. Our friends never showed up. Later, I paid.

John Cheever, Rest in Peace

HE'D NEVER READ a John Cheever story, so that couldn't have been the reason he traveled, dead of a massive heart attack, across his neighbors' backyards aboard the Bolens seventeen horsepower, forty-two-inch-cut riding lawn mower. And no one could explain later how Owe Posey's machine veered inexplicably from swimming pools, gardens, overgrown pergolas, gazebos, kiosks, birdbaths, scuppernong vineyards, ancient and unused swing sets, the occasional mean barking tethered pit bull. It happened on one of those midsummer Sunday mornings when *no one* in Gruel, South Carolina, performed manual labor—*for it was the Lord's day*—and everyone either drove twenty miles to the nearest church or hid their cars so people *thought* that they'd gone to Sunday school and eleven o'clock services.

Owe had turned the key without telling his wife, Carla, that he would only cut the one-acre backyard, that Monday after work he would finish up the front yard and weed-eat around the shrubs, crabapple trees, hand-placed brick walkway, and their own birdbath, kiosk, pergola, unused swing set, and vacant koi pond. The night before, Owe and his wife had celebrated their twenty-fifth anniversary at Roughhouse Billiards, on the square, and both of them drank too many cans of Pabst Blue Ribbon. Owe, for what it's worth, had said, "I swear to God on our thirtieth anniversary I'm going to splurge us with a night up in Greenville at the Holiday Inn Express, right on Main Street. They's a New Orleans–style restaurant within walking distance we can go eat shrimp."

He pronounced it "srimp."

Jeff the owner said, "Twenty-fifth anniversary's silver, right? Well these PBR cans are mostly colored silver."

Carla said, "Do you have any Goody's headache powders back there, Jeff? I got me a headache."

Owe's parents named him Owen, but some kind of snafu at Graywood Regional Memorial caused the birth certificate to come back "Owe Posey." His parents saw it as a sign and never fought the defect. Throughout his life, upon introducing himself, people thought he couldn't finish a sentence beyond pronoun and verb. Owe would say, "I'm Owe," and they'd expect him to continue: "I'mo go into town for a while," or "I'mo buy me a flyswatter and put some entomologists out of business," or "I'mo get me a beer—you want one?"

He'd gotten to be a local hero back when Ed McMahon yelled out "Hi-owe!" loudly to Johnny Carson on *The Tonight Show* whenever someone said anything a touch racy. In the 1970s, particularly, "Hi, Owe!" could be heard as he walked across Gruel's tiny square.

Jeff the owner shook his head. "We can't get aspirin anymore. Gruel Drugs got some, I hear, but they're closed." He turned to two men attempting trick shots at the pool table. "Any y'all got a aspirin for Ms. Posey?"

"I know it's our anniversary and all, Owe, but I need to go home. My head's banging. I just want to sleep, and sleep in tomorrow."

Owe wanted more booze. It wasn't but eleven o'clock. He said, "Sure, honey." To Jeff he said, "You think I can buy a few mini-bottles of bourbon off you? Me and Carla might have to celebrate in the morning, you know."

Jeff said, "This is the time when it's good to live in South Carolina. You go up to a place like New York where the bars sell drinks out of a regular quart bottle, you can't buy for take-out. And I read the other day *you can't smoke up there in a bar.*"

Owe Posey said, "Goddamn." He looked at his watch. "Goddamn. I'm glad it ain't midnight. That would make it Sunday."

The Poseys drove two blocks home and parked behind their house. Carla went upstairs to bed. Owe said he wanted to draw out some preliminary plans for some preliminary plans down in the kitchen. He kissed his wife for the last time, then alone and convinced that Carla slept, tried to direct his satellite dish toward a Dutch channel he'd discovered one time wherein women tended their gardens in the nude.

Both Owe and Carla worked at Park Seed Company, he as a horticulturalist and she in the catalog department. He watered everything from snapdragons to habaneros mostly, and Carla took care of mailing. Owe pulled off dead leaves. Carla took care of telephone orders. They lived in Gruel because disrepaired antebellum houses in a town gone bust since the mid-1960s could be bought for less than thirty grand, even in 2004. They got theirs—a two-story, ten-room house with hardwood floors and two bathrooms—in 1980 for fifteen. The foundation crumbled, the walls held termites, the attic housed a bat colony, and the yard seemed to be a mole/vole/shrew breeding ground, but Owe insisted that he could set aside some of his paycheck each month and, inevitably, resurrect the place. "I'm betting we can refurbish this house by 2005, and resell it for forty, fifty thousand," he said back in 1980. "Maybe more. If Graywood County ever grows and gets some industry, people will flock here. They'll want to live in the suburbs of Forty-Five. Who wants to live in a big city?"

And he was right, outside of industry coming into Graywood County. Owe had saved his money, remortared the foundation, and so on. Each year they paid more taxes due to their house's tax assessment.

"We have the best life possible," Owe said to the TV screen in their kitchen. "We have a better life than even you women picking tulips." He twisted off a one-and-a-half-ounce plastic Jim Beam bottle and held it upward, toward Carla directly above him. "What does anyone know."

Owe high-stepped out the back door, walked through the mudroom, and exited to his old empty koi pond. He sat on the rock edge and set his feet down in a mélange of unripe, fallen pecan husks, wild morning glory, and tulip poplar pods. His fish disappeared one day, and word was either some frat boys at Anders College over in Forty-Five underwent some kind of scavenger hunt or one of the poorer citizens of Gruel got hungry. It didn't matter to Owe. He just knew not to restock only to become disappointed.

In the moon- and starlight it looked like his feet rested in an olive green, orange, and purple swamp—as if he stood ankle-deep in his own septic tank. Owe looked to his right. An embankment of slightly tamed kudzu stood between his property and that of an abandoned house where, supposedly, Jefferson Davis once slept, a place owned by a man named Seabrook Pinckney who sent his kids up north. When the father died, no one returned to claim the house.

Owe looked to the left and thought, "I could take my car out of park and let it roll all the way down to Gruel Normal School, if I wanted."

He opened another mini-bottle, then a third. He said to no one, "Why don't these people ever admit that they drink a glass of wine every once in a while? What else could they do in Gruel? Some wine. Some claret. A gin and tonic, or julep." His wife turned on a bedside lamp upstairs for about two seconds—enough for Owe to see a bat flit close to his face—then she switched it off.

An hour after dawn, when Owe Posey woke up on the ground with his feet still in the ex-koi pond, he became oriented and thought, I want my wife. It's our anniversary! He thought, I'll start up the lawn mower and it won't seem like I woke her up on purpose.

Paula Purgason next door said that he waved to her as he left behind a forty-two-inch path through her crabgrass and clover. She said, "Oh, Owe had his head on the steering wheel, but I thought he only kidded around. You know how he *was* sometimes! I remember one day he told me about a stray cat that came around and drank a cup of gas that he used with a toothbrush to clean the carburetor of his lawn mower. He said that cat lapped up some gas, then ran around in circles until it fell over stiff. I asked Owe, 'It died?' He said, 'No, it only ran out of gas.'"

Dr. Bobba Lollis, the pharmacist at Gruel Drugs, said, "He came by here long before we went to church. We go to church, you see, and we leave at eight thirty. Anyway, I was out back putting sunflower seeds in the feeder, and Owe went by in a giant crescent, completely missing our little grandbaby's wading pool. I thought he was only being neighborly, you know, cutting everyone's grass. I thought he maybe thought it was Saturday."

"He's lucky I didn't shoot him," said Victor Dees. "I got me some Lugers from down at my army-navy store. Shit, man, I seen him coming across from over Bobba's house and the first thing I thought was 'head shot.' Then I thought, No, just go for his tires. But I drank my morning coffee. They's things I won't stop to do when I'm drinking the morning coffee."

Bekah Cathcart shrugged. "I thought at first my ex-husband had come back to haunt me. Not that he's dead that I know of. Of which I know. I'm merely glad that Owe Posey didn't disturb my Zen meditation garden. I yelled to Owe, 'Hey, you dumb SOB, don't run over my Zen meditation garden!' like that. In a weird way it looked like Owe tried to perform the cobra or sun salutation yoga pose. I have this sand pit, too, where I sweep circles. Some people use a rake, but I like to use a regular straw broom I bought from the Lions Club. Anyway, he drove *around* my special places. I didn't know Owe Posey all that well—he kind of kept to himself and declined joining the Gruel Association to Sanctify History like the rest of us who hoped to improve the town. But looking back, that doesn't make him a bad person. I think he was only shy."

Owe Posey ambled his way through a dozen backyards, up and down hills, then crossed Old Old Augusta Road. He cut hay dead for a good quarter mile through land no one claimed, and, finally, ran into a cement ex-silo at old Gruel Sand and Gravel, which now housed, partly, the Gruel Normal School. After headmaster Derrick Ouzts shook Owe Posey—and everyone in town wondered why Ouzts would be at Gruel Normal on a late Sunday morning—he called an ambulance. Ouzts also called Carla Posey and said, "I hate to disturb you, Mrs. Posey, but Owe showed up here on his lawn tractor and we needed to send him to the hospital."

Before he could say, "He seemed to've had a heart attack and didn't know where he was," Carla Posey said, "You sure it's Owe? Lawn tractor? He only had a Bolens seventeen horsepower, forty-two-inch-cut riding mower."

"Well, he showed up slumped over the steering wheel. That's all I know. He lodged himself accidentally up against the old sand silo."

Carla looked out of the upstairs bedroom window. She saw a serpentine strip of cut grass heading east.

And she laughed and laughed, though her head still throbbed.

At first, Owe thought he'd been shot in the chest. He wondered if one of Victor Dees's purported hand grenades lodged within his own rib cage and detonated. The coroner would later tell everyone down at Roughhouse Billiards that he'd never seen a heart that exploded such—that fragments of heart tissue catapulted into Owe's spleen, liver, and lungs. In actuality it wasn't quite the truth, but no one questioned the coroner's expertise.

In the split second between Owe Posey's heart attack and his head's subsequent thud onto the mower's steering wheel, he thought, I shouldn't have drunk that last mini-bottle; I shouldn't have fantasized fucking that Dutch girl in her tulip garden; the capital of Louisiana isn't New Orleans; I forgot to put Seven Dust on the Bigger Boy, Better Boy, La Rossa, Beefmaster, Early Girl, Mountain Delight, Early Cascade, and

Sixty-Five Day VFFNT Hybrid Whopper tomato plants in greenhouse one; wilt, nematodes, wilt, nematodes.

He thought, Carla deserved better than what I ever offered, and in his death ride he didn't so much envision bright light beckoning from afar as he foresaw a long, long, forty-two-inch wide path where the citizens of Gruel could skip and frolic and forget about all the pressures of a meaningless life.

The grass never grew back. When viewed from above it looked like a thin river Styx meandered between Owe Posey's back porch and the center of Gruel Normal. At first all of Carla Posey's neighbors wanted to sue her, or at least ask that she bring back some fescue from Park Seed. Then someone started the rumor that a man on his way to hell will leave a scorched mark on the earth at the point of his demise. Before long another rumor spread that Carla Posey practiced witchcraft, that she and Owe poisoned plants on their job, and that a bevy of hitchhikers could be found buried beneath their crawl space.

"I don't give a damn if she's a witch or serial killer," Paula Purgason finally said at an impromptu Chamber of Commerce meeting. "We can use Owe's dead path as a tourist attraction. Do y'all remember back thirty years ago when that little baby's headstone glowed at night over in Forty-Five? Everybody thought it meant that child was another messiah. They had people showing up from three states away to witness that thing. Hell, a busload of Mexicans showed up, and they're used to discovering Virgin Mary statues crying blood all the time."

Jeff the owner said, "I remember that tombstone. It ended up having some kind of phosphorous in the granite. The moon and nearby streetlight caused it to glow."

"We owe Owe," Paula said. "He might be frying in Hades right now, but instead of castigating Carla we need to get her on our side. Maybe we can hire her as a tour guide of sorts— you know, tell visitors all the bad things her husband did in life even if he didn't do them. It would be like one of those ghost tours in Charleston."

Victor Dees, dressed fully in camouflage, shook his head. "First off, Owe Posey was a decent man. He worked hard, paid his taxes, and didn't grow marijuana in his backyard even though he had the botanical abilities. Second, that death path to hell goes through my property, and I don't want no witch and her tourists traipsing across my place. Maybe I got some old claymore mines planted back there, y'all don't know."

Dr. Bobba Lollis said, "Oh shut up, Victor. I traipse around your backyard all the time when my dog gets loose. I vote we talk to Carla. I made the motion."

Paula seconded, and everyone in the makeshift unofficial Chamber of Commerce voted aye except for Victor Dees. He said, "Nolo contendere," the only Latin term he'd ever used.

In John Cheever's story "The Swimmer," as any college English professor teaching a sophomore-level course in Literature of the Supernatural can point out, Neddy Merrill's journey through the neighborhood pools goes from the Westerhazys' pale shade of green all the way to icy, icy water at the Gilmartins' house, then the Clydes' pool where he could only keep his hand on the curb. In between Neddy found himself in sapphire-colored water, a dry pool, the murk of a public pool, opaque cold water, cerulean water, and so on. Any college English professor worth his or her sheepskin will point out "symbolism" five minutes into class discussion, and how Neddy Merrill's awkward and visionary escapade imitated the stages of human life, et cetera.

But if the members of Gruel's volunteer Chamber of

Commerce, or the larger contingent of the Gruel Association to Sanctify History, had taken the time to consider Owe Posey's half-mile adventure they might have noticed how his backyard remained shaded to the appearance of dusk even at noon. And where he ended up, after the hay field, was a white sand-covered lot. In between were various shades of dark green, olive green, pale green, then yellow. Oh, if only one of the Gruel citizens had paid attention in college—or *gone* to an institution of higher learning that boasted an English department—then he or she would have no other choice but to sit in a corner and wonder if a philosopher might ever offer up any kind of valid epistemological answers in which to believe.

Luckily for Carla Posey, she took that sophomore-level course. She studied *Frankenstein*, and "Young Goodman Brown," and "The Swimmer" at Anders College. She understood that the townspeople's rumors were off base. Carla took a six-month leave of absence from Park Seed—her good boss said that he'd call it "maternity leave" since she'd never used one, since she'd been a loyal, committed, and trustworthy employee—and while grieving her husband's sudden and untimely death she took to reading again. Sometimes she took *The Stories of John Cheever* to Owe's grave site, sat on his nonilluminating tombstone, and read aloud. More than a few people noticed.

When Paula Purgason showed up finally with a platter of brownies baked by Maura-Lee Snipes at Gruel Bakery, Carla Posey's place was dark. The door was ajar, though, and Paula let herself in, chiming out, "Yoo-hoo, Carla? Are you home?" She thought, Has Carla gone to bed and forgotten to lock her door? Has she gone somewhere for supper?

But she heard foreign voices emanating from the far left side of the house, and walked toward the kitchen. Carla Posey sat on the floor, surrounded by only cabinets and appliances.

The TV set on the floor, too. Paula looked at the screen, which showed naked women, their hair in pigtails, tending to what looked like an island of blooming tulips. Paula said, "Carla? I brought you a little get-well something. I'm sorry it's taken me so long."

Carla didn't turn. She leaned forward and stared at the television, her face two feet away from it. Paula pounded on the doorjamb, but got no response. The women on television seemed to be talking about life and death, the way they held tulips upright, then turned them upside down. "We have a great proposition for you," Paula Purgason said. "It's a way for Owe to live forever. We want to give something to Owe."

Carla Posey didn't acknowledge her neighbor. She got up, turned off the TV, pulled her dress off above her head in one motion, and stood still there in the dark.

The next day Paula Purgason wouldn't say how she left the brownies balanced atop the staircase newel. She'd go to Roughhouse Billiards, order shot after shot of bourbon, and say how she could no longer sleep.

Acknowledgments

"Migration over Gruel" first appeared in *Black Warrior Review*. "Christmas in Gruel" first appeared in *20 Over 40*. "Soldiers in Gruel" and "Scotch and Dr Pepper" first appeared in the *Chattahoochee Review*. "Assurance" and "What Attracts Us to Gruel" first appeared in *River City*. "The Novels of Raymond Carver" first appeared in *Ninth Letter*. "Bluffs" and "Recovery" first appeared in *Arkansas Review*. "The Opposite of Zero" first appeared in *A Dixie Christmas*. "Polish" first appeared in *Shenandoah*. "Snipers" first appeared in the *Raleigh News & Observer*. "Lickers" first appeared in the *Kenyon Review*. "Shirts Against Skins" first appeared in *Verb*. "Slow Drink" first appeared in *Epoch*. "What If We Leave?" first appeared in *They Write Among Us*. "John Cheever, Rest in Peace" first appeared in the *Georgia Review*.

I would like to thank Liz Darhansoff, crocodile-wrestler and agent par excellence; Julie Marshall, Lynn Pierce, Tricia van Dockum, Dan Janeck, Patty Berg, and even André Bernard at Harcourt; my friends Scott Gould and Michael Parker; certainly the hardworking editors at the magazines and anthologies where these stories first appeared; brave and feisty Don O'Briant; Jim Dees and Ron Shapiro for watching my back; above all else, to Glenda Guion.